BEDLAM

DEREK LANDY

BEDLAM

HarperCollins *Children's Books*

First published in Great Britain by
HarperCollins *Children's Books* in 2019
HarperCollins *Children's Books* is a division of HarperCollins*Publishers* Ltd,
HarperCollins Publishers
1 London Bridge Street
London SE1 9GF

The HarperCollins website address is
www.harpercollins.co.uk
1

LIMITED EDITION ISBN 978–1–78517–587–9
HB ISBN 978–0–00–829366–6
TPB ISBN 978–0–00–829564–6
PB ISBN 978–0–00–829568–4

Derek Landy asserts the moral right to be identified as the author of the work.
A CIP catalogue record for this title is available from the British Library.

Typeset in Baskerville MT 11/13.5 pt by
Palimpsest Book Production Ltd, Falkirk, Stirlingshire

Printed and bound in England by CPI Group (UK) Ltd, Croydon, CR0 4YY

This b ... ™ paper

Fo ... green

This book is dedicated to Laura J.

Because apparently having a book dedicated to you doesn't count unless it's a Skulduggery book. Hey, I get it. I do. But does that mean I can never stop writing these? Because that's going to be pretty difficult, seeing as how everyone dies at the end of this one.

Aw, mannn... now look what you've made me do.
I've ruined the ending for all the nice people.

Don't worry, everyone, this book has a happy ending!
Super-happy, with rainbows!

(Do you think they bought it? Yeah, me, too. Phew.
That was a close one.)

(It's a good thing you're cute, it really is...)

*And from the everything came the universe, which grew and spread
and took its place beside the others.*

And life grew, and spread.

1

Magic.

The place dripped with the stuff. It gathered in the corner booths, spilled over the long, lacquered bar, and crawled its way across the floor, grinning its slow, idiot grin. It was in everything – the music, the drinks, the words spoken and the laughs they provoked. It was stitched into clothes and etched into jewellery. It was in the coiffed hair. The lipstick.

That's what sorcerers did now. Free from the old rules, they took their magic and they experimented. They pushed their powers into sigils scrawled on squares of paper. They shared and swapped, dipped in and dabbled. For some, it meant a night of unforgettable wonder. For others, it meant sinking into a cold, dark place with no walls and no floors and no way to climb out. But the party went on. The party always went on.

The sorcerers looked at Valkyrie when she walked in. They knew her. They all knew her. Valkyrie Cain, the Arbiter, the detective, her dark hair loose, still wearing her jacket, still cold from outside. Twenty-five years old, six feet tall and made of muscle and sinew, a pretty girl with a nasty streak.

And, where she was, *he* was, emerging from the other side of the bar. Skulduggery Pleasant, the Arbiter, the Skeleton Detective, wearing a black three-piece with a blue shirt and black tie, his hat pulled low over one eye socket. If bad news had a name, it answered to Skulduggery.

The conversation faded just for a moment, then swelled again, as if acting innocent was going to save anyone. They talked, and laughed, every one of them hoping that they weren't the person the Arbiters were looking for. Not tonight. Please, whatever god you believe in, not tonight.

Valkyrie took off her jacket. There were those who were impressed and those who weren't – but they all looked. They looked at her shoulders, carved from granite, and peeked at her abs when her T-shirt rode up, carved from marble. They saw the work she'd put in, the sacrifices she'd made. The punishment. Most of them would never know what it took to go through that. None of them knew the pain that drove her.

Christopher Reign, at least, knew of the effort involved. He was a man who loved his muscles as much as he loved his suits. The suits were from Italy. The muscles came straight from Detroit.

Valkyrie and Skulduggery sat at his table and didn't say anything. Skulduggery took off his hat.

Reign watched them. Smiled. Nodded to Valkyrie. "Thought you'd be bigger."

"No, you didn't," she said back.

He looked away, raised a hand. "I got a girl could bench-press you."

His girl stood up. She was taller than Valkyrie. Bigger arms. Her thighs stretched her trousers.

Valkyrie barely glanced at her. "I'm not here to outflex your gym buddies. I'm here to talk to you about Doctor Nye."

"I know you are," said Reign, and laughed. "Everyone knows you are. You been looking for that messed-up freak since before Christmas. That's over two months now. Why is that?"

"It's a family matter."

"A family matter involving Nye? Yowch." He chuckled. "Ever think that maybe it don't wanna be found?"

"We don't much care," said Valkyrie. "We're going to find it anyway. We've heard you might know where it is."

Reign shook his head. "I don't associate with the Crenga. They may talk like they're kinda human, but they're not. They're monsters. Intelligent monsters, hell, yeah, but monsters. You can't trust a monster."

Valkyrie put a square piece of paper on the table. It had a sigil drawn on it.

"I don't know what that is," said Reign.

"Of course you don't. People are calling it a Splash."

"Oh," said Reign. "Oh, I heard about this. Little jolts of magic shared between friends, am I right? Just enough to make you feel good?"

"Sure," Valkyrie said. "Completely harmless fun, if you don't count the potential side effects."

Reign's smile widened. "Side effects, Miss Detective? Oh, you're talking about those mages who lost control for a bit, right? Hurt a few people? Such a shame."

"Yes, it was," said Valkyrie. She tapped the piece of paper. "This is one of yours, isn't it? One you've sold?"

"What a positively outrageous accusation. I am deeply, deeply hurt."

"We talked to some people," said Valkyrie. "We did our homework. These little Splashes started appearing six weeks ago. We traced them right back here."

"Back here?" Reign said, eyebrows rising.

"Back here," said Valkyrie, nodding.

"Wow. I mean, I'm assuming you have evidence..."

"You've been watching too many mortal cop shows, Christopher. We don't need evidence. All we need is a suspicion, and then we let our Sensitives take a peek inside your mind."

"That would be worrying, if indeed I *was* involved in a criminal enterprise, and I didn't have the best psychic barriers that money can buy."

For the first time, Valkyrie smiled. "I'm a bit of a Sensitive myself," she said. "I've only just started to find out what I can do, but I bet I could break through those pesky barriers of yours."

"I think I'd like to see you try."

"How'd you do it, Christopher?"

His face fell. "Have we stopped flirting already?"

"Oh, that wasn't flirting. See, we know you don't have anyone in your crew who could come up with these Splashes. Something like this is relatively easy to replicate, but not at all easy to create. We think you had outside help."

"Ah," said Reign. "You think Doctor Nye is responsible."

"That's what we think."

"And so you're hoping that I still know where that gangly, no-nosed freak might be hiding out."

"That's exactly it."

Reign finished his drink and a waitress appeared, taking the empty glass and replacing it with a fresh one.

Skulduggery watched her hurry away. "Do you have mortals working in your bar, Mr Reign?" he asked.

"Sure do. I got a few of 'em. It's perfectly legal, and they're cheaper than hiring one of *us*. No mage wants to wait tables or scrub toilets, you know?"

"Back to Doctor Nye, Christopher," said Valkyrie.

"I told you, I don't associate with Crengarrions. I'm a business owner. I run a bar. I'm not a criminal. I don't deal drugs, magical or otherwise. I am a law-abiding citizen of Roarhaven, and I pay my taxes, the same as everyone else. Now, I just met you, and I like you, but right now I'm feeling... what's the word? Harassed. I feel like you're harassing me. You're welcome to buy yourself a drink and stay, chat, make new friends. I would love to see you loosen up. But I'm afraid I'm gonna have to call a halt to the interrogation."

"You don't have much of a say in it," said Valkyrie.

Reign's gym buddy came over then, the tall woman with all the muscles.

"This is Panthea," said Reign. "She's one of the door staff here. She is well within her rights to throw you outta this bar. All she needs is an excuse."

Valkyrie sighed, and stood. The chatter stopped. Only the music continued. Skulduggery started to rise, but Valkyrie put a hand on his shoulder as she stepped round him.

"You want to take the first swing?" she asked, looking up at Panthea.

Panthea sneered. "So you can arrest me for assaulting an Arbiter?"

"Oh, I wouldn't arrest you for something like that."

"So... I could knock you the hell out and I wouldn't land in a jail cell?"

"I doubt you'd be able to," said Valkyrie, "but sure."

Panthea smiled.

"So how do you want to do this?" Valkyrie asked. "Want to go outside, want to clear a space, want to just throw each other over tables?"

"I can do whatever you want."

"Not the third one," said Reign, "please. These tables cost money."

"I'll give you the first shot," Valkyrie said. "One clean shot, right across the jaw. See if you can knock me out."

Panthea grinned. "A shot like that, you'll be eating through a straw."

"If I could just interject," Skulduggery said, attempting to rise again.

Once more, Valkyrie put a hand on his shoulder, keeping him down. "Not right now," she said. "I'm having a conversation with the pretty lady."

Panthea arched an eyebrow. "You think I'm pretty?"

"You have gorgeous eyes."

"Compliments won't stop me from beating you up so bad you crawl home to your mammy."

"I wouldn't expect them to, beautiful."

Panthea folded her massive arms. "OK, well, you can stop, because I am many things, but beautiful is not one of them."

"Are you kidding?" Valkyrie said. "With your bone structure?"

"I've got a busted nose."

"Your nose has character. It's cute, and it makes the rest of you even cuter."

Panthea sneered again, and looked Valkyrie up and down. "Your arms are amazing," she said at last.

"You think so?"

"You're hitting all the right angles," Panthea said, nodding.

"Well, *your* arms are phenomenal."

"Yeah," said Panthea, "but it's hard to find clothes that fit."

"Oh, God, I know."

"I'm confused," said Reign. "I thought you two were gonna fight."

Panthea hesitated, then glanced at her boss. "I don't think I can, Mr Reign. I like her."

"*Awww*," Valkyrie said, "thank you. I like you, too. I'm looking for a gym to train at here in Roarhaven – where do you go?"

"Fit to Fight, down on Ascendance Street."

"Hey," said Reign, "I go there. I don't want her at my gym."

Valkyrie and Panthea ignored him.

"Actually," said Panthea, "I only work doors part time – the rest of my day I spend down there as a personal trainer, so..."

Valkyrie bit her lower lip. "Do you think you could fit me in?"

"Definitely."

Reign stood up. "OK, what the hell is going on?"

"We're flirting," said Valkyrie. "This is what flirting is, Christopher."

"Panthea, you can't flirt with her," Reign said, scowling. "She's an Arbiter and a... a customer."

Panthea frowned. "Is she a customer if she hasn't even bought a drink?"

"You have a boyfriend, Panthea."

"So what?" Valkyrie said. "I have a girlfriend. Doesn't mean we can't indulge in a little harmless flirting."

"Yeah," said Panthea, "lighten up, Christopher."

Skulduggery finally stood. "This night has not gone the way I had envisioned," he said. "Mr Reign – the whereabouts of Doctor Nye?"

"I don't know," Reign said, all trace of good humour having left his eyes. "I don't know where that freak is, and I don't care. If it did come up with the Splashes – and I'm not saying it did or that I'd even know if it did – then it took its money and it departed without leaving a forwarding address."

"And how did you contact the good doctor in the first place?"

"I told you, I'm not a criminal. But if I were a criminal, which I am *not*, then I'd still have nothing to tell you because *it* would have come to *me* with the proposal."

"I see," said Skulduggery. "Valkyrie, do you have anything to add?"

"Yeah," she said, and pointed to a man sitting at a table nearby. "*That* guy."

The man paled instantly and sat up straighter.

"You've been pretty handsy with the wait staff," Valkyrie said, walking over. "A little pat on the backside here, a little pinch there."

He shook his head quickly.

Valkyrie loomed over him. "You think that's a nice thing to do?" she asked. "You think that's acceptable?"

The man cleared his throat. "I... I..."

"Stand up, please," Valkyrie said.

The man hesitated, then stood.

"You mind if I give you a little pat?" she asked, and she slapped him, the heel of her hand crashing into the hinge of his jaw. He went up to his heels and toppled backwards, unconscious before he hit the ground.

"Aw, man," said Reign. "You can't do that. Panthea, she can't do that to a paying customer."

"The paying customer assaulted staff," Panthea said without moving.

"If you see Doctor Nye, please let us know," Skulduggery said, picking up his hat and walking to the door.

"Be sure to tip your waitress," Valkyrie said to the rest of the patrons, joining Skulduggery on his way to the exit. Panthea came up behind her, handed over her jacket. Valkyrie slipped it on, gave Panthea a wink and left.

"That," Panthea said once the door had closed, "was pretty badass."

2

"You're mad at me," Valkyrie said as they left the bar.

"I'm not mad at you," Skulduggery replied.

"I made the situation worse."

"Reign didn't know anything that could help us. We knew that was a possibility before we set foot in the place."

"I nearly started a fight."

"You did technically assault a man."

Valkyrie scowled. "Not him. Panthea. I almost started a fight with Panthea. I wanted to. I wanted to smack someone."

"You certainly managed that."

She stopped walking. It was a cold February night. They were saying it might snow. "There's something wrong with me," she said.

Skulduggery turned to her. "Yes. You've got a serious case of humanity. I'm afraid there's no cure."

"I'm not joking."

"Neither am I," Skulduggery said, and put his arm round her, pulling her into his chest. "You're coping as best you can with Alice's situation, but you're angry. Not with me, because no one could be angry with *me*, but with others. And yourself."

"Is that what we're calling it now? Alice's 'situation'?"

"What would you prefer to call it?"

Valkyrie didn't know. She doubted she could find a pithy way to encapsulate the killing of her own sister and the subsequent damaging of her soul. She shrugged. "Alice's situation is fine," she murmured, sagging against him. "But how are we going to find Nye *now*? We found it back in September when we weren't even looking for it – but now, when we *need* the bloody thing, it's vanished off every radar we can think of."

"We'll find Nye because that's what we do. We find things. Clues. Truth. Inappropriate humour at inappropriate times."

"Trouble," she said.

"Yes," said Skulduggery. "We find trouble."

"No," said Valkyrie, stepping away from his hug and nodding ahead of them. "*Trouble.*"

A City Guard patrol car was parked in the next street over. Its engine was silent, its lights off. Beside it was a small shop. The door had been kicked open. Crashes came from inside.

They ran across the road. Skulduggery was first through the door, Valkyrie right behind him. She readied herself for a fight, an unpleasant part of her hoping that the cops were heavily outnumbered and tonight was the night when she'd get to cut loose. She had a lot of anxiety to work through.

Instead, they arrived to find three City Guard officers trashing the place in the dark.

Two men and one woman. The woman noticed them, and hissed to the others. They stopped what they were doing and turned. Valkyrie recognised one of them – Sergeant Yonder. She didn't like him.

"Well," said Skulduggery, "this should be good."

Yonder didn't say anything for a few moments. When at last he spoke, what he said wasn't very convincing. "This is official City Guard business. You can't be here."

"We're Arbiters," Skulduggery said, stepping over the remains of a smashed shelf. "We can be anywhere we want to be."

Yonder bristled. "Your jurisdiction—"

"Is absolute. That's what you were going to say, wasn't it? You two – identify yourselves."

The woman squared her shoulders. "I'm Officer Lush," she said. "And I'm Officer Rattan," said the third cop.

"And what exactly is going on here?" Skulduggery asked.

"We had a report of a break-in," said Yonder. "We came to investigate."

Valkyrie picked her way across the floor. "Did you find anyone?"

Yonder glared. "The suspects had fled before we arrived."

"And the mess?"

"It was like this when we got here."

"Who owns this shop?" Skulduggery asked, and their attention switched back to him.

"I don't know," said Yonder.

"Do you think perhaps it might be a mortal?"

Yonder shrugged.

"Because we've heard stories," Valkyrie said, and they all looked at her. "You know all those pesky mortals from Dimension X?"

"The Leibniz Universe," Skulduggery corrected.

She ignored him. "You know how they were all given the empty houses in the West District? That's quite close to here, isn't it? They've only been there for five or six months, but they're already working hard to make a new life for themselves, away from Mevolent and all the nasty, nasty sorcerers from their home dimension. Well, we heard that there were some nasty sorcerers over *here*, too, and they were robbing these mortals."

"Not robbery," Skulduggery said. "Extortion."

Valkyrie snapped her fingers. "That's right. Extortion. Their little businesses would be targeted and threatened, and they'd have to pay these nasty sorcerers to not trash them."

Yonder didn't seem overly sympathetic. "That's too bad," he said. "Protection rackets are the bane of small business. Have these crimes been reported to the City Guard?"

"Well, that's the problem," Valkyrie said, passing Lush. "It seems the nasty sorcerers doing all this damage are City Guard officers. Like you guys."

"That's a serious accusation," Lush said.

Valkyrie smiled at her. "I'm in a serious mood."

Yonder's radio barked to life for a moment. When it went quiet, he nodded. "OK, duty calls. You two have a good night."

He went to walk out, but Skulduggery stood in his path.

Yonder narrowed his eyes. "You're impeding a sergeant of the City Guard."

"I'm just standing here."

Yonder went to walk round him, but Skulduggery stepped into his path again.

"*Now* I'm impeding you. Did I ever congratulate you, by the way? On your promotion? Congratulations. Sergeant Yonder, Officers Lush and Rattan – you're all under arrest. Surrender your weapons and we won't have to hurt you."

There was a heartbeat of silence, and then Yonder laughed, and looked at his friends and they laughed, too, as if Valkyrie and Skulduggery couldn't read the intent in their eyes. Yonder went for his gun and Lush went for hers and Valkyrie punched her in the throat and shoved her back. Rattan had his gun out and he was aiming at Skulduggery, but Skulduggery was throwing Yonder to the floor and Rattan couldn't get a clear shot so he switched targets, swinging the gun round to Valkyrie. Valkyrie's hand lit up and lightning streaked into his chest, blasting him backwards and filling the air with ozone.

Still gasping, Lush pulled her gun and Valkyrie grabbed her wrist with one hand and punched her in the face with the other. She ripped the gun away, tossing it into the shadows, and Lush snapped her hand out and a wall of air took Valkyrie off her feet.

She hit the ground and rolled, looked up in time to dodge a fireball. Energy crackled around her body. The fine hairs on her arms stood up. Lush threw another fireball and Valkyrie straightened, holding out her left hand, her magic becoming a shield that the fireball exploded against. Lush ran for her gun, but

Valkyrie caught her in the side with a streak of lightning that spun her sideways and sent her down.

Valkyrie pulled her magic back in and quelled it before it scorched her clothes. That was getting to be a problem.

Yonder was lying on his belly, his hands cuffed behind him.

"You can't do this!" he raged. "I'm an officer of the City Guard!"

"Not for long," Skulduggery said.

Yonder rolled on to his side so he could glare at him. "No one will believe you! Commander Hoc knows you've had it in for me from the beginning! He'll take my side!"

"He won't have a choice," Valkyrie said, walking over. "He'll do what Supreme Mage Sorrows tells him to."

Yonder snarled. "You're so smug, aren't you? You're in with the Supreme Mage, so you get to strut around, doing whatever you want. Let me tell you, let me be the one to tell you – that time is coming to an end. You hear me? Things are going to change around here."

Despite her worries, despite her anxiety, despite everything that had happened and everything she had done, Valkyrie looked down at Sergeant Yonder and found she still had the capacity to laugh at stupid people.

3

"Omen," Miss Gnosis said, leaning forward, her elbows on her desk and her fingertips pressed together. "We need to talk about your future."

Omen Darkly nodded. The office, filled with the morning sun, was nice and neat and smelled of some exotic spice that was not too pungent. Miss Gnosis had books everywhere. Her desk was packed full of stuff. She looked like she had a lot going on.

"Omen," she said.

He looked up. "Yes?"

"Your future. How do you envision it?"

"I haven't really thought about it too much."

"I realise that," Miss Gnosis said in that cool Scottish accent. She pushed a form towards him. "Do you know what this is?"

"It's the SYA."

"And what does SYA stand for?"

"Senior Years Agenda."

"Very good." Miss Gnosis sat back. "What age are you now, Omen?"

"Fifteen."

"So you've got another two years of school after this one, and maybe two years after *that* before your Surge. Do you have any idea yet what discipline you want to specialise in?"

"Well, I... I mean, I suppose being an Elemental would be, you know..." He trailed off.

"Do you want to be an Elemental?" Miss Gnosis asked. "You don't sound too enthused."

"Yes, no, I mean, sure."

"Is there anything else you'd rather be?"

Omen shrugged.

"Rack your brains, Omen. Is there any discipline other than Elemental magic that you would like to do for the rest of your life? Because that's what we're talking about here. The discipline you're focused on when you have your Surge is the discipline you're stuck with from then on." She hesitated. "You *do* know how the Surge works?"

"Yes, miss."

"Good, good."

"Like, it'd be cool to be a Teleporter," Omen said. "I'm always late for stuff and I get car sick on long journeys, so that would solve a lot of my problems."

"Teleportation is one of the tricky ones," Miss Gnosis replied. "You generally have to be born with the aptitude for it, like Never was."

"Yeah, I know," Omen said, a little glumly. "See, miss, the problem is I'm just not very good at most things."

"Ah, Omen, don't be so hard on yourself."

"It's true, though. I'm not. I'm no good at Energy Throwing or—"

"Proper names, please."

"Sorry. I'm no good at Ergokinesis and I did want to be a Signum Linguist, but I just find it hard to understand all the letters."

"Which is a problem when it comes to language," Miss Gnosis said. "But you've still got time to decide. What I want you to do is come up with a list of seven disciplines – *realistic* disciplines – to take into your final two years of school. Then you can figure out which one you want to specialise in."

"And what if I can't?"

"Then you'll still have two or three years after you leave in which to make your decision. You're putting a lot of pressure on yourself to have this worked out, but do you want to know a secret? Nobody has it worked out. We're all just playing it by ear. No one knows what the future has in store."

"Auger knows."

"Your brother's situation is slightly different."

"Sensitives know what's in store."

"No, they don't," Miss Gnosis said. "Sensitives can see *a* future – not necessarily *the* future. But what about that? What about becoming a Sensitive?"

Omen's face soured. "We're doing one of Miss Wicked's modules right now."

"And how's that going for you?"

"She paired me up with Auger, because siblings have a strong psychic connection, and twins have an even stronger one."

"I'm aware."

"And we did that test, you know the one, where we sit opposite each other and I look at a card with a pattern on it and he has to, like, read that pattern in my mind, and then we switch? Auger got every single one right."

"And how did you do?"

"I fell off my chair."

"Oh."

"I think it's a balance thing. Miss Wicked says psychic stuff can upset your equilibrium, so... Anyway, today we're going to try to talk to each other using only our minds."

"You might be better at that."

"I don't see how."

Miss Gnosis smiled. "Omen, come on. A little self-belief wouldn't hurt, now, would it?"

"It's just, we're the only set of twins in the class, and Auger can do it all brilliantly, and I'm kind of holding him back."

"I doubt he sees it that way."

Omen gave a little grunt.

Miss Gnosis let him out a few minutes early, which allowed him to get to the toilets without being caught in the sudden crush of students. In fact, he had time to take the scenic route to his next class, past both the North and the East Towers. He descended the staircase in the main building, quickening his pace ever so slightly, and arriving outside his next class just as the bell rang.

Doors opened and each room vomited forth a never-ending torrent of teenagers dressed in either black trousers or skirts with white shirts and black blazers. A few of Omen's fellow Fourth Years passed. Their blazers, like his, had green piping. He nodded to them. They ignored him. He shrugged.

He took his seat in the next class. Never came in, looking half dead from exhaustion, and sat next to him.

"You doing OK?" Omen asked.

"No," Never said, gazing blearily at her desk. "Did we have homework to do?"

Omen took out his books. "Yes. You didn't do it?"

Never gave a groan as an answer, and peered at Omen through one eye. "Why are you smiling?"

Omen shrugged. "It's just very unusual to have you being the one who's struggling while I'm doing all right, that's all. Maybe it's a sign that I'm finally getting my life in order, that I'm finally becoming the person I'm meant to be."

"Or," Never said, "this could not be about you, and actually be about *me*, and how hard it is to juggle being fabulous at school with being fabulous at having adventures. So, really, it could be either."

"All those adventures taking a toll, are they?"

Never laid her forehead on the desk so that her hair covered

17

her face. "I'm bruised. And battered. I get into fights now. Real, actual fights. Me. A pacifist."

"You're not a pacifist."

"Well, no, but I hate fighting. I hate the pain aspect. Also the effort aspect. Fighting would be so much easier if you could do it from your phone, you know?"

"Damn these physical bodies."

"Ah, now," Never said, sitting up and flicking her hair back, "I wouldn't go so far as to damn my physical body, Omen. I'm blessed with this form. See these cheekbones? I will never take these for granted. But I do ache. I mean, I can't be expected to follow your brother into every single battle, can I? He's the Chosen One. He's got the strength and the speed and the skill. I just have the bone structure and the attitude."

"Kase and Mahala aren't Chosen Ones," said Omen. "How do they do in these battles?"

"They've been doing this for longer," Never countered. "They're better at it than I am."

"There you go," Omen said. "You just have to give it time, and then you'll be as good as they are."

Never lolled her head back, and looked up at the ceiling. "Three days ago, we were fighting this guy, a Child of the Spider. Ever seen one of those people? They're creepy enough in their human form, but when they change..."

"You actually saw him transform?"

"Oh, yes," said Never. "It was gross. Like, seriously disgusting. He sprouted all these extra legs, his body contorted, his face became a spider face... and the sounds. Great Caesar's Ghost, the sounds! Squelching and tearing and popping and more squelching... And, at the end of it, he's twice as big as us, and a spider. A *spider*, Omen."

"You're not afraid of spiders, are you?"

"I tend to get slightly arachnophobic when they're three times the size of me."

"Understandable."

"So, we were fighting this giant spider, and I realised I'd forgotten to do the biology homework."

"You thought about biology when you were fighting a giant spider?"

"Well, yeah," said Never. "It just popped into my head – the module where we studied insects and arachnids – and then we had that chapter on the Children of the Spider and how we still don't really know how they came to, like, be spiders."

"Yes," said Omen, "I remember the lesson."

"Do you?"

Omen hesitated. "No."

"Thought not. Anyway, I asked Auger about the homework."

"While you were fighting?"

"Oh, wow, no. I've still got a long way to go before I can have light-hearted discussions while trying not to die. I just don't have the stamina. I'm out of breath the entire time. So I waited until after. And you know what he said?"

"He'd done the homework?"

"Well, yes, but do you know *how* he'd done the homework?"

"I would imagine by doing it in his spare time?"

"Will you please stop spoiling my stories by knowing what I'm going to say?"

"Sorry."

Never sighed, and continued. "He did it at night. The *previous* night, *after* we'd sneaked back to our dorm rooms. Four o'clock in the morning and he's making sure his homework's done. The same with Kase and Mahala."

"So... so why didn't you do that?"

Never frowned. "Because I was sleeping."

"But why didn't you—?"

"Because I was sleeping," Never repeated. "I love my sleep, Omen. It's one of the eight things that I do best. You can't expect me to not sleep because of homework. We all have our limits, the lines in the sand we do not cross. That is mine."

Omen nodded. "It's a great honour just to be around you sometimes."

Mr Chou walked in and closed the door.

"Can I copy off you?" Never whispered.

"Oh," Omen whispered back, "sorry, no. I didn't do the homework, either."

"Why the hell not?"

Omen shrugged. "I was thinking about other things."

Never glared.

"Right then," said Mr Chou, "let's start off with last night's prep. Who can give me the answer to the first question? Never?"

Never sagged.

4

Razzia was bent over the sink in the Ladies, doing her make-up, because that was practically the only room in the whole of Coldheart Prison where the light was good enough, and Abyssinia was in there with her, the two of them just spending time together, not bothering to talk, just two Sheilas hanging out, enjoying the silence, alone with their thoughts, and then Abyssinia said, "I don't know if I do."

Razzia stopped applying her mascara, and frowned. Had Abyssinia been speaking this whole time? Had Razzia been answering? Was this another one of those conversations she forgot she was having halfway through?

Strewth, as her dear old dad used to say. Her dear old dad used to say a lot of things, though. Her dear old dad could talk the hind legs off a kangaroo.

Was that a saying? Was that a popular phrase, back in Australia? She couldn't remember. Her past got so hazy sometimes. She wasn't even sure if she *had* a dear old dad, at least one that she'd known. She had a vague image of a nasty man, quick with his fists, but she didn't like that image, so it went away, and was replaced by Alf Stewart, the cranky but lovable old guy from *Home and Away*, the greatest television show ever made. Yep, a much better dad to have, she reckoned. Maybe. She hadn't seen that show in years. Did they still make it?

Oh, bloody hell. Abyssinia was still talking. Now Razzia had completely lost track of what was going on. The only thing she knew for sure was that her mascara wasn't all done, so she went back to applying it.

Knowing Abyssinia, she was probably talking about her long-lost-now-recently-recovered son, Caisson. She was always talking about him. Razzia got it. She totally understood. Caisson was family, after all. Nothing more important than family.

And it was nice seeing Abyssinia so happy. Those first few weeks, when Caisson didn't do a whole lot more than have bad dreams while sedated, were the happiest she'd ever seen Abyssinia. She was so proud of her son for sticking it out, for surviving all that pain.

It had reinvigorated her, too, having her son around. Suddenly her attention was back on the plan, because the plan secured Caisson's legacy. That focus had slipped a little, but now it was back on track. In less than two weeks, it would all kick off.

Razzia couldn't wait. She hadn't killed anyone in ages.

But, now that Caisson was up and about, it had quickly become clear to anyone paying attention that he was a weird one.

That wasn't easy for Razzia to admit. She'd always seen herself as the weird one in Abyssinia's little group of misfits, so to voluntarily hand over the title to a newcomer – even if he was the long-lost son of the boss – just felt wrong.

But there was no denying it: Caisson was an oddball.

She couldn't blame him, of course. He'd been tortured pretty much non-stop for ninety years. That would lead anyone to hop on an imaginary plane and take a sojourn from reality. His flesh was scarred, his silver hair – so like his mother's – grew only in clumps from a damaged scalp, and his eyes always seemed to be focused on something not quite in front of him, and not quite in the distance.

The fact was, though, he could have been a lot worse. According to Caisson, this was all down to his jailer, Serafina.

She knew that if he retreated deep enough into his mind there wouldn't be much point in torturing his body. So, every few weeks Caisson would be given the chance to recover, to get strong... and then it would happen all over again.

The whole thing was just so delightfully sadistic. Razzia hoped one day to meet Serafina. She'd been hitched to that Mevolent fella from ages ago, the one who'd caused all that bother with the war and all. Razzia reckoned she could learn a thing or two from someone like that.

Abyssinia sighed. "What do you think?"

Razzia blinked at her in the mirror. Abyssinia clearly wasn't asking about her hair, because it was the same as it always was – long and silver. The red bodysuit, maybe? Abyssinia's recently regrown body was still pretty new, and the suit did a lot to keep it maintained, but she'd been wearing variations of it for months and so Razzia didn't think she had chosen now to ask how she looked.

Must be Caisson again.

"Well," Razzia said, "the real question here, Abyssinia, is what do *you* think?"

Abyssinia exhaled. "I think we press ahead."

"Yeah," said Razzia. "Me too."

"This is what we've been working towards, and I shouldn't let new developments derail us from our goals. I've been promising you a new world for years, and I'm not going to abandon you, not when the end is finally in sight."

"Good to hear."

"But I just don't know what to do about the Darkly thing."

Razzia did her best to look concerned. She did this by pursing her lips and frowning at the ground. She didn't see what the problem was. The Darkly Prophecy foretold a battle between the King of the Darklands and the Chosen One, Auger Darkly, when the boy was seventeen years old. That was still something like two years away. Plenty of time to kill the Darkly kid before he could kill Caisson. It all seemed simple enough to Razzia.

Abyssinia, like most people, had a tendency to overthink things.

"Prophecies are dodgy," Razzia said, applying a bit of Redrum lipstick. "If a prophecy foretells what happens in the future, if nothing changes from this point onwards, then all you have to do to avert that prophecy is not do what you otherwise would have done. *Bam.* On the other hand, how can you be certain that what you *don't* do is in fact what leads to the prophecy being fulfilled? Fair dinkum, it's a complicated business, but, like most complicated businesses, it's also deceptively simple."

Abyssinia frowned. "I don't think that's entirely true, though."

"What do I know?" Razzia asked, shrugging. With the back of her hand, she smudged the lipstick to one side, then down to her chin. *Perfect.* "I'm nuts."

5

Valkyrie let herself into her parents' house, went straight to the kitchen and found her mother reading at the table.

"Oh, good God!" Melissa Edgley said, jerking upright.

Valkyrie laughed. "Sorry. Thought you'd heard me."

Melissa got up, hugged her. "You don't make a sound when you walk. I suppose that's all your ninja training."

"I don't have ninja training."

"Sorry," her mum said. "Your secret ninja training."

Valkyrie grinned, and eyed the notebook on the table. "What are you reading that has you so engrossed?"

"This," said Melissa, "is your great-grandfather's diary. One of several, in fact. Your dad found them in the attic, packed away with a load of junk."

"Ah, diaries," said Valkyrie. "The selfies of days gone by. What are they like?"

"They're beautiful, actually. Beautiful handwriting and beautiful writing."

"So that's where Gordon got his talent from."

"Well, he didn't lick it off a stone." Melissa hesitated, then looked up. "Your dad's in the other room. He's, uh... not in the best of moods."

"What's wrong?"

Melissa waved the diary. "He's flicked through a few of these.

25

Your great-granddad was a firm believer in the legend that the Edgleys are descended from the Ancient Ones."

"The Last of the Ancients," Valkyrie corrected. "But why does that make him grumpy? He knows it's all true now."

"And that," her mother said, "is the problem."

Valkyrie took a moment. "Ah," she said. "Maybe I should talk to him."

"That might help."

Valkyrie walked into the living room. Desmond was sitting in his usual chair. The cricket was on.

"Hello, Father," she said.

"Hello, Daughter," he responded, not taking his eyes off the screen.

She sat on the couch. "Enjoying this, are you?"

"Yes, actually."

"Who's playing?"

Desmond nodded at the TV. "They are."

"Good game?"

"Not sure."

"Who's winning?"

"Don't know."

"What are the rules?"

"No idea."

"I didn't know you even liked cricket."

He sat up straighter. "This is cricket?"

She settled back. "Mum told me about the diaries."

Desmond muted the TV. "My granddad had the best stories," he said. "The three of us would sit round his armchair and he'd just... I don't know. Regale us, I suppose. Regale us with family legends about magic men and women, doing all these crazy things, all because we were descended from the Last of the Ancients. But my father, well... he'd grown up with those stories and he was sick of them. He suffered from a, I suppose you'd call it a deficit of imagination. And he used to ridicule

26

the old man, every chance he got. In front of us. I didn't like that."

"Right," said Valkyrie.

"And Fergus followed suit. Turned his back on granddad and his stories. He'd always needed our father's approval more than Gordon or me, so siding with him against what they both saw as nonsense and fairy stories was one way of building a bond Fergus felt he was missing. I wonder what he'd say now if we told him the truth. I don't think I could do that to him."

Valkyrie didn't say anything to that. It wasn't her place.

"Me, I loved the stories," Desmond continued. "They meant something. They meant there was more to life than what I could see around me. They meant I could be more than what I was. Because of my granddad, I wasn't restricted like my friends were. I had, I suppose, a purpose, if I wanted to seize it."

"So you believed him," said Valkyrie.

"I did," Desmond said. "For a few years. When I was a kid. But I got to age ten, I think, and my dad sat me down and told me there were no such things as wizards and monsters. How wrong he was, eh?" Desmond smiled. "Gordon was the trouble-some one. Always had been. Even his name rankled our dad. Fergus and I had good strong Irish names – but Gordon... ha. My mother insisted on naming him after the doctor who delivered him. It was her first pregnancy and there were complications, but that doctor worked a miracle, and the future best-selling author came into the world and brightened it with every moment he was here. Our granddad passed all those stories, all that wonder, down to Gordon, and he just absorbed it. He believed, like I did, but unlike me he never allowed our father to trample that belief. That's what he had that I didn't, I suppose. A strength." Desmond shifted in his chair. "All those stories, they're in the diaries. You should read them."

"I will," said Valkyrie.

Desmond took in a breath. It was shaky. He expelled it slowly, and looked at her. "I'm glad we know about the magic," he said. "It's terrifying, knowing that you're out there, endangering your life, and it makes the world a scarier place, but I'm glad nonetheless. I wish I'd kept believing when I was younger, I really do. Still, I'm thankful Gordon did. Our granddad needed *someone* to believe him."

Valkyrie didn't know what to say, so she got up and hugged her dad. He hugged her back, and then shrugged himself out of his bad mood and turned off the TV.

"Cricket is a silly game," he said, "and none of it makes any sense. Where's your mum?"

"Kitchen," she said, and followed him out.

"Are you in a better mood?" Melissa asked when they walked in.

"I am," Desmond responded, kissing the top of her head. "Sorry for snapping at you earlier."

She looked up, surprised. "You snapped at me?"

"Didn't I?"

"When?"

"Earlier."

"I don't recall that."

"Well, maybe I didn't *snap*, as such, but I *was* curt, and for that you have my most sincere—"

"When were you curt?"

He frowned at her. "Earlier," he said again. "When we were talking. About the diaries. I was curt when we were talking about the diaries. You didn't notice?"

"I noticed you being a little grumpy."

He looked offended. "That wasn't me being grumpy. That was me being curt. That was my inner darkness shining through. Weren't you scared by the glimpse of the monster lurking beneath the surface?"

"Not... really."

"Oh."

"Sorry, dear, you're just too cuddly to be scary."

"I am frighteningly cuddly," he admitted. "But I'm sure I was dark, too, once upon a time."

"You were pretty dark that day you threw that guy through a window," Valkyrie said.

"That's what I'm thinking of," said Desmond, clicking his fingers. "I knew I'd done something cool."

"My cool dad," Valkyrie said wistfully. "So are you going to read the diaries?"

"I am," he replied. "I will. I owe it to my granddad. It might even give me an insight into what you get up to, saving the world every single day."

"I don't save the world every *single* day," Valkyrie responded. "I take time off. I go for walks. I go to the gym. I train."

"Wait now," said her mum. "Where's the part in that schedule where you have fun?"

"I have loads of fun."

"Do you have any friends? Do you go to the cinema? Go out for dinner? What about boys?"

Valkyrie opened her mouth to speak, but nothing came out.

Her dad narrowed his eyes. "You're hesitating. Why are you hesitating? It's because we're not going to approve, isn't it? What is he? Is he a werewolf? Is he a mummy?"

"Dad..."

"Is he a cannibal?"

"God, no. Why would I go out with a cannibal?"

"Love is blind, Stephanie. If you love someone, that means you're willing to overlook flaws in their character, like cannibalism and being too pretty. Your mother possesses one of those flaws. I'll leave it to you to figure out which one."

"Such a charmer," said Melissa.

"I'm not dating a cannibal," Valkyrie said.

"*Are* you dating someone?" her mum asked.

Valkyrie nodded.

"And? When are we going to meet him?"

It was on the tip of her tongue. *It's not a him.* So easy. Such an easy sentence to say. All she had to do was open her mouth and say it.

But she took too long, and now her dad was nudging her mother's shoulder. "It's your fault," he said. "She won't bring him home to meet us because she's afraid you'll embarrass her. This is always a problem when you have one really cool parent and one lame parent."

Melissa shook her head. "I preferred you when you were grumpy."

"I wasn't grumpy, I was *dark*."

"I'm going to say hi to Alice," Valkyrie said, turning on her heel.

"We're not finished with this boyfriend stuff!" her mum called out after her.

Valkyrie retreated, away from the possibility of disappointing her parents. Even though she knew they'd understand. They were liberal, progressive people, after all. They'd handled the truth about magic without unduly freaking out – she was sure they'd have no problem with the whole girlfriend situation.

But, even so, it made her tummy flip as she climbed the stairs.

6

Her sister's door was open. Alice sat in the corner of the room, peering into the hamster cage.

"Hey, you," Valkyrie said.

"Stephanie!" Alice cried, scrambling up and launching herself forward.

Valkyrie laughed and caught her and hugged her. "Hey, gorgeous girl."

"Are you staying for dinner?" Alice asked, face buried in Valkyrie's hip.

"I can't," Valkyrie said, prising her off. "I've got to go to work."

"With Skulduggery?"

"Yep. But I couldn't pass without calling in to say hi to the best little sister in the world."

"Do you want to see me dancing?"

"I'd love to, but I don't really have time. Did you learn any more moves?"

"Yeah, a few," Alice said. "Do you want to see them?"

"Tomorrow or the next day," said Valkyrie. "And bad dreams?"

Alice laughed. "You always ask me that!"

"I know I do. I'm interested."

"I never have bad dreams."

"Not even about the horrible man?"

"Ew," said Alice, making a face. "No. I don't think about him. He was smelly. I still haven't told Mum or Dad about him. It's still our little secret."

Valkyrie forced a smile. "Thank you," she said, feeling the guilt start to weigh down on her. She quickly walked over to the hamster cage, eager for a change of subject. "So how's SpongeBob?"

Alice laughed. "That's not his name."

"Is it not? Are you sure?"

"It's Starlight."

"Starlight the hamster... yes, I think I remember something about that. Where is he? Is he hiding?"

"There he is," said Alice, pointing at a lump of fur in the corner of the cage.

"Hello, you," Valkyrie said, hunkering down. She poked a finger through the cage and petted little Starlight. He was cold.

"He's dead," said Alice.

Valkyrie stopped petting him. She withdrew her finger and said, "Oh."

"He died during the night sometime," Alice continued. "Last night I fed him – well, Dad fed him – and I cleaned out his cage and I put new hay in and new newspaper because he likes playing in newspaper and he rips it all up sometimes, and then he died, I think."

Valkyrie let herself sit, her back against the wall. "And when did you find out that he'd died?"

"A few minutes ago," Alice said. "Like, ten. Or five. I can show you my dancing, if you like."

"Let's just wait a moment, sweetie. How are you feeling?"

Alice shrugged. "I'm fine."

"Did you love Starlight?"

Alice nodded.

"Did you love him a lot?"

"Like, loads," said Alice. "I used to close my bedroom door and let him out so he could run around and then he'd come over to me and climb on to my lap and I'd pet him. Like, I didn't love him as much as I love Mum and Dad and you, but I still loved him."

"Will you miss him?"

"Um, yes."

"Are you sad?"

"Yes," Alice said, and nodded again.

Valkyrie held out her hands, and when Alice took them she pulled her gently down. "Come here," she said. "Sit." When Alice was seated, Valkyrie gave her a soft smile. "When you say you're sad, do you actually mean you're sad, or are you saying it because you think I'm expecting you to say it?"

Alice didn't answer.

"It's OK," whispered Valkyrie. "You're not in trouble. I'm just interested."

"Um," Alice said, "I'm not really sad."

Valkyrie nodded, and kept nodding, waiting for the panic in her chest to settle down. "OK," she said. "OK, thank you for telling me. Will you miss him?"

"Yes," Alice said with absolute certainty. "I'm going to miss him loads."

"And do you know what missing him means? Have you ever missed anyone before?"

A shy smile broke out. "Not really," Alice said.

"Missing someone is when you get sad that somebody isn't there any more. Do you think you'll get sad now that Starlight isn't alive and you can't pet him and cuddle him?"

The tip of Alice's tongue came out and took up temporary residence at the corner of her lips. "Um... maybe."

Valkyrie switched on her aura-vision, reducing her sister to a dark outline, throbbing weakly with a dim, almost imperceptible orange. It was so spread out, so diffused, that it was barely there at all.

She switched off the aura-vision before it made her sick with guilt, pulled Alice in and wrapped her up in a hug. "You know what love is, don't you?"

"Of course," said Alice.

"And you love me?"

"With all my heart."

"And I love you, too, with all my heart."

They sat there, hugging.

"Is it OK that I don't get sad?" Alice asked softly.

Valkyrie kissed her head. "I'm going to fix that. You don't have anything to worry about. I'm going to find someone who can help you, and I'm going to fix everything."

Alice nodded and didn't respond, and Valkyrie hugged her closer and tried not to cry.

7

"It's nice here, isn't it?" Axelia Lukt said.

Omen looked up. He'd been daydreaming about being good at things, about being as cool as Skulduggery or as tough as Valkyrie or as capable as Auger. He hadn't even noticed the tram emptying the closer they got to the Humdrums. It was only Axelia and him left on it now.

He looked out of the window. "I suppose," he said, although to him this part of Roarhaven looked pretty similar to most of the other parts – apart from the fact that it was right beside the enormous wall that encircled the city. Was that what Axelia was talking about? Did she like walls?

"The wall's pretty," he tried.

"The wall's ugly," Axelia said immediately. "It's horrible and grey and horrible."

"That's what I meant."

"It blocks out the sun in the mornings for this whole part of town."

"It's so horrible," Omen agreed.

"But the rest of it," said Axelia, "it's so nice. It's peaceful, isn't it? Quiet."

Omen nodded, but he wasn't quite sure that was true. The Humdrums were where the mortals lived, the more than 18,000 refugees who had trudged through the portal from the Leibniz

Universe to escape their very own Mevolent, who was still alive and terrorising the ones left behind over there. Roarhaven had taken them in, mainly because there was nowhere else to keep them, and the High Sanctuary had assumed responsibility for turning them into productive members of society.

Axelia had grown up in a magical community in Iceland, where she'd had very limited interactions with mortals. Omen was beginning to think that maybe she viewed mortals, and these ones in particular, as quaint, somewhat primitive beings. It was ever-so-slightly condescending, he felt. And possibly ever-so-slightly racist.

The tram stopped and off they got. The Humdrums was definitely quieter than other parts of the city. No one here had cars, because no one could drive yet. Back in their own dimension, these mortals had been the serfs to the ruling class of mages. They'd lived in huts and hadn't had access to technology.

Here they were free. They worked and were paid. They'd been introduced to the delights of television and the Internet. They could walk the streets without being accosted by sorcerers.

"Hello," said Omen to a passing mortal. "Would you like a pamphlet?"

The mortal shrank back, but took a pamphlet and hurried on.

The bag over Omen's shoulder was weighed down with these pamphlets. This week, they were handing out information about the First Bank of Roarhaven, China Sorrows's pride and joy. Even mortals could save their money there, according to the pamphlets – it was perfectly safe and truly wonderful. Omen doubted this would work. The mortals here were more inclined to stash their money under their mattresses than hand it over to some huge institution where they didn't know the rules.

But volunteering for this stuff got Omen out of the last class of the day, so he didn't mind too much.

They folded pamphlets and stuck them through letterboxes and chatted whenever they regrouped at the end of a street. Axelia had already handed in her Senior Years Agenda. She wanted to be an Elemental, she said. There were a lot more of them flying these days, like Skulduggery did. She'd always wanted to fly.

Flying would be cool, Omen admitted. But he was wary of the fact that it required so much concentration. His mind was inclined to wander, after all.

They made their way to the square in the middle of the sector. It didn't have a name yet – the mortals intended to vote on one in the coming months. The High Sanctuary even offered to have a statue erected to someone they admired, mortal or mage. They were still deciding on that as well.

Aurnia was waiting for them with a few other mortals. She waved as they approached. Her companions, one girl and three guys, left her to it. As they passed, one of the guys rammed his shoulder into Omen's.

Before Omen knew what was happening, he was being loomed over and forced backwards.

"What?" said the guy who'd rammed him. "What?"

Omen blinked up at him. "What?"

"What?" demanded the rammer, his teeth bared, his eyes wide.

"I'm sorry?"

The guy's friends were pulling him back, and Axelia was suddenly standing between them and Aurnia was running up.

"Hey," Axelia said. "Hey! Back off!"

The guy glared at her, glared at Omen, and allowed himself to be dragged away.

"Are you OK?" Aurnia asked. "Omen, did he hurt you?"

"No," Omen lied, rubbing his shoulder. "Who was that?"

"That's Buach."

Axelia frowned. "Boo-ock?"

"Buach, yes," said Aurnia. "He's... I don't know. He doesn't like sorcerers, and he wants everyone to know it. He just gets very angry sometimes. Living here, surrounded by magic people... it makes him unhappy."

"Well, I'd stay away from him, if I were you," said Omen. "You really don't want to be around someone who's that volatile."

"He's my boyfriend," Aurnia said, wincing.

"*That's* your boyfriend? I thought your boyfriend was nice and sweet and happy. Didn't you tell me that?"

"And Buach is all of those things," Aurnia replied, "when sorcerers aren't around. Also, I think he doesn't like you because you wanted to kiss me."

"That's hardly fair," said Omen immediately. "When I wanted to kiss you, he wasn't your boyfriend. And why would you even tell him that? Of course he hates me now."

"Buach needs to learn that you are not his property," Axelia said.

"Oh, he knows," Aurnia replied. "He's just being stupid. He's really very sweet. And kind. He makes me happy." She sighed. "But what he did just now was terrible, and he'll either apologise to you or he won't have a girlfriend any more."

"You'd break up with him?" Axelia asked.

"*That's* the expression I was searching for," said Aurnia, pointing at her. "Break up with him, yes. I still don't know the proper phrases. In our culture, we don't even have equivalents. Anyway, yes, I'll break up with him if he doesn't say sorry."

"That's OK," said Omen. "It's no big deal. He doesn't have to."

Aurnia reached into Omen's bag, took out a handful of pamphlets and flicked through them. "Of course he does," she said. "There's a polite way to behave and a rude way. I'm not going to go out with someone who's rude."

Axelia grinned. "I like you more and more, every time I see you."

Aurnia grinned back. "I like you, too."

"Does anyone like me?" Omen asked hopefully.

"Sure we do," said Axelia. "You carry the bag."

8

The car hit a pothole and Valkyrie cursed, glared at nothing in particular and carried on. The roads around here were getting worse. No mortal officials bothered with them because, as far as they knew, these were tiny country roads that led nowhere, and no magical officials bothered with them because these were, technically, mortal roads, and mortals had to take care of themselves. Those were the rules.

Valkyrie slalomed very carefully round the next set of potholes, fully aware that she was using her irritation about the potholes to push her worries about Alice into the back of her mind. As long as it worked, she didn't much care.

She turned on to a wider road. An old man nodded to her. She nodded back. The road was better here. The giant potholes that Swiss-cheesed the surface were nothing but illusions – she could drive right over them and suffer not one jolt. The air shimmered ahead.

She drove through the cloaking shield, and the walled city of Roarhaven appeared before her.

The Cleavers let her through Shudder's Gate and she swiftly weaved her way towards the Circle. She gave Oldtown a miss – that was the only area where the traffic built up – and approached the High Sanctuary from the south. She took the ramp down into the car park, then walked across and stood on a tile and it shot off the ground, twirling as it ascended. It clicked into place in the floor of the marble foyer and she stepped off.

Skulduggery was waiting beyond the steady stream of mages, wearing a black three-piece, black shirt, red tie, with a red band on his black hat.

"You look like a gangster," she said, joining him.

"Good afternoon to you, too."

"Should I have dressed up? We get to see China so rarely these days that I feel I should have dressed up, maybe worn a hat of my own."

Skulduggery shrugged. "When in doubt, wear a hat, that's what I always say."

"You do always say that."

A young woman approached, well dressed, her fingers swiping a tablet screen. She tapped it off and held it by her side as she reached them. "Arbiters," she said, "please follow me. The Supreme Mage is waiting."

"Lead on," said Skulduggery, and they followed her from the foyer. "You're the new Administrator, are you?"

She glanced back. "I am. My name is Cerise."

"The Irish Sanctuary has not had the best of luck with Administrators," Valkyrie said. "They're like drummers in Spinal Tap, you know?"

"Spinal Tap, Detective Cain?"

"There's a high turnover is what I mean. You sure you want this job?"

"I have been a student of the Supreme Mage since I was sixteen years old," Cerise responded. "It is an honour to serve her now."

"But to handle the day-to-day running of the whole High Sanctuary..."

"The High Sanctuary is run by mages more talented and resourceful than I," Cerise said. "All I have to do is run *them*."

Valkyrie didn't say anything, but she thought that was a pretty good answer.

Cerise led them to a set of double doors – solid and plain – and she bowed again as they passed her. The chamber was small. There was a table at its centre with six chairs round it, four of which were occupied.

China Sorrows sat on the far side of the table, her posture perfect, her head up, her blue eyes unfocused.

"Detective Pleasant, Detective Cain, welcome," Aloysius Vespers said as soon as they entered. The English Grand Mage came over and shook their hands. He was one of the only sorcerers Valkyrie knew who wore actual robes, like a wizard in a movie. His white hair was long and his beard was braided. He had small teeth. "Please," he said, indicating the chairs, "sit."

The chairs were sturdy and hard. No padding. This was a chamber for doing business and making decisions, not for idle conversation and time-wasting.

The American Grand Mage, Gavin Praetor, poured them each a glass of water. He slid one to Valkyrie, started to slide the other to Skulduggery, then must have realised Skulduggery didn't drink, because he picked up the glass and took a sip from it himself without missing a beat.

"Should we begin?" Sturmun Drang said. "We are all busy, are we not? And time is not on our side."

"It never is," said China, blinking her way out of the Whispering and disconnecting from the city around her. "Skulduggery. Valkyrie. Thank you for coming."

"It's so hard getting an appointment to see you," Skulduggery replied, "so, when you call, we're all too happy to oblige. I assume you want to talk about the problem in the City Guard."

China waved her hand. "I'm meeting with Commander Hoc later today to discuss the fate of Yonder and his little friends, but I definitely see jail time in their future. That is not why I called you here, however."

She tapped the table and the wooden surface flickered, and small screens came to life beneath the grain. The screens showed a photograph of the American president, Martin Flanery, walking across the White House lawn, deep in conversation with a slight man in an ill-fitting suit. "The man next to the president is Bertram Wilkes, Flanery's personal aide. Grand Mage Praetor?"

"A little under six months ago," Praetor said, "Wilkes disappeared. The official line is that he resigned due to the workload, and planned to travel extensively in order to recharge his batteries. He has not, as far as we know, been seen since three days *before* he left his job, but that has been difficult to ascertain due to the fact that he has no family and, apparently, no friends to note his absence. It is our belief, however, that Wilkes was a mage, and we believe he was murdered."

Skulduggery shifted ever so slightly in his seat. "Go on."

Praetor tapped the table, and a black-and-white photograph appeared of a group of friends smiling for the camera. "We retrieved this from a woman we believe Detective Cain interviewed last year in San Francisco."

Valkyrie recognised a few of the faces – Richard Melior, Savant Vega, Azzedine Smoke and a friend of Temper's, Tessa somebody. Four others, too – one of them being Bertram Wilkes with radically different hair.

"We don't know his actual name," said Vespers. "All we know is this Wilkes persona which, as you can imagine, is a well-executed forgery. But, judging by the company he kept, it is not far-fetched to conclude that he may well be associated with Abyssinia."

"So you think Abyssinia sent him in undercover to the White House," Skulduggery said. "Why?"

"We don't know," China responded. "But we believe that the American president had him killed."

"You think Flanery knows about sorcerers?" Valkyrie asked.

"We do."

"So how bad is this situation?"

"We have had worse scenarios," said Drang. "World leaders,

42

law-enforcement officials, media organisations – they have all learned of our existence and we either find a way to guarantee their silence or we resort to more extreme measures to keep our secret."

Valkyrie frowned. "What do you mean, 'more extreme'?"

"Now is not the time," said China.

"How extreme have we gone?"

China sighed. "Lengths," she said. "Sanctuaries have gone to lengths to preserve our anonymity. We may have to go to lengths again here, as Flanery is not the most stable of mortal leaders."

"Whether Flanery knows about us or not," Skulduggery said, "we've got to find out why Abyssinia felt the need to send a spy into the Oval Office. Do we know anything at all about Bertram Wilkes?"

"The only lead we have is this person," China said, her fingernail tapping the table. A new photograph appeared. A tall man leaving a house, his dark hair shot through with grey. "We've identified him as Oberon Guile, an American sorcerer who has just completed a three-year sentence in Ironpoint Gaol for robbery. That is, roughly, the sum total of the information we have about him."

"This is Bertram Wilkes's house that Mr Guile is leaving," said Praetor. "We've been watching it for months and Mr Guile is the only person we've seen, coming or going. This photograph was taken three days ago, and we've been keeping discreet tabs on him since then in the hope that he leads us to something more concrete. But our feeling now is that we must act."

"Which is where we come in," Skulduggery said.

"I am fully aware that, as Arbiters, you do not work for me," China responded, "but I would greatly appreciate it if you would make contact with Mr Guile and find out what he knows and what he's after and how it connects back to Abyssinia and whatever dastardly plan she's hatching. Does that sound acceptable?"

"It sounds *positively* acceptable," Skulduggery said. "And in the meantime you're going to be looking into corruption in the City Guard and seeing how far it's spread, yes?"

China settled her gaze on him. "Yes," she said eventually, a hint of reluctant amusement in her voice. "I was just about to announce that."

Valkyrie and Skulduggery stood up to leave.

"One more thing," China said. "I have a favour to ask, actually."

Skulduggery tilted his head. "This should be interesting."

"I find myself somewhat conflicted of late," China began. "Abyssinia is, obviously, a threat that must be taken seriously. We don't know what her plans are, but we can rest assured that they will not be in our best interests. She sees herself as a ruler, the Princess of the Darklands and, I am sure, its future queen, and she will not stop until both the mortal world and the magical world are under her control."

Whereas China would only be happy once the magical world stayed under *her* control was something Valkyrie decided not to say out loud.

"Abyssinia's actions, and the actions of her little gang of killers, are to be condemned. However, I must admit to being cautiously happy that Caisson has been broken free from his almost-century-long torture. As everyone in this room knows, I raised him, and he was almost like a son to me."

Valkyrie kept her mouth shut.

"But more trouble is stirring," said China. "Serafina Dey wants Caisson back. She seems to think that because he killed her dearly departed husband, she *owns* the poor boy. So, as part of her efforts to recover him, she's coming here."

"I don't suppose she's planning a quiet visit, is she?" Skulduggery asked.

China smiled. "Not entirely. She expects crowds, a red carpet, a reception, dinners... And that is what I have to request of you."

"I don't eat dinner," Skulduggery said.

"And you don't have to," China responded. "I'm going to be greeting her on the front steps of the High Sanctuary on Saturday at noon. My esteemed Council of Advisors will be in attendance, of course, and I would greatly appreciate it if you two would be there also."

"Why?" Valkyrie asked.

"A show of strength," China said. "A show of solidarity."

"And also because we're Arbiters," Skulduggery said, "and we operate outside the jurisdiction of any one Sanctuary. In theory, we're the only people with the authority to challenge someone like Serafina Dey."

"There is that, too," China conceded.

Skulduggery looked at Valkyrie, and she shrugged.

"We'll be there," she said. "I'm not going to pass up the opportunity to meet the woman who married Mevolent. I can only imagine what kind of freak she's going to be."

9

"Mr President, we were thinking that maybe you need a cat."

Martin Flanery, the President of the United States of America, the most powerful man in the world, the most important man in the world, and the most famous man in the world, swivelled his chair round and looked at the aide who had spoken.

The Oval Office was full of people. His Chief of Staff, his Directors of Communication, his Press Secretary, aides and advisors and assistants and one or two others. All their voices blurred into one after half an hour. This guy had caught his attention.

"What?" he said.

"A cat," the aide repeated. Flanery didn't know his name. Aides' names were rarely important. "Or a dog. A pet, basically. We feel it might soften your image."

"What's wrong with my image?"

The aide paled. "Nothing."

Flanery leaned forward, elbows on his desk. "Then why do I need to soften it?"

The aide looked around for help. None came. That pleased Flanery. He liked to see people flounder.

"We just thought," the aide said, not nearly so confident now, "that it might be a good idea to present a, uh, a more relatable image to the voters."

"They seemed to relate to me fine when they voted for me,"

Flanery said. "You think they've forgotten that? You think they've forgotten who I am?"

"I... I didn't mean anything by it, sir."

"You know your problem? The lot of you? You're approaching it all wrong. People don't want to relate to me. They want to emulate me. They want to *be* me. I offer them what nobody else does. I offer them glamour. Celebrity. I offer them opulence, and that's what they want. When they're paying for groceries or standing in line for a hot dog or watching the game, they think about me and they know that if they put in the time and the effort, they could have what I have."

This was a lie, of course. In order to have what Flanery had, they'd need his money and his keen understanding of power, a talent that allowed him to take risks that the average person couldn't even *begin* to comprehend. He was so far beyond them that it had stopped being funny a long time ago – but the fantasy seemed to keep them happy.

The conversation turned to matters of policy, and Flanery's mind drifted to Dan Tucker, the vice-president, and the interview he'd given that made it sound like he was mocking Flanery's intelligence. Flanery would have to talk to him about that. Or get his Chief of Staff to talk to him. He was sure it had just been a mistake. It had to have been.

Then he thought about the Big Plan that he'd come up with, and he thought about Abyssinia and about how much he despised her. She was a witch, and she treated him with disrespect. Because of that, he didn't like talking to her. He quite enjoyed it when she rang his private phone and he didn't answer. That was a power move. His father had taught him all about power moves, and Flanery had added a few of his own over the years. He was an expert at power moves.

When the meeting was done, he dismissed them all and left the Oval Office. He went down the corridor and kept going until he entered the Residence. He went into the dining room and shut the door, then turned on the TV to find out what the press was saying about this whole Dan Tucker mess.

It was not good.

"Everything OK, Martin?"

Flanery yelled and jumped. Crepuscular Vies sat at the table, halfway through a meal. His shirtsleeves were rolled up and he wasn't wearing his hat. His bow tie had butterflies on it.

Flanery didn't like to see him eating. Having no lips made it unpleasant. "How did you get that food?" he asked, looking away.

"I picked up the phone and ordered it," Crepuscular answered, and then, in a startlingly precise impression of Flanery's own voice, said, "Bring me a steak, fried to a crisp, with some fries. No vegetables.' You're not a difficult man to impersonate, Martin, even though I was restricted to the terrible orders you regularly make. Steak, well done? That's a crime against cattle."

With no idea how to respond to that, Flanery decided to let it go. To cover up this momentary weakness, he jabbed a finger at the TV. "You hear this crap? You hear what they're saying?"

Crepuscular sawed through another bit of meat, then popped it between his teeth. "I did."

"They're saying Tucker insulted me," Flanery said, feeling the anger rise again. "They're saying he called me stupid. He's the vice-president! He wouldn't do that. I'm the one in charge. He wouldn't be vice-president if it wasn't for me picking his name out of a hat!"

"You might not want to tell him *that* part."

"You're supposed to help me," Flanery grumbled. "Isn't that what you said you'd do? Isn't that what you promised?"

Crepuscular didn't say anything. Good. That meant Flanery had him on the back foot. Not responding to a challenge showed weakness, which was why Flanery always responded to opponents with insults or scorn. Crepuscular, for all his arrogance, hadn't learned that yet.

"As far as I can see," Flanery continued, "you haven't lived up to your part of the deal. This shouldn't be happening. The media shouldn't be reporting this stuff. What are you going to do about it? I get enough incompetence with my staff, I do not need it from you!"

Flanery stopped, and waited for Crepuscular to respond.

Crepuscular finished eating, and dabbed at his lipless mouth with a napkin before he stood. He pushed the chair back into place and unfolded his shirtsleeves, buttoning them at the wrist as he came forward. He reached out and his hand closed round Flanery's throat and he walked him backwards.

"You seem to be mistaking me for someone else," Crepuscular said.

Flanery wasn't a particularly athletic man, and he'd never played sport or learned how to box or wrestle, and in many respects he'd never had to actually lift anything heavy in his life, but even so he was surprised at the ease with which Crepuscular pinned him to the wall. His height, his weight, his importance – none of it meant anything. To Crepuscular, Flanery was nothing but a weakling.

"You seem to be mistaking me for Mr Wilkes," Crepuscular continued. "He was the one you barked at, and complained to, and insulted. He was the one who scurried after you. Do you think I'm him, Martin? Is that what you think?"

Flanery tried to answer, but all he could do was gurgle. He could barely shake his head.

"I'm the one who killed him, Martin," Crepuscular said. "I'm the one who snapped his neck after he'd finally had enough. I remember the look on your face when he stood up to you. Your bullying didn't seem to work on him then, did it?"

Darkness clouded Flanery's vision. He was aware of his own spittle on his chin. He was aware of the ridiculous sounds he was making. He was aware of his hands, tapping weakly against the scary man's arm. His head pounded. His legs were jelly.

And then Crepuscular moved him away from the wall and

swung him round, and the backs of his knees hit something and he collapsed into a chair and Crepuscular was walking away.

Flanery doubled over, gasping for air.

"You're doing a great job, Mr President," Crepuscular said, his voice coming from somewhere behind the drumming of Flanery's own heartbeat. "Don't let the liberal media get you down. They don't understand you. They don't see why the people love you. And they *do* love you. More than any other president since Lincoln."

Nodding, Flanery straightened up in his chair.

Crepuscular had put his jacket on. He was wearing another one of those checked suits he liked so much. He put on his hat and straightened his bow tie. "Ten days," he said. "Ten days and your plan goes into action. Ten days and the world changes, sir, and you go down in history. Are you looking forward to that?"

Flanery nodded quickly.

"Then who cares what they say on the news? And who cares what Vice-President Tucker may or may not have called you? None of it matters. The only thing that will matter, in ten days' time, is the small naval base in Whitley, Oregon, and all the people who died there."

10

It was a messy business, crying.

Sebastian hated it. His tears would fog up the lenses on his mask and his face would get all wet and dribbly and there wasn't anything he could do about it except wait. Eventually, the mask would soak it all up, just like it did when he perspired. Or sneezed.

Sneezing was the worst. Well, sneezing was the worst *so far*. Every night, before he went to sleep, he prayed that there would be no reason for him to throw up the next day.

His suit. God, he hated that thing. The beaked mask that made him look like a crow. The heavy coat. The hat. Why was there even a hat? Why was the hat necessary?

He hated it all. He longed to touch his own skin, to rake his fingers through his hair. Ever since he'd put the suit on, he'd been unable to scratch himself. Itches drove him mad.

And breathing. Oh, how he missed fresh air. How he missed the taste of it. And the feel of it. A breeze. What he wouldn't give to feel the slightest breeze against his face.

But the worst thing about this whole mission was the loneliness. The sheer, terrifying loneliness of his situation. Every other day, he'd get an update on the continuing search for Darquesse. He'd stand there and nod while Forby took him through the details of what he was doing, pretending to grasp at least some of the fundamentals when it came to scanning an infinite number of dimensions for the slightest trace of Darquesse's energy signature. He was sure Forby now regarded him as an idiot, and probably regretted voting for him to be the leader of their little group, but for Sebastian it was one of the few chances he got to interact with a real live person, so he loved it. He loved every mind-numbingly confusing second of it.

And, every week, they'd have their meeting. They'd all get together at Bennet's, or Lily's, or Kimora's. Never at Ulysses's house, because his wife didn't approve, and never at Tarry's, because he said his place was always a dump, but they got together and they chatted and either Ulysses or Lily would bring cake, and even though Sebastian didn't need food – his suit took care of his nourishment – and he couldn't eat even if he wanted to, it was good. He had friends.

But then the meeting would end, and they'd all head back to their families and to their lives, and Sebastian would return to the empty house he'd made his own, and sit there. In the dark. In the silence.

Metaphorically, of course. Every house in Roarhaven came fully furnished and hooked up to electricity, so he actually sat in a warm, brightly lit house, watching TV or reading a book.

But no amount of TV and no amount of books, as wonderful as they were, could ever provide him with the friendship he needed – that he'd once had, but he'd left behind. For the mission. For the damn mission.

For the mission he was failing at.

Of course he was going to fail. It was inevitable. He was going to let them all down. The world needed Darquesse. They needed her power, even if they didn't realise it. And it was all up to him to find her. All up to Sebastian Tao, the Plague Doctor, the Idiot Who Was Going To Ruin Everything.

There was a doomsday clock, somewhere in the world, and it was ticking steadily down.

A knock on the door snapped him out of his melancholy. He opened it. Bennet stood there, holding two bottles of beer.

"Hey, buddy," Bennet said. "I was passing, and..."

Sebastian frowned behind his mask. "There's nothing beyond this house except more empty houses."

"Well, I meant I was in the neighbourhood and..." Bennet sagged. "The fact is, my TV packed up on me, and there's a game on tonight that I've been looking forward to, so I was wondering if I could watch it with you...?"

"Sure," Sebastian said, the brightness in his voice surprising him. "Come on in. I'm afraid I can't offer you anything, because I don't eat or drink."

"That's why I brought these," said Bennet as they walked into the living room. "They're non-alcoholic, don't worry. I have to drive home."

"Wise man," said Sebastian. He sat in the armchair, searching for the remote, while Bennet took up his position on the couch. "I'm pretty sure I have the sports channels. I vaguely remember flicking past a football game once." He found the remote and sat back.

"It's nice and quiet here," Bennet said.

"Yeah," Sebastian responded. "No traffic outside. No neighbours."

Bennet sipped his beer. "It's been pretty quiet at my place, too. Christmas was particularly hard. I'm just used to, you know, decorations and the tree, and the music and all the fuss and the... the *feeling*, you know? But the house was very quiet this year. Very quiet. I didn't bother with any of the... things. That was Odetta's area."

"How *is* Odetta?"

"She's good," Bennet said with a sad smile. "She really seems to be happy with Conrad. He doesn't say much, you know. Or anything, really. Apparently, Hollow Men can grunt, if they churn their gases in a certain way? But I've never heard him make a sound. He treats her well, though. I think. I don't know. He doesn't do a whole lot except stand there."

"Right."

"Makes you wonder how bad a husband I must have been if Odetta chose a Hollow Man over me, eh?" Bennet said, and laughed. "But naw, she's good. She's happier. And Kase is living with them. He's doing well at school. He's a good kid."

"He is," Sebastian agreed. "Do you spend much time with him?"

"Not as much as I'd like. And now, with my new job and all, I've got to focus on not getting fired, so that cuts down on the father-son thing."

"You want my advice?" Sebastian said. "Spend more time with him. He deserves all the attention he can get from parents who love him."

"Yeah..."

"We never know how much time we have left, Bennet."

Bennet took another sip of his beer. "This is true."

"If I had family, I'd be cherishing every moment I had with them."

"You don't have family?"

"Not any more."

"You... want to talk about it?"

"Not especially."

"Sore subject?"

"Yeah."

"OK," said Bennet. "But, if you ever do need to talk, that's what friends are for."

"Thank you," Sebastian said, fighting the sudden rush of warmth that threatened to bring tears to his eyes. He clicked on the TV. "So what channel is the game on?"

"Do you ever doubt what we're doing?"

Sebastian lowered the remote. "What do you mean?"

"What Forby's doing with the machine and all?"

"Looking for Darquesse?"

"No. Well, yes, but not the search itself – just the likelihood of finding her."

Sebastian sighed. "It's tricky," he admitted. "I've got this little voice in my head and every day it whispers to me, *Maybe Darquesse is dead. Maybe the Faceless Ones tore her apart years ago.*"

"Or maybe, if we find her, she won't want to come back."

Sebastian frowned. "You think that's a possibility?"

"Don't you?"

"I don't know. It never occurred to me that she might not want to return. I mean, this is her home."

"That she left."

"Well, yeah, but she left under false pretences, didn't she?"

"Which brings me to my next point," Bennet said. "What if she comes back to finish the job? If we find her, if we tell her that she was fooled into thinking she'd ended all life on earth... what if she only comes back to do it for real?"

"That," said Sebastian, "is a possibility. We all know that. But do you believe it?"

"No," said Bennet. "But can I be trusted? Can any of us be trusted? We saw what Darquesse can do. We saw her power and it unlocked something in us, a love and a devotion that could quite possibly be self-destructive. I don't think she'd kill us if she returned. But I might be wrong. We all might be wrong."

"Sounds like you're going through a crisis of faith, my friend."

Bennet suddenly looked flustered, like he'd miscalculated. "I mean... I mean, I'm still devoted to—"

Sebastian held up a hand. "I didn't mean it as an accusation. Of course you're doubting all this. Everything you've said is one hundred per cent true. These are the thoughts that go through my mind a thousand times a day."

Bennet relaxed. "So how do you handle it?"

"I... believe, I suppose. I choose to believe that it'll work out, that we'll find her, we'll bring her home, and that everything will be OK. You're not alone here, Bennet."

Bennet finished his first beer, and put the empty bottle on the coffee table. "Well, neither are you. I hope you know that."

Sebastian smiled. "Thank you. So, which channel is the game on?"

"I don't know," Bennet answered. "I don't even like football. I came over here because I was lonely and I thought we could hang out. Do you have any video games? I'm pretty good at—"

Bennet's phone beeped at the same time as Sebastian's buzzed. They looked at their screens at the same time. It was a message. From Forby.

I think I've found Darquesse.

11

Valkyrie got back to Grimwood House at a little past nine. She got out of the car and Xena ran up to her and they cuddled until the dog calmed down enough for Valkyrie to open the front door.

She flicked on the lights, dumped the day's post on the hall table and fed Xena. She ate leftovers in the quiet kitchen, washed the plate and put it away, then went upstairs to have a shower. Her phone chimed when she got out. It was Temper Fray, asking them to meet him the next day. She messaged him back, then dressed in pyjama bottoms and a light top. On her way back down the stairs, the doorbell rang.

She padded across the hall in her bare feet, and opened the door.

Tanith Low stood there in jeans and a warm coat open over a Prince T-shirt, her blonde hair tousled.

Valkyrie leaped forward, wrapping her in the biggest hug she could muster.

"Holy crap," Tanith wheezed.

"I missed you," Valkyrie said into her shoulder.

"I miss my lungs," said Tanith. "I'm sure they were there a second ago..."

Valkyrie released her and jumped back, looked her up and down. "Your hair's shorter. I love it. Where have you been?"

"Away."

"What have you been doing?"

"Things."

"How are you?"

"Tormented."

"I want to hear every last little detail."

She made them each a cup of tea and they sat on the couch, legs curled beneath them.

"Look at you," Tanith said. "Right up until you answered that door, I still had this picture in my head of you as a... not a kid, but... a girl. But you're a proper grown-up, aren't you?"

"Technically."

"How's Skulduggery?"

"Same as ever. We've been dealing with a bit of a thing lately. Abyssinia, you heard of her?"

Tanith nodded. "I try to keep up with what's happening. Is it true she's Skulduggery's ex?"

"That is true, yes."

"Wow. Must have been quite a shock to learn he had an ex-girlfriend back on the scene. How about you?"

"How about me what?"

"Any boyfriends I should know about?"

"Not right now," said Valkyrie. She took a breath. "There is a girlfriend, though."

"Really?" Tanith said, drawing the word out as her eyes got wider. "You dark horse, you. When did this happen?"

"Few months ago. Her name's Militsa Gnosis. She's a teacher at Corrival Academy. Necromancer."

"Oooh," said Tanith, "a bad girl."

Valkyrie laughed. "Not really."

"So is this it? The full switch, girls-only from now on?"

"Ah, I still like boys, too."

"You played that close to the chest, didn't you? I'm usually good at picking up on things like this, but you've surprised me."

Valkyrie shrugged. "You meet the right person at the right time, and you discover brand-new things about yourself. I was a little surprised, too, to be honest, but there you go."

"Have you told your folks?"

Valkyrie hesitated.

Tanith smiled. "Yeah, that tends to be the hard part. Coming out to other sorcerers isn't a big deal – we're all at it. But those limited life spans mean that mortals tend to be a little more conservative. Some of them."

"They're going to be cool about it," Valkyrie said.

"Of course they are."

"But I'm still nervous."

"Course you are."

"How about you?" Valkyrie asked, sitting back. "Boys? Girls? Both?"

"Neither," said Tanith. "Been too busy for distractions."

"Is that why you're back in Ireland?"

Tanith sipped her tea, then put the cup on the saucer and the saucer on the coffee table. "Yeah."

"Are you in trouble?"

"When am I not?"

"Anything I can do to help?"

Tanith shook her head. "I got myself into this, Val. I'm going to get myself out."

"How brave," said Valkyrie. "How noble. How dumb. If I can help, let me help. You have friends."

"I know I do," Tanith said, her voice quiet. She let a few seconds go by before speaking again. "Have you heard of Black Sand?"

"Sure," Valkyrie said. "The terrorist group in Africa."

Tanith did not appreciate that. "They're not terrorists, Val. You can't believe everything the Sanctuaries tell you. They're a resistance group."

"And what are they resisting?"

"OK," Tanith said, shifting slightly, "China wants control of the African and Australian Sanctuaries, right? I mean, that's fairly obvious."

"Of course," said Valkyrie. "She already controls one Cradle of Magic – she'd love to control all three."

"But she's not actually doing anything about it, is she? She would *like* control – but she's not trying to *take* control. That would be like declaring war on your allies, and she's not going to do that."

"Right."

"Except she *is*."

"Tanith—"

"Just listen. I could get you proof, but this isn't your fight. I need you to understand why I'm doing what I'm doing. She can't just take them over, as much as she'd love to, so she's being sneaky about it. As far as I can tell, she's focusing on the three African Sanctuaries first. She's got spies and double agents working in a, quite frankly, *bewildering* array of schemes designed to usurp the Council of Elders, and replace them with her own people. Then they'll bow to China as their Supreme Mage, and she can focus her attention on Australia."

"And Black Sand...?"

"Black Sand are resisting," Tanith said. "They're targeting her schemes and disrupting them wherever they can."

"And you're involved with them, aren't you?"

"They needed fighters and I..."

"You needed somewhere to go," Valkyrie finished.

Tanith looked away. "I was lost," she said. "With what happened to Ghastly, and Billy-Ray... I couldn't stick around, you know? I was looking for a fight, and they offered me one.

"But, a few months ago, Sanctuary forces rounded up a load of friends and families of Black Sand members. Innocent people, Val."

Valkyrie frowned. "They would have been interrogated by Sensitives," she said. "They can't be *that* innocent."

"They knew what was happening, but they had no part in it. And now the Sanctuaries – who have no idea we're doing all this for *them*, to keep *them* independent – have decided to make an example out of them by sentencing them to thirty years in prison. Each."

"So you're here to convince China to release them?"

"No," said Tanith, "that'd never work, and she wouldn't be interested anyway. I'm here to offer up the Black Sand leader in exchange for the people they've imprisoned."

"The Black Sand leader," Valkyrie repeated.

"Yes."

Valkyrie closed her eyes. "Tanith, please tell me you're not the Black Sand leader."

"I can't exactly do that, Val."

Valkyrie groaned. She put her cup on the coffee table and leaned forward. "They'll throw you in prison. Not one of the good ones, either. Ironpoint, maybe, or Coldheart, if it was under Sanctuary control."

"I know."

"The other convicts will kill you," Valkyrie said. "You won't last a week."

"Oh, ye of little faith," Tanith said with an unconvincing smile. "I give myself two, easy."

"Let me talk to China. Me and Skulduggery. We'll sort it out."

"You won't be able to," Tanith said. "This is bigger than your friendship with her, Val. You know her. I know her. From her point of view, she'll have no choice but to be seen as ruthless, and lock me away in the worst prison she has. The fact that she hates me and I hate her will have nothing to do with it. She's set herself on this course, just like I have."

Valkyrie blinked. "But... OK, wait, so why are you here? I mean, what's the plan?"

"I told you the plan."

"No, you told me the stupid plan where you go to prison. I

mean the good plan where all this is taken care of and you stay *out* of prison."

"That plan doesn't exist."

"Not yet it doesn't, but that's because you've just come to me about it. I'll come up with a good plan. Skulduggery will... well, he'll watch as I come up with a good plan."

"Skulduggery's not very good with plans," Tanith agreed.

"Don't do this yet," said Valkyrie. "Promise me that, OK? Give me a little time to think of something."

"Val, I appreciate the offer, but there's really nothing you can do."

"Give me time."

"Innocent people are in jail cells as we speak."

"A few more days isn't going to matter," Valkyrie said. "It'll give them time to maybe work out in the yard or something. Start a diet. Make new friends. Don't rush into this."

"No one's rushing, believe me."

Valkyrie clutched Tanith's hand. "Help us."

"Help you what?"

"Help us with this thing," she said. "This Abyssinia thing. We need all the help we can get. There are bad guys all over the place – more of them than there are of us. Help us with this, and then if your thing hasn't been sorted or we don't at least have a good plan, then you can continue with your stupid one."

"Val..."

"Give me a chance to help you. Please."

Tanith sighed, and Valkyrie grinned.

12

Tanith got on her motorbike and rode away, and Valkyrie locked up the house and went to bed, Xena curled up on the floor beside her.

She woke almost two hours later to Xena barking madly at two people stumbling through the bedroom.

Valkyrie sprang out of bed, hands crackling with energy. Her bedroom was not her bedroom. Her bedroom was a town, at night. Cars were on fire. Bodies lay on the streets. Gunshots and screams in the distance. The stumbling figures were the Darkly brothers.

She shook the magic from her hands, and knelt beside the dog. "It's OK," she said. "It's not real. It's OK."

Xena stopped barking but kept growling.

The brothers changed direction and the town shifted around Valkyrie, keeping them in view. The effect was dizzying.

She'd seen this before – it was part of a vision of the future she'd had multiple times – but never like this, never focusing on just this one event. Something was different about it. It felt... more real. It felt more urgent.

She knew why. It was closer. It was going to happen, and it was going to happen soon.

Auger was bleeding badly. Omen dragged him on. The people in the helmets and black body armour came after them, guns up, swarming across the road. Professional. Relentless.

They opened fire. Three bullets struck Omen and he went straight down without even crying out, and Auger turned to help him and another burst of bullets sent him spinning.

"Stop," Valkyrie snarled. *"Stop."*

The vision slowed, and then froze.

Valkyrie stood.

This was new. She'd never done this before. She'd never even considered that she *could* do this.

Xena came forward, too, sniffing at Omen, confused when she detected nothing but empty space.

Valkyrie moved towards the people with the guns, but they were beyond the walls of the bedroom, and, as much as she tried to shift the vision to bring them closer, it wouldn't budge. She doubted she'd be able to glean anything new from them anyway. They wore no badges, no patches, no identifying markings. The only thing she knew about them was that they were well armed and that they killed teenagers.

The vision flickered. It was breaking down, and giving her a headache while it did so. Grimacing against the pain, she looked around for a clue as to where she was, where this was happening. Was *going* to happen.

There was a car parked by the side of the road just beyond the wall behind her bed. The vision flickered again.

She just had time to glimpse the licence plate before the vision washed away, leaving her pressed against the wall.

Oregon.

Omen Darkly was going to die in America.

13

Lunchtime. Omen finished eating, grabbed his bottle of rock shandy and went looking for someone to talk to. Mr Peccant passed and scowled for no reason other than scowling at Omen was what he did. Omen was pretty sure it was becoming Peccant's favourite hobby.

He found Never on one of the benches in the second-floor corridor, talking to Grey Keller. They laughed, and Grey got up and made another joke, then laughed again as he walked away.

Omen sauntered over, took Grey's place on the bench and wiggled his eyebrows.

Never frowned at him. "What's your face doing? It's weird and I don't like it."

"My face is asking you a question," said Omen. "It's asking, is there anything going on that I should be aware of?"

"And my answer is, undoubtedly," Never said. "Like, a serious amount is going on that you should be aware of. Schoolwork is only the beginning of it."

"I mean about Grey."

"What about Grey?"

"You and Grey."

"Oh," said Never, taking a drink from his bottle of water. "Naw. Grey is lovely and everything, and undeniably cute, but he isn't interested in me."

"You want me to talk to him?"

Never looked horrified. "About me? Great googly moogly, no. Why would you even suggest that?"

"I have a few classes with him. We chat occasionally. I could tell him how cool you are."

"First of all, he knows how cool I am. Everyone knows how cool I am. Look at me. Second, he's not interested in me because, from what I can tell, he's not interested in anyone. Being interested in people is just not his thing."

"Huh," said Omen. "I wonder what that's like."

Never grunted. "I'm sure it has its problems, the same as everything else. Speaking of everything else, any movement in *your* love life?"

"Not really," Omen admitted. "I met Aurnia's boyfriend yesterday."

"Aurnia..." Never said, squinting. He clicked his fingers. "Mortal girl from Mevolent's dimension! Got it! Yes, and how *was* her boyfriend?"

"Large," said Omen, "and I'm pretty sure he wanted to fight me."

"Well, he *did* just meet you, so I can understand the impulse."

"Oh, cheers for that."

Never grinned. "Did you puff out your chest and square up to him?"

"No," Omen said, frowning. "Was I supposed to?"

"Not really. Good boy, Omen. I'm proud of you."

"I'm not sure what for, but OK."

A Fifth Year girl whose name Omen didn't know walked by. She smiled at Never. Never winked back.

Omen frowned. "Is *that* something I should be aware of?"

"We're just friends," Never said casually.

"That was a flirty look she gave you."

"How would you know?"

"I've seen them in movies," Omen replied, a little defensively.

"You *are* surprisingly well versed in romantic comedies," said Never. "But we're just friends, really. It might lead to something more, or it might not. Whatever."

Omen sagged. "You're so lucky."

"I know," said Never. "But remind me – how, exactly?"

"You're bisexual. I wish *I* was bisexual."

Never laughed. "Feeling cheated, are we?"

"Well, yeah. I mean, it's like I'm cutting off half my potential love interests without even thinking about it. If I liked boys as much as I liked girls, I'd at least have the chance to... to... Well, to be turned down by more people. But that's not the point."

"I wouldn't worry about it, Omen. Most sorcerers eventually turn bi because they grow tired of viewing relationships from a traditional, mortal perspective. They gradually allow themselves to be free – the key word being *gradually*. It just takes a little time."

"But what if I'm not bi?" Omen asked, keeping his voice low. "What if I'm one of those sorcerers who's, like, straight or gay their entire lives?"

Never patted his shoulder. "It won't be so bad. I'll still invite you to parties."

"You promise?"

"Omen, I'm going to be having so many parties you won't know what to do with yourself, and I want you there, standing in the background, maybe handing out canapés. The dream."

"The dream," Omen said, and they tapped their bottles together just as the bell rang.

"Aw, crap," Omen muttered.

"You just remembered what class we have now, didn't you?"

Omen grumbled in reply, and got up and trudged after Never. They made it to their seats just as Miss Wicked walked in.

Omen liked Miss Wicked. She was scary, but in a good way. Or at least a mostly good way. But this latest module was not proving to be a strong point for him.

The class went quiet before the door had even closed behind her. She went to her desk, turned on her heels and watched them.

Madcap Fenton, a self-proclaimed class clown, stood, a confused expression on his face, and walked to the front of the class and started to write on the board. Omen glanced at Never, then at Auger. They both looked as mystified as Omen felt.

Madcap wrote TELEPATHY and then returned to his seat.

Omen, and everyone else, stared at him. After a moment, Madcap blinked and said, "Whoa."

Miss Wicked flicked her wrist, and her telescopic pointer shot out to full length. The tip, covered with a tiny rubber ball, quivered mere centimetres from Diana Whist's eye. Miss Wicked swept her arm back, and tapped the board.

"Telepathy," she said. "The transmission of information from one person to another via psychic link. This can take the form of images or words or simple feelings – or all three at the same time. Entire conversations can be held and distance is no obstacle. Minds can be read. Secrets can be unlocked. Control can be taken."

She whipped the pointer away from the board, and levelled it at Madcap. "Why did you write this word?"

"I... I don't know," he answered.

"You wrote it because I told you to," Miss Wicked said. "I entered your mind and I gave you an instruction."

October Klein's hand went up, somewhat tentatively. "Excuse me, miss? Isn't that, like, not allowed?"

Miss Wicked looked at her.

October swallowed, but managed to continue. "Aren't you supposed to, kind of, ask a student's permission? Before you enter their mind?"

"You gave me your permission when we began this module," Miss Wicked said, "or at least your guardians did. Did none of you read the form you took home for them to sign? No one? You disappoint me, class. I thought you were strong, independent individuals. It appears I was mistaken."

October frowned. "My parents had no right to give permission for something like that."

"Indeed, they didn't," said Miss Wicked. "But they did it anyway, didn't they? Because until you grow up, take responsibility for yourselves and everything that comes with it – including, but not limited to, reading the small print – then other people are going to continue to make your decisions for you. In this case, they granted me permission to enter your minds for the purposes of this module. Which means I can read your thoughts from the moment you step into this room, and I can do so without warning. So, and I mean this quite sincerely, clean up your thoughts, everyone."

A blush wave passed over the class, and hit Omen particularly hard. Even Auger took to just staring at his desk.

"We'll touch on other aspects that a fully rounded Sensitive would need in later modules," Miss Wicked continued. "You'll be given the chance to try out telekinesis, pyrokinesis and astral projection. But telepathy is where we begin because telepathy is where the real power lies. Apart from communication, apart from reading somebody's thoughts and controlling their minds, you can alter an enemy's memory, take possession of their body, and change their very personality." She smiled. "What's throwing a little ball of energy compared to something like that?" She whacked the pointer against her desk. "Pair up. This next hour is going to be interesting."

14

Around the corner from Decapitation Row, tucked under an arch, was a charming little café with cakes in the window. It had a bell above the door that tinkled when Valkyrie entered. The place only had five tables, and only one of them was occupied, right at the very back.

Militsa stood as Valkyrie walked over.

"Hey, you," Valkyrie said, kissing her. "Am I late?"

"Not at all," Militsa answered.

"Really?"

"Of course you're late. You're always late. But that's all right."

They sat, and Valkyrie looked around. "I've never been here before. Is it good?"

"I have no idea."

"Hello there," the waiter said, appearing at their table. He smiled as he handed them the menus. "The soup of the day is leek and potato. Could I get you some drinks to start?"

"I'll have a glass of still water," Militsa said.

"Me too," said Valkyrie.

The waiter smiled again. "Absolutely. Coming right up."

He gave a little bow, which transformed into a turn, and then he swept away. A little dramatic for a café in the early afternoon, but fair enough.

"How did your meeting with Temper go?" Militsa asked.

"We haven't had it yet," Valkyrie said.

"Oh, I thought it was this morning. Any idea what it's about?"

"None at all. He was being cagey, though." She shrugged. "I'll find out soon enough."

"And then you're heading off to America?"

Valkyrie nodded. "We shouldn't be too long. We just have to find this Oberon Guile guy and work out if he's got anything to do with that missing White House aide. Just a normal day at work, all in all." She gave Militsa a smile.

Militsa tucked a strand of red hair behind her ear. "Something's up."

Valkyrie frowned at her. "How can you tell?"

"You just have that look about you. So what's on your mind, pretty lady?"

Valkyrie sighed. "Ah, I don't know. Everything? I've got so much going on that it's hard to keep it all straight."

"Then tell me what's uppermost in your mind."

"Well, I suppose, right now, that would be Omen and Auger. I'm worried about them."

Militsa leaned forward slightly. "Is this the vision again?"

"I had another one last night. It's about to happen."

"Any idea when?"

"Soon. Weeks. Maybe days. Omen's going to be shot and killed. Auger's going to be shot. I don't know what happens after that."

"Any other details?"

"It happens in America."

Militsa frowned. "OK, then we make sure they don't go to America in the next few weeks and *boom*, lives saved."

"I don't think it's that easy."

"Of course it is," Militsa said. "You know better than anyone how much future timelines can change because of the slightest alteration. Actively *stopping them* from leaving the country? That entire timeline will probably be rewritten just like that." She clicked her fingers.

"Maybe," said Valkyrie.

The waiter came back, produced the bottle of water with a flourish, and filled their glasses. "Have you decided what you'd like to order?" he asked.

Valkyrie snatched up the menu. "Oh, sorry, let's see..."

"Take your time," said the waiter. "Take all the time you need."

"How are the wings here?" Militsa asked.

The waiter shrugged. "Fine."

Militsa smiled. "You don't sound overly enthused."

He sighed. "They're grand. Order them if you want."

Valkyrie raised an eyebrow.

"OK," Militsa said slowly. "Then I'll have the wings, I suppose."

The waiter made a note.

Valkyrie closed the menu and handed it back to him. "And I'll have the chicken."

"What a wonderful choice," he responded, smiling broadly. He bowed, backed away, turned and disappeared into the kitchen.

"I think he fancies you," Militsa said.

"Oh, then that's a wonderful way to impress me, by being rude to my girlfriend."

"I do like it when you call me that."

"I know," Valkyrie said, giving her a smile before getting back to the subject. "So what are the Darkly boys getting up to these days?"

"You don't know?"

"I haven't spoken to Omen in weeks."

"You really should, you know," said Militsa. This is when the teacher in her came out – when she used that disapproving tone. "He's such a nice lad, and it's not really fair that you only check in on him when you've wrapped him up in whatever might get him killed next."

"I don't *only* talk to him then," Valkyrie answered, a little defensively. "I just... I don't have a reason to talk to him at any other time."

"Friendliness isn't a reason?"

"We're not exactly friends, though, are we? He's fourteen."

"Fifteen."

"When did he turn fifteen?"

"New Year's Day."

Valkyrie winced. "You think I should send him a birthday card?"

"Almost two months late? Probably not. And you don't have to be friends in order to be friendly."

Valkyrie sighed. "Yeah... maybe. So are you going to tell me how they've been?"

"Omen's struggling with classwork because he doesn't put in the effort, as per usual, and he's also trying to figure out what he wants to do with his life. And Auger... Auger's the Chosen One. He's off doing Chosen One things, having adventures, risking his life, fighting bad guys..."

"How does the school allow that stuff to keep happening?"

Militsa shrugged. "What choice do we have? Besides, everyone – and I mean the school and his own parents – sees this as a vital part of Auger's training and development. This is all building up to that momentous day when he'll have to confront the King of the Darklands."

"Don't worry," said Valkyrie, "we're keeping an eye out for anything to do with Abyssinia and, if Caisson *does* graduate from Prince of the Darklands to King, we'll step in."

"And do what?"

"And do something incredibly drastic and foolhardy that will alter the future so Auger won't have to confront anyone."

"But that's if you can *find* Caisson," Militsa countered. "Unless I'm very much mistaken, Coldheart Prison is still flying about somewhere and none of you lot even know where to look."

"Finding hijacked prisons is not my job."

The door opened and a man came into the café. Militsa had her back to the door, but her eyes widened and she sat up straighter.

"Death," she whispered.

Valkyrie reached forward, patting her hand. "It's OK," she said. "There's no danger. It's just a vampire."

The vampire walked over. Dark-haired, with delicate features, and a thin scar running down one side of his face. He stopped beside their table. His tone was quiet. "Please forgive the intrusion."

"It's been a while," Valkyrie said. "Militsa, this is Dusk. He's tried to kill me a few times, and he bit me once. I didn't turn into a vampire, though. Obviously. We're cool now, though. I think. Aren't we cool?"

"We are," Dusk said, "*cool.*"

Militsa smiled up at him. "Hello."

"Hello," said Dusk. "Valkyrie, even though we are... cool... I feel I must apologise for my past behaviour."

"You're here to say sorry?"

"No," said Dusk, "but I am making amends for my mistakes, and I take my opportunities when I can."

"Don't worry about it," Valkyrie said. "I mean, who hasn't tried to kill me, really?"

A tight smile. "That may indeed be the case, but when we first met I was undergoing a process for which we vampires don't have a name."

"Oooh," Militsa said, and then blushed.

Dusk looked uncomfortable, and Valkyrie frowned. "What? What is it?"

"I've... I've heard of this," Militsa said. She winced at Dusk. "Sorry."

"Don't apologise to him," said Valkyrie. "He tried to kill me, remember?"

Militsa leaned forward and kept her voice low. "For roughly three or four weeks every year, a vampire's human side will become dominant. It's, uh, something they don't like to talk about."

"In polite society," said Dusk.

Valkyrie folded her arms. "So your human side was dominant

when we first met? Then why were you so intent on murdering me?"

Dusk hesitated to answer. Instead, he looked at Militsa.

She cleared her throat. "Vampires are rather cold creatures, both physically and... emotionally. If Mr Dusk was intent on murdering you, like you say, then that was probably due more to his human side than his vampire side."

"Seriously?" Valkyrie said. "The worst thing about a vampire is his humanity?"

"I'm afraid so," said Dusk.

"Wow," Valkyrie said. "That's depressing for pretty much all of the human race."

"I was wondering if I could have a word with you," said Dusk. "In private, if you don't mind. It will not take long, I assure you."

Militsa stood. "I have to pee," she announced, and walked away.

Valkyrie motioned to the chair, and Dusk sat. "What's on your mind?" she asked.

"A gentleman came to see me," he said. "He said his name was Caisson."

Valkyrie sat up straighter. "You're working with Abyssinia?"

"No," Dusk answered. "I stay out of human affairs as much as possible. The Supreme Mage uses me and my fellow vampires when she needs us, but by and large she – and, by extension, the City Guards – leaves our district alone. I like this arrangement. I do not wish to see it change."

"Then why did Caisson go to see you?"

"He came to see me because he heard of our interactions, and he wants to see you," Dusk said. "He asked me to pass on the message."

"Why does he want to see me?"

"I do not know."

"Why does he think I'd say yes?"

"He merely stated that you two are not actually enemies, so you have no reason not to."

"Huh," said Valkyrie. He had a point.

"He would like to meet you at ten a.m. on Saturday, in the Fangs. The directions are written here." He slid her a folded piece of paper. "Naturally, he would expect you to come alone."

"Naturally."

He stood. "I apologise again for my behaviour in the past."

"Well... I suppose I'm sorry for, you know..." She indicated his face.

Dusk smiled. "My scar is hardly your fault. I blame Billy-Ray Sanguine and that straight razor of his, the scars from which never fade."

Valkyrie showed him the palm of her right hand. "Believe me, I know."

Dusk nodded to her, and turned to leave.

"What did you see?" she asked suddenly.

He stopped moving.

"When you bit me," she said. "You told Billy-Ray Sanguine that you saw something in my blood. He said it was punishment enough. What was it?"

Dusk's response was slow. Measured. "It is perhaps best if you do not know."

She laughed. "Well, *that's* not going to work."

"There are secrets we hide, Valkyrie, even from ourselves. We need to, in order to survive this world."

"Seriously? Even now, after Darquesse, after all that? You're saying there's something worse?"

"I will tell you if you truly wish to know. But I advise against it. Strongly."

Valkyrie had to smile. "There's really not a whole lot left that could upset me."

He looked at her. "Take some time. In a few days, if you still believe you should know, come and find me. I'll tell you what I saw."

The waiter came over before Valkyrie could respond, and Dusk took that opportunity to leave. The waiter dumped Militsa's plate on her side, then gently laid Valkyrie's in front of her.

"There you go," he said warmly. "Have your friends left?"

"My girlfriend is just in the bathroom."

His smile widened. "In that case, can I just say, and I hope I'm not being out of line here or anything, that I am a huge, huge fan. The idea that I'm even talking to you right now is blowing my mind."

"Right," said Valkyrie.

"Could I be incredibly cheeky and ask you to sign an autograph for me? Is that terrible? It's probably terrible." He put his notebook and pen into her hands and waited there, still beaming.

Militsa retook her seat. The waiter ignored her. She did her best not to laugh.

"Sure," Valkyrie said reluctantly. "Who'll I make it out to?"

"Haecce. H A E C C E. Thank you."

"To Haecce," she murmured as she wrote.

He peered at what she was writing. "And could you maybe sign it Darquesse?"

The pen stopped. Valkyrie looked up. "I don't do that."

"Aw, just this once!"

She closed the notebook, held it out for him. "I don't do that," she repeated.

His smile faded. "I'm just asking you to write your name."

"That isn't her name," Militsa said.

"Are we talking to you?" the waiter said angrily.

Valkyrie was out of her seat before she knew what was happening and the waiter was bent backwards over a table with her hand on his throat and energy burning behind her eyes. She became aware of Militsa tugging at her, trying to pull her back.

She released her hold and the waiter slipped sideways and fell off the table, sending chairs crashing into each other.

"We'll eat somewhere else," Militsa told him as he tried to right himself. "We're not paying for this food, by the way. You can explain that to your manager. Also, you're not getting a tip. I always tip, because I appreciate floor staff and kitchen staff, and I realise that, generally, you're not paid an awful lot, but you're getting nothing this time. I think you know why. Sweetie, shall we take our leave?"

"Yeah," Valkyrie said quietly. "Let's go."

Militsa linked arms with her, and marched her out on to the street.

Once they were out of view, Militsa stopped and turned. "Are you OK?" she asked. "You don't usually fly off the handle like that."

"I'm good," said Valkyrie. "I'm fine. Just... just got a little angry."

Militsa hugged her. "Want to go somewhere else? I still have half an hour left of my break. Are you still hungry? What do you want?"

"I want a muffin," Valkyrie mumbled into her shoulder.

"My baby wants a muffin," Militsa said, "my baby gets a muffin. Come on." They started walking. "So what did tall, dead and handsome want to talk to you about?"

Valkyrie smiled. "'Tall, dead and handsome'. That's good."

"Isn't it? I thought of it when I was peeing."

"You're very clever."

"I *am* a teacher."

They walked on, looking for somewhere that sold muffins.

15

Temper Fray left his sword and his City Guard uniform in his locker and dressed in civilian clothes for the meeting. He slipped his badge into his back pocket and his gun into the holster beneath his jacket. If there was one good thing about winter, it gave cops like him a good excuse to wear bulky coats.

He took the tram across the city. He liked the tram. It was smooth, efficient and good for the environment. Just like him.

He grinned to himself. That was funny.

The store where he'd arranged to meet the guy was called *The Cabinet of Curiosities*. If it had existed in any mortal city around the world, it would have been one of those weird little shops that attracted only the most discerning customer, those with dark sensibilities pursuing arcane delights.

But, because it was in Roarhaven, it was just another store that sold magical junk.

Temper nodded to the guy behind the counter and walked to the back, where an over-the-hill surfer type with shaggy hair was trying on lacquered masks over his sunglasses. When he saw Temper coming, he tried to stuff the masks on to a nearby shelf. One of them fell, hit the floor and broke into two pieces.

"*Awwwwwww,*" the surfer said.

"Adam Brate?" Temper asked.

"Yeah," Brate said, eyes still on the broken pieces. "Aw, man."

"Don't worry about it," Temper said quickly. "I'll pay for the damage."

"That's a Necromancer ceremonial mask," Brate responded. "It's worth more than my house."

"In that case, let's talk over here," Temper said, and led the way to the far corner. "You know who I am."

"Yeah, dude, I know who you are. Of course I do. I mean, I got in touch with you, didn't I? You're the traitor."

Temper let that one slide. "I guess I am."

"That's, uh, that's why I called. I figured you'd understand the, well, the implications of what I have to tell you."

"Sounds ominous."

"Oh, it is," said Brate. "I mean, I think it is. I don't have the full story, and you'll certainly know more about this than I do, but... but I had to tell someone. For years, I've been... I mean, I have been *devout*, you know? My family have worshipped the Faceless Ones, we've gone to church, we've done the prayers, the offerings, read the Book of Tears..."

"I've got some friends coming," Temper said. "They'll want to hear this, too."

Brate frowned. "What friends?"

"Trusted friends. Don't worry, you're quite safe with them."

"I don't know, man. I find it very hard to trust people. I'm a naturally paranoid person, you know?" He spun suddenly. "What the hell is that?"

"That's a wall, Adam."

"Oh," said Brate, calming down. "Sorry. I've also taken a buttload of drugs over my lifetime? So I kinda see things that aren't really there?"

"Good to know. Ah, here are my friends now."

Brate turned as Skulduggery and Valkyrie walked in.

"That's... that's Skulduggery Pleasant."

"Yes," said Temper.

"That's Skulduggery Pleasant and Valkyrie Cain."

"It is."

"Oh, I don't know about this," said Brate. "I don't know. I mean, these guys... Trouble follows these guys around, you know? I don't wanna get *killed*, man."

"You won't."

They came over, and Temper nodded to them. "Skulduggery, Valkyrie, this is the gentleman I asked you here to meet."

Brate stuck out his hand. Skulduggery shook it. "Dude. Adam Brate's my name. I know who you are, of course, and I've waited a long time for this moment."

Skulduggery tilted his head. "Is that so?"

"You have no idea, man. No idea at all. I just need someone to take me seriously, you know? Someone to believe me. I've been warning people about this for years, but no one has listened. Now, after all this time, I have the three of *you*." He switched his attention to Valkyrie, shook her hand vigorously. "I feel like I know you already, I really do. Oh, hey, I apologise for wearing the sunglasses, you know? Not making eye contact? See, I'm in disguise. I think it's safer for me if you don't know who I am."

Valkyrie frowned. "But you just told us your name."

Brate stopped shaking her hand. "Aw, hell."

"Adam has some important information to share," Temper said quickly. "That's what you told me, right, Adam? Why don't we get down to business?"

"Yeah, man," said Brate, "OK. Well. I'm... I was telling Temper here that I am, or I was, up until recently, a devout member of the Church of the Faceless. My family, back in California, were fanatical, and that's how I was raised. I kinda drifted away in my adult years, but a few years ago the True Teachings were introduced, and I came back."

Valkyrie frowned. "The True Teachings?"

"Peace and love," said Brate. "The idea that the Faceless Ones were bringers of warmth and harmony instead of, you know, oppression and death."

"Ah," said Valkyrie. "You're talking about the Great Pivot."

"Am I?"

"It's what we call it," Skulduggery said. "The Church needed to soften its philosophies in order to be allowed to practise, and suddenly they were all about sweetness and light."

Brate seemed a bit put out by that. "That's a... that's a cynical way to view what happened, man. Warmth and harmony have always been part of what the Faceless Ones promised us."

"Providing we worship them," Skulduggery said.

"Well, yeah," said Brate. "But that's the same with all religions, right? Obey our rules, worship our gods, and you'll be rewarded, and the non-believers will burn in whatever hell we imagine there to be."

"I think we're getting a little sidetracked here," said Temper.

"Yeah, sorry," Brate said. "My thoughts and feelings towards my religion are not actually relevant to what I have to say. I don't think they are anyway. I dunno. I'm conflicted. But I have to do what I think is right."

Temper hoped his smile was both patient and reassuring. "Why did you bring us here, Adam?"

"Arch-Canon Creed," said Brate, squaring his shoulders. "He's resumed his search for the Child of the Faceless Ones."

Temper's chin dipped to his chest. "Damn."

"I'm sorry," Valkyrie said. "The search for who?"

"The Child of the Faceless Ones," said Brate. "The offspring. The heir."

Valkyrie frowned. "The Faceless Ones had a kid?"

"Temper," Skulduggery said, "do you want to take this?"

"I guess," Temper muttered. He took a breath before speaking again. "OK, so, according to the legends, back when the Faceless Ones ruled the earth, before the Ancients rose up against them, they didn't need human vessels. Back then, for whatever reason, they could survive in this reality in their true forms. But then the Ancients did something to turn the environment inhospitable, and, from that point on, the Faceless Ones needed to possess human bodies."

Valkyrie nodded. "I've seen that happen. Continue."

"The vessels didn't exactly last too long, so most of the time the bodies would burn themselves out and the Faceless Ones would vacate them, move on to the next, and then the next, leaving a trail of burnt-out corpses behind. But sometimes they vacated the body *before* it burned out, and, if that happened, the person would return to normal."

"I've understood all of this so far," Valkyrie said. "This is good. Go on."

"So we're left with a few ex-vessels getting back to their old lives," said Temper, "and, for the most part, everything is the same – except for the slight alteration that has been made to their DNA. Nothing obvious. Nothing that changes their appearance or behaviour, nothing that changes their personalities. Nothing to mark them out. These ex-vessels have children, and pass on this particular strain of DNA. Generation after countless generation. We emerge from the mists of time, venture into recorded history, and still we go on. Generation after generation."

Valkyrie frowned. "So there are people out there, in the world, with Faceless Ones DNA? Seriously?"

Temper nodded. "And Arch-Canon Creed wants to find them."

"One, actually," Skulduggery interjected.

"Yes," said Temper. "He's looking for one in particular."

"To do what?" Valkyrie asked.

"Bring about the end of the world," said Brate, eager to get involved in the conversation again. "Call the Faceless Ones *back*, man. Have them wipe the earth clean and allow their disciples to live in ecstasy for all eternity – while the rest of you heathens burn and die." His smile faltered. "Which is, obviously, not cool."

Valkyrie stood there with her hands on her hips – one of those hips cocked. "How many?" she asked. "How many people are out there who are, you know, actually descended from insane supergods?"

"It's estimated that one in seven people carry this particular strand of DNA," said Temper.

Valkyrie stared at him. "That's... that's, like, a billion people. There are a billion people with Faceless Ones genes walking around? Well... Jesus. I mean, how do we stop Creed from finding them?"

"Oh," said Temper, "he's already found them."

"What?"

"He found thousands of them before his experiments were shut down. Tens of thousands. More, probably. He'd been conducting experiments for centuries. We didn't have the terminology we do now, but essentially what he was doing, even back then, was Activating these latent genes. There's someone out there, statistically there *has* to be, with a strong enough DNA strand to become the Child of the Faceless Ones. Once they're Activated, they'll be able to call their cousins home. Creed just hasn't found the right subject."

"And what happened to all the people he's experimented on?"

"We call them the Kith," said Skulduggery. "Creed Activated their genes, which led to a certain transformation. Their faces were... lost."

"Lost?" Valkyrie echoed.

"They melted away," said Temper. "They were left with, I don't know, smoothness. No hair, no features, no eyes or ears, no mouth. And, from what we could tell, their minds were wiped. After they were Activated, they didn't need to eat or drink. They didn't communicate. They just... stood there. Some of my best friends are still standing in a bunker somewhere."

"Your friends?"

Temper smiled weakly. "I was a Disciple. You knew that already, right?"

"Pretty much."

"I followed Creed. I was young, and stupid, and I needed somewhere to belong. Out of all my friends, he said I was one of his favourites. This gene had been detected in us, and it was strong. We were prime specimens. Creed would Activate others, develop this technique or that approach, and then take what he'd learned and apply it to us, one by one. He failed, over and over again. Like I said, my friends... I watched them being led away, excited at the possibility of being turned into the Child of the Faceless Ones. Next time I saw them, they'd be standing in a row, without a face, and the Activations and the experiments would continue. So I left. I renounced it all and ran."

"Years later, in order to take over the Church," Skulduggery said, "Creed had to prove that he'd left his old ways behind. No more Activations. No more Kith."

"But he's doing it again," said Brate. "This Religious Freedom Act that was passed last year? It's letting him get away with more and more."

"Where is it happening?" Skulduggery asked. "If we can catch him in the act, or at the very least find some of these new Kith, Supreme Mage Sorrows will have all she needs to have Creed arrested."

"We wouldn't arrest him ourselves?" Valkyrie asked.

"We could, but for something like this, something this big, it would be wise to have the support of the Sanctuaries."

"I don't know that I can be of any, like, assistance, man," said Brate. "I don't know where the latest Activations are taking place. It might be in the Dark Cathedral; it could be in a whole different country. The Church of the Faceless, they got, like, places *everywhere.*"

"Can you poke around?" Temper asked. "Nothing too aggressive. Just chat to people. See what they think. No one in the Church will speak to me any more, and they certainly won't speak to these two."

"He has a point," said Skulduggery. "Adam, we need to make this quite clear – we are not asking you to put yourself in any danger. We're not even asking you to be a spy. We're asking you to have a few casual conversations with people who might know something. Do you understand?"

"I understand, man," said Brate. "So do I need, like, a code name?"

"I don't think you understand."

"No, I get it, I do."

"OK."

"But..."

"No."

"But," Brate continued, "I think a code name might be a good idea. Like... Condor. Or Rattlesnake. Or, uh..."

"You won't need a code name because you're not a spy," Valkyrie told him.

"I could wear a disguise."

"No."

"I'm really good with disguises. I bet if I wore a disguise you wouldn't even recognise me. I'm not talking about sunglasses, even. I'm talking about a proper, full-on *disguise*. Like a moustache, or something."

"You don't need a disguise," said Valkyrie, "because you'll be chatting to people who already know you. They wouldn't chat to you if they didn't recognise you, would they?"

"Ah. Yeah. I guess not."

"Maybe this isn't a good idea," Skulduggery murmured.

"No, dude," Brate said quickly. "I can do it. I can. I won't mess it up. No one has ever believed in me. No one has ever trusted me with something this important. No one has ever trusted me with *anything*, man. But you guys do. You guys see something in me. Potential, maybe. True courage, perhaps. A steely-eyed determination, no doubt. I will not let you down. Skulduggery, Valkyrie and Temper – you're, like, my Three Musketeers, you know? And I would be honoured to be your d'Artagnan in this time of need."

Temper looked at Skulduggery, and Skulduggery looked at Valkyrie, and Valkyrie looked fed up.

"Fine," she said. "You can be our d'Artagnan."

"One for all!" Brate cheered.

"Don't do that," said Skulduggery.

"Sorry."

16

"Empty your mind," Miss Wicked said, and someone muttered, "That was fast."

Omen grinned as the class chuckled. Everyone shut up quickly and Omen knew that Miss Wicked had just used one of her glares. He couldn't see it, of course. He was too busy sitting there with his eyes closed.

He heard them all around him. The shuffling of feet. The creaking of desks. The entire class was watching Auger and him sitting opposite each other, trying to speak to each other without making a sound.

All he had to do was concentrate, Miss Wicked had said. Focus. Twins had a higher chance than most of getting this right. For once, Omen could be ahead of everyone else. If he could just manage this one simple thing.

Oh, God. He wasn't concentrating. He was thinking too much.
He stopped thinking.
Stopped.

It wasn't easy.

Every time he tried to stop thinking, it was like a thousand thoughts were knocking on the door of his mind, screaming to be let in.

He was doing it again. He was thinking about his thoughts. Dammit. OK. He was definitely going to stop now. Definitely.

Was Miss Wicked reading his thoughts right now? Was she checking on him? No. That could interfere with what they were trying to do. She wouldn't do that. He hoped she wasn't doing that. He hoped.

But what if she was?

So many thoughts about her, so many images, getting worse, filling his mind, one after the other, an unstoppable flow of images and thoughts and—

Take a breath.

She wasn't reading his mind. Relax. Focus. Empty the mind.

Empty as a tin can. An empty tin can, not a tin can full of peas or something. Maybe it once had peas, but now it didn't have anything. It was just—

That wasn't working.

Not a can, then. A box. A box was better. An empty box. Obviously, an empty box. Maybe it had once been full, but now it was empty. Maybe it had been full of cans of peas.

Peas again. Why peas? Why was he thinking of—

OMEN!

Omen shrieked and fell out of his chair.

He hit the floor, eyes open, and Auger stood up, a delighted smile on his face.

"You heard that, right?" Auger asked. "You heard that?"

"I... I heard it," said Omen.

"That was so cool," Auger said, pulling him to his feet. "It was like there was a tunnel between us. Did you feel it?"

"Well done, gentlemen," Miss Wicked said. "Auger, you spoke to Omen. Omen, did you answer?"

Omen hesitated.

"I think he was about to," Auger said quickly. "I could feel him about to say something, but I think I did something wrong and I broke the link."

"Is that so?" Miss Wicked murmured. "Omen, do you think you could re-establish that link?"

"Probably not," he said.

"Could you try?"

"I... suppose."

There was a knock on the door. Kase poked his head in.

"Miss Wicked, excuse me," he said, "but could I, uh... Auger and Never are needed in the... the, um... They're needed."

Miss Wicked raised an eyebrow. "Are they now?"

Kase nodded. "Urgently. Please, miss."

She sighed. "Auger, Never – it would appear that you're needed elsewhere. I trust you won't be long."

"We'll try not to be," said Auger, suddenly all business, and the class watched as he followed Never out of the door.

They all knew what was going on. There was something happening, something terrible and something dangerous, and only Auger Darkly and his friends could stop it and save the day. The rest of them had to just sigh with envy and get back to work.

Except Omen didn't really sigh with envy any more. He'd been in the thick of the action and he didn't really want to be there again. Saving the day, in his experience, usually meant a lot of running and quite a bit of hiding, with some really scary bits in between. He was fifteen years old and in school. He had enough running, hiding and scary bits as it was.

17

Valkyrie roamed the halls of Corrival Academy, listening to the voices that rumbled behind the classroom doors. She wondered how differently she'd have turned out if this place had been around when she was a teenager. Maybe it would have steered her clear of the trouble that had lain ahead of her. Maybe it would have made things worse. Maybe she would have made some friends her own age. *That* would have been weird.

She'd tried to get Skulduggery to come with her to talk to Omen while they waited for Fletcher to become available. He'd tilted his head, told her he had someone else to talk to, but wouldn't tell her who, and strode away.

She'd shrugged and walked in the opposite direction. For all she knew, he didn't have anyone to talk to and he was just being mysterious. Probably hiding in a toilet cubicle somewhere, waiting for the time to pass.

The thought amused Valkyrie for a brief moment, because the truth was she was quietly happy that he'd gone off.

There were a lot of things she hadn't got round to telling him yet, but the idea that she should let him know about her upcoming meeting with Caisson was pulling on her thoughts.

But no – as awful as it was to keep something from him, she couldn't risk him scaring Caisson away. There was a part of Valkyrie that wanted to spring a trap on him herself – having

Caisson in shackles would bring Abyssinia to her knees – but if there was even the slightest chance that meeting with Caisson could offer a solution to everything that had been going on...

Besides, as Dusk had mentioned, Caisson wasn't actually an enemy. As far as Valkyrie knew, Caisson had done nothing wrong. In fact, he could conceivably be labelled a hero. He did kill Mevolent all those years ago, after all.

So she was going to keep it a secret, for just a little while longer. She'd tell Skulduggery afterwards. He'd understand – she was sure of it.

Militsa had told her where to go, so when the bell rang she was standing right outside Omen's classroom. They came out, the chattering youth, and their eyes widened as they passed her. Some stared in wonder, others in fear.

Yeah, she could understand that.

And then Omen was there, standing in front of her. He'd grown taller since she'd seen him last.

"Happy birthday," she said.

He looked puzzled. "Thank you?"

"I was just passing so I thought I'd drop by, see how you're doing."

"You... you dropped by to see *me*?"

"Well, we're waiting until Fletcher – that's Mr Renn to you – can take us somewhere, but yeah, I came to see you while I wait. Is that OK?"

"Sure," Omen said. "I'm just... surprised."

"Why? We're friends, aren't we?"

He blinked. "Are we?"

"Aren't we?"

"I mean, yes, OK, we can be friends, sure."

"Good." They started walking. The crowds parted for them. "So how are things?"

"Great," Omen said. "Yeah, great. Just... great."

"Girlfriends? Boyfriends?"

"Neither."

"Pets?"

"None."

"You getting nervous about the exams?"

"They're not till June."

"You should do what I did – get a reflection to do the studying for you and then absorb all the information afterwards. Or just get the reflection to sit the exams."

"Yeah, that'd be cool. But we're not allowed. They have ways of stopping reflections from helping us with that stuff."

"So you have to do all the work yourself?"

"Yeah."

"Well, that sucks."

"It really does."

They walked on.

"How's Never?" Valkyrie asked.

"Good. Spending a lot of time with Auger and the others."

"A good Teleporter *is* hard to find," she said. "Do you ever join them on their adventures?"

Omen gave a little smile. "No. That's not for me, I don't think."

Valkyrie raised an eyebrow. "This is a change."

"I just don't think I'm any good at it, really. I'm not like Auger, and I'm not like you. You guys are special, and determined, and all those cool things, and I'm just... ordinary."

"Nothing wrong with being ordinary, Omen."

"Yeah, I know."

"So," Valkyrie said, figuring she'd skipped round the subject long enough, "any plans?"

"Plans?"

"To go away anywhere."

"Like holiday plans? Um, no. It's the school term, and..."

"Of course," said Valkyrie. "Of course. Hey, can you do me a favour? Can you stay out of trouble?"

"Sorry?"

"Trouble," she said. "If you could stay out of it, that would be great."

"What trouble am I in?"

"None," she said.

"So... what trouble am I going to be in?"

She laughed. "None! Wow, you are *paranoid*!"

"I'm not sure I understand what you're asking me to do."

Valkyrie turned to him. "OK, look. There's something going on. A case. It's got something to do with America, or, at the very least, Americans."

He looked doubtful. "Do you need my help?"

"No. In fact, we need the opposite."

"You need my... hindrance?"

"We need you to stay out of it."

This was puzzling Omen. That was plain to see. "But I'm not *in* it," he said. "I don't know anything about it. This is the first I'm hearing of it. I don't even know what it *is*."

"I realise that this might be confusing."

"Oh, good. I was worried."

"But I need you to promise me."

"I... I promise," he said. "Can I ask a question, though?"

"No."

"Just one."

"If you know anything at all about it," Valkyrie said, "telling you might involve you, and we don't want that, do we?"

"I suppose not."

"You just focus on having a boring, ordinary few weeks, and I'll explain it all to you when it's over, deal?"

"I... suppose so."

She smiled. Finally, she'd done something right. "OK then, buddy. You'd better get back to class."

"School's over."

"Oh," she said. "Don't you usually have detention, or something?"

He sagged. "Yeah," he said, and trudged off.

18

Valkyrie knocked on the staffroom door.

Militsa opened it, and grinned. "Well, this is a lovely surprise! My girlfriend's come to pick me up from work!"

Valkyrie winced. "Actually, I'm here to see Fletcher."

"No!" Militsa gasped, clutching her heart. "Mr Renn! Are you trying to sneak away with my woman?"

"I'll win her back if it's the last thing I do!" Fletcher warbled from somewhere Valkyrie couldn't see.

Militsa grinned again, and gave Valkyrie a peck on the cheek. "He'll be with you in a second," she said. "I've got some students that need extra tutoring, though, so I shall see you tomorrow, my petal."

"Yes, you will," said Valkyrie, giving her a squeeze before she let her walk away.

The door opened further and Fletcher stood there with his ridiculous hair. "Hey," he said.

"Hey."

"Haven't seen you in a while. Is it just you?"

Valkyrie shook her head. "Skulduggery will be here once he's stopped being mysterious."

"Fair enough," Fletcher said, ushering her into the otherwise empty staffroom. "You want anything? We're out of tea, but I can make you a coffee."

"Ha, no thanks. I've heard about the coffee here. So how are things going? How's life?"

"Ticking along," he said. "And actually, now that you're here... I have a question."

"OK."

He hesitated. "So... we dated."

"Yes, we did."

"We had fun."

"Loads of fun."

"You were my first serious girlfriend."

"And you were my first serious boyfriend."

"It didn't end too well."

"This is true."

"You kind of cheated on me."

"Not my proudest moment."

"With a vampire."

"Which turned out to be a huge mistake."

Fletcher nodded. "It's good of you to acknowledge that."

"Haven't we been over this, though?" Valkyrie asked. "I'm pretty sure I apologised about a million times."

"Three times," Fletcher corrected.

"Is that all?"

"I counted."

"Three times seems... less than I remember."

"Well, that's how many it was."

"I'll take your word for it." She smiled. "I feel like you're skirting round a subject, however, and it's not about Caelan the sulky vampire."

"Did I, um... did I turn you gay?"

Valkyrie laughed. Really, really laughed. She hadn't laughed like that in a long time.

"No," she said when she'd finished. "No, you didn't, you muppet."

"Because you never indicated that you were, you know, interested in girls when we were dating."

"I don't see why I would have."

"Well, yeah," said Fletcher, "but... like, is this a new thing? I mean, I'm thrilled for you, I really am. Militsa is so cool and so, so nice. I'm happy you're happy, basically. But did you... was there an awakening or...?"

"Wow," said Valkyrie. "An *awakening*."

"I don't really know what I'm trying to say."

"Do you want me to sit you down and go through it all?"

Fletcher brightened. "Would you?"

"No," said Valkyrie. "I liked boys. And I appreciated how girls looked, but they never really registered with me in that way until I got a bit older."

"So there was no big bombshell moment when you realised?"

"Not really. Just a growing certainty."

"And is Militsa your first—"

"Not going to go into too much detail, Fletch."

"Right, yes, of course. Boundaries."

She smiled. "I have no boundaries, you should know that by now. But I'm not going to go into detail because Skulduggery's just arrived."

"Ah," said Fletcher, and turned to Skulduggery, standing in the doorway. "Skulduggery, I know you don't indulge in small talk, so all I'll ask is: where do you need to go?"

"Seattle," Skulduggery said.

"Seattle," Fletcher repeated, clapping his hands. "Home to Nirvana, Soundgarden and Jimi Hendrix. I can take you to the site of the first Starbucks, which is no longer there, or the Space Needle, which is still there, or the airport. Which is still there, too."

"We'll need to rent a car," Skulduggery said, "so the airport would be handier."

"You got it," said Fletcher, and narrowed his eyes.

After a moment, Valkyrie asked, "Is everything OK?"

"I've been trying to do what Nero does," Fletcher said. "He

doesn't need to be in physical contact with other people in order to teleport with them. I can't seem to figure out how he does it, though."

"Nero's a Neoteric," Skulduggery said. "That means even he doesn't know how he does it. You should stick to the old-fashioned method." He put his hand on Fletcher's shoulder. "It's what you do best."

Fletcher looked at his hand, then smiled. "Thanks, Skulduggery. Your support means a lot to me."

"I'm just waiting for you to teleport."

"Oh," Fletcher said, and Valkyrie laughed at him.

19

Fletcher took them to Sea-Tac Airport and then teleported away, leaving them to rent a car. There was snow on the ground, turned to brown mud by the side of the roads. Once they were driving, Valkyrie was able to tell Skulduggery about Tanith's arrival, and Alice's hamster, and the rerun of the vision about Omen and Auger.

She didn't tell him about Caisson, though. She was going to keep that to herself until after their meeting.

"I've been having this vision since before Abyssinia returned," she said, "and not a whole lot about it has changed. Auger's still injured. Omen still dies."

"The more information we get about it, the better our chances of averting it," Skulduggery responded. "The latest detail you picked up was that it happens here, in America – possibly in Oregon. It stands to reason – though I make no assumptions – that what we are investigating now is somehow linked to what happens to the Darkly brothers in an indeterminate amount of time. So I would suggest that we continue as we are, and learn as much as we can about what's going on."

"But we've got so many things going on," Valkyrie countered. "We've got Alice's soul to heal, President Flanery's missing aide to investigate and now we have Temper's melty-face people to find."

"Kith."

"Melty-face people is more descriptive. My point is, we can't do everything."

"Of course we can," Skulduggery said. "We're Arbiters. We're detectives. We have incredible bone structure."

"All that is undeniable, but aren't we in danger of missing something if we have all these different things calling out for our attention? I don't want to lose a chance to find Doctor Nye because we're chasing down a lead on Flanery's assistant."

He shook his head. "Flitting between investigations will keep us sharp, and prevent us from developing tunnel vision. It's a good thing to be so busy."

"I told Omen to stay out of America for the next few weeks," Valkyrie said. "Do you think that was a good idea?"

"Yes."

"OK."

"Unless by telling him to stay out of America you've inadvertently set him on a collision course with the events you saw in your vision."

"Oh, God. Do you think I have?"

"Probably not."

"Phew."

"But maybe."

"Skulduggery, I swear to God..."

They turned right at a junction. "When it comes to visions of the future, we can't know anything," he said. "We could continue on exactly as we are and not one thing you saw will actually come true. Or we could second-guess every decision we make from now until then, and the future would happen just as you foresaw. From what we know, there are an infinite amount of possible futures that stem from any given moment. Sensitives can glimpse one of these possible futures, but there's no way of knowing how close it is to what will eventually transpire."

Valkyrie let his words soak in. They didn't make her feel any better. In fact, they made her glum. Which in turn made her wonder.

"Am I as much fun as I used to be?" she suddenly asked.

"No," Skulduggery said immediately.

She shot him a look. "You could have taken a little more time to think about it."

"You've had a lot on your mind for the last thirteen years," he responded. "First you found out that your uncle had been murdered, then you had to help save the world, then you met some transdimensional supergods, after which you found out that you were this Darquesse person that all the Sensitives were so worried about. Then you thought you were going to be the Death Bringer, then Darquesse emerged, and then she took over your body, and then you died, and then you had to fight her, and then you were in America for five years to recover, and now you've come back and you've had to rescue your sister from a serial killer who blamed you for the death of his serial-killer apprentice, and now this whole thing with Alice's soul... But I think there was maybe a three-week gap somewhere in there, before things got too serious, when you were what could be considered *fun*."

She grunted. "We've been busy."

"Yes, we have."

"And do you think I've become too... serious?"

"It's a serious world."

"That doesn't answer the question."

"You're as serious as you need to be," said Skulduggery. "And you're as flippant as you need to be. It's a balancing act. If you tip too far one way or the other, you fall off the wire. People like us, Valkyrie, it's our purpose in life to walk that wire."

She nodded, and looked out of the window. "I don't think I'm as happy as I used to be."

"It would astonish me if you were."

"I've got issues. About everything that's happened. I think I need to talk to someone."

"You can talk to me."

She smiled. "Thank you. But I think I have to talk to someone else. You're... I don't mean this in a bad way, but—"

"But I'm a part of the problem," Skulduggery said.

"Yes. Sorry."

"Don't be. I'm a bad influence, and I always have been. You need a professional. China has a few on her staff at the High Sanctuary."

Valkyrie looked at him. "I might make an appointment, so."

He nodded. "That's probably a good idea."

"Would you ever consider it?"

He flicked the indicator and they overtook a slow-moving truck. "I'm too far gone, I'm afraid," he said. "I have my demons, but they work to keep each other in check at all times. My mind is in a permanent state of finely tuned chaos that I would be loath to disrupt."

"And you don't think it's too late for me?"

He angled his head towards her. "Your traumas have made you who you are, but they don't define you. You can live with them, I have no doubt."

Valkyrie nodded. She was satisfied with that. For the moment.

They got where they were going a little over an hour later. An operative from the American Sanctuary indicated the car on the other side of the street, the one Oberon Guile was sitting in. Valkyrie nodded her thanks to the operative, who ignored her, and drove off.

"I don't think that guy appreciated handing this case over to us," Valkyrie said as they parked. "Can we send him a muffin basket or something?"

"No."

"Then can *we* get muffins?"

"Sure."

They got out and Valkyrie crossed the road, approaching

Oberon's car with a bright smile on her face. She motioned for him to wind down the window, and as she reached the car Skulduggery slipped in the passenger side, gun levelled at Oberon's midsection.

Valkyrie leaned in. "Hands on the dash, if you wouldn't mind."

"This is really not a good time," Oberon said, complying. He was stubbly, and even better-looking in person, and he had a nice accent and a nice voice. It had an edge to it.

"Who are they?" Valkyrie asked. "The people in the house you're watching?"

"I'm not watching anyone, Miss Cain," Oberon said. "I'm just sitting here in my car."

"You know who I am."

"I may not be the most sociable of sorcerers," said Oberon, "but I've heard of the Skeleton Detective and the girl who almost killed the world."

"My nickname sucks."

Oberon looked at Skulduggery. "You can put the gun away. I'm not your enemy."

"I'll decide what you are," Skulduggery replied. "My partner asked you a question that you haven't answered."

Oberon drummed the dashboard with his fingertips. "The people in that house are of no concern to you. You want something – tell me what it is so I can get back to sitting here. But, Miss Cain, would you mind getting in the car? I'm trying not to draw attention to myself."

Valkyrie got in the back, then scooted over so she could look at Oberon while they talked. His car was very clean.

"Bertram Wilkes," Skulduggery said. "You were in his house last week."

"So?"

"So why were you there?"

"Maybe I was his guest."

"For you to be his guest, he would have to have invited you

in. That would be rather hard to do, seeing as how he's been missing for six months."

"OK then, I broke in," said Oberon. "He owes me money."

"How much?"

"Few hundred."

"Did you get it?"

"No."

"When was the last time you spoke to him?"

"Well," Oberon said, "how long did you say he's been missing? Six months? So, let's say that I haven't spoken to him in six and a half."

"Why are you lying to us?" Skulduggery asked.

"I don't really see a reason why I should answer any questions at all, to be honest. I'm not part of your Sanctuary thing. You got no jurisdiction over me."

"We can arrest you."

"For what?"

"Obstructing an investigation. Wasting our time. Not being forthcoming."

Oberon gave a little laugh. "That's a crime now, is it?"

"We're Arbiters," Skulduggery said. "That means we can make up our own crimes."

Oberon sighed and scratched his cheek.

"OK," he said at last, "I'll tell you the truth. But you gotta do something for me in return. You gotta help me raid that house."

Valkyrie sat forward. "Who's in there?"

"Bad guys," he answered. "I think they might have my son. I haven't been able to confirm that because there's one of me and nine of them – but, with you two, I could probably make a go of it."

"Why would they have your son?" Skulduggery asked.

"You know who Wilkes was, right? His job?"

"President Flanery's personal aide."

"My ex, Magenta, that's Robbie's mom, she's a Sensitive, the kind that specialises in persuading people to do things, oftentimes against their own interests. That's a very particular talent to have, and it's one of the reasons we broke up. She's not a bad person by any stretch, but I don't think she could resist some small manipulations to get her way every now and then. That's got nothing to do with anything, though.

"Four years ago, right after we split, she mentioned something about taking a job for a mortal politician – Flanery. It paid good money and it wasn't overly time-consuming, so she could give Robbie the support and attention he needed. I wasn't around much, so I got to see him at weekends and whenever I was back this way. It wasn't perfect, but it worked.

"Magenta was used to convince senators to vote a certain way, to push judges to make favourable decisions, that kinda thing. She said Flanery had an advisor, a sorcerer."

"Wilkes," said Valkyrie.

"No," said Oberon. "Wilkes came later. I don't think Flanery knew that Wilkes was a mage. Or maybe he did, I don't know – but his advisor was somebody else."

"Where does your child come into all this?" Skulduggery asked.

A muscle flexed in Oberon's jaw. "When Flanery started his bid for the presidency, he needed Magenta more and more. She resisted. She was talking about quitting. That's when Robbie was taken."

Valkyrie's eyes widened. "Your son has been missing since before Flanery became president?"

"Three years now," Oberon said. "Every two or three days, Magenta gets to spend a few hours with him. As I'm sure you know, I spent most of that time in a prison cell, so I didn't know that Robbie had been snatched until I got out of Ironpoint and received a letter she'd left for me."

"Why were you in Wilkes's house?"

"I was trying to find what you detectives call a clue. Am I pronouncing that right? Clue?"

"Surely your wife could help you...?"

"I haven't been able to speak to Magenta," Oberon said. "I haven't been able to get close. She's got the Seven-As-One guarding her."

Skulduggery grunted, then turned to Valkyrie. "The Seven-As-One are—"

"Seven Sensitive siblings," Valkyrie said, "who maintain a psychic link at all times. They're used to guard people and places, making it almost impossible for anyone to sneak up on them without the alarm being raised."

Skulduggery tilted his head. "How do you know all that?"

"I do get out every now and then," she said, returning her attention to Oberon. "So you think your son is being held in the house across the road."

"I don't know," Oberon said, deflating slightly. "I only know that the people over there are sorcerers, and they're involved. Maybe they have Robbie in there, maybe they don't. But they definitely know more about what's going on here than I do, so, if you wanna know who's behind all of this, I'd say that helping me bust in there is a great place to start. And I ain't gonna give you much of a choice in the matter. I'm going in."

He got out of the car and started striding across the road.

"Oh, I like him," Valkyrie said.

"I thought you might," said Skulduggery. "Go round the back, will you? Let's at least *pretend* like we're professionals."

20

Valkyrie put her boot to the door and it burst open and in she went, shock sticks swinging, catching the first guy in the jaw and the second guy in the knee, the back, and then the face. They both fell and she moved out of the kitchen, down the short corridor. There were a lot of crashes coming from the front of the house. Lot of cries of pain.

A woman came hurtling out of a doorway, not even looking where she was going. Valkyrie jabbed her in her chest with both sticks and there was a flash and she went flying back.

"Clear," she heard Skulduggery say.

"Clear," she responded.

She put her sticks away, forming a cross on her back, and stepped into the living room. Five unconscious people in here – one still conscious, bleeding from a busted nose and sitting on a chair. Skulduggery and Oberon stood over him.

"What's your name?" Skulduggery asked. The man twisted his lip as he was about to answer and Skulduggery hit him. "Rudeness will not be tolerated – let's just make that clear right at the start. I'm Skulduggery, she's Valkyrie, he's Oberon. What's your name?"

The man spat out a tooth. "Sleave," he said.

"Where's my son?" Oberon demanded.

Sleave frowned. "How the hell would I know? Who's your son?"

"Robbie," said Oberon. "His name's Robbie."

"Ah," Sleave said, "you're his dad, are you? Not much of a family resemblance, if I'm being honest."

"Where is he?"

Sleave held up his hands. "I refer you to my earlier reply. To wit: how the hell would I know?"

"You move him around, don't you?"

"I *did*," said Sleave, "with the rest of these mooks. Every week, we'd take the kid somewhere new and guard him, feed him, put up with his nonsense and take him to see his mommy two or three times a week. But recently we were informed that our services were no longer required. Sadly, I have been made redundant." His voice suddenly filled with hope. "I don't suppose you have any other kids we could kidnap, do you?"

Oberon lunged and Skulduggery held him back, and Sleave laughed.

Valkyrie hunkered down in front of him. "How long were you on this particular job?" she asked.

Sleave shrugged. "Four months, maybe five."

"So you're not the first to keep him moving around."

"And we're not the last, either."

"Who's your boss?"

"We're freelance. We don't have a *boss*."

"Then who hired you? Who gave you your instructions? Who did you report to?"

Sleave grinned. "The answer to all those questions is the same name, and I'll tell you what it is – providing you let us go."

"I'm afraid that's not how it works."

"Then you should probably change how it works, because you may have come in here and kicked all our asses, and some of them twice, but, from where I'm sitting, I'm the one in the position of power."

"Careful now," Valkyrie said. "We can always send a Sensitive into your head, and who knows what they might scramble while they're in there."

Sleave didn't look too worried. "You don't think I've got defences for that sorta thing? Sure, those defences don't last forever, but I'd hold out for as long as I could, just out of spite. Let us go. All of us. Even the stupid ones. Then I'll tell you the name of the man you're looking for."

With Oberon now at the other side of the room, Skulduggery straightened his tie. "We won't do that," he said. "But you tell us his name, and, when we've verified that you told us the truth, *then* we'll let you go."

"That's more like it!" said Sleave. "See, girl, this is how you negotiate! May I stand?"

"By all means," said Skulduggery.

Sleave stood. "I like your counter-offer, Mr Pleasant. It shows potential. But we're not gonna be able to accept this whole *being released afterwards* thing. The problem is, yeah, we're criminals, and so decidedly untrustworthy – but you're Sanctuary folk, and so you're *absolutely* untrustworthy."

"You obviously haven't heard," said Valkyrie. "We're Arbiters now. We don't report to anyone."

"Huh," said Sleave. "I didn't know the Arbiters were still a thing."

"They weren't," Skulduggery said. "They are now."

"But you're still working with the Sanctuaries," Sleave said, "which means you're bound by their rules."

"Not all of them."

"Then you can let us go, and once you do that I'll tell you his name. If I don't, or if I lie, you feel free to hunt us down. Contrary to what you might be thinking, we're really not that smart, so you won't have too much trouble finding us."

Skulduggery looked at Oberon, and then at Valkyrie. She shrugged.

"OK," Skulduggery said. "We won't arrest you."

Another smile broke out across Sleave's face. "Knew you were a man with an open mind. I could see it in your eye sockets."

He kicked one of his unconscious friends until they stirred. "Hey! Hey, get up. Wake the others or drag 'em out. You got two minutes."

They stood silently while Sleave's friends were either revived or hauled out through the back door. It took a lot longer than two minutes.

When they were gone, and only Sleave remained, he pulled on his jacket. "It was very nice to meet all of you," he said. "Detective Pleasant, you're a surprisingly reasonable fellow for a bunch of bones in a suit. Detective Cain, you're a scary lady and that's all I'll say about that. Robbie's dad, I don't know anything else about you, so all I'll say is that you just need to calm down in general and maybe people will like you more."

Skulduggery took out his gun and aimed it at Sleave's head. "The name."

Sleave raised his hands slowly. "We only met him once," he said. "He came to see us, told us what he expected, told us when and where to move, and explained how we'd be getting paid. We never saw him again, never saw anyone else working for him."

"His name."

"Crepuscular Vies."

Skulduggery glanced at Valkyrie, then at Oberon.

"Never heard of him," Oberon said.

"I'm not surprised," said Sleave. "I didn't have a clue who he was, either, and I still don't. He's tall, about the same height as you fellas, and wears a suit, bow tie and a hat. But I wouldn't worry about what he's wearing, because his face is... It's just wrong. You'll know it when you see it."

"Nationality?" Valkyrie asked.

Sleave laughed. "Don't you know? Irish, of course. The most evil people in the world are Irish."

21

"What do you think of him?" Valkyrie asked as they waited in the diner for Fletcher to come and pick them up.

One eyebrow rose on Skulduggery's façade. "The waiter?"

"Oberon," she said, and took a sip of coffee. It was not good.

"He seems capable," Skulduggery said. He had a glass of water before him that he was never going to touch. "He threw around some of Sleave's people without too much bother."

"Do you believe him?"

"I have no reason not to. You?"

"Yeah, I believe him."

"Well, OK then."

It was pitch-black outside, and the diner was empty of customers apart from them and a drunk guy in the corner booth who kept getting up to play sad country songs on the jukebox.

Valkyrie took another sip of her coffee. It wasn't getting any better. "Do you think he'll be able to find out anything about this Crepuscular Vies?"

"Probably not," Skulduggery said. "Oberon's motivations may be pure, and he could have useful contacts in the criminal under-world that might provide a lead, but we'll probably have to devote some time to it ourselves after our show of strength for Serafina tomorrow. Once all this is out of the way, I promise we'll come up with a way to find Doctor Nye."

Valkyrie nodded and took another sip, hoping he wouldn't spot the look of guilt that flashed across her face.

Fletcher came in. Valkyrie scooched over so he could sit beside her. "Everything good? Everyone unharmed? Sorry I'm late. Had a bit of trouble finding the place. How's the coffee?"

"Wonderful," said Valkyrie. "You should get some."

"Naw, caffeine makes me jumpy, and I'm going straight back to sleep after this."

She winced. "We're sorry for getting you out of bed. Aren't we, Skulduggery?"

"Absolutely," Skulduggery said.

"And we appreciate you doing this, don't we, Skulduggery?"

"Thoroughly."

Fletcher smiled. "The way I look at it, I'm not only helping you, I'm also helping the environment. That's one of the great tragedies about keeping magic a secret, isn't it? If everyone knew about us, Teleporters could transport people all round the world without a single harmful emission. Makes you wonder if we should just tell them for the sake of the planet."

"I'm not entirely sure that the war that would inevitably follow wouldn't damage the environment all over again," Skulduggery said.

"You should have more faith in mortals," Fletcher countered. "Not all of them are war-hungry simpletons, you know."

"No," Skulduggery said, "but they do tend to scare easily and, when people are scared, they lash out."

Fletcher adjusted his hair slightly. "You have such a dim view of the people you fight every day to protect."

"I'm just waiting for them to prove me wrong."

Fletcher looked at Valkyrie. "Please tell me you have a cheerier outlook on life. You can't be as miserable as him. You just can't."

She smiled. "I believe that people are good."

"Thank you," Fletcher responded.

"Most of them anyway."

"OK."

"I mean, not any that *I've* met, but—"

"You can stop there," he said. "Wow, the two of you must have fun saving the world for people you don't even like."

"I'm joking," said Valkyrie.

"I'm not," said Skulduggery.

"I believe people are good," Valkyrie continued, "though flawed, and, given all the information and enough time, they will do the right thing."

Skulduggery picked up his hat from the seat, and put it on the table. "And I believe that life is arbitrary and when time moves on it will be as if we never existed. Do you want any pie?"

"No," said Valkyrie.

"Then we should probably get going."

"You've changed," Fletcher said, not moving. "The both of you. You have. Remember when we used to be a team? Remember the energy? The excitement? The laughs? Whatever happened to all that?"

"When who used to be a team?" Skulduggery asked.

"The three of us," said Fletcher. "And Tanith and Ghastly."

"And you?"

"Yes, me. You never took me seriously, but I was a vital part of the team."

"You were the bus."

Valkyrie laughed and Fletcher smirked.

"I helped out more than that and you know it," he said. "You just don't want to admit that I've grown. Hey, I understand. You knew me when I was a kid. Now I'm an adult, and I have a job, educating young people, moulding young minds. I have responsibilities. Obligations. We're both alphas. You probably feel threatened by me. Also, you're jealous of my hair. I get it. I'd be jealous of it, too. But I propose, right now, that we leave the past in the past and, from this day on, treat each other as equals. What do you say, Skulduggery?"

Fletcher stuck out his hand. Skulduggery observed it for a moment, then extended his own hand – and picked up his hat.

"You're funny," Fletcher said, nodding as Skulduggery put the hat on and stood. "That was well done."

"Thank you," Skulduggery said.

Valkyrie left a tip and got out of the booth after Fletcher, and they went outside and he teleported them home. He dropped Skulduggery beside the Bentley, and then left Valkyrie in her living room. She gave him a hug and he vanished, and Xena came bounding in.

Valkyrie had a few hours' sleep, and then drove to Roarhaven to meet the Prince of the Darklands.

22

The Fangs was quiet this time of the morning. Vampires may not have been harmed by the sun, but they weren't known to be early risers. The only people on the streets were those coming back from a night shift.

She followed the directions Dusk had given her and came to a theatre, a few years old and never used. She went round the back, found the opened door and climbed the stairs. With each step, she took the next one slower.

This could be a trap, of course. This was very likely a trap. It was so likely a trap that Abyssinia would have known that Valkyrie would be thinking that and would then dismiss it because of how likely it was, so then the possibility of this being a trap became even more likely.

Eventually, her thoughts became so confusing that she just marched up the rest of the stairs and emerged on to the roof of the theatre.

There was a man standing here, waiting. He was thin and had tightly-shaven silver hair, and pale scars on his pale skin.

"You must be Caisson," said Valkyrie.

His smile was fleeting. Uncertain.

There was a nervous energy about him, like an animal getting ready to bolt.

Valkyrie proceeded with caution. "How are you coping with being back in circulation?"

"I have good days and... bad ones," he said. He had a soft voice. "I'm having a good day now, in case you were wondering. I'm not going to attack you, or anything like that. I keep thinking I should attack you because... because we're on different sides."

"I keep thinking that, too."

"Isn't that odd? How we think that? How we're almost ready to... to do that? For no reason other than the people we associate with."

"It is strange, yes."

Caisson's eyes dipped. "You're friends with the skeleton," he mumbled.

"I am."

"The skeleton murdered my mother."

"He killed her, yes. But she came back."

His eyes flickered up, and he gave another faltering smile. "I'm very confused," he said.

"I don't blame you."

He was seized, all of a sudden, by an intensity that made Valkyrie want to step back. "The skeleton took my mother away from me!" he raged. "When I needed her! He hurt her! *He killed her!* She's only alive today because he was too weak to finish the job! I hate him and I want to kill him and everyone he knows!"

And, as suddenly as it had arrived, the rage passed.

He started crying.

Valkyrie waited a moment. "What can I do for you, Caisson?" she asked softly. "Why are we here?"

It took him a moment to answer. It was a moment he spent wrestling with thoughts she'd never be able to understand.

"My mother," he said eventually, "she has spies. I heard one of them say that you're looking for someone. Some*thing*. A Crengarrion."

She frowned. "Doctor Nye. Yes."

"I know where it is. I heard my mother say."

Valkyrie forced herself to wait.

"Is it important that you find this creature?" Caisson continued. "If it's important, then I'll tell you, but you need to tell me something first."

"It's important. I need Nye to help my sister. What do you want to know?"

"Greymire Asylum," Caisson said. "Where is it?"

"I've never heard of it."

"But you can find out, can't you? You're a detective. You can ask someone. Maybe the skeleton knows."

"I can find out, sure. You tell me where Nye is and I'll find where—"

"*No!*" Caisson screamed. "You tell me where Greymire Asylum is and *then* I help you! You *first*! *You!*"

Valkyrie held up her hands. "OK! OK, I'll do that. I will."

Caisson hugged himself and shook his head, muttering.

"What's in there that's so important for you?" she asked.

Caisson tapped his forehead. "It's for my mind. My mind is... I can be quite erratic, and..."

"And there's a cure for you in the asylum?"

He nodded. "A cure, yes. A cure for me in Greymire. K-49."

"I know some really good doctors I could introduce you to. So does China, for that matter."

Caisson blinked. "China..."

"China Sorrows. She raised you, right? She took you in and she raised you like you were her own child."

His face contorted, hatred etched into every line and hollow. "China betrayed me. China gave me to Serafina to torture. She lies. She is nothing but darkness and coldness and lies. I'm going to kill her. We're going to hunt her down and kill her, and kill

118

anyone who stands with her. We're going to tear her *apart*. We're going to make her *scream*. We're going to make her *bleed*. We're going to—"

He stopped, breathing quickly, forcing himself to calm down. "No," he said. "My only hope is K-49. My only hope is in Greymire Asylum. Find out where it is, and I'll tell you where the Crenga is working now. Meet me here in two days. But... at night. I don't like the day, it's too... Meet me at night."

"Monday night, then," she said. "When it's dark? Ten o'clock?"

"Yes. Yes, ten o'clock. At ten o'clock you will tell me what I need to know, and I will tell you how to find the creature you seek."

23

All things considered, that had gone pretty well.

Valkyrie checked the time. Serafina wasn't due to arrive for another ten minutes, and the High Sanctuary was only five minutes away. She'd make it over there by noon, no problem.

China had told her to dress formally, but she hadn't quite known what that meant in this instance. She wasn't going to be wearing a dress, she'd known that much. Nothing with heels, either. In the end, she had decided that black jeans and a smart coat were formal enough – plus, they allowed her to fight to the death if the situation called for it. Which was always a bonus.

This was a good day, Valkyrie decided. She hadn't walked into a trap, and she'd managed to strike a deal with a guy who looked like he was barely keeping it together. If Skulduggery had been with her, she just knew he'd have said the wrong thing and it would all have imploded.

It was a good thing she hadn't told him. It was definitely a good thing, and he would totally understand.

Totally.

She came round a corner, and braked.

There was traffic. There was actual traffic.

"No, no, no," she muttered, craning her neck to see past the line of cars.

This was unheard of. For one thing, apart from Oldtown, the

streets of Roarhaven were designed to flow unimpeded. That had long been a bragging point, another area where mages could feel smug when discussing their mortal cousins and their constant traffic woes.

For another, Valkyrie hadn't even known that there were enough cars in Roarhaven to *form* a traffic jam. Most people here used the tram system.

"Why didn't you all take the tram?" she shouted, even though no one could hear her.

People walked by. People crossed the road, darting between Valkyrie's slow-moving car and the slow-moving car in front. Large groups of people. Very large groups. Some of them held signs.

She finally got closer, and a City Guard officer checked her Sanctuary tags and waved her into the Circle zone, and she sped down the ramp to the parking area beneath the High Sanctuary, then sprinted for the elevator tiles.

She rose up, into the foyer, looking around for someone she recognised. There were City Guard officers and Cleavers everywhere. Sanctuary staff rushed to and fro. The air had a nervous energy to it.

Cerise, holding a clipboard, saw her immediately, despite the chaos, and swept over to her, taking her gently by the arm. "You are required outside," she said, the calm at the centre of this storm. "The High Superior is approaching Shudder's Gate."

"I'm so sorry I'm late," Valkyrie said. "I didn't expect the traffic. There are a lot of people out there."

"Yes," said Cerise. "There are."

The doors opened and a blast of noise hit them. It looked like the entire Circle zone was filled with people, divided by a thin line of Cleavers. More people joined either side. They waved placards. They shouted.

Cerise left her at the top of the steps and Valkyrie crossed an actual red carpet to hurry over to Skulduggery. He was in a dark blue three-piece with a crisp white shirt and a blue tie. His hat was perfectly placed.

"Just in time," he said.

"This is a bigger deal than I'd thought," she responded, actually having to raise her voice to be heard over the restless crowd.

"People have come from all over the world for this. Serafina Dey hasn't been spotted in public for decades."

"She has a lot of fans."

He shook his head. "Only half of them are here supporting her. The others are protesting."

Valkyrie took another look, and realised one half of the crowd was arguing with the other. She turned back to Skulduggery. "Cerise called Serafina the High Superior."

Skulduggery said something that Valkyrie didn't hear.

"What?" she said.

He stepped closer and extended his hands to either side, and the air around them rippled. Her ears popped slightly as the sound of the crowd was muted. "Is that better?" he asked, keeping his hands where they were.

"Much," she said, speaking at normal volume again.

"Serafina is the head of a different branch of Faceless Ones disciples," he told her. "The Legion of Judgement."

Valkyrie nodded. "Now that sounds like a fun and accepting place of worship."

"The Legion views Mevolent as their messiah, and reckons that his interpretation of their teachings – and I would use air quotes here if my hands were free and if I were the sort of person to use air quotes – is the *true way*. Creed, on the other hand, has a supposedly gentler approach."

"But Creed denounced Mevolent during the war for being too soft."

"And yet now the Church is all about fluffiness and acceptance. Makes you wonder if Arch-Canon Creed is being entirely honest, doesn't it?"

"He must love the fact that Serafina's visiting."

"The visit has, I've heard, caused something of a split within his congregation, but I'm sure there's a part of him, tucked away somewhere, that will be happy to see his little sister after all these years."

Valkyrie's eyes widened. "They're brother and sister? Did everyone know this except me?"

"Probably."

She glared. "You did this before."

"Did I?"

"With China and Mr Bliss. You didn't tell me they were brother and sister until, like... Well, I don't think you *did* tell me. I think someone else did."

"Magical society is a small world," Skulduggery said. "People have brothers and sisters all over the place, right where you least expect them. Parents, too. Cousins, aunts and uncles."

"And everyone looks the same age," Valkyrie said. "I'll never get used to that part of it. So which is bigger – the Legion of Judgement or the Church of the Faceless?"

"The Church has more physical places of worship, but most worshippers keep their membership secret, so it's very hard to say which is bigger – and more and more mages are turning to the Faceless Ones with every week that passes."

Valkyrie made a face. "Why?"

"People need something to believe in. Even sorcerers. The more they learn, the more they uncover about life and magic and alternate universes, the more they search for a greater meaning."

"But the Faceless Ones don't care about any of them."

"People are strange," Skulduggery said, and brought his hands back together, and the noise closed in on them once more.

The three Elders arrived, nodded to Skulduggery and Valkyrie, and took up their positions in front of them. Then China came out, looking amazing. She winked at Valkyrie and took her place at the very top of the stairs.

The crowd went quiet as Serafina's convoy came into view – black cars and SUVs, reinforced with armour and with protective sigils engraved into their doors. The Cleavers directed them round and then through the Circle, making sure they stayed clear of the grasping, clutching hands of the people. As they neared, colour washed across the air, and Valkyrie realised that the High Sanctuary's force field had been extended. A section opened so that the convoy could pass through.

It stopped at the base of the steps. One of Serafina's security people, a woman in black, opened the door to the middle car, and Serafina Dey stepped out.

24

She was... glorious.

Tall and solid and strong, Serafina wore a red dress, stained black at the edges. The skirt wrapped tightly around her waist and flared out at the ends. The bodice had a ribcage – made of actual ribs – and it opened at the chest to reveal a necklace of finger bones. Bracelets, also made of bone, rattled on her left wrist. Her long chestnut hair was held back by a headpiece formed from what looked like a human skull.

"Jeepers," Valkyrie whispered.

Half the crowd cheered with bottomless adoration. The other half hurled insults and obscenities. It would have been amusing if the wide-eyed fanaticism wasn't so scary.

Serafina ascended the stairs alone. Once at the top, she embraced China.

"My magnificent girl," Serafina said. "It's so good to see you again after all these years."

"You look radiant," China responded.

Serafina kissed both China's cheeks. "As do you. Belated congratulations on your new position. You thoroughly deserve it. If anyone can whip the Sanctuaries into shape, it's you."

China smiled. "You're far too kind. Allow me to introduce you to my Council of Advisors. This is Grand Mage Aloysius Vespers of the English Sanctuary."

Vespers shuffled forward and struggled to bow. "Welcome to Roarhaven, High Superior! The tales of your legendary beauty are all true, I see, even to old eyes such as mine."

Serafina bowed slightly. "Have we not met before, Grand Mage? You seem familiar to me. Perhaps without the beard..."

Vespers chuckled. "I am afraid not, High Superior. I would remember meeting someone as striking as you."

He shuffled back and Praetor stepped forward.

"This is Grand Mage Gavin Praetor," said China, "of the American Sanctuary."

Praetor bowed deeply, but kept his eyes locked on Serafina's. "It is an honour, High Superior, to be in the presence of someone so bewitching."

"Surely, Grand Mage, you are used to it by now," Serafina responded. "Is the Supreme Mage not more bewitching than I? Is she not the most beautiful woman you've ever laid eyes upon?"

Praetor smiled. "I would certainly not like to choose between you, High Superior."

"How thoroughly gracious," Serafina said.

"And this is Grand Mage Sturmun Drang, of the German Sanctuary," said China. "I believe you know each other."

Drang gave a curt bow. "High Superior."

Serafina smiled. "No exaltations about my timeless beauty, Sturmun? I can call you that, can't I? I believe once you make an attempt on someone's life you grant that person permission to use your first name."

Drang remained impassive. "That was a long time ago."

Serafina's smile grew smaller, but somehow even more glorious. "Was it?"

China seized this moment to step between them, and steered Serafina towards Skulduggery. "And you remember Skulduggery Pleasant, of course."

"How could I forget a man such as this?" Serafina said, and tapped her finger-bone necklace. "I believe one of these is yours."

"I believe you may be right," Skulduggery said. Coolly.

"And this," said Serafina, "must be the infamous Valkyrie Cain, the girl who very nearly destroyed us all."

"I suppose I am," Valkyrie responded. "How do you do?"

"Very well, thank you," Serafina answered, and swept her arm back. Her security person, the woman dressed in black, came up the steps. "Allow me to introduce my sister, Rune."

Rune was as tall as Skulduggery, and she had broad shoulders, an impressively square jaw and flat, expressionless eyes. Her dark hair was tied back in a functional bun, and she managed to make the suit she wore seem like a military uniform.

"We've met before," Skulduggery said.

"I'm aware," said Rune.

A silence followed.

"How was the journey?" China asked.

"Long," said Serafina. "How I miss the days when everyone had a Teleporter at their disposal."

"You miss them when they're gone, don't you? But don't worry. Corrival Academy is training up the next generation of Teleporters and I'm sure they'll be available to hire in a few short years."

"Quite," said Serafina, and her smile dimmed a fraction before returning, as brilliant as ever.

"Please come inside," China said. "It's far too cold to be standing out here like this."

Serafina gave a gentle nod, turned to the crowd and waved. This drove her supporters into a frenzy. It didn't go down well with the protestors.

One of them threw a bottle of water. It bounced harmlessly off the force field. Serafina blew a kiss.

Valkyrie stood with Skulduggery, watching the procession as it threaded its way into the High Sanctuary. "Are we done now?" she asked once they were alone.

"We are," he said.

The crowd started chanting competing slogans at each other as the Cleavers moved to break them up.

"I talked to Caisson," Valkyrie blurted.

Skulduggery tilted his head at her.

"I didn't know how else to say it," she said. "I thought blurting might be the best option." She looked at the crowd. It was showing no signs of dispersing.

"You must be talking about some other Caisson..." Skulduggery said slowly.

"Nope," she replied. "It's the one you're thinking of. You know, your *son* Caisson. He wanted to meet me and we met."

"First of all," Skulduggery said, "he's not my son."

"You don't know that. You told me yourself, there are all kinds of magical ways to make a baby that don't require the usual process."

"I'm going to say it again: he's not my son. Second of all... why didn't you tell me?"

"I am telling you."

"Why didn't you tell me before you met him? It could have been a trap."

"That's why I didn't tell you. It was a risk, but it was a risk I was ready to take. He had a proposal that he wanted to talk to me about. It was all very fine and undramatic. I mean, he's obviously a very traumatised person, but he didn't try to kill me or anything."

"Well... that's a good start, I suppose."

"He did say he wanted to kill *you*, though."

"That hardly seems fair. The only bad thing I ever did to him was kill his mother, and she came back."

"That's what I told him," Valkyrie said. "I think he's conflicted about the whole thing, but he still wants to kill you. So, this proposal of his. He claims to know how to find Doctor Nye, and he says he'll tell me if I tell him where Greymire Asylum is."

Skulduggery tilted his head to the other side. "Greymire, eh?"

"He says there's a cure there – I think it's called K-49 – that'll help soothe his mind. So do you know where Greymire is?"

"Not exactly."

"Can you find it?"

"I don't know."

Valkyrie frowned. "Is that doubt in your voice?"

"Greymire Asylum doesn't exist," Skulduggery said. "Not officially anyway. It has no staff and it has no patients. No one knows anyone who's ever worked there."

"OK, so it's a secret psychiatric hospital."

"No," Skulduggery said. "It's not a psychiatric hospital at all. It's what was once called a lunatic asylum, as barbaric as that sounds. Sorcerers driven mad by magic were sent there. Only the most dangerous. Only the worst cases. They were locked away so that the rest of us could forget about them."

"China would know where it is, wouldn't she?"

"She won't tell us. I wouldn't tell us, either. Greymire is best left forgotten."

"Well," said Valkyrie, "that's not really going to work for me."

"We'll grab Caisson," Skulduggery said. "The next time he comes to visit, we'll grab him and send someone into his head. We'll find out what he knows."

"No."

"Valkyrie—"

"We've been looking for Nye for months and we haven't come close to it. Caisson is our only lead, and I'm not going to risk that by trying something sneaky. Besides, his head is so messed up that I doubt a Sensitive would be able to learn anything useful, even if we did grab him. Caisson came to me with a proposal and I've accepted."

"It sounds like you've already decided."

"And it sounds like you're trying to overrule me."

"You can't tell him where Greymire is," Skulduggery said.

"Even if you knew, you couldn't tell him. That information is too dangerous to be let out into the world. We'll find Nye on our own. It's just a matter of time."

"Too much time has passed already. Alice is eight years old. She deserves a normal life."

"We'll give it to her, I promise. We just need another way."

"The other ways aren't working. Your ways aren't working. This is my way. Are you going to help me, or will I have to do it alone?"

He looked at her. "I'll help you. Of course I will. But you must understand what we'll be doing. Greymire Asylum contains the worst of the worst, Valkyrie – sorcerers whose names you've never heard because no one wants to utter them aloud. To pass this information to someone like Caisson... If we're discovered, we'll be arrested for treason."

"They wouldn't arrest *us*. Who'd order it – China? China wouldn't arrest *us*."

"Not without good reason. Which this would be."

Valkyrie looked at the crowd, then raised an eyebrow. "And what, do you think, would the punishment be for breaking into Greymire Asylum?"

"Why would we do that?"

"If we found this K-49 thing, we wouldn't have to tell Caisson where Greymire is, would we? We give him his cure, he tells us where Nye is."

"That could work."

"So, if China won't tell us where Greymire is, how do we find it?"

"The only place I can think of where it would be written down is in the diaries of the Grand Mages – but they were all destroyed when the Desolation Engine went off in the old Sanctuary."

"There has to be someone apart from China who knows."

"There may be one person..."

"There you go," said Valkyrie, grinning. "I knew you'd think of something."

25

The crowd that filled the Circle zone a few hours earlier had finally dispersed. There had been a lot of shouting and sign-waving, but Omen didn't have a clue what had been going on. Someone was visiting, he reckoned. Someone important.

He waited beside the fountain, his coat zipped all the way up to his chin. He should have worn the coat he'd got here in the city, the one guaranteed to keep you warm no matter what, but instead he'd chosen the other coat, the one made by mortals, because it did a better job of hiding the extra weight he was still lugging around. This was a dreadful coat. He was freezing.

At a little past four, the mortal ambassadors came out of the High Sanctuary and down the steps. Aurnia parted company with them before they got on the tram that would take them back to the Humdrums. She was wearing a coat made by sorcerers. She didn't look chilly in the slightest.

"I'm so sorry I'm late," she said. "The reception got in the way of everything and the meeting ran over and it was just, it was bedlam. Have you been waiting long?"

"No," he said. "Not long at all."

She glanced at the clock. "I can't even go for coffee with you," she said. "I told my parents I'd be back by half four to help with the shop. You came out here for nothing."

"Not for nothing," said Omen. "It's always good to see you. And I can ride back with you."

"But that's really out of your way."

"It's Saturday. What else have I got to do?"

She laughed, and they caught the next tram, and settled in their seats.

"Who was the reception for?" Omen asked.

Aurnia soured. "The wife of Mevolent – Serafina Dey. In my dimension, she's been dead since before I was born. But, here, she lives, and it is Mevolent who is dead. Which, of course, is far preferable."

"Did you get to meet her?"

She frowned. "No. Why would I want to meet anyone like that?"

"I just thought it would be... I don't know, actually. So, um, the meeting you had. What was it about?"

Aurnia shrugged. "The usual. It was us, voicing the concerns of the people in our community, and the High Sanctuary's... um... what's the word? People who love rules and filling out forms?"

"Oh, I know it. I know the word you're thinking of. It's... It begins with a b..."

"Bureaucrats!" said Aurnia. "Yes! Us on one side, the High Sanctuary's bureaucrats on the other. They make notes and lists and tell us no, using every other word *but* no."

"Sounds annoying."

"It can be. But it's how things get done here and, to be honest with you, it's still far, far better than what we had back home. What day did you say it is again?"

"Saturday."

She nodded. "So it's once more time to thank you for making me an ambassador."

He laughed. "I get the feeling you're good at it."

"I do enjoy it, I have to say. Some of the other ambassadors got bored or too busy so they're not coming to the meetings any more, but I really like it. I like making a difference, and I like people paying attention to what I have to say. I'm the youngest ambassador we have. It's, uh, it's cool."

"I'm glad," Omen said, smiling. "How's the shop?"

"It's doing OK," Aurnia replied. "It's smaller than the one we used to have, but it's obviously in a much safer neighbourhood. Well, usually."

"What do you mean?"

Aurnia shrugged. "There are people – sorcerers – who have started coming into the Humdrums and, you know..."

"What?"

"They offer to protect our businesses for money, but, if you don't pay, bad things happen."

"Seriously?" Omen asked, keeping his voice low. "Have you told the City Guard?"

"The City Guard are, usually, the ones doing it."

Omen stared at her. Then sat back.

"You hadn't heard?" Aurnia asked. "About any of this?"

"No," said Omen. "I mean... I don't pay that much attention to the Network, but I'm sure I'd remember something like that."

"It hasn't been reported. The Supreme Mage would prefer to handle this without causing a scandal. She says sorcerers still like to congratulate themselves on taking us in, even if they do hide us away in a corner of the city where nobody else goes. She says they would not appreciate these unfortunate developments."

"But that's awful."

"Yes."

"But that's, like, *really* awful. Everyone should know about this. It can't be allowed. If people knew what was going on, it would stop immediately."

"Would it?" Aurnia asked. "We're setting up our businesses and our shops and our services, and everyone my age is going to school, but, for the vast majority of us, we're working for sorcerers. We're cleaning their houses and taking care of their children and preparing their food. They don't really care about the bad things that are going on because they don't..."

"Don't what?"

"They don't view us as equals," Aurnia said. "I don't mean you. And I don't mean all sorcerers. But... a lot of them."

Omen didn't know what to say. "Wow."

"Yeah."

"We're horrible."

"No, you're not."

"We are horrible, terrible people."

"You're cool," said Aurnia, smiling again. "Many sorcerers are cool. But some are not. What's the Frank Sinatra song? 'That's Life'."

"You know Frank Sinatra?"

She grinned. "We're making our way through the music of this dimension. At first, it was all noise and none of it made sense – but the more we listen, the more we love. My father is a big fan of Frank Sinatra. He hopes to see him in concert one day. My mother, she's into the Beatles and the Monkees."

"Great bands," Omen said, nodding.

"Of the Beatles, she loves John the most. She wants to write him a letter."

"Uh... I think John Lennon is dead."

"Oh," said Aurnia. "Oh, she will be disappointed."

"Frank Sinatra's dead, too."

Aurnia winced. "My father will not be happy."

"What about you?" Omen asked. "Do you have a favourite band or singer or whatever?"

She hesitated, then shook her head. "I'm not going to say her name, in case you tell me that she's also dead. I'd rather live in a world with her in it, thank you very much."

"Well, OK," said Omen, smiling. "That sounds fair enough."

There were very few people travelling this line today, so it didn't take long to reach the Humdrums. Aurnia pressed the button to stop, and she stood.

"Thanks for coming out," she said. "Sorry we didn't have time to do anything."

"That's OK," Omen said. He tried to think of a funny line to part with, but by the time he'd come up with something Aurnia was already waving and hopping off.

The tram pulled away, and he shrugged. It hadn't been that funny anyway.

The only other passenger on the tram, a girl in a big coat who had been sitting at the other end, got up and walked over – and sat beside him. Actually sat *beside* him.

He felt his face go red, and felt his heart in his chest. She was going to chat him up. *She* was going to chat *him* up.

He decided, then and there, that he didn't care what she looked like under that hood – he was going to say yes when she asked him out.

She pulled down the hood and he shrieked.

"Quiet!" Colleen Stint said, punching his arm.

"Ow!" he yelled.

"What part of *quiet* didn't you understand?"

They stared at each other.

Then he leaped up, spun round, expecting the other members of First Wave to charge at him.

Colleen sighed. "There's no one else here."

"Where are they?" he demanded. "Where's Jenan?"

"I'm the only one who came. Would you please stop freaking out? It's embarrassing for you."

Pretty sure that they were, in fact, alone, Omen glared at her and backed away. He sat down opposite.

"What are you doing here?" he asked. "How did you even get past Shudder's Gate?"

"Nero," she said. "Don't worry, he doesn't know it's you I came

135

to see. I asked if I could tag along the next time he teleported into Roarhaven. He's been, I don't know, distracted lately, so he didn't ask any questions."

Omen frowned at her. "Why has he been teleporting into Roarhaven?"

"You really think they'd tell us?"

He narrowed his eyes. "What do you *want*, Colleen?"

"We need your help. Me, Perpetua, Sabre and Disdain – we want to get away from Abyssinia."

"But you *are* away from Abyssinia. You're here. Why didn't the others come with you?"

Colleen made a face. "We don't want to come to *Roarhaven*. Everyone here knows that we left with Jenan and joined up with Abyssinia. Can you imagine the way they'd look at us? Can you imagine what they'd say about us?"

"Then where do you want to go?"

"Nowhere with sorcerers," Colleen responded. "We just want a few years away from all this craziness. When it's over, when people calm down, maybe then we'll come back, but right now we want to blend in with the mortals, maybe somewhere in Australia, or California. Somewhere with a beach."

"Why?"

"Why do we want a beach?"

"Why are you leaving Abyssinia?"

Colleen hugged herself. "We never wanted to be there. We thought we did. We let Mr Lilt convince us that we were bigger and better than everyone else, and that Abyssinia would let us take what was ours."

"And what *is* yours?"

"I don't even know," Colleen said, her shoulders slumping. "I think we just wanted to be respected, and we didn't want to wait for it. We wanted it now. We wanted to be on the winning side. Does that sound stupid?"

"Very much so."

"I don't know why we fell for it, Omen. OK? Maybe because we were in a gang, and we all thought we were cool, and then Lethe told us we were awesome, that we were First Wave, and Razzia was there, and Nero, back when he was behaving normally, and it was all exciting and cool and fun."

"You were hanging around with murderers."

"Yes, I know," Colleen snapped. "Thank you, Omen, for stating the bloody obvious."

"Well, you were," Omen mumbled.

Colleen looked away. "Isidora's dead."

Something turned in Omen's chest. "Oh."

"Yeah."

He'd never had someone he knew die before – not one of his contemporaries, at least. Someone his own age. Someone he'd passed in the corridor. "How?"

Colleen cleared her throat. "Jenan killed her."

"What?"

"She tried to leave," said Colleen. "In fact, no, she didn't try. She just wanted to. She was finding out how she could, but Abyssinia... Well. Abyssinia can read your mind, you know?"

"Jenan did it?"

"Yes. Sort of."

"What do you mean?"

"There was this whole big ceremony," Colleen said. "You know that round thing that hovers over the energy field in Coldheart?"

"The dais."

"Is that what it's called? I didn't know that. Anyway, yeah, the dais. We were all on it. The convicts were looking down at us, Abyssinia was making a speech, and Isidora was standing right on the edge of the dais. She was crying. I was crying. She was apologising and begging and... and Abyssinia told Jenan to push her off."

"And he did it?"

137

"Yes. I think Abyssinia helped. I think she maybe got into his head, maybe gave him encouragement. Maybe took over, I don't know. But yes. He pushed Isidora off. She was my best friend. Since then, we've all been too scared to try anything."

"So why now?" Omen asked.

"Something's about to happen. They won't tell us what, but we're going to have to hurt some people, I think. We don't have any time left. We have to get out in the next few days. We need your help."

Omen nodded. "Tell me everything. I can get Skulduggery and Valkyrie to—"

"No," Colleen said sharply.

"Why not?"

"They'll use us to get to Abyssinia, or they'll get us to answer questions or whatever. But all we want to do is get out, and then disappear."

"They'll help you."

"They'll also help themselves. Omen, come on – that's what they do. If they know that something bad is about to happen, they'll have to, like, solve the problem, won't they?"

"I suppose..."

"We've got no interest in that. It's too dangerous as it is – we're not going to risk anything more. You can't tell them about this. You can't tell your brother, either – he's just like them. Promise me, Omen."

"Colleen, you can trust them."

"Promise me, or I'm getting off this tram and you'll never see me again."

Omen sighed. "I promise. What do you need?"

"Papers," she said.

"Aw, Colleen."

"Birth certificates, medical histories, all the mortal papers we've been taught how to replicate."

"Colleen, I'm the worst forger in class. You know that. I barely scrape by, I never do the homework and I cheat on all the tests – very, very badly."

Colleen squinted. "Didn't you get an A on your end-of-year assignment?"

Omen went red. "I didn't forge that. I just submitted the real certificate."

"Oh, Omen."

"I'm really not the person you want for this."

"You can do it," Colleen said.

"Well, it's nice that you have faith in me..."

"You *have* to do it," Colleen continued. "We have no other choice. We are completely and hopelessly desperate. I wouldn't be here if I had, literally, any other option."

"Right. Thanks."

"Please?" said Colleen. "I know we're not friends. I know we've never spoken more than a few words to each other, and not all of them have been overly nice. But you're the only one we can trust to do this. Please. Our lives are at stake."

"Fine."

"Thank you," Colleen said. She took a folder from her coat and passed it to him.

"Just the four of you?" Omen asked.

Colleen nodded. "Jenan's in too deep to come out. I think the thing with Isidora... He pushed her over the edge, but I think it pushed *him* over the edge, too. He's changed. He's not right in the head."

"He was never right in the head."

"Yeah, maybe."

"What about Lapse and Gall?"

A look of disgust came over her face. "Gall would follow Jenan into hell, and I think Lapse is actually enjoying himself. He was always a bit of a mindless thug, and now he's in his element. The rest of us are just terrified."

"I'll get it done. But how will I get them to you?"

"I won't be able to get back into Roarhaven, but I'll be able to get to Dublin, if you could sneak out of Corrival and meet me there? Thursday, maybe? How about the Spire, at three o'clock?"

Omen nodded. "I can do that."

Colleen pressed the stop button and the tram slowed. Before she stepped off, she turned to him and said, "Help us, Omen-one Kenobi. You're our only hope."

And then she was gone.

He'd been Star Wars-ed.

26

Feeling better now that she had confessed all to Skulduggery, Valkyrie listened to the radio while they drove. Skulduggery preferred to drive in silence, but she needed the distraction. Silence made it easier to hear the voices in her head, and that stirred her anxiety. She didn't like that. Anxiety split her in two and hid the stronger part away. Until she found Nye, until she had healed Alice's soul, she couldn't afford to be anything but strong. When she was strong, she was unbeatable. When she was strong, she got things done.

"Are you OK?" Skulduggery asked. His hat was on the back seat and his façade was up. It was one she'd seen before. A dark-haired man with nice eyes.

"Of course," Valkyrie said. "Why do you ask?"

"You're humming."

"Was I?"

"You were."

She hadn't realised. She shrugged. "So what? I was humming along to the music."

"No," he said. "The music was playing, but you were humming a single, continuous note."

She didn't remember doing that. It would have worried her if she'd let it take root in her mind. "So who are we going to see?" she asked.

"Are you sure you're all right?"

"Skulduggery, Jesus, I'm grand. I'm sorry my tuneless humming offended your sensitive ear cavities. I was miles away and... and that's it. No big deal. So – this person we're going to visit. Who is it?"

"Her name is Mellifluous Golding," he said. "She collects secrets. I'm hoping that the location of Greymire Asylum is one she has in her possession."

"You're hoping?"

"Hope is what we have, Valkyrie, and it has served us well in the past. I am nothing if not a very optimistic pessimist."

"You're a pessimist?"

"By nature."

"But you're always so cheerful."

"My pessimism has nothing to do with my disposition."

"I'm an optimist."

"Good for you."

"I think. Is there a test?"

"Indeed there is," said Skulduggery. "Do you always expect the best in any situation? Do you have unwavering faith in your fellow human beings? Are you reassured by the certainty that life has a true and intrinsic value?"

"No, no and yes. What does that make me?"

He smiled thinly. "Conflicted."

Valkyrie rolled her eyes. "Yeah, I could have told you that. So you're a pessimist, then. Do *you* expect the best in any situation?"

"Generally, no. I try not to have any expectations about anything. That can be quite difficult to do, of course, but it helps me keep an open mind."

"And what about the unwavering belief in our fellow human beings?"

"If you don't expect anything good from people, you are rarely disappointed. That said, I do have unwavering belief in *you*, Valkyrie. But you've always been the exception."

She smiled at that. "And what about the third one? What was it?"

He looked at her. "Am I reassured by the certainty that life has a true and intrinsic value?"

"Yeah, that. Are you?"

"Not at all," he said, and looked back to the road.

They passed through a set of gates, took a well-paved road up through a landscaped woodland. When the trees stopped – suddenly, like someone had taken a slice from a pie – the house came into view.

It was tall, and smooth, and exceedingly narrow, no wider than Valkyrie's living room. It curved and sprouted offshoots that linked up with each other. There were few windows.

Valkyrie and Skulduggery got out of the Bentley. As they walked towards the double doors of the entrance, Valkyrie called for her magic to blast her upwards, high over the house. She hovered there, a little unsteadily, and looked down. It was as she'd thought.

She descended, landing heavily beside Skulduggery. "It's a sigil," she said. "The entire house is a huge sigil. Why? What does it do?"

"Nobody knows, except for Mellifluous," he said. "Maybe you should ask her."

They climbed the three steps and the doors opened, and they were greeted by a striking woman in an emerald green dress with Grace Kelly hair.

"Skulduggery," she said. "Valkyrie. My day is instantly brighter." She stepped forward, shook Valkyrie's hand. "Mellifluous Golding, my dear. You are a tall one, aren't you?"

Valkyrie smiled. "Very nice to meet you."

"And so polite." Mellifluous winked at her, and ushered them in. "*Entrez, entrez, s'il vous plaît.* Welcome to Clockwork House."

The floors were polished and the ceilings were high. The light came in through the skylights. The walls...

The walls were covered with burnished cogs of various sizes. They formed one long trail that flowed up and around and back on itself. There didn't appear to be 190-degree turns in this house – all the corners were rounded, which allowed the trail to move from wall to wall.

Mellifluous chatted to Skulduggery as she took them through. Wide-open, arched doorways led from one insanely long room to another.

They came to what was presumably a living room, and sat. All the furniture looked expensive.

Mellifluous crossed her legs and adjusted her skirt over her knee. "So what can I do for you?"

"We need to get to Greymire Asylum," Skulduggery said.

She raised an eyebrow. "My, my. That's an unusual one. Very few people have even heard of that God-awful place."

"Do you know where it is?" Valkyrie asked.

"Me personally? Not a clue, darling. Nor do I want to. Even thinking about Greymire Asylum gives me the heebie-jeebies. I have a policy of staying away from places full of people who'd want to kill me and wear my face." She laughed. "Morbid. I love it."

"Is it here?" Skulduggery asked. "Is it one of your secrets?"

"Very possibly," said Mellifluous. "You may ask."

Skulduggery looked around. "I wish to know the location of Greymire Asylum," he said loudly.

A sheen ran across the surface of the cogs.

"You're in luck," Mellifluous said, and got up quickly. "This way."

They followed the sheen as it moved across the cogs, out of the room. Through two more doorways they passed until finally they came to the cog in the middle of a wall where the sheen had settled.

"I do indeed possess that secret," Mellifluous said. "I will need two secrets in return, one from each of you."

Valkyrie frowned. "I don't get it."

Mellifluous led the way into another room. "Every cog contains a secret. Some are little secrets, some are big – but all are secret for a reason. The reason is what matters. This secret," she said, tapping a random cog, "could be the truth behind who killed JFK, while this secret," she tapped another, "could be an exam that somebody cheated on twenty years ago. So long as it's important to you, the secret has meaning. It has power."

They came to a room with four closed doors along one wall, and Valkyrie realised these were the first interior doors she'd seen.

"Are any of *your* secrets here?" she asked.

"Oh, my secret is in the very first cog," said Mellifluous. "It's how I started it all. And again, in the grand scheme of things, it wasn't a secret that would change the world – but it was a secret that changed *my* world. It was my first taken name, from back when I was a man. I took a new taken name and a new gender and I was reborn as this fabulous creature you see before you. Secrets are secrets. As long as they matter to someone, they matter. So tell me, Valkyrie – do you have a secret?"

"And that would be where I come in," the splinter of Darquesse whispered into Valkyrie's ear.

27

Valkyrie jumped, then tried to disguise the jump with a cough.

Mellifluous smiled. "Is everything all right, my dear?"

"Yes," Valkyrie said, smiling back. She glared at Kes, then looked away, made a show of examining various cogs. Kes walked right by Skulduggery and Mellifluous, and they had no idea she was even there.

"And there's a reason you haven't told anyone about me," Kes continued. "If people knew I was hanging around, after all those people Darquesse killed, they'd find a way to make me corporeal just so they could execute me. I think that makes me a particularly *juicy* secret."

"I do have one," Valkyrie said, turning to Mellifluous. "A secret, I mean. I think it should do."

"Excellent," Mellifluous said, and motioned to the doors. "Valkyrie, you will find your cog in the first room. Skulduggery, yours is in the second. Bring them to me when you've finished."

Valkyrie hesitated. "Who will hear it?"

"Nobody," Mellifluous responded. "Not even me. If someone listens to a secret, it's no longer a secret, is it?"

Valkyrie glanced at Skulduggery, reassured by the slight nod he gave.

"The cog will know if you're lying," Mellifluous said.

The room Valkyrie stepped into was bare apart from a table,

on which sat a cog, average-sized but duller than the cogs on the walls. She shut the door behind her, and a moment later Kes walked through the wall.

Valkyrie raised an eyebrow at her. "I haven't seen you in a while."

"No offence," Kes said, approaching the cog, "but you've been a little bit of a misery guts lately. I mean, ever since you saw the damage you'd done to Alice's soul, it's been pretty bleak to be around you."

Valkyrie stared. "Wow."

"I'm just being honest."

"You could be a little less honest."

"Where's the fun in that? But I've been keeping tabs on you, you know, keeping up to date. On things." She grinned. "How's Militsa?"

"She's great, thank you."

"I bet she is."

Ignoring the tease, Valkyrie joined her at the table, and looked down at the cog. "What do I do? Is there a microphone or something? Or do I just, like, talk?"

Kes had moved over to the wall that separated this room from the room Skulduggery entered. "Think I should stick my head in?" she asked.

"Why would you do that?"

"So I can hear Skulduggery's secret."

"No," Valkyrie said immediately, looking up. "God, no."

"But aren't you curious? He's had so many huge secrets so far, what can he have left?"

"He's four hundred and fifty years old. I'm sure he's got loads of secrets left. And you're not going to listen because it's private."

"That's not an actual reason, though, is it?"

"Then how about this? If you listen to his secret while he tells the cog, it's no longer a secret."

Kes sighed. "You're no fun."

Valkyrie picked up the cog and brought it close to her lips.

"Hi," she whispered. "So... when Darquesse left, a part of her stayed behind. I'm the only one who can see or hear her."

"Lucky girl," Kes said happily.

Valkyrie glared, then went back to whispering. "That's it. That's the secret. Nobody else knows, so... That's it. Is that OK? I hope it is. Anyway, uh, bye."

She looked at the cog.

Kes peered at it. "Did it work?"

"I have no idea."

"Did it beep?"

"Why would it beep?"

"I don't know," Kes said, a little hotly. "Things beep when you leave messages."

"It's not voicemail, Kes. It's part of a magical... thingy."

"I love it when you get technical."

"I think it's done," Valkyrie said. "I mean, I told it the secret. There's nothing left to actually do. So... it's done. Right?"

"Yes," said Kes. "Maybe."

"Maybe?"

"Maybe the secret isn't big enough."

"You said it was."

Kes made a face. "What do I know? I'm a version of you, like, three times removed. I'm essentially an idiot."

"Oh, cheers."

"Maybe I'm just not that big a secret."

"But it matters to me," said Valkyrie, "and that's what's important. Mellifluous made that perfectly clear."

"Meh," said Kes.

"OK then, what should I do?"

Kes shrugged. "Tell it another secret?"

"I don't have any other secrets."

"Sure you do," Kes said. "You've got loads of things you haven't told anyone. Deeply, hilariously personal things."

Valkyrie frowned. "None of them are nearly in the same category as being the only person able to see a splinter of a genocidal god."

"Hey. Don't underestimate your own patheticness."

"Doubt that's a word."

"Of course it's a word. It's the state of being pathetic. Which you are."

"Are you going to stand there and hurl insults or are you going to help me come up with something?"

"I can't do both? Fine. Can you think of anything else? Anything bigger? A secret you're keeping even from yourself?"

"If I were keeping a secret from myself, how would I know?"

"I'd know," Kes said, grinning.

"So you know a secret that I'm keeping from myself?"

"I know one that you're not admitting to."

"About what?"

"Well, if I tell you, would it still be a secret?"

Valkyrie stared at her. Then shook her head. "I don't want to know."

"What?"

"If I'm keeping it from myself, then there's probably a very good reason." She hefted the cog and walked to the door – but stopped before she reached it, and turned. "So what have you been doing if you haven't been around me?"

"Not a whole lot I *can* do," Kes replied. "I've just focused on staying alive."

"What do you mean?"

Kes hesitated. "You've got plenty of problems as it is."

"That's absolutely true, but that doesn't mean you shouldn't tell me yours."

"Well, I'm... I'm kind of losing my strength a little bit."

Valkyrie frowned. "How much is a little bit?"

"Like... a big bit."

"And what does it mean when you lose strength?"

"There isn't a guidebook to any of this," said Kes, "so I'm

149

really not sure, but I reckon if I lose enough strength then I'm going to... stop."

"Stop what?"

"Stop existing."

"What?"

Kes tried a smile. "Kes go *poof*."

"But... but no," said Valkyrie, walking over to her. "You can't. You can't just... stop *existing*. That's stupid."

Kes nodded. "I agree. One hundred per cent. That *is* stupid. But, like I said, it seems to be what's going to happen."

"There has to be something I can do."

"Nothing springs to mind."

"You've taken all this time off and you have no thoughts on how to save yourself?"

"Short of heading off after Darquesse and rejoining her? Not a clue. So, sorry I haven't been around. It takes a lot out of me to find you and get to you and then actually interact with you."

"Then save your strength," Valkyrie said. "Don't appear to me any more."

Kes laughed. "Are you nuts? You're the only person I can have a conversation with. I love talking to you. It gives me meaning. Also, and I don't want you to take this the wrong way, what with your new relationship status and all, you're pretty easy on the eyes."

Valkyrie had to laugh, and Kes grinned.

"I'll be OK," Kes said. "We'll work something out before it's too late. But right now you've got to focus on helping our little sister. That's what's most important."

"All right," Valkyrie said. "I... I wish I could hug you."

"Yeah," said Kes. "Me too."

And she vanished.

Valkyrie took a moment, then left the room. Skulduggery and Mellifluous were waiting for her. Mellifluous held a cog identical to Valkyrie's.

"Well now," Mellifluous said, "that must have been a very detailed secret."

"Sorry," Valkyrie said. "I was having something of an internal debate."

"They're the best kind," Mellifluous said.

They moved through the house, following the trail of cogs. So many of them. There must have been tens of thousands on those walls. Maybe hundreds of thousands.

They finally came to the end of the trail. No more cogs – just spokes sticking out from the wall. Mellifluous slid the cog that Skulduggery had given her on to the next spoke in line. It locked into the cog beside it with a satisfying click and a sudden sheen swept over its surface, changing the colour ever so slightly.

"That will do," she said quietly. "Come."

She led the way back through the rooms, back to the cog with the secret they were looking for. Mellifluous took that cog off the wall and replaced it with Valkyrie's. The cog clicked. There was a second where Valkyrie thought nothing was going to happen, but then the sheen spread across it.

"Is that... is that it?" she asked.

"That's it," said Mellifluous. "Come this way."

They followed her. "And what happens if someone finds out one of these secrets?" Valkyrie asked.

"You mean out there, in the world?" Mellifluous replied. "If that happens, then the secret isn't a secret, and the cog containing it will turn dull, and I'll have to find a new secret to replace the one I lost." She shrugged. "I don't take it personally. These secrets, they don't belong to me."

They came to another door. The room within was small. No cogs on the walls. At its centre sat a contraption. That's the word that sprang into Valkyrie's head. Not a machine, not a device. A contraption. It had pulleys and levers and a gramophone horn, and it was built round a network of dull cogs. Mellifluous slid the secret on to the spoke, spent a few moments rearranging the other cogs round it so that they'd fit, and then stepped away.

"Pull this lever," she said, and left the room.

When the door was closed, Skulduggery reached out his hand.

"I want to do it," Valkyrie said.

"I can understand that," he said, moving back. "The desire to be the instigator on every step of what is a very personal mission."

"Yes," Valkyrie said. "Also, I want to pull the lever of the whirry thing."

She pulled. It gave a deep, satisfying clunk. The gears started moving. It did indeed whir.

A hiss emerged from the gramophone horn, and then a voice.

"I... I have a secret," the voice said. "It, it's... I shouldn't. I can't. I..."

Another hesitation. There was a sob.

"Greymire Asylum," the voice said. "It's on... on Inis Trá Thuathail. It's hidden there. It's... Oh, God. Oh, God, forgive me."

The recording ended, and the cog turned dull.

Valkyrie looked at Skulduggery. "Inis a what?"

"Inis Trá Thuathail," he said, "or you may know it by its anglicised name of Inishtrahull."

"Yeah," said Valkyrie, "never heard of it."

"It's an island about ten kilometres off the Donegal coast. Uninhabited since 1929 or thereabouts. That must be where they built the asylum. Maybe underground."

"When can we go? Can we go now?"

"You need sleep," he said. "We'll go in the morning."

Valkyrie wanted to insist – but she was too exhausted to argue.

Mellifluous was waiting for them in the living room. "Do you have what you need?" she asked.

"We do," Skulduggery said. "Thank you."

"Whatever I can do to further the cause of whatever your cause is, I am willing to do in exchange for more secrets. Tell your friends."

She walked them out, and stood in the doorway as they went to the Bentley.

Valkyrie turned before she got in. "What's it all for?" she asked. "What are all those cogs going to do when they start turning? What's the point of it all?"

Mellifluous smiled. "Oh, Valkyrie," she said. "Haven't you guessed? That's a secret, too."

28

It was two in the morning, and the peaks of Coldheart Prison skimmed the clouds, leaving a swirling trail as it continued on its new course. Every week, it was set upon a different loop, of varying distances and at varying heights and speed.

Razzia enjoyed watching the birds, up here where nothing could touch them, as they passed through the cloaking shield and an entire island prison suddenly appeared before them. Most of those birds panicked and, after a great deal of flapping, veered sharply away. Some of them, if they were approaching from a particularly unfortunate angle, just didn't have time, and flew straight into the side of the buildings. The rocky area behind the Beast – the tallest and most imposing of the prison's structures – was littered with broken, feathered bodies.

Razzia liked to climb along those rocks. It was risky – one unexpected gust of wind would pluck her off her feet and then she'd be falling forever – but worth it for the fresh snacks her pets could enjoy.

More than once she'd had to cling to those rocks as whoever was up in the control room had to jolt the invisible prison out of the path of an approaching passenger jet. Those jets could get so incredibly close, and Razzia would laugh and holler as the engines roared by and wave at the people with their heads resting against those little windows, even though they couldn't see her. They always looked so warm.

Sitting on the rocks of Coldheart, Razzia was anything but warm, but it was worth it to see Hansel and Gretel so happy. They snapped at the bird carcasses, swallowing chunks of meat and feathers before retracting into her palms like well-fed, psychopathic snakes.

She clambered back the way she'd come and hopped over the wall. A convict in one of the watchtowers shouted something down to her that was lost in the wind. It was probably something disrespectful. No matter how many of them she killed, there was always one more willing to say stupid things. She thought about going up there and killing him now, but Abyssinia wanted her to come along when they visited the White House. Razzia glanced at her watch. She didn't really have time to kill the convict. Abyssinia liked people to be punctual.

Razzia made a note of which watchtower it was, and then hurried through the heavy doors. The convicts inside were mostly asleep, although a few were wandering around, talking among themselves. They were all pretty excited about the plan. In one week's time, they'd get to wallow in violence and blood and death, and they were very much looking forward to it.

She got to the control room. Abyssinia and Nero were already there.

"Sorry I'm late," Razzia said. "I was feeding the littl'uns."

"You're forgiven," said Abyssinia. "Nero's just been... Nero, what's the phrase?"

"Doing a recce," Nero told her.

Abyssinia nodded. "Nero's just been doing a recce. It's nine o'clock in the evening back in Washington, and President Flanery is still in the Oval Office."

Razzia grinned. "Alone?"

"Indeed. Nero, if you wouldn't mind...?"

Nero nodded, and within an eyeblink they were standing in

front of Martin Flanery's desk and the president was lurching backwards off his chair.

Razzia giggled.

"You can't be here!" Flanery said, straightening up. "You can't just beam down without telling me!"

"Calm down, Martin," Abyssinia said. "Tell your receptionist not to disturb you for the next few minutes."

"What if someone had been in here with me?" Flanery raged. "What if the press had been here? I sign a lot of bills at that desk and there are photographers—"

"Tell your receptionist," Razzia said, right into his ear.

Flanery flinched, and fumbled for the right button to push.

"No one is to interrupt me," he commanded, and then made a show of fixing his tie. "What do you want?"

Razzia didn't know how Abyssinia stood the man. If it was her, she'd have pulled out whatever was there in place of his spine months ago.

"You haven't been keeping me updated, Martin," Abyssinia said, taking a seat and crossing her legs. "We agreed that you would. We agreed that it was important."

"I can take care of my part of the plan," Flanery said, his upper lip curling.

Razzia resisted the urge to rip that lip away from his face. She'd done that once, to a really annoying bloke from Japan, but admittedly she'd needed a knife to remove it completely. Today she was willing to see if she could do it barehanded.

Abyssinia smiled. "I'm concerned about you, Martin. I have my friends to confide in, and advise me, and talk to, but you... you don't have anyone now that your little assistant is gone. Did you ever find out what happened to Mr Wilkes?"

Flanery shrugged. "He left. People leave their jobs all the time. The pressure got too much for him. He wasn't up to it. And I don't need anyone to advise me. I have the best advisor right here, in my brain." He tapped his head for emphasis.

Razzia wanted to snap that finger back on itself.

"I'm just worried about you," said Abyssinia.

Razzia had been thinking a lot of very violent thoughts lately.

"You should worry about yourself," Flanery shot back.

Was this normal?

"I'm a perfectionist," Abyssinia said. "I'm sure you know all about that, Martin. So I worry. As long as everything is in place, the plan will go smoothly – but if even one element is misaligned…"

For Razzia, of course, normal was relative. Normal changed with each mood. She was a violent person. It stood to reason she'd think violent thoughts. But was there something more?

"I told you, everyone on my side is ready," Flanery said. "They're moving out on Thursday. They'll be in position when we need them."

She'd been feeling odd lately. Unmoored. The certainty that had been hers a year ago had abandoned her. Nero was the only one left of her squad. Lethe had been deprogrammed. Smoke had been incinerated. Cadaverous was dead. Destrier was too busy working on his little projects. Now it was only Razzia and Nero, and Nero was no longer the amusingly arrogant pup he'd once been. It seemed like his magic, wild and unwieldy, was starting to infect his mind – but such was the curse of the Neoteric.

Abyssinia looked around. "I do so like this room," she said. "Great presidents have stood here. Made great decisions." Flanery puffed himself up. "Some terrible decisions, too, of course, and some terrible presidents."

Flanery bristled. "My approval ratings are up," he said.

Abyssinia smiled. "Are they?"

"Everywhere that matters. The country can see that what I'm doing is working. They're not believing the lies they're being told by the liberal media. No one understands the working men and women of this country like I do. No one understands—"

"Will you shut up?" Nero shouted. "Will you please just shut up?"

Flanery's face went bright red, all but his lips, which were pursed together in a tight, pale line. What Razzia wouldn't give to smash that face in.

And there were those violent urges again. The tendency to break things – and people – that had been with her for her entire adult life was now becoming something she had to actively quash. No matter how much she wanted to, she knew she couldn't just wander around killing idiots because they annoyed her. Strewth, leaving a trail of corpses in her wake was not how she had been raised. She was better than that.

And yet...

No. Indiscriminate killing was what got people thrown in prison for the rest of their lives. She couldn't handle that. Stuck in a cell, cut off from her magic, cut off from the world... And, of course, they'd take her pets. She wouldn't be allowed to keep them.

In all this craziness, in all this uncertainty, Hansel and Gretel were the only things keeping her relatively sane. Even now, she could feel them in her arms, moving slightly between the muscle and the flesh and the veins. Her palms itched where they emerged. They wanted to come out, to burrow through Flanery's head like an arrow or, at the very least, to bite that nose off his face. She smiled. They were adorable.

She realised Nero was still hurling abuse at the president. For all his wicked ways, Nero was a liberal at heart, and he'd been storing up this anti-Flanery rhetoric since Abyssinia had first told them the full extent of her plan. Abyssinia, for her part, wore a quiet smile as Nero went on and on about how stupid Flanery was, how ignorant, how buffoonish.

"Nero," Abyssinia said at last. "That's enough."

Nero went quiet. Flanery quivered with rage. Razzia doubted he'd actually say anything, though. She'd seen his type before, and figured he was incapable of standing up to anyone who stood up to him.

She was right.

"I have to take a meeting," Flanery said, his voice shaking.

Abyssinia stood. "Of course," she said. "You're a busy man, Martin. You've got a country to run."

Flanery nodded.

"But I will need to do a quick scan of your mind," she continued. "Just to make sure the Sanctuaries haven't got to you. I've told you how sneaky they can be. Their psychics could be influencing you even now and you wouldn't know."

"Right," said Flanery. "OK."

Abyssinia held out her hand, and smiled. "Would you mind?"

Flanery hesitated, then came forward.

"You're such a tall man, Mr President," Abyssinia said, lowering her hand. "Could I ask you to...?"

Another hesitation, then Flanery got to his knees, and Abyssinia placed her hand on his head.

"Perfect," she said.

Razzia hid the smirk that wanted to spread across her face.

Abyssinia took her hand off Flanery's head. "Everything seems to be in order, and I know I've said this before, but what a wonderful mind you have, Mr President. One of the greatest, I would imagine."

Flanery nodded up at her.

"And can we agree that you'll be keeping me up to date on any and all developments?" she asked. "We are at a crucial stage of the plan, and I really need to know that you're doing everything I need you to be doing."

Flanery nodded again, and started to stand.

"Oh, don't get up on our account, Martin," said Abyssinia. "We'll see you soon."

And then they were out of the Oval Office and back in the Coldheart control room.

"That man's mind is impressively twisted," Abyssinia said, wiping the hand she'd touched him with. "Thoroughly uninspired, but impressively twisted."

"Abyssinia, I'm sorry," said Nero. "I didn't mean to have a go at him like that."

"Perfectly understandable," she responded, giving him a smile. "Martin Flanery represents every bad thing about mortals – their greed, their corruption, their destructive pathology. He's why we're doing what we're doing. Personally, I can't wait until I set off the bomb and we watch the life get sucked out of his body live on air."

"And the bodies of every living thing in a three-kilometre radius," said Razzia.

Abyssinia nodded. "That's definitely going to be the highlight of *my* day."

29

Emerging from a troubled sleep, Valkyrie sat up in bed slowly, her hair over her face and her eyes half shut. She could hear the dog on the other side of her locked bedroom door, snuffling at the ground.

She checked the time. She had another hour before Skulduggery got here. The sun wasn't even up.

She pulled on a pair of tracksuit bottoms and a warm hoody, tied her hair back into a ponytail and went downstairs, Xena leading the way. She did a few stretches in the hall, and went for a run.

When she was done, she fed the dog, showered and dressed and had breakfast. She let Xena out of the house and free to roam, and Skulduggery pulled up a few minutes later. She put on a warm coat and got in the Bentley, and immediately turned on the heater.

"This car is freezing," she said.

"Good morning to you, too," Skulduggery responded.

It took a little over three hours of driving fast to get to Malin Head in Donegal. They parked by the coast. It was raining. It was windy. Valkyrie wrapped a scarf round her neck, yanked a woollen hat down past her ears, and pulled on a pair of thick gloves. They left the warmth of the car and looked out to sea.

"Do you know where Inishtrahull is?" she asked.

"I do. Would you like to follow me, or...?"

"Flying burns through my clothes," she said. "I'll take a lift with you, if you don't mind."

"Not at all."

She made sure there was no one to see them, then wrapped her arms round him. They lifted off the ground, drifted over the grass, drifted over the rocks, and, once they were over the water, they started to pick up speed.

God, it was cold up there.

The wind grew stronger and, instead of fighting it, Skulduggery let it twirl them as they caught a ride on the air currents. They flew beside seagulls, then dipped low over the heads of the grey seals looking up at them from the churning water.

Inishtrahull was small and rocky. It had a lighthouse, painted white, and a handful of stone houses, many of them missing their roofs.

They touched down, and Valkyrie jammed her hands in her coat pockets and stomped her feet to get some feeling back. "OK," she said, "we're looking for the entrance to an underground psychiatric institution, right? So, there'll be a door."

"There'll be a door," Skulduggery responded. "Or a cave. Or a hole in the ground."

Valkyrie looked around. "This place is small, but it's not *that* small. This is going to take us *days*."

"Not necessarily," Skulduggery said, holding up his hand and splaying his fingers. "The air is behaving curiously. It's moving around something large."

Valkyrie turned, looked over at the empty expanse of grass and rock. She knew what that meant. The asylum wasn't under-ground at all – it was invisible, cloaked by the same magic that protected Roarhaven from prying mortal eyes.

"Well then, let's go," she said.

They started walking, guided by the disturbances in the air, until finally Skulduggery told her to stop.

She looked down. Her right elbow was missing. She took her hand from her pocket and moved it away from her body and it, too, disappeared. She was standing on the edge of a cloaking bubble.

"Look at me," she said, "finding clues wherever I—"

Huge hands emerged from nothing, grabbing her, and a Hollow Man lunged into sight, forcing her backwards. More Hollow Men came through, surrounding her, pulling at her, their rough, leathery fingers scratching at her face, getting tangled in her hair, seizing her head, trying to twist it off. She glimpsed Skulduggery, fire in his hands, getting swarmed by the lumbering paper men.

"Get off!" she yelled, her magic darting from her fingertips, and a half-dozen of them burst apart where they stood. She was instantly rewarded by green gas blasting into her face.

Gagging, coughing, blinded and trying not to throw up, Valkyrie reeled, reaching out, bursting every Hollow Man she came into contact with. She dropped to her knees, tears streaming, and heavy feet tried to stomp on her. She curled up, focused on the feeling in her chest, letting it expand, letting it flow through and out of her body. She could feel it around her, forming a bubble. She heard Hollow Men burst as they came close. She heard the hiss of their gas escaping.

The hissing died down. The bursting stopped.

"Time to stand up now," Skulduggery said.

"I hate that gas," she said, letting him pull her to her feet. She blinked rapidly until her sight returned. Her hat was gone and so was her scarf, and she'd burned through her gloves. She'd liked those gloves.

They passed through the cloaking sphere, and Greymire Asylum loomed darkly before them.

Tall and narrow, it was a building that seemed to consist mostly of spires and spikes and towers, with small, barred windows set unevenly into its thick stone walls. It was as if a dozen different architects had all tried to build a section at the same time, and none of them had bothered to check if any of it fitted.

The place unsettled Valkyrie. It made her queasy.

They walked up the winding path. The doors opened when they approached, groaning on their hinges like a bad horror movie. Noise drifted out. Voices – talking, shouting and screaming – were layered over each other, becoming denser the closer they got.

The reception area of Greymire Asylum was vast, edged on both sides by steel stairs that curled upwards into the ceiling. The floor was fitted entirely with white tiles, apart from the strange black pattern that they had to walk over to get to the desk, set behind a cage. There was no one sitting there. By the looks of it, the reception area was not a well-travelled part of the asylum.

The doors closed behind them. Slowly, with much groaning.

Footsteps on those steel steps. They walked over to the stairs on their left as a man in robes came down. He wore a mask. Black cloth, eyeholes and two small holes for the nostrils and a hole at the mouth, big enough to fit a straw. His watery eyes peered out at them.

"Visitors," he said. He sounded surprised.

"Hello," said Skulduggery. "I'm Detective Pleasant, this is Detective Cain. We're from the Arbiter Corps. We'd like to speak to whoever's in charge."

The man made a small noise behind his mask, and nodded. "My name is Brother Boo," he said. "I suppose I am the one in charge. Please, come this way."

They followed him up the stairs. It was slow going. He was a small man with short legs. He didn't move very far very fast.

At the top of the stairs they came to a corridor that led to another corridor and then to another. The paint on the walls was faded. The walls themselves were damp. There were sections of the floors and ceilings that were just metal grilles. Beneath them and above them, people cried and begged and threatened.

Brother Boo took them to his office. It was small, and smelled of sour sweat. There was a window behind his desk that looked out on to storm clouds.

He sat. They sat.

"Oh," he said, like he'd just remembered he was wearing a mask. He took it off. His face was round and pale and his hair was decidedly sparse.

"Well now," he said, "this is interesting. As you can imagine, we don't have many visitors to the island. We certainly don't have many skeletons stopping by. It's one thing to hear tales of you, Detective Pleasant, but quite another to see you in the flesh. So to speak."

"I hope I don't disappoint," Skulduggery said, as if they were old friends. "Can I ask, Brother Boo, to what order you belong?"

"Of course, of course," Brother Boo replied. "I am one of the surviving members of the Order of the Void. There used to be more of us, but I'm afraid time is a whittler. We have our faith, and we have our duties – chief among them, at present, being the asylum itself. May I ask you a question now? How did you find us? It's no small feat, what you have managed."

"I confess," Skulduggery said, "I read of your location in one of the diaries of Eachan Meritorious."

Brother Boo frowned. "Were the diaries not lost, some years ago? News is slow to reach us out here on the island, but I seem to remember reports of the Sanctuary being destroyed."

Skulduggery nodded. "The old Sanctuary is gone, as are the diaries, but I read this some time before we lost them."

"Ah," said Brother Boo. "That explains it. And for what purpose have you travelled here?"

"We're searching for a cure," said Valkyrie. "An associate of ours has been left badly traumatised by years of torture, and we're here looking for a way to soothe his mind. We heard that we might be able to find such a cure here. Something called K-49?"

"I see," said Brother Boo.

"Do you know what that is?"

"I'm afraid you have been misled," said Brother Boo. "We do not so much *cure* the afflicted here as contain them. We have our doctors, and they work extremely hard, but many of our patients are far too dangerous to risk treatment. Their insanity is the most wicked, the most insidious. They can never be released because they can never be cured."

"How many patients do you have?" asked Valkyrie.

"We have one hundred and eight in total."

"And what do they do all day if you're not treating them?"

"What do they do? I'm... I'm afraid I don't understand. They do nothing. They stay in their cells."

"All day? All day, every day?"

"Yes. We could never let them out, Detective Cain. These are dangerous people."

"And you don't even try to help them?"

Brother Boo smiled patiently. "We're helping everyone else by keeping them safely within these walls."

"That's... that's barbaric."

"No, no. It's the patients who are the barbarians. They have committed crimes so unspeakable no gaol or prison in the world would take them. Greymire Asylum is their home."

"They're ill," Valkyrie said. "They need help."

"They need chains, Miss Cain."

"If I may interrupt," Skulduggery said. "Brother Boo, this K-49 that our associate is seeking. What is it?"

"I'm afraid I am not required to help you," Brother Boo answered. "Greymire Asylum falls outside of any Sanctuary's jurisdiction."

"We don't work for the Sanctuaries," said Valkyrie.

"No, but you work within their system of governance and control. Greymire, as an institution, is separate from all that. The Sanctuaries have never wanted to take responsibility for the patients we house, and are only too happy to let us continue to work without interference."

"Well," Valkyrie said, "we're interfering now."

Brother Boo smiled again. "Indeed."

She clenched her fists to stop her hands from grabbing him.

"Brother Boo," said Skulduggery, "we're on a mission of some importance. Whatever K-49 is, we need it. Greymire Asylum is obviously one of the most remote magical institutions in the world. You've cut yourself off from the rest of us, probably with good reason. But there must be something you need. Something, either magical or mortal, that we can get for you. Whatever it is."

"I thank you for your kind offer," said Brother Boo. "But the Order of the Void is entirely self-sufficient."

Skulduggery tilted his head. "Everyone needs something," he said, good humour in his voice.

Brother Boo chuckled. "Those of us in the Order have a motto, Detective Pleasant. In the original tongue, it is *ensa varden ne reviar*. In a language you would understand? *We require nothing*. I am sorry, but regrettably you must leave without the thing you seek."

Brother Boo stood, as did Skulduggery.

Valkyrie stayed seated. "So you're not going to share it with us," she said.

"It was very nice meeting you both."

"If it's a potion or whatever, you could just tell us how to make it. We don't have to take any of yours."

"Brother Bear will show you out."

A large man in robes, wearing the cloth mask, appeared behind them.

Skulduggery looked at Valkyrie. She sighed heavily.

"Fine," she said, standing. "Obviously, we're not going to get what we came here for."

Brother Boo smiled. "I'm glad you understand."

"Before I go, though, could I use the convenience?"

"I'm sorry?" said Brother Boo.

"The bathroom," she said. "The jacks. The bog. The loo. The toilet."

Brother Boo frowned. "The lavatory?"

"Yes," said Valkyrie, "could I use the lavatory?"

"Of course," said Brother Boo. "Brother Bear, please escort Detective Cain to the lavatory."

Brother Bear turned and Valkyrie followed him. She winked to Skulduggery as she passed. She had a plan.

30

Brother Bear led Valkyrie down another long corridor. The sounds of sobbing dimmed slightly.

"Thank you very much," Valkyrie said when they came to a door. She pushed it open. The stench made her gag. Holding her hand over her nose and mouth, she entered.

There were three wooden stalls set up inside, and exactly zero windows to climb out of. This was dismaying. Her entire plan consisted of sneaking out of a window. So far, it wasn't going well.

Brother Bear came in behind her. She looked at him.

"Right," she said.

She chose the middle stall, and went in. There was a plank of wood with a hole cut into it. Valkyrie stared in horror.

The plank did seem to be clean, though.

She turned. Brother Bear looked at her, his hands clasped before him. She closed the door, securing it with a simple latch, and stood there. Well, this was a brilliant waste of time.

She looked at the plank, and sighed. Now that she was here, she realised that she did actually have to go.

She undid her jeans and sat. The door didn't go all the way to the ground, and the stall was barely taller than she was.

"Hello?" she called.

Brother Bear didn't respond.

She continued. "Could you make some noise? I'm just very

aware that you can hear everything, and... Could you hum, or something? Is there a sink out there? Maybe if you turned the tap on I'd be able to go."

He didn't answer. He didn't move. No tap was turned on.

Glowering, Valkyrie took out her phone, selected the first song that came up – "Time is Running Out" by Muse – and played it really, really loudly. She closed her eyes and sang along. When she was done, she left the stall.

"Thank you for your help," she said to Brother Bear. "Oh, look, there *is* a sink."

She washed her hands, dried them on her coat, and left the room. Skulduggery and Brother Boo were waiting outside. Skulduggery tilted his head at her. She rolled her eyes in response.

Brother Boo swept his hand towards a corridor. "The exit is this way."

Valkyrie trudged after them. Down one long corridor after another. "This place have a gift shop?" she asked.

"I'm afraid I don't understand," said Brother Boo.

Of course he didn't.

His office was just ahead. They were almost out. But she couldn't just leave. She needed K-49, whatever the hell it was. They passed a corridor on their right.

"Oh, what's down here?" Valkyrie said as she strode through.

"Excuse me," Brother Boo said from behind her, "the exit is this way. Excuse me!"

Brother Bear was thundering after her. She turned a corner and sprinted to the next and turned and energy crackled as she shot off her feet, blasting straight up and then she cut off her magic suddenly, letting her momentum carry her to the grilled ceiling. She managed to get her fingers through the grille and curled them, gritting her teeth against the pain as she hung there.

Brother Bear came running. He passed underneath. Then Brother Boo, scuttling after him. Skulduggery followed.

"Where is she?" asked Brother Boo, a little panic edging through his smug demeanour. "Where did she go?"

"Oh, that girl," Skulduggery said. "She'd get lost in her own house, she really would."

Brother Boo whirled to him. "*Where is she?*"

"I have no idea," Skulduggery said. "She does tend to wander off, but don't worry – she will turn up eventually."

Her fingers were on fire. Her arms were on fire. Someone walked by above and almost trod on her.

"You," Brother Boo said to Brother Bear, "go that way. If you find her, drag her out of here, do you understand? Detective Pleasant, you will stay with me, and we'll go this way."

"Excellent plan," Skulduggery said. "She won't go too far. The moment she gets hungry, she'll come running back, you mark my words."

Valkyrie waited until they had gone, then she let herself drop. Using her magic to control her descent, she landed quietly and shook out her hands, wincing at the pain.

She hadn't sneaked through any windows, but this was the next best thing.

She went exploring.

31

After ten minutes of exploring, she'd come to the conclusion that exploring was stupid and she hated it, and that this level of the asylum held nothing of interest for her. The only way to the level above, she reckoned, was probably through a heavy wooden door with an army of gargoyles etched into it – a heavy wooden door that wouldn't open for her. It didn't even have a lock that she could pick. Stupid door.

The handle rattled and Valkyrie jumped behind a weird old statue of a weird old man. The door opened and a Brother emerged, holding a narrow metal rod. On the other end of that metal rod was a collar, secured round the neck of a shuffling patient.

He had someone on an actual leash.

The Brother led the patient onwards, and the door opened again and a woman came through, dressed in drab grey scrubs and reading through notes. Valkyrie sneaked out from behind the statue, got a hand to the door before it closed. She checked to make sure no one was coming, then sneaked in, found some stairs leading up and crept onwards.

She watched from behind cover as Brothers transferred patients from room to room. Not all of the patients were on leashes, but some of them struggled so much they required two Brothers to escort them.

Valkyrie found more stairs. She was almost to the top when another man in grey scrubs appeared. He frowned when he saw her there, frozen as she was on the steps.

Valkyrie put on a smile and continued up. "Hello there," she said. "You are...?"

"Doctor Derleth," he said hesitantly as she reached him and shook his hand.

"Ah, Doctor Derleth! There you are! I got myself a little lost, if I'm being honest with you. I'm sure I'm not where I'm supposed to be, and I'm probably where I'm not *meant* to be."

She laughed, started to walk, pulling him alongside her before she released his hand. "Now then," she continued, "hopefully, you can help me. Brother Boo told me I could pick up some K-49. He wasn't overly thrilled about the prospect, said something about *that's not how we do things in Greymire*, but I persuaded him that I couldn't leave without it, and what can I tell you? I can be very persuasive when I want to be!" She laughed again.

Derleth smiled politely. "Um... of course. And how much do you require?"

"Just enough for one."

"One patient," the doctor murmured. "A single vial of K-49 should suffice, I presume?"

"Hey," Valkyrie said, "you're the expert, am I right? I barely know what I'm doing, but don't tell anyone else that!" She laughed. "If a single vial will be enough for one person, then yes, a single vial will definitely suit my needs."

"Well then," Derleth said, "our store is this way." He took the lead and she walked alongside. "What, um, what do you *do*, exactly?"

"Me? I do a little bit of everything, quite frankly, but, if I'm being honest with you, I'd say my true talent lies in administration."

"Is that so?"

"Yes, it is," Valkyrie said. "I can administrate pretty much anything. Show me a spreadsheet and watch me go, as my mother used to say. As long as I don't have to do it *here*. I don't want to insult you or anything... but all that screaming..."

She made a face and he chuckled.

"I understand," he said. "It can get to you at first. After a few months, however, I have to say you barely notice it. And if you leave, for whatever reason? It sounds demented, but you miss it when it's gone."

He chuckled and she chuckled and they both chuckled.

"One thing I was wondering, though," Valkyrie said, because she couldn't help herself, "is what is the point of having an asylum if its aim isn't to help people?"

Derleth made a sound, halfway between a laugh and a grunt. "Ah, yes, you've heard Brother Boo's edict of *contain, not cure*... That isn't strictly true, of course. The Order of the Void, well, they are who they are, but we doctors do try to help those we feel could benefit from our attention – but they are few and decidedly far between. Mostly, as Brother Boo likes to say, we contain."

They turned down another corridor. This place was just one damn corridor after another.

"How many are you trying to help?" Valkyrie asked.

The doctor looked pained. "At this moment? Unfortunately, there are no inmates interesting enough."

Valkyrie was struggling to find excuses to pretend to laugh. "So why are there even doctors here if you're not out to help anyone?"

"Oh, because who could turn down such an opportunity to conduct this level of research?"

"To what end?"

"For the advancement of psychology, psychiatry... for magic itself."

"What does magic have to do with madness?"

More stairs. Up they went.

"Well, our power is constrained by our minds, is it not?" Derleth said. "The limits we impose on ourselves are far more effective than anything imposed from without. This is where we explore possibilities. There are rooms, there are entire *floors* that are designed to open up a patient's very psyche, to give form to whim and to fancy and, through these forms, decode the essence of what makes us who we are."

It was quieter up here. Almost still.

"I'm not sure I understand," Valkyrie said.

"No?" Derleth replied, peering at her. "But you seem like such a bright girl."

Valkyrie didn't like the way he said that. "I mean, I think I understand," she clarified, "but I'm probably wrong. Because it sounds like you're saying there are rooms you can walk into in this place where your thoughts become real."

"Yes," said the doctor, "that is exactly what I'm saying."

"But these people seem disturbed and... fragile. Wouldn't that do them more harm than good?"

Derleth smiled again. "We have limited interest in doing them 'good', my dear."

"And this is legal? What you're doing here? Because, to be honest with you, it sounds a lot like you're torturing these people."

"Is that what it sounds like?" Derleth said, frowning. "That is interesting. As for whether our work is legal, I'm afraid such questions don't enter into this conversation. The asylum is beyond the laws of any nation or Sanctuary."

They stopped at a blue door.

"You'll find what you're looking for through here," said the doctor.

"You're not coming with me?" Valkyrie asked.

"I'm afraid not," he said, smiling. "We have a new patient with us today. It's time I began the examination."

She didn't like his smile. It was a smile just for her, and she didn't trust it. They shook hands and Derleth walked away, and Valkyrie hesitated a moment before opening the door and walking through. She stepped into a large room, empty white walls, white floor, white ceiling, with another blue door opposite. The air smelled funny in here. She crossed the room and went through.

Another white room, a little smaller this time. Another blue door. That same smell. She walked through.

White room. Blue door. She walked through.

The rooms got smaller and smaller the further she went. Valkyrie tried turning back, but they were locking behind her, so she kept going. She could always blast her way out, if it came to that. If this was all some kind of trap.

It wasn't normal, that was for sure. Door after door, room after room with nothing in them. Not normal. Not right. The closer the white walls drew, the more her shoulders brushed against them, the tighter the knot in her chest became. She stopped for a minute, closed her eyes and pictured herself on the beach back in Haggard. The beach and the sand and the sea and all that sky. All the lovely, empty space.

She took a deep breath and let it out slowly, and passed into the next room. She ignored how narrow it was – no bigger than a broom closet. But there was a way out. There was always a way out. That calmed her.

On she went, two more blue doors. They weren't even opening fully now – just enough to squeeze through. She pushed open the next one. She turned sideways. Her left leg went first and she shifted her hips after it, got jammed a little, but managed. She sucked in a breath, scraped her ribcage between the door and the frame. She brought her hands up to flatten herself as much as she could. For a moment, she was stuck and panic flashed, but it was just her coat bunching up. Once she'd yanked it down, she could turn her head and then she was through, jammed into the corner of this tiny space.

She manoeuvred herself round as she struggled to close the door. It shut and locked and she reached for the next one and it didn't open. She tried again. Didn't even budge.

Her throat went tight.

She knocked. This had to be the last door. It had to be. If the room beyond it was any smaller than the one she was in, then the door wouldn't even open. It had to be the last door and, as such, there was probably someone on the other side who was coming forward to turn that handle even now.

She knocked again. "Hello?" she called.

It wasn't a call, though. It was a cry. It was panic, edged with hysteria.

"Could you open up, please? Hello? Open the door, please. Please open the door."

The door didn't open.

Valkyrie's skin prickled. She was suddenly so very warm. She pulled her coat off her shoulders, banging her elbows as she did so. It got stuck, trapping her arms behind her. Sweating now. Whimpering slightly, she twisted and tore one hand free, then the other, and threw the coat on the ground.

It was going to be fine. It was going to be fine.

She gripped the door handle and let her magic flow into it. It didn't explode, like she'd hoped. It didn't even spark. It certainly didn't open.

She slid away from it a little and let the lightning fly. The door absorbed it. No damage. Nothing.

"Open the door!" she screamed. "Open this goddamn door!"

She slammed her forearm into it, kicked it, beat her fists against it, screamed again, screamed for Skulduggery. All the while, this little voice in her head telling her to stay calm, to not panic. This isn't permanent. There's a way out. There has to be. There always is.

Door in front won't open. Door behind won't open. Valkyrie looked up. The ceiling, twice the height of her. Could she punch through it? Fly through it? Raised her T-shirt to wipe her face, then focused. Magic crackled. She jumped. Landed. Didn't fly.

Covered face with hands. Breathing shallow. Quick. Magic

wouldn't work if she panicked. Always the way. She couldn't panic. Mustn't panic. Made herself be calm. Forced it.

Magic crackled and burst out of her.

It hit the door in front and the door behind and hit the floor and ceiling and it crackled and did nothing and it hit the walls and did nothing.

She pulled it in, cut it off, closed her eyes, lips pressed together, making rhythmic murmurs that hummed against her teeth while she tapped her forehead against the door. *Tap-tap-tap-tap*. Fists clenched. Tapping. *Tap-tap*. Hurting now. Too fast, too hard. Stopped herself. Blinking. Eyes stinging with sweat.

In all this white, a piece of dark.

It caught her eye. The wall to her right. It was singed – just slightly.

Hope surged. Magic surged. Tendrils of energy hit the wall and burned. Broke through to the darkness on the other side.

Turning as much as she could, she kicked, stomped, bashed the opening bigger.

Fresh air. She felt fresh air.

Put a leg through, ducked, slid sideways into the dark. Cooler here. Still tight. Still too tight. But cooler.

Her eyes adjusted. The darkness got lighter up ahead. Black turned to grey.

Started moving sideways. Walls got closer. Squeezing now, her breath held. The walls dragged at her clothes. Just a bit more. Little bit more.

Hips stuck. Chest stuck. Head stuck.

Whimpering. Trying. Reaching for the grey.

The grey went out. Fresh air stopped. Trap. It was a trap. It was a trap and now she was stuck.

Tried moving back, back the way she'd come. No use. Couldn't even turn her head.

The walls. The walls were wooden. She could feel that now. A moment ago, they'd been smooth. Now they were rough and wooden. She did all she could to wonder about that, to occupy her mind with that. Wooden. Her hands, fluttering like moths, felt the wood. Felt the splinters. Felt the sharp tips of nails.

Valkyrie heard something behind her, in the dark. Twisted her neck as much as she could, jammed her skull between the wooden boards in front and behind.

"Help me," she whispered.

She reached out and hit a wall. A wall to the left of her. A wall, of that same rough wood, that hadn't been there a moment ago. With her other hand, she reached into the blackness, and touched that same rough wood to the right of her.

"Help me," she said again.

It sounded different, her voice. Closer. She stopped trying to turn her head. She couldn't see anything anyway. There was nothing to see. Only darkness.

Valkyrie could hear her own breathing now. It was loud.

She was in a box.

32

Suddenly there was light streaming through the cracks in the wood, and the box tilted and she cried out as it fell backwards. It hit the floor. Painfully.

"Let me out!" she shouted. "Let me out!"

Figures moved, their shadows dancing. People meant enemies. She was used to enemies. She could deal with enemies.

Magic flared, filled the box with sizzling, spitting energy, but didn't do any good. Didn't break through.

"We're going to try to help you," said a voice. The doctor.

"Let me out," Valkyrie ordered from inside the box, keeping her voice as steady as she could.

"No," said Dr Derleth from outside the box. "That's not how we'll help you. But, while your body may be trapped, the air you're breathing will allow your mind to loosen in all the ways we need it to. You're an interesting case, Detective Cain. Yes, yes, I know who you are. You've tasted godhood and yet you choose to wallow in human guilt. We'd like to examine that."

"I don't want to be examined."

"I'm sure you don't."

More figures moved. The box was lifted off the ground. Carried.

"This is pointless," Valkyrie said. "You think Skulduggery Pleasant is going to let this happen? You think he isn't demanding to know where I am right this second?"

"I don't care about the skeleton," said Derleth.

"You should," said Valkyrie.

"I care about you, Detective Cain. I care about getting to the bottom of *you*. Of what makes you who you are. Aren't you interested in that?"

"I know who I am."

Derleth laughed. "Oh, I'm afraid you don't, dear girl. None of us do. Not until we've passed through the crucible. Not until we've succumbed to our greatest fears."

They were going down now, down some stairs. The light changed from the steady wash of a bulb to the flickering of flames.

"Listen to me," Valkyrie said. "Listen very carefully. This is important. This is very important and you should listen, because this is your last chance. Let me out. Put the box down and let me out and I won't hurt you. This is your last chance."

They reached the bottom of the stairs. The footsteps became muted. They were walking on earth. Derleth said something that Valkyrie didn't hear.

"What?" Valkyrie said.

"I said it isn't a box," Derleth told her.

"Well, whatever it is," Valkyrie said, as they came to a stop.

"It's a coffin," said Derleth, and the figures lowered Valkyrie into a deep and dark hole.

Valkyrie screamed.

They were filling in the hole. Covering it with dirt.

Valkyrie screamed.

She lay in the dark.

Some of the dirt had slipped through the cracks in the coffin, fallen on to her cheek. Her chin. Her neck. She didn't turn her head, didn't shake it off. She felt the dirt on her skin until she couldn't feel it any more. It became a part of her. Or she became a part of it.

Her body was still, and cold, and heavy. Like a corpse. Like a corpse, she lay there with her eyes open, staring at a blackness so black she couldn't tell the difference when she blinked. Like a corpse, she'd be here forever, lying in a coffin in the dirt. This was where death would catch up to her. She'd slipped away once, but not again.

Death didn't forget.

She screamed again.

It came on like a passing train, and she screamed and kicked and banged and cried and begged, and then the train moved on and her stillness returned.

Time didn't pass. It didn't stay still, either. In the box, time didn't exist. Only Valkyrie existed, a ghost inhabiting the house of bone and meat that she'd been born into. She was her own haunted house. The thought might have made her smile if her mouth still moved.

She wasn't panicking any more. The panic had left her. Meat didn't panic. Meat was meat. Panic was for the living.

She remembered living, but only dimly. She remembered her life, but only faintly.

All those struggles. All that fighting and running. All that talking and thinking. She knocked on China's door. Walked up a hill with Skulduggery. Ran across a field with a man chasing her. Fell to her knees with her guts torn out. Slipped in the snow. Crawled away from a Hollow Man. Laughed with her parents. Sang to her sister. Died.

The air.

They'd done something to the air, Derleth had said so. They wanted to loosen her mind. What did that mean?

She felt her mind squirming. Is that what Derleth had meant? Is this what they wanted?

It squirmed and squirmed and wriggled in her skull. The folds of her brain turned in on themselves. She couldn't see anything in the darkness so instead she saw her brain, glistening and wet and moving like many snakes.

She pulled back and saw herself. The darkness wasn't a problem any more. She could see everything. Her face was placid. Her eyes were closed. She opened them, and looked at herself watching herself. Then she closed them again. She looked so dead.

So

very

dead.

In the dark.

                    In

                            the
            dark.

    Her mind went
              a

                 w

                    a

                       y.

In the dark.

Something scratched against the wood beneath her. Rats. Something worse. Scratching and scraping. Soon they'd be inside the coffin with her. Crawling over her. Biting. Burrowing.

The wood broke. She heard it splinter. She felt hands, in the dark, arms wrapping round her and then there was cracking and more splintering and down she went, out of the coffin, into the cold, the earth rumbling, dirt in her hair, dirt in her ears and her eyes and her nose.

She didn't mind. She was already dead. Already a corpse.

The grip tightened, and now they were going sideways, and then upwards. She was pulled along and she didn't think about it. Her thoughts had left her head. There was a pleasing numbness up there now, like everything had gone soft, so, when the tangled tumbleweeds of guilt and shame and loathing came rolling in, their thorns had nothing to scrape against.

Through the darkness they rumbled for what could have been a minute or what could have been a month, and then they exploded up into light and Valkyrie sprawled on to something wet. Grass.

Her body took in air. She hadn't asked it to. Her own weight rolled her on to her back. Her eyes were open. There was darkness overhead, but it was layered, and it had pinpricks of light. Stars.

"You're home," Billy-Ray Sanguine said, pulling her to her feet. He wasn't wearing his sunglasses. That was odd. "I brought you home. You'll be safe here."

They were in the back garden of her parents' house.

"Go on," said Billy-Ray.

Her legs didn't move. This didn't surprise her. A corpse's legs rarely moved of their own accord.

Billy-Ray nudged her. Her body put out a foot to stop itself from tipping over.

"Hey," Billy-Ray said, moving round, holding her shoulders. He frowned at her, looked at her with eyes he didn't have. "Is this it? Is it over? Have you given up?"

She looked at him because that's where her eyes were pointed.

"I thought you were formidable," Billy-Ray said. "Thought you were unbeatable. What happened to that girl?"

She didn't answer because corpses didn't answer. Generally.

"Go on now," Billy-Ray said. "Your family is waitin' for you. You'll be safe at home." He sank into the ground and left her alone.

Home.

Her body moved its head away. She didn't want to look at the house she'd grown up in, because she wasn't there. She was still in the coffin. This was all some cruel, sadistic trick. That hadn't even been Billy-Ray. Billy-Ray was...

She frowned. Billy-Ray was something. She couldn't remember what.

It made no difference. She was trapped in a wooden box and she was dead, and this was a trick. She wasn't here and this wasn't her house, and her parents weren't in there and her sister wasn't in there and all the love and support and the understanding that she'd grown up with, none of that was in there, either.

She missed it. She missed it all. It was so tempting to let herself believe this was real because then she'd be able to feel something again, if only a lie and if only for a moment. Was that so wrong?

She moved a foot. Then she moved the other one.

One foot and then the other, slowly and heavily, that was how Valkyrie traversed the few steps to the back door. Steering the corpse like an unresponsive car, she reached out its hand and turned the handle. Her body caught its toes on the step through the door. It stumbled. Righted itself. Closed the door behind it.

The cruel trick continued. She stood in the kitchen she'd grown up in. Beyond the cold shell of flesh, there was warmth. It didn't quite reach her, she was tucked away too deeply for that, but she knew it was there and that was enough.

The kitchen was dark. Red digits glowed at her from the oven. The fridge started to hum. Otherwise the house was silent.

She left the kitchen behind her as she moved into the hall. Photographs on the wall. The vase on the side table, and the dish where her parents kept their keys. Unopened letters. Bills, probably.

Her body took a breath in through its nose, and Valkyrie smelled the house. It smelled right. It smelled like home.

Maybe this was real.

She got to the stairs. Up there, her parents would be sleeping. Her sister would be sleeping. Up there was her old bedroom, the room where she could be alone and be herself. Up there, she was alive.

Her body put a foot on to the first step, and Valkyrie felt something, deep in her body's chest.

It took another step, and there it was again. A heartbeat.

Gripping the banister with one cold hand, her body took the next step, and the next, and Valkyrie could feel her lungs again, and how empty they were. The higher she climbed, the more she felt. Her head was dizzy. Her hands and feet tingled as blood remembered to flow through her veins.

Up she went, and each step brought her closer to life, until finally she reached the top and gulped in a mouthful of air.

Stumbling drunkenly, she made it to her room without waking her family. She closed the door gently, wincing as it clicked, and switched on the light. Posters on the walls. Books scattered. Clothes strewn, poking out from beneath the bed. The room she'd had when she'd been a teenager.

She went to the bed and sat. She was alive. Alive. That was good. That was promising. Did that mean all this was real? Call Skulduggery. She should call Skulduggery and he'd be able to tell her what was real and what wasn't.

Another adventure, then. Another secret she'd have to keep from her parents. She was getting used to it by now. She crossed to the wardrobe, opened it. Her reflection looked back at her. She didn't look like a teenager. She looked older. That didn't make any sense. She touched the glass and stepped back, and the reflection blinked, like it was awakening from a dream.

Valkyrie smiled at it, and stepped forward, and then stepped through the glass.

She emerged on the other side and the other Valkyrie stepped back to allow her through, and Valkyrie shook her head suddenly because this wasn't how it was supposed to happen.

"This isn't right," she mumbled.

"What isn't?" said the other Valkyrie.

"This isn't how it works."

"Of course it is," the other Valkyrie said. "I touch the mirror and you come through."

"But I'm not the reflection," Valkyrie said. "You are."

The other Valkyrie peered at her. "I think you're broken."

"No. I'm not. I'm just... I touched the glass. You're meant to—"

"*I* touched the glass," the other Valkyrie said. "I did. You just copied me because you're my reflection. Do you... do you think you're real?"

Valkyrie narrowed her eyes. "I *am* real."

"I should call Skulduggery," the other Valkyrie said, and took a phone from her pocket.

Valkyrie didn't know why, but she slapped the phone out of the other Valkyrie's hand.

"OK," the other Valkyrie said, "you're going to have to get back in the mirror while I figure this out. Did you hear me? Get back in there."

The thought of going back through the mirror suddenly filled Valkyrie with terror. She couldn't go back there. All the bad feelings were back there. All the coldness and the numbness were back there.

She shook her head. "*You're* the reflection," she said.

The other Valkyrie picked up her phone, slipped it back in her pocket. "You stepped through."

"Yes, I did, but... but something went wrong. I'm Valkyrie Cain. I'm the *real* Valkyrie. I was just... I was with Skulduggery, in Greymire, and—"

"And then I went through doors and I was in a coffin and Billy-Ray pulled me out and brought me here," the other Valkyrie said. "Yeah, I know. That happened to *me*, not you."

Valkyrie shook her head harder. "You're getting confused."

"Oh, I am way past confused," the other Valkyrie said. "I don't know what's real and what isn't. They did something to me. The air. It made me... it loosened my mind. Maybe this has something to do with that. It probably has, because this doesn't make any sense. But I do know one thing. You are the one who stepped through the mirror. You're the reflection. I'm sorry, but you're not real, and you're going back into that mirror, even if I have to throw you in myself."

The other Valkyrie put a hand on Valkyrie's shoulder.

Valkyrie hit her, latched on to her, hit her again as she fell back. The other Valkyrie went low, grabbed her around the waist, holding on for a few seconds to recover while Valkyrie tried to get at her. Then the other Valkyrie lifted, ran forward, and Valkyrie's back hit the wardrobe door and her elbow went through the mirror. The other Valkyrie got a hand to her face and pushed her head into the glass. It was like being pushed underwater.

Valkyrie took hold of the other Valkyrie's T-shirt and let herself fall backwards through the mirror, slamming the other Valkyrie's face hard into the glass. While the other Valkyrie went reeling, the real Valkyrie scrambled out of the mirror again. She shut the wardrobe door.

The other Valkyrie straightened. Blood ran from her nose.

Valkyrie raised her hands and so did the other one and lightning crackled and flew between them, and Valkyrie winced because she expected it to hurt like hell, but it just tingled. The other Valkyrie snarled.

They charged at each other. Valkyrie threw a punch that

crunched painfully off a forearm. In return, she got an elbow to the jaw that rocked her skull. The other Valkyrie's hands grasped at her, yanked her over a hip and Valkyrie's face hit the floor and her arm nearly broke. She covered up as the hammers came down, tried to turn, but the other Valkyrie was kneeling on her ribs, keeping her in place. So this was what it felt like.

Energy crackled around Valkyrie's body and she shot out from beneath her, across the floor, crashing into the wall and demolishing the desk. The other Valkyrie stumbled and Valkyrie got to one knee, magic crackling again, and this time she flew upwards, hitting the other Valkyrie like a cannonball, spinning her into the corner while Valkyrie collided with the wall beside the door.

Valkyrie collapsed again, clutching her right shoulder. Something was broken.

"Jesus," the other Valkyrie said. "You broke my ribs."

Valkyrie groaned, turned over, got up.

The other Valkyrie, her face a mask of pain and blood, came forward and threw a right cross that nearly took Valkyrie's head off.

"You're not real," the other Valkyrie said. "You're my reflection. Do you get that? Do you?"

Valkyrie lunged at her, tried to grab her, tried to sink her teeth into her neck, but the other Valkyrie caught her with a hook just behind her left ear and all the bones left Valkyrie's body and she fell, a useless heap. Her hand closed around the other Valkyrie's ankle. She got a knee in the cheek for her effort and her head hit the wall and the room darkened.

33

Valkyrie stepped back as the reflection slumped into unconsciousness. When she was sure it wasn't going to pop up again, she sat on the footboard of the bed and probed her left side. Her ribs were definitely broken. Every breath she took sent a dozen knives stabbing into her, and the leaves she usually took for pain were in the coat that she'd dropped back in the last of the white rooms.

She heaved herself to a standing position. The reflection was still unconscious, but she crept past it anyway, closing the door behind her. She shuffled to the bathroom. It was a minor miracle she hadn't woken her family with all that crashing around.

She waited for her nose to stop bleeding and then washed the blood from her face. She took out her phone, but before she could dial there was a knock on the door and Cassandra Pharos stepped in.

"You have to hurry," she said.

"I'm just going to call Skulduggery," Valkyrie said, but Cassandra was shaking her head as she pulled Valkyrie gently out of the bathroom.

"No time," she said. "No time. You're not safe here."

"But this is my home."

Finbar Wrong was waiting on the landing. "She can get to you here," he told her. "We didn't think she could but she can. You have to keep going before she gets you."

"Before who gets me?"

"The Nemesis of Greymire."

"I don't know who that is."

They brought her to the top of the stairs.

"It's her," said Cassandra.

The Nemesis of Greymire came slowly up the steps. She was thin, and dressed in rags. Her head was covered in a cloth mask, like the kind they wore in the asylum. She carried a sledgehammer, the long handle balanced on one shoulder.

"What does she want?" Valkyrie asked.

"To punish you," said Finbar, "for all the bad things you've done."

They backed away from the stairs, and a baby started to cry in Alice's room.

"Go on," Cassandra said. "Take your sister. Run. We'll try to delay the Nemesis."

"She'll kill us," Finbar said to Cassandra.

Cassandra shrugged. "It won't be the first time we've died because of Valkyrie."

He nodded his agreement, and they stayed where they were while Valkyrie hurried to Alice's bedroom. She went straight to her sister's cot, wrapped her in her blanket and scooped her up.

"It's OK," Valkyrie whispered, kissing the baby's forehead. "I'll keep you safe."

Alice stopped crying.

Valkyrie stepped out of the bedroom as the Nemesis reached the top of the stairs. Cassandra and Finbar ran at her and the Nemesis swung the hammer, caught them both with the same swing. Their skulls crunched. The Nemesis flicked the hammer up and around and balanced it once again on her shoulder. She stepped over their bodies.

Clutching Alice tight to her chest, Valkyrie ran through a corridor she didn't remember existing and kicked open the door at the end. She caught her foot on a rock and tripped, went stumbling, fell to one knee. The grass was wet, and quickly soaked into her jeans. She was in a graveyard. The sky was grey. Clouds blocked out the sun.

She turned to close the door, but the door wasn't there any more. There was only the Nemesis, walking towards her. Valkyrie tried blasting it with everything she could muster, but the lightning just hit the creature's skin and then it was gone. There was nothing burnt, nothing singed, nothing damaged in any way whatsoever. The Nemesis of Greymire ate up the lightning and carried on regardless.

Valkyrie ran between the graves. It was a large cemetery, on a hill. The headstones were in lines, like hundreds of dominoes. Valkyrie slipped on the grass, went sliding down for a bit. She came up in a crouch, Alice still safe in her arms. She didn't recognise the name on the headstone beside her, but she recognised the date. Devastation Day. The day Darquesse murdered all those people in Roarhaven.

She started running again. Every headstone on either side had the same date carved into the granite.

She turned right, ran straight across. Took a left. Went diagonally.

Everyone. Everyone in this cemetery died on the same day.

"This way!" someone shouted. They waved at her. "Hurry!"

She checked behind her. The Nemesis wasn't moving quickly, but she was closing in all the same.

Valkyrie ran towards the waving figure. She almost laughed with relief when she reached him.

"In trouble again, I see," Kenspeckle Grouse said. "And you've managed to drag your little sister into this mess with you. How proud you must feel."

Valkyrie's relief washed away. "I'm helping her," she said.

"Oh, is that what you're doing?"

"Her life is in danger."

Kenspeckle nodded. "It is, yes. You know, I told Skulduggery the same thing all those years ago. I told him involving you was obscenely irresponsible."

"He didn't have much of a choice."

"Nonsense. He just didn't want to listen, and neither did you. You had your whole life ahead of you, Valkyrie. You could have been happy. Instead, you chose *this*. And now you want to subject your sister to the same horrors you experienced?"

"I'm saving her," Valkyrie said, anger rising.

"You can't save anyone," Kenspeckle responded. "You couldn't save me, could you?"

Alice started to cry again. Valkyrie patted her, swaying, and kissed her forehead. "I'm going to save her," she said.

There was movement out of the corner of her eye and Valkyrie threw herself down, protecting Alice as she rolled. The Nemesis of Greymire's hammer swung lazily into Kenspeckle's chest, lifting him and flinging him over the headstones. Valkyrie slipped and hands grabbed her, pulled her up.

"Come on," said Anton Shudder, and led her away from the Nemesis.

"I don't understand any of this," Valkyrie said as they ran.

"The Nemesis is here to punish you," Shudder told her, not looking back.

"For what?"

"For everything."

"Why is she after Alice?"

"She's not."

"She's chasing her."

"She's chasing you. You're endangering your sister by bringing her with you."

"I couldn't just *leave* her there."

"Why not?"

There was a strange sound, a deep throb getting louder, and the Nemesis of Greymire's hammer came spinning by Valkyrie's ear and hit Shudder in the back. He was propelled forward, off his feet. He fell face down as the hammer thudded to the grass.

Valkyrie skidded to her knees beside him. He blinked at her.

"Run," he said.

She hooked her free hand under his arm. "Get up."

"I can't move," he said.

"Then I'll carry you."

"You're carrying your sister. Run, Valkyrie."

"I'm not going to leave you here."

"Get to Ghastly," Shudder said. "He'll take you to safety. Go now. Go."

She had no choice. The Nemesis was already stooping to pick up the hammer.

"I'm sorry," said Valkyrie, and ran on. She glanced over her shoulder to see the hammer swinging down towards Shudder's head, but averted her eyes before it hit.

There was a church ahead of her. It was small, made of black stone. The door was open.

She ran in, closed the door, turned as her eyes adjusted to the new gloom. Pews, an altar, and a man sitting in the front row with perfectly symmetrical scars running down his head.

34

Ghastly Bespoke looked round. His smile was tired. "I've been waiting for you."

"The Nemesis is chasing me," Valkyrie said.

"She won't be able to break through that door," Ghastly responded. "Sit."

She sat beside him. Alice gurgled happily.

"Do you know what's happening?" Ghastly asked. "Do you know where you are?"

Valkyrie did her best to focus on a thought that flitted through her mind too fast to catch. "Not really," she said.

"You're in Greymire Asylum," Ghastly told her. "Do you remember Greymire?"

"Yes," she said. Of course she did. She was there right now, looking for K-49. "They're doing something to my mind."

"Sort of."

"They're making me go crazy."

"Just a little."

"They gassed me. So this isn't real. This is in my head."

"No," said Ghastly, "it's real. I'm not the real me, but you're the real you, and you're sitting in a real church. But it's a church that didn't exist until you saw it.

"This floor of the asylum, it transforms to reflect the inner workings of your mind. The longer you stay here, the deeper it goes, and the harder it is to find your way out. It's how they examine their patients."

"And why do they send the Nemesis?"

He looked at her. "They don't. The Nemesis just appears."

A hammer pounded on the church door.

"She wants to get in," Ghastly said, standing. "I should let her."

Valkyrie jumped up. "What?"

"I have to let her in," said Ghastly, walking towards the door.

Valkyrie ran round him, planting herself in his path. "Why would you do that?"

"She's here to punish you."

"I don't want to be punished."

Ghastly smiled for the first time. "Of course you do. The Nemesis wouldn't be here if you didn't. There are one thousand, three hundred and fifty-one graves out there because of you."

"I didn't kill them. Darquesse did."

"It happened because of you," Ghastly said. "They all died because of you."

"I can't be held responsible for—"

"You were warned about her. The Sensitives had the dreams. They had the visions. They told us she was coming, and they told us all the horrible things she was going to do. And you knew that was your future self. You knew that if you stayed on this path, if you stayed with magic, with Skulduggery, then you would become her. But, instead of turning away, you stayed. You couldn't even consider depriving yourself of the adventure. Of the wonder. You wanted so much to be different, to be exceptional, to be important, that you walked right into that future and you allowed it to happen. The people in those graves, they died because of your arrogance. Finbar and Cassandra, Kenspeckle and Anton and even Billy-Ray Sanguine, they died because of your hubris. I died because of your ego – and so did she."

Valkyrie frowned. "So did who?"

Ghastly moved past her and walked towards the door. The pounding was getting heavier, shaking the door on its hinges.

"So did who?" Valkyrie shouted, and noticed that Alice wasn't gurgling any more.

She pulled the blanket aside, but there was just another fold beneath. She pulled that fold down, pulled down the next one, held Alice away from her so she could figure out how to get at her, and then the blanket slipped from her grip and unravelled as it fell and the bones of her sister clattered to the stone floor.

Valkyrie sucked in a groan and fell backwards, crashed into a pew, her hands scrabbling for purchase, trying to keep herself upright.

Daylight, dim and cold, slanted across the church and the Nemesis of Greymire came inside, and Ghastly turned to Valkyrie. "You deserve this," he said.

There was a door behind her. Valkyrie sobbed and shouldered it open, went stumbling into darkness. She lit up her hands. Stone walls on either side. She ran.

None of this could be real. Ghastly, the others, they were dead. And Alice... Alice wasn't a baby any more. That was wrong. Her thoughts were wrong.

She tried to slow her mind down, but it was travelling too fast. She couldn't focus. Couldn't do it.

So she stopped running, and she held her sister's face in her mind. This was all for Alice. All of it. Helping her. Healing her. Saving her. Making her whole again. That's what this was. That was the only thing that mattered.

She burned that image into her thoughts until that's all there was. Until nothing distracted her. Nothing tugged at her. Her sister was all that mattered. Her sister was her whole world.

She could think now. Her thoughts travelled the path they were supposed to travel. This was better. This was sanity.

She opened her eyes.

She was in a large room with white walls. She turned.

Doctor Derleth was standing there. "You *are* interesting," he said.

35

Valkyrie shoved him, sent him hurtling off his feet, feeling the power that burned in her eyes.

"What did you do to me?" she snarled.

He gazed up at her curiously. "I took a peek into your mind," he said. "Just a quick one. Just to see if you were filled with all the interesting things I suspected. And you were. It was delightful."

"You gassed me."

"A paltry amount," Derleth said. "Barely worth mentioning. All the gas did was unscrew the lid. Whatever happened after that was all you."

"It wasn't real."

"That's right."

"It was a hallucination."

"Oh, no," Derleth replied. "No, no, no. You went insane."

Valkyrie pulled the magic out of her eyes, drew it back inside her. "Bull," she said. "That's a load of... It was an illusion."

"Your mind broke, my dear," said Derleth. "Snapped like a twig. That's what this place does to people, even us doctors." He smiled. "You're one of us now."

Valkyrie picked him up by his coat. "Give me what I came for."

"Forgive me," Derleth said, "but you have no *idea* what you came for. You think K-49 is a pill, or a serum, or a treatment?

You are stumbling around in the dark, my dear, attempting to interfere in matters you simply do not comprehend. You'd be far better off—"

Valkyrie slugged him across the jaw and the doctor crumpled.

"Do not patronise me," she said to his unconscious form, then stepped over him.

She left the room through the blue door and hurried down the first set of stairs she came to. Avoiding the doctors and the Brothers, she slipped through a rusted door where all the crying and moaning was coming from. There were metal doors on either side of her. Cell doors.

She started walking. The patients couldn't know she was there, and yet there were suddenly a hundred fists hammering on those doors and she quickened her pace, hands at her ears, trying to block out the cacophony that followed her.

This place was insane. Every corner she took led to more moaning and crying and hollering, more metal doors with their numbers peeling off.

Valkyrie stopped.

The door beside her had a number: 84.

She stepped back, looked around. There, on the wall. The letter N.

K-49 wasn't a cure. It was a *cell*.

She ran back the way she'd come, back to the stairs, and she went down.

Down again.

And down again.

She kept going until she came to floor K, and she found a map on the wall, covered in grime. She wiped it as clean as she could, and found K-49 with her finger. It was coloured differently from the others. It was green.

Valkyrie stepped back. On the floor, there was a faint green line.

She followed it through a series of rooms, and the air began to taste cleaner, fresher, and she kept going, until finally she burst out into the lashing rain and above her the tallest of the asylum's towers loomed against the grey clouds. K-49.

Valkyrie hurried over. The tower appeared to have only one window, right at the very top. She reckoned she could make it all the way up there before her clothes started to scorch. Probably.

She crouched slightly, and drew in her magic, feeling it in the pit of her stomach. She straightened as she released it and burst upwards, trailing a stream of white energy. The ground fell away and the tower flitted by, and then she was at the window, grabbing the bars with one hand while she sat, one bum cheek on the ledge, letting the energy fade.

The wind pulled at her hair.

Valkyrie prised open the window and slipped inside. A grey-haired old woman sat in a chair beside the bed. It was warm in here, and there was a small music box open on a side table. It played a tune Valkyrie couldn't place.

It was beautiful. Hypnotic, almost.

She shook her head to wake herself up. "Excuse me," she said softly. "Sorry. Hello?"

She moved round until she was standing directly in the old woman's line of sight, but those old eyes didn't even register her presence.

Valkyrie knelt by her. "Hello? My name's Valkyrie. I'm looking for something in this room, something that would..." She didn't know exactly how to put this. "Something that would help soothe a troubled mind. Do you know what that could be?"

The old woman didn't bother to respond.

Valkyrie knew how she felt. She could have stayed here listening to that music for the rest of her life, too.

But there was something... Something she had to do...

Alice.

Valkyrie slapped herself in the face to wake up, and, as discreetly as she could, she searched the old woman and the chair she sat upon. Next she went to the bed, then the dresser. She picked up the music box, checked it for hidden compartments. It was wooden, and had a studded metal disc that turned in its centre. The lid closed and the music stopped and the old woman murmured.

"Hello?" Valkyrie said softly.

The old woman shook her head and made a noise. An angry noise. Valkyrie felt a buzzing at the base of her skull. Her thoughts clouded.

Then there was pain.

She dropped to her hands and knees, and the music box fell open on the ground beside her and the music resumed playing.

The pain went away and the buzzing stopped, and a moment later the old woman settled down.

Valkyrie stared at the music box, then picked it up and stood. "I'm going to have to take this," she said. "I'm sorry. I don't want to upset you, I don't want to hurt you, but I know someone who needs this urgently. I'm sure the doctors here have another one they can get for you. You're going to be fine. You're going to be OK."

She went to the window, opened it, sat up on the sill and swung her legs out.

She looked back at the old woman sitting in the chair. "I'm really sorry," she said, and closed the lid and let herself fall.

Before her magic had a chance to start crackling around her, Skulduggery swooped in, caught her and kept going, rising higher into the darkening sky, leaving Greymire Asylum behind.

36

Corrival Academy slept.

The floorboards creaked. The ceilings groaned. The classrooms and corridors, the cafeteria and cloakrooms, stood empty and dark, waiting to be filled, and Omen Darkly crept like a fat ninja through the shadows.

No. Damn it. Not fat. That was mean – even he had to admit that. He wasn't fat any more, for a start. Well, he *was*, but not as much as he used to be. The word *fat* was unnecessarily harsh. He had to work at being kinder to himself, that's what Axelia said, and that started with cutting out the insults his mind lobbed at him when he did stupid things like sneak through school at night.

He knew full well why his mind tossed these words at him. It was all a defence mechanism. He used them so that when other people called him names it didn't hurt as much. Pretty basic psychology. But that didn't mean it was any better for his self-esteem. He needed to watch that. His self-esteem was hooked up to life support as it was. It didn't need Omen tipping it out of its bed.

Corrival was different at night. Without the students, without the constant murmur of conversation, Omen realised just how big the place was. The corridors were ridiculously long and strangely wide. The stairs swept upwards at odd angles. The rooms had a weird symmetry to them, their placement eccentric yet precise. No doubt it was all in order to channel the energies of its students, to focus their minds and their magics, but in the dark like this it was just... spooky.

Also, the place played tricks the further Omen crept. He was sure there was someone watching him. Someone following him.

He hurried on.

Up the main stairs he went, on to the first floor. He slowed at every corner, peered round in case a teacher had been working late. For all he knew, some of his teachers *lived* in their offices. Peccant, for instance. There was a man who slept at his desk, Omen was sure – or, at the very least, hung from his ceiling. He definitely didn't go home. He didn't have a wife or kids waiting for him, or a dog that would sit in the hall with its tail wagging whenever it heard his keys in the door. Peccant lived for his job – you could tell from the lines etched into his grim face. Peccant's very existence was one long experiment to see how humourless a living person could actually be.

Omen turned, frowning into the gloom. He was sure... That time, he was sure he'd heard something.

But, if it had been a teacher, they wouldn't be sneaking around behind him. They'd be calling his name and issuing a detention. So, if he *was* being followed, he wasn't being followed by a member of staff.

Which was a thought that in no way made him feel safer.

He continued on. It might have been a student. Maybe Gerontius or Morven had been awake when he'd sneaked out of their dorm room. Maybe they were both following him, wondering where the hell he was going at this time of night.

That was likely. Well, kind of likely. It's just that they had both looked sound asleep when Omen had slipped out.

Or maybe it was no one. Maybe it was Omen's imagination. Maybe he was paranoid because he was doing something that he could get into a lot of trouble for. More than a lot. He was, after all, about to help some actual wanted fugitives.

He slowed down. Oh, God. Oh, what the hell was he thinking?

The classroom was right ahead. Beyond that door was all the equipment he'd need to start forging the documents Colleen and the others were waiting for.

But going through that door, turning on those machines... that could get him arrested. Actually arrested.

He turned. Walked back the way he'd come. He couldn't do it. He couldn't. They were fugitives. They had thrown their lot in with Abyssinia. Jenan had tried to *kill him*, for God's sake.

Of course, he wasn't doing this for Jenan. He was doing this for the others, who had realised what a mistake they'd made. Everyone made mistakes. Omen made plenty. Was he prepared to point at their latest mistake and say, *This is the one that will define you?*

Or was he going to help them get past it?

He had stopped walking. Of course he had. He turned again, muttering to himself, and trudged on to the door. He raised his hand to turn the handle. Such an ordinary door. Such a plain and ordinary door. Beyond it lay unimaginable risk. Beyond it, his freedom hung in the balance – as did the lives of a bunch of people who never particularly liked him, but who needed him right now. Who were depending on him.

All that behind this one, plain, ordinary, boring old door.

Omen steeled himself. Grasped the handle, turned it, opened the door and stepped in.

Nope, wrong door.

37

There was a buzz of excitement Sebastian hadn't felt in a long time. Forby had been keeping them all informed over the last few days, detailing how he was closing in on Darquesse's signal. Sebastian doubted anyone in the group knew what Forby was talking about, but no one was in the mood to complain.

They'd gathered in Lily's front room. Forby was the only one standing. Kimora was squeezed between Bennet and Ulysses on the couch. Tarry perched on the left arm of the chair in which Demure was curled. Sebastian sat in the other armchair – leaning forward. Waiting.

"Lily!" Demure screeched.

"Coming, coming," Lily said, hurrying in from the kitchen with a tray of finger food. "Would anyone like some sandwiches? I've got ham, cucumber and egg. Kimora, I've got gluten-free sandwiches for you. I found this fantastic recipe—"

"Lily," Kimora interrupted. "Thank you for caring, but I swear to God, if you don't sit down right this second..."

"Sorry, sorry," Lily said. She put the tray on the coffee table and went to sit on the arm of Sebastian's chair.

He leaped up immediately. "It's your chair – you sit, I'll stand."

"Nonsense," Lily said. "You're the guest."

"I prefer standing, honestly."

"Will you both stop being so damned polite and sit down?" Ulysses barked.

Lily perched. Sebastian sat. "Um," he said, "I suppose I hereby call this special meeting of the Darquesse Society to order. Forby, please update us on how the search is going."

Forby smiled. "The search is *not* going," he said. "The search is over. I found her."

Cheers broke out. Everyone jumped to their feet, started hugging each other. Only Sebastian kept his eyes on Forby.

"Tell us," he said.

"I managed to zero in on her signature," Forby said, "just like I'd hoped. I won't bore you with the details – I know how you all love my details – but essentially what I did was build a scanner based on the device we'd recovered from the Leibniz Universe, a device that kept open a portal between dimensions. A few days ago, I got a spike in readings that I told you about, which was my first indication that I'd found the dimension we'd been looking for. I repeated the scans eight times, just to be absolutely sure."

"And you are?" Demure asked. "You're absolutely sure that she's there?"

"I am."

"And, if you're reading her energy signature, that means she's alive, right?"

"No," Forby said. "Her energy signature is merely her presence. I've got no way to check for life signs."

"Any... *other* signatures?" Sebastian asked.

Forby hesitated. "Yes," he said at last. "Many."

"And could these energy signatures belong to Faceless Ones?"

"There's a high probability, yes."

The house went silent, until Lily clapped her hands.

"But that doesn't mean they're alive, now does it?" she said. "It might be an entire reality full of the corpses of Faceless Ones, with Darquesse sitting on top."

"Absolutely," said Sebastian. "So now that we know where she is – how do we get to her?"

"We can use the portal device, can't we?" Tarry asked.

"That's where we've hit a snag," Forby said. "I thought I could use the device to open a portal without requiring a Shunter. Unfortunately, that has proven to be beyond my capabilities."

"It's not the end of the world," said Lily, shrugging. "I'm sure we can club together to pay a Shunter to open the portal, can't we? Then your little doohickey will keep it open while we search."

"We can't pay a Shunter the same as the High Sanctuary does," said Forby. "And they're all on exclusive contracts, anyway. I doubt we'll find one willing to do some illicit freelance work."

"I might know of one," said Ulysses.

They all looked at him.

"You know one of the Shunters working for the Supreme Mage?" Sebastian asked.

"No," Ulysses answered, "not one of those. But I do know another. I kind of reached out to him when Forby picked up the first trace."

Demure narrowed her eyes. "How much is he charging?"

"Nothing, actually."

"He'll open the portal for free?"

Ulysses nodded. "That's what he said. All we have to do is sneak him in past the walls."

"Why doesn't he shunt in?" Bennet asked. "He can't be much good if he can't even shunt into the city."

"Actually," Forby said, "nobody can shunt in. The High Sanctuary has set up blockers all over Roarhaven to stop Mevolent's forces from doing just that should they decide to invade."

"I'd like to see them try once we've got Darquesse back," Tarry said, folding his arms. "She'd wipe them out with a wave of her hand."

There were a few laughs, a few nodding heads.

Sebastian kept his eyes on Forby. "Will the Shunter be able to open the portal with the blockers in place?"

Forby allowed himself a small smile. "He will. I helped build the blockers, so I know a way to block them. I'm pretty sure nobody will even notice there's a gap."

"So if we sneak this Shunter guy in," Sebastian said, "he'll open the portal right here and the device will keep it open. Then what do we do?"

Forby let out a long, long breath. "Then one of us, maybe two, goes through."

"Into another dimension?" Demure asked, suddenly unsure.

"Yes," said Forby. "Probably not me, though. I mean, I would, but someone has to stay here and make sure the device doesn't break down."

"What would we need?" Bennet asked. "Like, spacesuits or something?"

"I don't know yet," Forby answered. "It's entirely possible, I suppose. The environment could be toxic. It could be hazardous. And it could be overrun with Faceless Ones. So... yes, it might be unfriendly."

"And how do we find Darquesse? We'd be stepping into a whole other universe. She might be on a completely different planet."

"She won't be," said Forby. "In fact, from my calculations, she should be within one hundred kilometres of where the portal opens. If you're lucky, you could emerge and be right beside her. There's no way of judging. Sorry."

Lily looked around. "So Darquesse is within one hundred kilometres of where we're standing right now?"

"Yes," Forby said. "One hundred kilometres and, you know, a few hundred million dimensions that way." He pointed left.

Everyone oohed softly. Everyone except Sebastian.

"That's assuming there'll even be a planet on the other side of that portal," he said. "We might step through into empty space."

Forby gave a little cough. "It's possible," he said. "But, if there is a surface for you to walk on, you'll be carrying a portable scanner that should lead you right to her. You'd need to take food, supplies..."

"This suit takes care of all that for me. I'll have to go. Alone."

"No," said Bennet. "We can't let you do that. It's too dangerous."

Sebastian didn't answer for a bit. Then he nodded. "Yeah, you're right."

"Although," Forby said, "your suit does make you the perfect candidate."

Sebastian made a face beneath his mask. "Does it, though? Couldn't we rustle up a spacesuit for, I don't know, Tarry?"

"I can't go," said Tarry. "I have a job. They'd never let me take the time off."

"Have you asked?"

"You're really the only one of us who could go through," Forby said.

"We don't know that," Sebastian responded. "That version of earth might have a breathable atmosphere and abundant food and water. It might be amazing."

Lily stepped over to him, put a hand on his shoulder, and said, "You're the Plague Doctor. You're our leader, and you have our respect. But you *are* going."

Sebastian sighed. "Yeah, I know."

"I'll go with you," said Bennet.

"Thanks, dude, but no. I'm the only one dressed like an idiot, so I'll have to do this alone." He turned to Ulysses. "Looks like it's a plan. When will your Shunter be available?"

"He's ready now," said Ulysses. "It'll take him a day or two to get here, though."

"I'll need that time to build a portable scanner," Forby said.

"And I think I can get my hands on a sub-machine gun," said Demure.

Sebastian frowned. "How can you get a sub-machine gun, and why would I need one?"

"I have a shady past," Demure said, "and that world might have monsters you'll need to shoot."

"Oh," said Sebastian. "Oh, yeah. Good point."

"Who is your Shunter friend anyway?" Lily asked.

Ulysses hesitated. Everyone looked at him.

"He's not a friend," said Ulysses. "I've never actually spoken to him. He's more... a friend of a colleague of an acquaintance of someone I used to know."

"Ulysses," said Sebastian. "Who is he?"

"Nadir," said Ulysses. "It's Silas Nadir."

38

Omen was exhausted.

He'd been up all night, forging those documents, and he still wasn't finished. He had one more night of work ahead of him – maybe two. It was bad enough when he was doing that stuff to get a passing grade – but it was so much harder when there were people actually depending on him not to mess it up.

Pressure. Omen wasn't good with pressure.

He also wasn't good with sneaking around and breaking the rules and helping known fugitives. The school day hadn't even started and already he was a paranoid wreck, imagining that everyone was staring at him and whispering about him. Every corner he turned, he expected Cleavers to be waiting on the other side, or worse still – Skulduggery and Valkyrie. But that was nonsense. No one had seen him. No one knew what he was up to. Nobody at all.

"Hello, Omen," said Skulduggery, and Omen screamed.

Everyone else in the corridor stared. Skulduggery tilted his head.

"You seem... jumpy," he said.

Oh, God. Oh, God.

"I'm fine," Omen responded.

What was the point of lying? Skulduggery knew. Obviously, he knew. Why else would he be here? It would be better for Omen if he confessed now, immediately. Just got it all out there.

"Wauuggh," said Omen.

"I'm sorry?"

Oh, God. He'd forgotten how to speak. His limbs were suddenly so incredibly heavy and his tongue was an alien creature in his mouth over which he had no control.

"Would you like to have a chat, Omen?" Skulduggery asked.

He couldn't cry. He wouldn't. Everyone was watching. If he started blubbering, that would be the only thing anyone would ever say about him. *When Omen Darkly was arrested, he cried like a stupid little baby.* No. Omen would not be remembered like that. He would maintain his dignity. He would be cool at all times.

"You're taking an awfully long time to answer my question," Skulduggery said.

"Sorry!" Omen blurted.

"That's OK."

"I'm so sorry!"

"It's fine, really. Valkyrie asked me to stop by and I think she said 'chat', so here I am. My apologies for arriving before your classes have even begun, but my days tend to fill up fast, so I'd really like to get this out of the way as soon as possible."

Omen frowned. "You... you want to chat?"

"Yes."

"Um, about what?"

"You can pick the topic," Skulduggery said, starting to walk. Omen hurried to keep up. "Or we don't have to chat about anything in particular. That's what's so nice about chatting. It's not as formal as a talk, and you can flit from subject to subject as you wish."

"Oh," said Omen, the panic receding. "Cool. Uh, I could... I could talk to you about school, about how my lessons are going?"

"No," said Skulduggery, "that's boring. I don't want to do that."

"Right. Sorry."

"Valkyrie seems to think you might be feeling left out of things. *Are* you feeling left out of things? Because you should be. It's safer for you that way, and also safer for us, as we don't have to worry about where you are and if you're dying or something dreadful like that. To put it mildly, I'm really not sure why I'm here, but the fact remains that here I *am*, and so, if there's anything you want to get off your chest, then..." He waved his hand.

"Thank you," said Omen.

"You're quite welcome. While I wouldn't go so far as to say that you're like a son to me, Omen, or a nephew, or even the nephew of a close family friend, I do, nevertheless, view you as a young person who has entered into my orbit and who I now must deal with."

"That's very sweet of you."

"I am surprisingly sweet. People often say that."

A First Year boy ran up. "My great-great-grandfather fought beside you in the war," he announced breathlessly. "He still talks about it. You probably wouldn't remember him. It was so long ago and you fought beside so many people."

"But I also have a marvellous memory," said Skulduggery. "What's his name?"

"Bernan Howbeit."

"Howbeit," Skulduggery murmured. "Yes, I do remember him. He fought at the Siege of Lions, didn't he?"

"Yes, sir," the boy said, beaming.

"He was dreadful," Skulduggery said.

"Oh," said the boy.

"How is he? Is he doing well?"

"He's... he's doing fine, sir."

"Excellent," Skulduggery said, and marched on.

"What's it like," Omen said, keeping up, "to have everyone staring at you wherever you go?"

"It can be trying, especially if it interferes with an investigation. There are times when it's intrusive and unwelcome, and there are times when all I want is to be left alone. But you must keep in mind that it doesn't happen outside Roarhaven or the magical communities. In the mortal world, I get to wear a disguise."

"You could wear a disguise here, too."

"I could," Skulduggery said, "but then how would people recognise me?"

They reached the stairs as the bell rang, and by the time they reached the bottom the corridors were emptying.

"What class do you have now?" Skulduggery asked.

"Maths," Omen said, "with Mr Peccant. He doesn't like it when I'm late."

"I'll talk to him – it'll be fine. Which way's the cafeteria?"

Omen pointed and followed as Skulduggery strode on. The Dining Hall was empty apart from the catering staff behind the counter, clearing up the last of breakfast. Omen took a seat while Skulduggery went to ask for something. He came over a moment later with a carton of juice, which he put in front of Omen, and then sat.

Omen frowned at the carton. "Thank you."

"I find that people like to drink when they chat," Skulduggery said. "It gives them something to do while they listen and formulate responses. It's blackberry. Do you like blackberry?"

"That's fine," said Omen. "It's just... This is something you'd give to a kid, isn't it?"

Skulduggery nodded.

Omen tried a smile. "Only... I'm not a kid. I mean, you wouldn't have given a carton of juice to Valkyrie when she was fifteen, would you?"

"Dear me, no," Skulduggery said.

"So you kind of, you see me as a kid, then."

"Yes."

"Right."

"Does that upset you?"

"No," Omen said. "Well, a little, yes. Like, you don't view me as an adult."

"Because you're not an adult."

"But you viewed Valkyrie as an adult."

221

Skulduggery nodded.

"So you viewed Valkyrie as an adult when she was fifteen, but you don't view me as an adult when I'm fifteen."

"Exactly," said Skulduggery.

"Why not?"

"Valkyrie had, to borrow a phrase, the weight of the world on her shoulders when she was fifteen years old. She had been offered a glimpse into her own future that was little more than a nightmare. She had to grow up a lot faster than normal, and I certainly didn't help matters, the way I acted." A moment passed. "If you don't want the juice, I can take it back."

"No," Omen said quickly, "I'll drink it." He popped it open and took a sip. Refreshing. "Would you change any of it?" he asked. "With Valkyrie? If you could?"

Skulduggery put both elbows on the table and interlaced his gloved fingers. "From a practical point of view? No. She was integral to saving the world on multiple occasions. But do I wish I could change some things, looking back? Yes. I don't regret introducing her to our world – her entire existence opened up from that point onwards. But if somehow I could simultaneously have allowed her to grow up in her own way, at her own pace, to experience the things that she needed to experience? I would have.

"Those experiences are important. You're young, Omen. You think adulthood will never get here. You want all this strife, all this uncertainty, to be over, yes?"

Omen nodded.

"It's never over. It's just replaced by different sorts of strife and different sorts of uncertainty. And don't believe anyone who tells you that their childhood days were the best years of their life. I'd hate to have to go through mine again, and I much prefer being an adult. Even one without any flesh."

"But if everyone's so uncertain all the time," Omen said, "how do they know what to do with their lives? Like, right now everyone in my class is filling out these Senior Years Agenda forms, where you're basically deciding what discipline you want to focus on."

Skulduggery tilted his head. "That's a part of your curriculum? They've made that into something you can be tested on?"

"Pretty much."

Skulduggery took off his hat and put it on the table beside him. "The people here at the Academy are trying to figure out the optimal way to teach the next generation of sorcerers. They want you to be the best and the brightest. Something like this, a school on this scale, with these resources, has never been attempted before. Because of this, they're going to make mistakes."

"You think the SYAs are a mistake?"

"Choosing your discipline is a personal matter," Skulduggery said. "You have practically all of them at your fingertips right now, but at a fraction of their potential. By the time your Surge hits, you'll either have figured it out, or you won't. If you're not specialising in one thing in particular, you'll be an Elemental. I, personally, chose this discipline and, I have to say, it's not so bad."

"You can fly," said Omen, grinning.

"I can fly, indeed. And I've passed on that knowledge so now other Elementals are flying, too. What I'm telling you is that it sorts itself out. You don't need to fill out a form to decide what you want to be. You just need to listen to yourself."

"Flying wouldn't be so bad, maybe."

"It does grant you a fresh perspective on things."

"I just don't know what I'm going to do," said Omen. "I don't want to disappoint my parents even more than I already have."

"Quite a couple, your parents."

"Do you know them?"

"I met them at the last Requiem Ball, almost ten years ago now. They were..."

"Intense?"

"Yes."

"That sounds like them, all right." Omen slurped some more

juice. "Could I ask if, when you were a kid, you liked your parents?"

Skulduggery hesitated. "I liked my mother. I'd even go as far as to say I *loved* my mother. I had... disagreements with my father."

"I didn't mean to make it sound like I don't love my parents," Omen said quickly. "I do. Of course I do. I'm just... I'm just not really sure if they love me."

Skulduggery's head tilted again.

"Sorry," said Omen, giving a shaky laugh. "You probably think that sounds really pathetic."

"Parents should love their children," Skulduggery said. "It doesn't always happen that way, unfortunately. Things go wrong. Some people aren't built for it. But you're not pathetic for wanting something that should naturally be yours, Omen, and never be afraid to be sad. The wind does not break a tree that bends."

"That's... wow. Is that, like, some ancient proverb that you picked up on your travels, hundreds of years ago?"

"It is," Skulduggery said. "Also it's written on the back of your juice carton." His phone buzzed, and he read the message, then picked up his hat and stood. "I have to go now, Omen. I'm under instructions to remind you to stay away from America. Will you do that for me?"

"Yes. I mean, I already promised Valkyrie, but yeah, I'll stay away. Can I ask why, though?"

"I'm sure Valkyrie will tell you once it's all over. For now, you should really get to class."

Omen paled. "But aren't you coming with me to talk to Mr Peccant, to tell him why I'm late?"

"You'll be fine," Skulduggery said, walking away. "Uther Peccant is a very understanding man."

"I don't think you know him very well."

But Skulduggery was already gone.

"Aw, dammit," said Omen.

39

When the dreams came, Valkyrie was trapped in that coffin again, being buried alive by all the people who'd died because of her. She screamed and begged and pleaded and all they did was laugh and throw down more dirt.

She woke, hot and tangled in sweat-soaked sheets. She sat up and cried until her insides quivered.

When she was all cried out, she dragged herself into the shower and stood under the hot spray until she'd stopped shaking. She put on some clothes, fed Xena and herself, and then she worked out, ignoring her phone when it rang. She had another shower, a longer one, and dried her hair and dressed properly.

The phone rang again. She didn't answer it. A message came through from Skulduggery, telling her that Oberon Guile had a lead regarding Crepuscular Vies. She should have answered it, but she didn't want to go anywhere, didn't want to leave the house, so she lifted the lid of the music box and sat on the edge of her bed, staring at the wall.

The jingly-jangly thoughts quietened, and fell obediently into place.

The vision involving Omen and Auger was still on track to happen the way Valkyrie had seen. They were still in danger. Working with Oberon Guile could possibly help to avert that future.

She stood. Helping Oberon meant helping Omen. That was her priority right now. Well, one of them.

Valkyrie frowned. Was today Monday? Today was Monday, she was pretty sure. She'd arranged to meet Caisson tonight. Could she get to America and back before ten? With Fletcher she could. He was so handy.

The phone was ringing again. How long had it been ringing? How long had she been sitting there?

She closed the lid of the music box. Time to get back to work.

Forty minutes later, she was standing with Skulduggery and Oberon Guile outside an apartment building in Tucson, Arizona. Skulduggery was wearing a façade. Valkyrie was wearing a coat and holding a photograph of a man in a military uniform staring straight at the camera.

"His name's Thomas Bolton," Oberon said. "He spent twelve years in the US Army and then he quit to join a private company. No one I've talked to seems to know *which* private army, however."

Valkyrie passed the photo to Skulduggery. "We could find that out pretty easily," she said.

"I have no doubt," Oberon responded, taking the photo back. "My detective skills only go so far before they fall over and die. From what I've been able to gather, though, he's making a living as a mercenary these days."

"And what links him to Crepuscular Vies?" Skulduggery asked.

"A very thin thread," Oberon admitted. "I know a lot of ex-cons, a lot of disreputable people, but only one of them had even *heard* about a sorcerer matching Vies's description. So I followed that trail, shaky as it was. Talked to one person who sent me to another who sent me to another, and eventually I got chatting to a plumber from Philadelphia. I mean, he's a sorcerer, too, but he needs to earn a living, you know? Anyway, Bolton's his ex-brother-in-law, a real dirtbag from what I been told. Thanksgiving before last, the plumber starts to get the feeling that Bolton knows about us – you know, the magic thing? He reckons Bolton's new employers know about us, too, so a few days later he follows him, ends up sneaking around a warehouse where a bunch of military guys are congregating. But he's a lot better at plumbing than he is at sneaking, so he gets discovered, and a guy with a 'freaky-looking face' – his words, not mine – and answering to the name of Crepuscular proceeds to beat the living hell out of him. He manages to run, and Bolton doesn't see him, so the plumber goes home, convinces his sister to finally end her crappy marriage, and gets on with his life."

"That's actually pretty good detective work," said Valkyrie.

"You think so?"

"You show potential," Skulduggery said, and looked up at the apartment building. It was a rather nice building, as buildings went. "Is Mr Bolton at home right now?"

"As far as I can tell, yes, he is," Oberon replied. "And I'm pretty sure he's alone."

They took the elevator up. Valkyrie used to be nervous stepping into elevators, especially old ones, paranoid that they'd break down between floors and she'd be trapped for hours.

Right now, she wasn't worried too much. About anything. It was nice.

Skulduggery led the way to Bolton's apartment. He pushed at the air and the door burst open, and he went in first.

The apartment was open-plan. Doors to their right and left – the bedroom and bathroom, presumably – and then the kitchen and the living room sharing the same space. Everything was stylish and expensive. Whoever Bolton worked for, they obviously paid a hell of a lot of money.

Thomas Bolton came running out of the bedroom with a gun in his hand and Skulduggery waved and a wall of air hurled Bolton backwards. He landed on a coffee table and bounced off, hit the TV, the gun clattering into the corner.

"We have some questions," Skulduggery said, but Bolton's hand was at his ankle, and when he stood he had another gun and he was firing. Oberon dodged back out of the apartment while Valkyrie threw herself behind the kitchen island. Skulduggery grunted as bullets pulled at his jacket, and he spun and went down on one knee, hand clutching his shoulder.

The firing stopped. There was the click of a magazine being ejected and Valkyrie stood, hands crackling. Bolton saw her mid-reload and barely dodged the lightning she sent his way. It scorched the wall behind him.

Bolton scrambled for the window, firing without looking, forcing Valkyrie to duck. When she looked up, he was already climbing out.

She hurried over to Skulduggery as Oberon ran in.

"I'm OK," Skulduggery said. "Catch him before he gets away."

Valkyrie knelt, tried to pull his hand away from his shoulder. "Did he shoot you? Did he hit you?"

"He damaged my jacket," Skulduggery said, but, when she managed to pull his hand away, his façade's skin was rippling and fragments of bone fell to the floor. "It's just my clavicle," he said. "I have a spare. Valkyrie, we can't let him get away."

She nodded, straightened, backed up so she could see out of the window. Bolton was running across a neighbour's roof.

Anger curling her lip, she crouched, energy crackling around her whole body. Then she launched herself forward, out through the window, across the roof, her fists out in front, and at the last moment she brought her hands in and slammed her shoulder into Bolton's back and he flipped, windmilling off the roof while Valkyrie flew on.

She applied the brakes and got her legs under her, feet slapping the rooftop at a run. When she finally stopped, she let herself slide down the roof and then jumped, landing in the same back garden in which Bolton was just getting to his feet.

He rushed her without hesitation. She could have blasted him, but she let him come, let him grab her, let him try to hit her and then she hit him, an elbow straight to the chin. He grunted. Stepped back. Realised she was gripping his sleeve. He tried to pull his arm free and Valkyrie stepped into him, the point of her elbow to the sweet spot at his sternum. He gasped and she hammered her fist into his nose, then hit him three more times, all to the jaw.

His knees crumpled and she thought he was going down, but instead his arms encircled her just below the hips. She could do nothing as he picked her up and then threw her down again, hard. The breath left her lungs and he was on top, and it was all Valkyrie could do to hold on to him, to pull him close. He struggled to get free, struggled to get some distance to throw a punch, but she had one arm wrapped around the back of his neck and the other wrapped around his right arm, while her ankles locked together around his waist.

Bolton struggled and cursed. Valkyrie held on, and sucked in a welcome breath of cold air.

"I'll kill you," Bolton snarled through gritted teeth. "Kill you. Freak. Kill all of you."

He spat. Right in her face.

She roared and seized his head with both hands and put enough juice into her palms to throw him backwards. He landed and rolled and she was up, stalking over, ready to fry him, ready to cook him where he lay.

Then Oberon was jumping down, stepping in between them, his hands up, and he was saying something and blocking her way and all she wanted to do was throw him aside and kill this piece of—

She stopped.

She didn't want to kill him. She didn't want to kill anyone.

Valkyrie backed off, hands at her head, and Skulduggery was there, holding his shoulder.

"I need to get home," she muttered to him. "I need to get home before I hurt him."

"I'll call Fletcher," Skulduggery said. "Oberon, can you handle Mr Bolton from here?"

Oberon looked uncertain. "You want me to... question him?"

"Interrogating a suspect is no big deal," Skulduggery began, and went on to say something funny that Valkyrie was only half listening to.

The voices in her head... they were screaming at her.

40

Fletcher teleported them to Skulduggery's house on Cemetery Road. Valkyrie had recovered enough to insist on helping Skulduggery with his injury.

"I want to see your Clavicle Room," she said to him after Fletcher had left them, injecting more frivolity into her voice than she was feeling.

"I don't *have* a Clavicle Room," Skulduggery insisted. Valkyrie was pretty sure he was lying.

The house was, as always, immaculate. The living room had a large TV that was only used when Valkyrie was around. There were two armchairs. The fireplace was empty. The kitchen was stark. There were no photographs anywhere. No keepsakes. No curios.

Skulduggery took off his jacket as he walked deeper into the house. There were bullet holes in his waistcoat, too.

"Does it hurt?" Valkyrie asked, following.

"Not any more," he said.

"Is your façade damaged?"

"It'll be fine in a few hours. You really don't have to worry about me." He looked back at her. "How are you?"

She smiled and frowned at the same time. "Me? I'm fine..."

"That's some temper you're developing."

"He spat at me, Skulduggery. Also, come on, he shot through you *and* your jacket, and it's a nice jacket."

"It *is* a nice jacket," Skulduggery murmured.

The first room on the left was, essentially, a giant walk-in wardrobe. It was one of three in the house. This one had three-piece suits, of varying shades of blue and black. The greys and charcoals were in the room across the hall.

Skulduggery chose a suit of the deepest, darkest blue, and laid it on a small table. "If you wouldn't mind?" he said, taking off his tie.

Valkyrie flashed him a smile. "I don't mind at all."

He folded the tie, put it away in his tie drawer, and took his smashed clavicle from his pocket and looked at it for a moment before tossing it in a box. "Pick another one out for me, would you?"

"Sure," she said. "Where?"

"The library," he said. "Gordon's first book."

Valkyrie left him to change clothes. She went to one of the largest rooms in the house, a library with bookcases on every wall. She found her uncle's books, pulled out a rare first edition of the cult horror *Caterpillars*, and reached into the space it had occupied.

She located the hidden lever with her fingers and pulled it, and the bookcase swung open. Valkyrie stepped into a room lined with mirrors. In the centre of the room, on a series of glass shelves that rose from floor level to head-height, there were enough bones to build a complete skeleton many times over.

Valkyrie traced her finger over the clavicles, and picked up the longest as Skulduggery came in behind her. He held out his hand, but she stepped up.

"I'll do it," she said. She unbuttoned his shirt a little and pulled it gently to one side. Flicking on her aura-vision, she watched as his aura shrank away from the clavicle as she moved it in. Then, quite suddenly, it latched on, and the bone clicked, jerking out of her grip slightly and settling into place.

"Thank you," Skulduggery said, buttoning his shirt.

"Dare I ask where you got all these spare parts?"

"A lot of them I've picked up along the way," he said. "Some have been donated by friends."

"Does that happen? Friends give you their bones?"

"They *leave* me their bones, yes."

"That's weird. Nice but weird. But mainly nice. Wouldn't it be cool if we could heal Alice so easily? What do you think it'll do to her? Healing her, I mean."

Skulduggery hesitated. "I don't know."

"It might be fine," Valkyrie said. "She mightn't even notice."

"That's a possibility."

"Or it might traumatise her, right?"

"Another possibility."

Valkyrie started walking and he followed. "No matter what I do, I always seem to be about to hurt my sister. I mean, how can that be fair? How can healing her damage her in a whole new way? It shouldn't be allowed."

"No, it shouldn't."

"Do you think I should do it?"

"We've had this conversation."

"Yes, but now we're closer to it happening, so do you think I should do it?"

"It's not my—"

She turned to him. "Skulduggery, please. Just tell me. Should I do it?"

"Yes."

"Even with everything that could go wrong?"

"She's broken," Skulduggery said. "You can fix her."

"Is she, though? Is she broken? I mean, she's *her*. This is who she is, and it's who she's been for the last six years."

"But she's not who she was born to be," he countered. "Permanently happy is not a natural state."

"It should be," said Valkyrie. "God, how great would that be? You go through life with a smile on your face and even when

233

things go bad and you lose people... none of it makes any difference. Because you're happy. All the time."

"But she's not whole."

"You keep saying that like it's a terrible thing, but it doesn't have to be. I mean, if you lose a part of yourself, you come in here. You pick up a spare bone and you slot it in and then you walk out and you're still the same you. It's not like that with the rest of us. We're not so easy to put back together. If we lose a part of ourselves, it's gone for good."

His head slowly tilted. "If you could heal yourself, would you?"

"I... I don't..."

"If you could throw away the guilt you're carrying around, would you do it?"

"We're not talking about me," she said, annoyed.

"We're talking about healing."

"This isn't—"

"Would you wipe away all the bad thoughts in your head?"

"It doesn't matter what—"

"Would you wipe away—"

"No!" she snapped, as energy crackled from her eyes. "OK? I wouldn't. But there's a difference between Alice and me. Alice doesn't deserve any of this. None of it was her choice."

"And you think you deserve to suffer?"

"How many times do I have to tell you that this isn't about *me?*" She tried to bury the anger, but it kept growing. "You're twisting this. You want me to say something or admit to something and I don't know what you want."

She spun, walked out. She had to. The anger was boiling, magic darting between her fingertips. Getting hard to see. Had to get outside. Had to fly.

Skulduggery's hand on her arm. "You don't deserve to suffer, Valkyrie."

"Let go."

"It's not your—"

Her magic flexed and hurled Skulduggery back and Valkyrie ran for the back door and it opened to let her out and then she was flying, screaming at the sky.

41

She flew back to Grimwood because her clothes were in tatters. Another outfit ruined. She dumped the remains in the outside bin and let herself into the house. Xena followed her in, squirming between her legs as she tried to walk. Finally, Valkyrie sat on the stairs and cuddled her, eyes fixed on the floor.

It was like she'd been out drinking and lost control and did something horrendously stupid from which there was no recovery. Except she didn't drink, and she had no one to blame but herself. Her phone remained silent. No messages. No calls.

He was OK. She was sure he was OK. She hadn't blasted him that hard – she didn't think.

No, he was fine. She knew he was. The reason he wasn't calling to check up on her was undoubtedly because he was furious with her. Or he hated her. Or he was disappointed in her. She didn't know which one was worse.

She moaned into Xena's neck. Xena licked her face.

Valkyrie gathered the embarrassment and shame and guilt and self-loathing and, as she always did, wrapped them in a ball and kicked them into a corner of her mind. They'd roll back again the moment she weakened, but she couldn't afford to feel them right now. She had to meet Caisson.

She patted Xena, went up to her bedroom and instead of

pulling on some fresh clothes she went straight to the music box and opened the lid.

The tune washed through her mind. That ball of guilt and whatever else was swept out to sea. She wouldn't be seeing it any time soon. She smiled. She was breathing normally again. This was good. This was nice. She could have stayed there all evening, listening to that music. It was a shame she had to give the box to Caisson.

Valkyrie frowned. Caisson. Something to do with Caisson.

Her eyes snapped open wide. She checked the time, staring at her phone in disbelief. She'd been standing there for two hours. Impossible. That was impossible.

She closed the lid. The music stopped. She was going to be late.

She pulled on fresh clothes, grabbed the music box, and jumped in the car.

By the time she got to the Fangs, she was very late. Music box in hand, she jumped out of the car, but instead of running up the stairs she blasted off her feet, landing on the theatre roof.

It was empty. She'd missed him.

Bizarrely, she didn't panic. This was a problem, yes, a serious one, but she could still hear the tune from the music box in her head, and it kept the panic at bay.

Options. She had options. The obvious one was to find Dusk and see if he had any way of contacting Caisson. Failing that, she'd wait. It wasn't the most dynamic of strategies, but she had something that Caisson needed, and he would find a way to approach her again. And if he didn't? She'd find Nye herself, and hang on to the music box. Which wasn't a bad consolation prize.

"You're late," said a voice from behind her.

Valkyrie hadn't even heard him approach. The music in her head had possibly made her too calm. Smiling at that, she turned.

"Sorry," she said. "But I'm here now."

If it was possible, Caisson looked even more frazzled now than he had when she'd first seen him. Poor guy. He'd feel better soon, though, yes, he would.

"Did you do it?" he asked. "Did you find out where it is?"

"Of course I did," said Valkyrie. "It wasn't easy. I mean, the whole process, from beginning to end, it was – and I do not use this word lightly – fraught."

Caisson tugged at his sleeve. "Where is it?" he asked. "Tell me where the asylum is."

"I can do better than that," said Valkyrie, holding up the music box.

Caisson looked at it for no more than a moment, then his eyes flickered to hers. "What's that?"

"It's your cure," she said. Such a silly boy. "This is what they use to soothe the voices in your head. It's what you wanted."

"I don't want that," Caisson said, frowning. "My cure isn't a... it isn't a *music box*." That familiar rage gripped him and he screamed, "It's not something you can *hand me*!"

"Whoa!" said Valkyrie. She was starting to panic. "Wait a second here. Calm down, all right? This is what I found. This is... this is it – it has to be! It soothes the mind!"

"That's not what I need!"

"But I took this from K-49!"

His eyes widened. "You found it?" he asked, his voice suddenly soft. "You were at Greymire? Where is it?"

"I... I can't tell you."

"It's what we agreed."

Valkyrie didn't understand this. She shook her head. "I thought if I brought you the cure, you'd—"

"There is no cure!" he roared. "There is no music box or antidote that can help me!"

"I can't tell you," she repeated, trying to be calm. "It's too dangerous for someone like you to know. The patients in that place... If they got out..."

Caisson came forward quickly, both hands closing around her

left wrist. He was suddenly so calm, but he talked really fast. "I thought you wanted to help your sister," he said.

"If you... if you tell me where Nye is, I'll—"

"No more deals," said Caisson. "We had a deal and you broke it. That makes you a deal-breaker. I can't trust a deal-breaker. That Crengarrion you want. I'll get a message to it, tell it you're closing in, tell it to move on. You'll never see it again. Never ever."

"There's got to be something else I can do for you."

"I've spent decades being tortured, Valkyrie. My needs are simple. There is nothing you can give me that I could possibly want – except for Greymire Asylum."

He released her wrist and stepped back.

"Don't go," she said.

He started to walk away. "Say hello to your sister for me."

"What's the cure?"

Caisson turned.

"If it's not the music box," she said, "or it's not a serum or an antidote or whatever... then what is it?"

"It's a person."

"A doctor?"

Caisson shook his head.

"A patient, then. The woman."

He didn't respond.

Valkyrie chewed her bottom lip. "If I tell you where Greymire is," she said at last, "you'll only break her out?"

"I have no interest in any of the others."

"I have your word on that? You let that one woman out? The rest stay where they are?"

"You have my word."

"And you'll tell me where Nye is?"

"I promise."

"OK," she said. "OK, I'll tell you."

*

239

Valkyrie sat on the roof and listened to the music box.

She had panicked. That was unlike her. It was understandable, of course. She had a lot on her plate. And a lot on her mind. And a lot everywhere. Plus, she was still fragile. Greymire Asylum had done a number on her, and no mistake.

But it was fine now. The music box was making it all fine now.

Valkyrie took out her phone and called Skulduggery. Waited for him to answer.

"Hello," he said.

She closed the music box so she could think properly. "I'm sorry," she said.

"OK."

"No," she said, "I'm *really* sorry. I'm so, so sorry. I didn't mean to do it. It just... it just flashed out of me and I couldn't stop it."

"That's OK," he said. "I should have let you leave when you wanted to leave."

"Did I hurt you?"

"No."

"It looked like I hurt you."

"Only a little bit."

"Are you around? Can I see you? I'm in Roarhaven."

"I'm still at home."

"Ah, right." She sighed. "I messed everything up, didn't I?"

"Not everything," he said. "I take it you met Caisson? Was the music box what he wanted?"

"No. Skulduggery, I... I had to tell him where Greymire Asylum was."

He paused. "OK," he said. "OK. We'll say Abyssinia broke into your mind. You'll have to reinforce that idea in your head because China will be using the best Sensitives she's got to find out what went wrong, so your defences better be in place."

"I don't really have any defences, though."

"Then you need lessons. I know some people who can—"

"Skulduggery, I'm telling you, it's not as bad as you think. Caisson just wants to break the old woman out."

"What old woman?"

"The old woman in the tower. She's all he wants."

"Who is she?"

"He didn't say. Can you... can you forgive me?"

"Of course." Without hesitation.

"Thank you," she said, and then put some energy in her voice. "Because I'm going to need your help."

"You definitely are."

Valkyrie smiled. "I know you're freaking out about this, but I really don't think it's going to be that big a deal. Why would China even think it was me who told him where the asylum was? I know I shouldn't have, I know you told me not to, but, I mean... OK, so what? I think you're worrying too much."

"And what about Nye?"

The smile turned to a grin. "I know where it is. You'll never guess. Try, though. You'll never get it. But try."

"I'm really not in a guessing mood."

"Go on, try."

He sighed. "OK, let's see... is it—"

"An underwater lab!" she shrieked.

"What?"

She jumped up. "An underwater laboratory! Under the water! In the ocean! Can you believe it? Isn't that so cool? Have you ever been to an underwater lab before?"

"I'll be honest with you," Skulduggery said. "I have not."

"And haven't you always wanted to?"

"Very much so."

She twirled on the rooftop. "Then tomorrow we're going to an underwater lab! Don't we have just the coolest job *ever?*"

42

The whole class was silent and sat in twos, staring at each other, straining to broadcast a single word into the mind of their partner. A metronome tocked. Miss Wicked stood and watched.

Tock. Tock. Tock.

Omen sat opposite his brother. Auger's left eye was bruised. He had a cut along his cheek that was already half healed. Some of his hair appeared to be singed. None of that mattered. What mattered was the word. The word was Hello.

Miss Wicked clicked her heel against the floor. Everyone's eyes immediately closed. Omen breathed slowly, in and out. He visualised a tunnel opening in his mind. On the other end of that tunnel was his brother. There was nothing else. There was only the tunnel.

Tock. Tock.

The metronome.

The tunnel.

Tock.

The tunnel.

Hands went up. Omen heard the rustling of movement. He ignored it. He focused. He could do this. All he had to do was broadcast the word.

Hello. Hello. Hello.

More rustling. More hands going up.

Omen ignored them. It didn't matter to him how many other people in the room were managing to do what they'd been assigned. It only mattered what Omen managed to do.

The tunnel. Auger sat at the other end of it, Omen knew. He was just sitting there, waiting, his mind open, ready for Omen to throw that word in there.

That was a little bit of pressure, Omen wasn't going to lie. And the pressure was actually a little distracting. Kind of made it hard to focus on what he had to do.

But he ignored it, just like he was ignoring the rustling of movement and the idea that everyone else in the class had already done this and they were all waiting for him. Just like he was ignoring his itchy ankle and his itchy cheek. That was maddening. The itchiness. The more he avoided thinking about it, the more the need grew.

Tock.

Breathing. That was important. Breathing was as important as emptying the mind. Maybe more important. Whether the mind was empty or full, you still needed to breathe. Of course, too much attention could be paid to the breathing. Right now, for instance, all of Omen's concentration was on taking air into his lungs and then blowing it back out again. This wasn't what he needed to be focusing on. He needed to be focusing on the task at hand. He needed to be focusing on the fact that Miss Wicked expected him to do well.

Miss Wicked.

No. No. He focused on the tunnel. On the tunnel. Not on Miss Wicked. On the tunnel. On telepathy. On the word. Not on Miss Wicked. Not on—

Dammit.

"Auger," Miss Wicked said, "are you receiving anything?"

"Um..." said Auger.

"Any words?" Miss Wicked pressed. "Any images, even?"

Omen opened his eyes. The whole class was looking at him,

Auger included. Auger's eyebrows were raised slightly, but he suppressed a grin as he turned to Miss Wicked. "Not really, miss. Almost, though. We're getting closer."

"OK," Miss Wicked said, stopping the metronome. "We've done enough for today. We're going to be continuing with this for the rest of the week, until every one of you can broadcast at least a couple of words. Once that's done, we shall venture out of the classroom and continue somewhere that is not a controlled environment. It all becomes a lot trickier when you have distractions all around you. Any questions?"

Axelia raised her hand. "Will we be taught how to stop people from reading our minds?"

Miss Wicked nodded. "Yes, but not in this module. First, you learn how to do it, then you learn how to stop it. Anyone else? No? Good. Dismissed."

Omen picked up his bag as everyone started filing out. He turned to Auger. "What?" he said, a little more defensively than he'd intended.

"Nothing," Auger responded.

"Then why are you grinning?"

"I'm just happy," Auger said. He passed Omen, put a hand on his shoulder and leaned in. "I will never look at Miss Wicked in the same way again, I swear to God."

Omen sagged and Auger walked out, grinning even more broadly. Omen followed him, aware that Miss Wicked was watching him leave. He glanced up, saw the unimpressed look on her face, and hurried on.

43

Skulduggery was waiting for her on the pier in Haggard.

Valkyrie was feeling better this morning. Less manic. She'd had the music box on all night as she slept, and as a result she was a lot more... steady.

"I'm sorry," she said. "I know I apologised, but I am sorry for yesterday."

"It's OK."

"I didn't mean to do it."

"I know."

"I didn't want to do it. It just happened."

"You lost control of your magic," Skulduggery said. "I understand that. You don't have to apologise. I've already forgiven you."

"Thank you," she said. "Can I have a hug?"

"Of course you can," he said, and they hugged. "Feel better?"

"Much," she said, and looked at the sea. "So where is it?"

"Where's what?"

"This boat you said we're getting. I assume it's a boat, and not a submarine or something? I don't think I'd like being in a submarine. Very... enclosed."

"It's a boat," Skulduggery said, nodding. "Or a ship, to be more precise. They're very touchy about things like that."

"Who are?"

"Pirates."

She gaped at him. "We're getting a lift with pirates?"

"It's a pirate ship. It stands to reason that there'll be pirates on it."

Her eyes narrowed. "What kind of pirates? The modern kind, or the—"

"The old-fashioned kind."

"With the eyepatches and the cutlasses and the parrots?"

"Yes. Also they're ghosts."

"It's a ghost ship?"

"It's a *cursed* ship, and they're ghost *pirates*. A cursed ship is different to a ghost ship for a variety of reasons, but mostly because we wouldn't be able to travel on a ghost ship. We'd just fall right through the deck."

"Are they friendly?"

"Ghost pirates? As a rule, no. As a matter of fact, I'm a little surprised that they agreed to do this. I always thought they hated me."

"Why would they hate you?"

Skulduggery shrugged. "We all do things in our youth that would not be considered wise. I'm no different."

"What did you do?"

"I was sixteen years old. In London, William Shakespeare was putting the finishing touches to *Romeo and Juliet*. France had declared war on Spain. The steering wheel had just been invented, but wouldn't come into common usage for another three hundred and two years. And I had stowed away on a merchant ship in search of adventure – as was the custom at the time."

"Wait," Valkyrie said, "is this where you first met Ghastly?"

"It is indeed," Skulduggery replied. "We were both arrogant, brash young men back then. Insufferable, really."

"Wow. You've changed so much."

He ignored that. "Bonds are formed when you stow away on the same ship, you know. Friendships are forged."

"Get to the pirates."

"Three weeks into our voyage, we were set upon by the *King's Fury* – the most feared ship on the seven seas, captained by Edgar Dudgeon, a man with a heart as black as coal. The ship and its crew had been cursed – they needed to find the Treasure of Bravo Cortes within a year or they would spend eternity as wraiths upon the waves. By the time they boarded our little merchant vessel, they had eleven days left in which to find this treasure. They were desperate, raiding every ship they passed, killing everyone they found if they didn't know anything that could help them. And nobody did.

"Ghastly and I managed to convince Captain Dudgeon that we knew where the Treasure of Bravo Cortes was hidden. In exchange for our crew's freedom, we'd take them there."

"And where did you actually take them?"

He shrugged. "Left a bit, right a bit, straight on. Essentially, we led them nowhere for eight days. On the ninth day, however, we performed a spectacular escape, after which we were promptly recaptured."

Valkyrie frowned. "Can it really be called an escape if you're caught again immediately?"

"Yes."

"I don't think it can."

"This is my story, Valkyrie. You can have your own story where things can be called whatever you want them to be called. Right now, this is mine, and this is how it happened. So, on the tenth day, we escaped for a second time, and were recaptured once more. There are limited places to run on a ship. On the eleventh day, when it became clear that we didn't know anything, Captain Dudgeon prepared to kill us."

"By making you walk the plank?"

"By getting us stabbed with swords."

"Oh."

"You look so disappointed."

"Naw, it's fine."

"We were surrounded, sharpened blades levelled at our hearts, snarling faces—"

"It's just," Valkyrie said, "what's the point of being a pirate and doing pirate stuff if you don't take advantage of the fact that you have a sea, and you have a plank, and you can make people walk off that plank into that sea? That's all I'm saying. It seems like it'd be a missed opportunity to do anything else."

"I think you've become overly fixated on the plank."

"They're pirates, though. They're not... highwaymen, or..."

"Can I finish my story?"

Valkyrie sighed. "Sure."

"Thank you. Where was I?"

"They had you surrounded but obviously you escaped."

He tilted his head. "Don't say it like that."

"Like what?"

"Like that. Dismissively. It was a wonderful escape. There was fighting and swordplay and fireballs and clambering up the rigging and swinging from masts... It was very, *very* exciting."

"OK," said Valkyrie, "so tell me about that."

"Well... I just did."

"Oh."

"Just there."

"You were right," Valkyrie said. "It *was* very exciting."

He was starting to sound grumpy. "So we fought them until the deadline passed and the curse hit, and that's the end."

"How did you get off the ship?"

"It doesn't matter."

"No, Skulduggery, it does matter. I'm sorry if I ruined your story. Please tell me how it ends."

He didn't respond.

"Please?" she asked.

"We jumped off and swam."

She blinked. "That's it?"

"It was a long swim. Even with our magic, we could have drowned."

"OK."

"I was almost eaten by a shark."

"Yeah?"

"I mean... it was a small one, but... yes."

"Didn't you once tell me that the story of how you met Ghastly wasn't very exciting at all? And yet it's full of fighting and escape attempts."

He shrugged. "We'd just met. I didn't want to appear to be bragging."

"Yes," she said, "because that would have totally given me the wrong impression of you."

They looked at each other.

"They're here," Skulduggery said, and Valkyrie turned to watch a thick fog rolling in.

There was a shape within that fog, a darkness, and that darkness sharpened to a point as a prow burst through the fog and the *King's Fury* came after it, a huge ship with black sails and the Jolly Roger fluttering from the highest mast.

"Awesome," Valkyrie whispered.

The *King's Fury* veered away from the pier and Skulduggery wrapped an arm round Valkyrie's waist and they lifted off the ground. They landed on deck as the ship turned back to open waters, not slowing down even for a moment.

Grizzled ghost pirates stared. Valkyrie could just about see through them. It was weird.

"Captain Dudgeon," Skulduggery said, nodding to a pirate with a long black beard and a three-cornered hat, "very good to see you again."

Dudgeon peered at them. "I don't seem to be understanding," he said.

Skulduggery tilted his head. "What would be the problem?"

Dudgeon bared his teeth in confusion. The upper row was golden. The lower row was rotten. Valkyrie didn't want to know how he'd ever eaten anything. "We're here to facilitate passage for a landlubber named Skulduggery Pleasant and his companion," Dudgeon said. "At no stage did anyone mention a talking skeleton."

"Skeletons are bad luck on ships," said one of the other pirates. "Probably."

"Throw it over the side," said another.

"Ah, no," Skulduggery said. "You see, I *am* Skulduggery Pleasant. It's *me*, captain."

Dudgeon frowned. "You're the boy?"

"Indeed I am."

"What happened to you?"

"I was killed," Skulduggery said, "and I came back to life without my flesh. Highly unconventional, I grant you, but then I've led a highly unconventional life. As have we all, have we not?"

He looked around, nodding to the pirates. They just gazed back.

"You're alive, then?" Dudgeon asked.

"In a manner of speaking."

A pirate raised his hand. "How come you don't fall apart?"

"Magic."

"And where's that other fella?" Dudgeon asked. "The scarred fella? Did he change, too?" He looked at Valkyrie. "Did he turn into you?"

"Not quite," she responded. "My name's Valkyrie Cain. Thank you for welcoming us on to your fine ship."

Dudgeon grunted. "Fine ship, indeed. Most feared ship on the seven seas, so it is."

"I've heard. You must be very proud."

The captain peered at her. "Aye," he said again, then turned and shouted. "All right, ye scurvy-ridden seadogs! You know where we're going! Make haste!"

Valkyrie smiled to herself as the ghost pirates hurried back to work all around her. Every now and then, life definitely had a way of delighting her.

44

"They're going to kill us, aren't they?" Valkyrie murmured to Skulduggery two hours later as they stood together on the prow of the ship. The *King's Fury* cut through the waves faster than it had any right to, blowing her hair back off her face. She was freezing. Her clothes were damp with sea spray, and she tasted salt on her tongue.

"They're going to try," Skulduggery responded.

She sighed. "Are we at least getting close to Nye's underwater lab?"

"Judging by our speed and our trajectory, we should be approaching the coordinates Caisson gave you as we speak."

"I just wish we could meet people who didn't want to attack us all the time."

"It's a sad state of affairs, all right."

She tied her hair into a ponytail. "OK then," she said, "we may as well get it over with."

They turned, to face Captain Dudgeon and his crew, their cutlasses already drawn.

"I'd like to say this is entirely unexpected," Skulduggery announced, "but unfortunately it is not."

Dudgeon grinned. "Surprised?"

Skulduggery tilted his head. "No. I just... I just said that."

"When?"

"Just then."

Dudgeon scowled. "Well, I didn't hear you."

"You're right in front of me."

"It's hard to hear every little word over the wind and the sea and the... Anyway, you'll be wanting to shut up now. You're our prisoners, and you remember the policy for prisoners on the *King's Fury*, don't you?"

"If I recall correctly, they don't last long."

"Right you are," said Dudgeon. "Over four hundred years ago, you tricked us into an eternity trapped as ghosts. For four hundred years, we've been planning our revenge."

"But... I came to you."

"And now you're in our grasp."

"No," Skulduggery said, "my point is, in all these four hundred years, you had to wait until I came to you. That's not very good planning."

"We didn't have much of a choice," Dudgeon snarled. "We were cursed to never again set foot on land. Thanks to you and your scarred friend."

"You can't blame Skulduggery and Ghastly for what happened, though," said Valkyrie. "You got the curse put on yourselves. You spent a year trying, and failing, to find the treasure of whoever."

"Bravo Cortes," came a chorus from the pirates.

"In the last, what, eleven days, Skulduggery and Ghastly may have led you on a wild goose chase, or whatever the nautical equivalent of that is, but if you're honest with yourselves, you'd have to admit that you wouldn't have found the treasure anyway."

"In fact," Skulduggery chimed in, "because you believed us when we told you we knew where it was hidden, your last few days as mortals were happy ones. We gave you that. We gave you that happiness."

The pirates frowned. Started muttering amongst themselves. Finally, Dudgeon shook his head.

"No," he said. "You gave us false hope, and that's the worst kind of hope there is. It's entirely possible that we'd have found someone who genuinely knew where the treasure was buried. Instead, we put our faith in two hornswagglers."

The ghost-pirates repeated that word – *hornswagglers* – and shook their fists and their cutlasses and generally looked very, very angry. There was no talking their way out of this situation – Valkyrie could see that now. The pirate closest to her looked away to grouch to his friend, and Valkyrie stepped in with a right hook to the jaw.

In theory.

In practice, her fist passed through his head and he jumped back, startled.

Everyone else fell silent.

"You can't do that!" he shouted. "You can't just put your hands through me! My body is a sovereign entity!"

Another pirate, a particularly thin one, sighed. "You don't have a body, Triston."

"I have the form of one! I have the memory of one!"

"I didn't mean to put my hand through you," Valkyrie clarified. "I just meant to punch you. I didn't know that would happen. I'm sorry."

"Yeah," said a pirate from the back of the crowd, "calm down, Triston."

"Shut up, Bernard!" Triston screeched.

"Please excuse me," Valkyrie said. "I haven't had a lot of experience with ghosts. I didn't know the rules. I'm genuinely sorry."

Triston took a deep breath, and nodded. "Very well," he said. "I'm willing to forget this. It was a shock, and it was very distressing, but... but I just want to put it behind me and move on. I forgive you."

"Thank you," said Valkyrie.

"Are you both quite finished?" asked Dudgeon. "Because, if you don't mind, I'd rather like to get to the killing part of the afternoon."

Valkyrie frowned. "How are you going to kill us if we can't touch each other?"

Dudgeon smiled an unpretty smile and stepped forward, his finger raised. "You can't touch us, girly. But we can touch you." He poked Valkyrie in the chest. She felt it.

"Well," said Valkyrie, "that hardly seems fair."

"Life isn't fair," said the captain. "Life isn't designed to be fair. We're born unequal. Some are strong, some are weak, some fast, some slow, some clever, some not. Some have the luck about them, others wallow in misfortune. Fairness means nothing, and so you must take your opportunities when they present themselves. And I intend to take this opportunity to kill the man who condemned us to this fresh hell."

Valkyrie raised a hand. "Does that mean I can go?"

Dudgeon considered it. "No."

"But I wasn't even there. I had nothing to do with any of this."

"We're still going to kill you, though."

"Aw, man," Valkyrie muttered.

"Captain!" a pirate yelled from the crow's nest on the very top of the main mast. "Ship to starboard! Closing fast! It's the *Savagery*!"

They all turned. A large patch of impossibly dense fog was moving towards them fast.

"Ah, bugger," muttered Dudgeon, then he shouted, "Avast ye, lads! Prepare for battle!"

The deck was suddenly a scramble of ghostly bodies, some of them passing through Valkyrie. She shivered every single time.

"The *Savagery*?" she asked Skulduggery.

"Another cursed ship," he told her, "captained by a bloodthirsty maniac and crewed by the most merciless killers on the seven seas."

"I thought the *King's Fury* had the most merciless killers on the seven seas."

He shook his head. "The *King's Fury* is the most feared *ship*. The *Savagery* has the most merciless *killers*."

"Which is worse?"

He shrugged. "Much of a muchness, really."

45

The *Savagery* loomed out of the fog, a great beast with a sharp prow. Her masts were taller than the masts on *King's Fury* and she was longer and fatter. Valkyrie could see the leering, screaming faces of the crew and the cutlasses they waved over their heads.

She frowned. "Are they going to hit us?"

The *Savagery* collided with *King's Fury* and Valkyrie was thrown backwards. She slammed against a couple of barrels, her heart lurching as violently as the ship itself. The two ships sailed onwards side by side, ploughing through the waters. Ropes were thrown from the *Savagery*. Ghost ropes.

The *Savagery*'s crew boarded. Suddenly the ghost pirates were screaming and shouting and trying to kill each other. Valkyrie watched them fight, watched them hack and slash and stab and swing. It was hard to keep track of it all. She switched on her aura-vision and that was better.

Skulduggery pulled her to her feet, and they dodged between the fighting, those cutlasses coming awfully close. One of the pirates, she couldn't tell which side he was on, saw her and decided he wanted to kill something made of good old-fashioned flesh and blood. He came for her, and she watched her hand rise, watched her lightning leap from her fingertips and connect with the pirate's aura. The aura convulsed and exploded into noth-ingness, taking the pirate with it.

The other pirates stopped fighting. They stared at her. Valkyrie switched off her aura-vision.

"You killed him," said someone.

"She can't have," said someone else. "You can't kill what's dead."

"She did," a pirate close to her whispered.

Skulduggery stepped forward. "We should probably be leaving now," he announced. "Captain Dudgeon, thank you for the ride. It was very much appreciated. To everyone else, feel free to get back to the fighting."

But the pirates weren't looking at her any more.

Valkyrie turned as something swooped down, bony arms wrapping round her, then heaved her off the deck and away from the ship. She looked down, to the sea churning below, to the long serpent body that disappeared beneath the waves. Long hair, wet and knotted and twisted with seaweed, whipped across her face. Valkyrie pulled one arm free, used it to push herself back, but the creature's grip was too strong.

A long face appeared between that curtain of hair, old and lined, the cheeks hollow, the nose hooked, the eyes sunken but bright. The Sea Hag gave her a smile of rotting teeth and breath that stank of fish, and then they plummeted into the water.

46

Oh, it was cold.

She had thought she was cold before, standing on the deck of the *King's Fury*. But that was nothing. That was a summer's breeze compared to this.

The cold surrounded her. It seeped into her. It divided her mind and cleaved her thoughts, then swept them to one side and filled what was left with the cold and the dark and the wet.

Valkyrie focused on what little she could still feel: the arms round her, the body against her. She opened her eyes, but her vision was obscured by dark hair – her own or the Sea Hag's, she couldn't tell.

The Sea Hag. From all those years ago.

She turned her head, saw the Hag's serpent body, long and writhing, coiling into the dark. She saw Skulduggery, moving towards her like a torpedo, but the serpent body convulsed and slammed into him and the Sea Hag pulled Valkyrie away and brought her twisting downwards.

For the first time, she thought about air, and thought about how little of it she had in her lungs.

Her instinct was to struggle and bite, to reach up and plunge her thumb into the Sea Hag's eye – but the Sea Hag was drowning her, and desperate exertions were only going to use up whatever oxygen she had left. So she calmed the hell down, and brought her magic out to play.

Her whole body crackled and the Sea Hag released her in an instant, screaming as she recoiled, and Valkyrie broke away, flying now through the water.

Her lungs burned. She fought the urge to suck in a breath.

She piled on the speed. Any moment now she'd burst into the air. Any moment now. Any moment.

But it was dark. Dark and getting darker.

Dimly, she knew she'd been twisted around, had lost her sense of up and down. But the darkness meant that she was going down, getting deeper.

Valkyrie arched her back, swung her arms up, pulled out of the dive and headed in the opposite direction. The darkness was following her now. It was dark everywhere. Her lungs were steel traps, but they burned, they were on fire, and they were setting off fireworks in her brain.

The crackling faded. She was slowing. Didn't know where she was.

The crackling stopped. She drifted. The cold came in again, but it was nice this time. It soothed her. It played with her hair and prised at her lungs. *Open up. Just a little.* After everything she'd done, all the terrible things, all she had to do was open up and let the water in and she wouldn't have to feel bad any more.

A shape moved in the darkness. Long hair. Serpent tail.

Hands gripped her. A face. A mouth. On hers. A kiss.

Sweet oxygen rushed down her throat to her lungs, inflating them, expanding them. Strength exploded within her, ran to her numb toes and the tips of her tingling fingers. It filled her mind with thoughts.

The kiss broke off. Valkyrie raised her hand and lit it up like a lantern. It wasn't the Sea Hag who held her but a young woman with soft lips, beautiful eyes and glorious hair. Valkyrie couldn't help it – she looked down, down past the torso, down to where the hips swelled and the fish tail began.

A fish tail. Not a serpent tail. A fish tail.

A mermaid. A proper mermaid.

The mermaid kissed her again and Valkyrie took what oxygen she could, and then they were travelling, moving astonishingly fast with apparently very little effort. As tightly as the mermaid was holding her, Valkyrie was aware of every rhythmic swish and sway. The way the creature moved was hypnotic.

There was a light in the dark, then more lights as they drew closer.

The underwater laboratory was a series of brightly lit glass bubbles, like upturned goldfish bowls as big as houses.

The mermaid took Valkyrie to the smallest bowl, and they swooped in underneath and slowed as they came up, breaking through to the surface.

Valkyrie gasped, sucked in air, blinking quickly to clear her vision. The mermaid took her to the edge of the pool and gave her a little push up out of the water. Valkyrie's hands and knees were suddenly on dry, solid ground. It was warm here, too, and filled with plants. They grew from pots and hung low from the domed glass ceiling. A path of stone led to a door.

Valkyrie stood, and turned. The mermaid rested both arms on the edge of the platform and smiled up at her.

"Hello," the mermaid said.

"Hi."

"My name is Una. What's your name?"

"Valkyrie."

"That's not your real name."

"No," said Valkyrie. "It's my taken name."

"Oh," said Una. "We only have one name down here. It's simpler."

"It's very nice to meet you, Una. You saved my life."

Una shrugged her bare shoulders. "Are you here to see Doctor Nye?"

"I am. Is it here?"

Una nodded.

"Do you work for it?" Valkyrie asked.

Una laughed. "We don't work for anyone."

"How many of you are there?"

"There are enough."

"I don't want to be rude or anything, but could I ask what you are?"

"What do I look like?"

"A mermaid."

Another smile. "I am a Maiden of the Sea. You can call me a mermaid if you like."

Valkyrie took off her coat, looked around for somewhere to hang it, then just laid it wetly on the ground. "Thank you for saving me."

"You're welcome. The Sea Hag is unpleasant."

"She certainly hasn't changed much since we first met."

Una raised an eyebrow. "Do you know her?"

"Not really, but the first time I met her she was living in a lake."

Una laughed. "Yes, we heard about that. It is indeed a pity she didn't stay there. I don't think she likes you."

"I think you might be right."

"Are you feeling unwell? You're shivering."

"The water's pretty cold. But I can warm up," Valkyrie said, and held out her arms, letting her magic crackle. Una stared in wonder, her eyes reflecting the light show.

Valkyrie stopped before her clothes began to scorch. She was warmer, and a lot drier, even if her clothes and hair were still damp.

"That was beautiful," Una said.

"Did you happen to see my friend before you saved me?" Valkyrie asked. "He's a skeleton. In a suit."

"A suit of clothes?"

"Yes."

"Your skeletons wear clothes?"

"Just him."

"That is most odd," Una said. "But then I find the human obsession with clothes to be a source of endless puzzlement. When I was on the surface, humans followed me around and insisted on covering me with fabric. They were very insistent."

"You were on the surface?"

"Long ago," said Una.

"Did you... did you have legs?"

"Oh, yes," Una said. "With feet and everything. On the surface, we have legs; in the seas, we revert to our natural state."

"Wow."

"But I have never understood clothes."

"They have their uses. They keep us warm and dry, and shoes protect our feet, and pockets are cool."

"Pockets?"

"They're where we keep stuff. But my friend, the skeleton. Have you seen him?"

"Is that him there?" Una asked, looking over Valkyrie's shoulder.

She turned. Skulduggery waved to her from outside the bubble.

She pointed at the pool and he nodded and sank from sight, and a moment later he broke through the surface of the water and rose up until he could step off on to the platform.

"You're alive," he said to her.

"You lost your hat," she replied.

"I did, and that is unfortunate." He moved his hands away from his body and the water drifted from him in droplets. He guided them back to the pool, then brushed at his jacket. "But I would choose you over a hat every time."

"What?"

"I'm just saying that I'd—"

"It would be a choice?"

He stopped brushing, and looked at her. "Sorry?"

"You'd need to actually *choose* between me and your hat? It wouldn't be an automatic thing? You'd have to pause and consider the options?"

"Huh," Skulduggery said. "I had thought that what I'd said was a good thing. Now I see that it wasn't. I apologise, and will now change the subject." He stepped towards Una, hand outstretched. "Hello."

Una rose up and shook his hand. "You are Skulduggery," she said. "I am Una. I take it you are here to see Doctor Nye also?"

"Indeed. Is it in?"

"That depends," said Una. "Do you promise not to kill it?"

"I can't actually promise that, no."

Una pointed at the door. "In which case, the doctor is through there," she said, and smiled.

47

Beyond the door was a passageway of glass, a tunnel encircled by water. Fish pulsed around Valkyrie and Skulduggery as they walked, slashes of colour emerging from the dark and then sinking back into it once again. It was hypnotic. Restful.

Valkyrie's eyes refocused on her reflection and she scowled. "My hair's gone frizzy."

"I didn't want to say anything," Skulduggery responded.

"I was talking to the pretty mermaid with her glorious hair while I looked like I'd electrocuted myself. Which I suppose I kinda had." She did her best to smooth her hair down, but it didn't do much good.

There was a circular door ahead of them, metal, almost as wide as the tunnel itself, with a wheel in its centre. Skulduggery gestured for Valkyrie to go ahead, so she spun the wheel and heard a click, and had to put her shoulder to it to get it to move. Once she had it moving, the door swung freely, and she stepped over the lip and into a large, brightly lit glass dome, which housed the laboratory. Music was playing. Something classical.

Doctor Nye didn't look up from the microscope it was stooped over. "Of course," it said. "Of course you're here. Of course you would find me. Of course you could not leave me in peace."

"Hello, Doc," Valkyrie said, all smiles as she wandered over. Nye wasn't wearing its surgical cap today so its mottled scalp, decorated with a few wispy strands of hair, was hers to examine the closer she got. There were some sores on that scalp. A few had scabbed over. A few were open, and weeping.

Nye raised its head. Its eyes, yellow and small and far apart, blinked quickly, and its long, thin mouth twisted at one corner in annoyance. It didn't have a nose. Just another open wound.

"Is Whisper here?" Valkyrie asked. "She's cool. I liked her. I know I've only met her once, and that was when I was threatening you and demanding to know where Abyssinia was, but I think we could be friends."

"She hated you," said Nye.

"I don't think that's true."

"She despised you. She told me so."

Valkyrie shrugged. "First impressions aren't really that important, though. That's what I always say. It's on the third or fourth impression that you really start to build up an idea of who a person is. So is she here?"

"I have switched patrons," said Nye, "so Whisper is no longer my bodyguard."

"Switched, eh?" Skulduggery said. "So you're no longer working for Serafina Dey. Did you know that's who you were working for, up there in that castle, in those mountains?"

"At the time, I did not," said Nye.

"And who are you working for now?"

Nye looked at them both. "Why are you here?" it asked. "Is this about Abyssinia again? I do not know where that woman is and I have no wish to ever see her again."

"It's not about Abyssinia," said Valkyrie. "It's about your work."

"And what work would that be?"

"Your work on the soul."

Nye nodded, and stood. It was about ten feet tall – not nearly as tall as it had been when Valkyrie had first encountered it. Crengarrions of a certain age tended to shrink, apparently, right up until their death. Nye picked up a tray of Petri dishes with its long-fingered hands, and took it to a nearby desk. "And if I help you?"

"We leave," Valkyrie said. "We just walk out of here, without putting you in shackles and slinging you back into Ironpoint Gaol."

"Very well," it said. "Please make this quick. I have a lot of work to do."

"We want to know how to heal a soul," Valkyrie said.

"Hmm," said Nye, and didn't move for a moment. Then it looked up. "You don't. You can't. A soul is not a physical thing, and so it cannot be hurt. If it cannot be hurt, it cannot be healed. But a soul can be broken. Pieces go missing. It is then a matter of finding the missing pieces, and allowing it to put itself back together."

"And how do we do that?"

"That all depends on the type of death experienced. Some souls dissipate, some roam, some barely move from the spot where the death occurred. I cannot say why one death is different to another, and even my studies have yielded contradictory results. The secrets of the soul, I think, were never meant for the likes of us." Nye smiled. "That doesn't mean I will not seize them when I can, of course."

"I'm looking to repair my sister's soul," Valkyrie said. "Where do I start?"

"First, tell me where and how she died."

"She died in Roarhaven, killed by the Deathtouch Gauntlet," Valkyrie said. "Revived with a Sunburst."

"Interesting," said Nye. "Not the Sunburst. The Sunburst is just a tool. But the gauntlet was designed to kill even those who would normally be able to recover from the slight inconvenience of death. At a single touch, it stops the body and the brain from functioning and eradicates any magic that might circumvent one's mortality. It does this by scattering the soul. The essence of who we are splinters and vacates the physical form."

"That didn't happen with Darquesse," Valkyrie said.

"I'm sorry?"

"Darquesse had taken over my body. The gauntlet was used to kill me and to kick her out. She wasn't splintered."

"I would imagine Darquesse's soul to be vastly different to other people's," Nye said. "I would have loved to have examined her."

"Yeah," said Valkyrie. "I'd have loved to see you try."

"If the gauntlet scattered Alice's soul," Skulduggery said, "then where are the pieces?"

Nye sat back. "I assume the girl is responsive? Aware?"

"She's completely normal," said Valkyrie, "apart from the fact that she never gets sad."

"Then she was revived in time for at least part of her soul to return to her body. If you can retrieve the other fragment or fragments, I believe you can reattach them. But I find it interesting that you wish to pursue this course at all. Your sister cannot get sad, yes? That sounds like a happy life. Why would you want to reunite her with the aspect of her soul that brings sorrow?"

"She's damaged," said Valkyrie. "I need to fix her."

"Perhaps she would argue that she doesn't need to be fixed."

"I'm not having this conversation with you," Valkyrie said. "I'm responsible for breaking her apart, and I'm going to put her back together. You're going to tell me how to do that."

"First we need to know how to find the fragments," Skulduggery said. "Do you have a way for us to do that?"

Nye hesitated.

"You do," Skulduggery said, "but you don't want to tell us what it is."

"It's not that," said Nye. "It's merely..."

"It's a device. And you don't want to part with it."

Nye sagged.

Valkyrie picked up a box with wires poking out of it. "Is this it?"

266

"No," said Nye.

She dropped it. It smashed on the ground and Nye gasped as she picked up something else. "Is this it?"

"Here it is!" Nye said quickly, scuttling over to an old globe in a brass stand. "Please don't break anything else!"

Skulduggery took the globe. It was about the size of a football. "How do we use it?" he asked.

"It will need to latch on to what remains of the girl's soul," Nye answered. "Once it has done this, it will find whatever fragments there are and direct you to them."

"And once we've located the fragments, how do we retrieve them?"

"A simple Soul Catcher should suffice. Once you have collected all the errant fragments, you will need to isolate your sister and then simply break the Soul Catcher. The fragments will return home."

"And the soul will put itself back together once they're inside her?"

"Indeed."

"It's that easy?"

"The process should be straightforward, yes."

Valkyrie smiled. Laughed. "Well... OK then. OK. This is good. This is great!"

"And now," said Nye, "a warning."

48

Valkyrie's smile failed. "A warning?"

"It is entirely possible that the fragments have remained independent," Doctor Nye said. "If, however, a fragment has found a host, then it is inside a living being with a soul of its own. Because of the damage it has sustained, there is a possibility that the fragment will have merged with this other soul in order to maintain its integrity."

"If this has happened," Skulduggery said, "how do we separate it from its host?"

"If it has merged fully with its host's soul," said the doctor, "there will be nothing you can do. That fragment is now gone. If, however, it has not merged fully, then the sister will need to be nearby. Her presence should pull the fragment to her."

Valkyrie looked at Skulduggery. "We have to go."

Instead, Skulduggery folded his arms. He tapped a finger against his chin.

"Skulduggery—"

"Doctor," Skulduggery said, "Valkyrie can see souls."

Nye's small eyes widened. "She can?"

"I can see auras," she corrected.

"Same thing," Skulduggery said. "What's more, Doctor, her powers seem to be directly attuned to them. Just a short time ago, I witnessed what appeared to be the full dispersal of a ghost."

Nye stared at Valkyrie. "You killed a ghost?"

"No," she said immediately. "I mean... I don't think so. You can't kill a ghost. Can you?"

"Instead of bringing her sister with us to coax out the fragment, couldn't Valkyrie do it?" Skulduggery continued. "If she can *see* the soul, and *touch* the soul... surely she'd be able to *separate* the soul."

"Yes," Nye whispered. "Yes, this would be entirely possible. In theory. I... I should go with you. To observe. This could help my research in innumerable—"

"Forget it," Valkyrie said. "We're not teaming up. Skulduggery, we have to go."

Skulduggery nodded. "I just have a few more questions for the good doctor."

She put her hand on his arm. "For all we know, a part of Alice's soul is just about to merge with someone else. We have to go *now*. Skulduggery, please."

"You go say your goodbyes to the mermaid," he responded. "I need to know how to work this globe."

"One minute," said Valkyrie.

"I promise."

She nodded, and hurried out the way she came.

Una still rested her elbows on the edge of the platform.

"She's been waiting," she said, rolling her eyes as the Sea Hag rose up from the water behind her.

"I don't have time for you," Valkyrie said.

The Sea Hag's sneer was not a thing of beauty. "You think you can dismiss me so easily? After what you've done?"

"What have I done?" Valkyrie said. "Really, now? What have I done that's so terrible that you're still trying to kill me? Is it really that I was rude to you over ten years ago? Seriously?"

The Sea Hag said nothing.

"I don't have time for these little vendettas that people like you seem to love. I've got enough going on without adding your drama to the list. So, allow me to say I'm sorry. I'm so dreadfully sorry for being rude to you once upon a time. Are we over it now? Are we?"

The Sea Hag folded her long arms, and a mermaid's head broke the surface of the pool behind her. Blonde hair. Beautiful. Another appeared beside her. And another. All looking at the Sea Hag. All intent. All focused.

Valkyrie frowned. "Hold on a second," she said.

They burst upwards, and they had spears in their hands – harpoons – and they drove them into the Sea Hag's torso and the Sea Hag thrashed and screeched. Valkyrie jumped back as the mermaids kept their grip on the weapons, keeping the Sea Hag from swimming away. With gritted teeth and bulging muscles, they forced her backwards, moving her torso out of the pool and on to the platform. Another mermaid rose, handed a harpoon to Una, and with a kick Una propelled herself out of the water completely, her fish tail splitting, forming human legs that drank in and swallowed the scales, and she dropped, the harpoon aimed at the Sea Hag's heart.

Valkyrie lunged, colliding with Una after she landed, but before the harpoon could sink into the Sea Hag's chest. They went rolling. The harpoon fell. Una's hand closed around Valkyrie's throat and Una came up to her feet and lifted Valkyrie, slamming her against the glass wall. Valkyrie brought both fists down on to Una's arm and buckled the elbow, but Una went to grab her again with her left hand and Valkyrie kicked at her newly formed knee, twirled her round and snaked her arm under her chin.

"Calm down," she said into Una's ear. Una struggled and Valkyrie tightened the stranglehold until she stopped.

The other mermaids were glaring at Valkyrie, but they were too busy holding on to the harpoons that pinned the Sea Hag to do anything about it.

"She hates you," Una managed to garble. "She tried to *kill* you."

"Lots of people try to kill me," Valkyrie replied. "If I took it all personally, I wouldn't have any friends. No one dies because of me, not if I can help it."

Skulduggery walked in, the globe tucked under his arm and a Soul Catcher in his hand. He surveyed the situation. "I see," he said, put down the globe and took out his gun. He waved it at the mermaids. "Move away, please. Thank you. Move away."

One by one, the mermaids withdrew their harpoons and swayed backwards.

"I'm going to release you now," Valkyrie said to Una. "If you try anything, it won't go well for you."

Una said nothing until Valkyrie let her go and stepped away. The mermaid glared. "This is a mistake."

"Probably."

"You will come to regret this. Some day in the future you will need the help of the Maidens of the Sea and you will not have it."

"I think I'll cope."

The mermaids disappeared under the water. Una glared once again, and then let herself fall backwards. The water claimed her and she was gone.

Skulduggery put away his gun and handed the Soul Catcher to Valkyrie.

"Doctor Nye had a spare one of these lying around," he said. "Your friendship with the mermaids didn't last particularly long."

"Just once," she said, "I'd like to meet a new group of people and not be their enemy."

"Why?" the Sea Hag said weakly. "Why did you help me?"

"Helping people is what we do," Valkyrie said. "Are you OK? Do you need a doctor?"

"I will heal," said the Sea Hag, lifting herself up. She started swaying. "But I do not understand. You hate me."

"No, I don't."

The Sea Hag shook her head. "None of this makes any sense."

"I'm not going to just stand around and watch someone get murdered, OK? I don't care who they are."

"I... I may have misjudged you."

"That's OK."

From the tangle of her hair, the Sea Hag drew a small golden bell. Grimacing in pain, she leaned forward, placing it in Valkyrie's hand. "I owe you a debt," she said.

"Don't worry about it," said Valkyrie. "Just heal your wounds and carry on with your life."

"I will." The Sea Hag's smile was awful and smelled of fish. "Thank you."

"Why did they try to kill you anyway?" Skulduggery asked, picking up the globe.

The Sea Hag swayed back to the pool. "They have always hated me and mocked me for how I look. I'm not beautiful, like they are. I don't have a dainty fish tail, like they do. I also eat their young."

"I'm sorry?" Valkyrie said.

"Their young," said the Sea Hag. "The eggs they lay. I eat them sometimes."

Valkyrie stared.

"Thank you again," the Sea Hag said. "If you ever need my help, ring my bell and I will be there."

She sank into the water, and was gone.

"Huh," Skulduggery said.

"Oh, God," said Valkyrie.

"You may have allied yourself with the wrong side," Skulduggery said, rising off his feet and drifting over the pool.

Valkyrie jumped and he caught her, his arm round her waist. "It's just she's so ugly," she said, "and they're all so pretty, so I naturally assumed they were secretly the bad guys because they were ganging up on the ugly one. I thought... I thought..."

"A common mistake," Skulduggery said as they sank down. The water rushed out of their way and surrounded the bubble of oxygen the lower they went. "Just because someone is ugly on the outside doesn't mean they're not even uglier on the inside. The reverse is also true for the beautiful. The trick, you see—"

"Is to never assume anything," she finished.

"Quite."

With Valkyrie holding the Soul Catcher, and Skulduggery holding the globe and Valkyrie, they moved down and then sideways, away from the glass domes of the laboratory, away from the light and the warmth. They travelled into the cold and the dark, the water flowing all around them, and Valkyrie stopped talking. To talk was to use up oxygen, and to risk distracting Skulduggery. She looked at the bell in her hand, then put it in her pocket, careful not to let it ring.

49

Serial killers, it had to be said, were not among Sebastian's favourite people in the world.

They were scary, and nasty, and on occasion in the past had tried to kill him. Silas Nadir, in particular, had a habit of trying to do just that.

But things were different now. Sebastian was now the Plague Doctor, his face hidden behind a mask, his voice distorted. Nadir wouldn't see the fear, wouldn't hear the tremor. Sebastian was bigger, stronger, and better than he had been the last time they'd tangled. He hoped.

Nadir stood in Demure's living room, smiling to himself as Forby got the portal machine ready. He had a beard. He hadn't had a beard when Sebastian had seen him last.

No one said anything. Everyone, apart from Nadir himself, was looking decidedly grumpy.

"OK," Forby said, "we're ready."

"Before we do this," Demure said, stepping forward, "I just want to make sure you understand, Mr Nadir: I do not approve of your lifestyle."

Nadir raised a lazy eyebrow. "My lifestyle?"

Demure cleared her throat. "Your serial killing. I don't approve of it."

"Wow," said Nadir. "That's actually pretty powerful, you saying that to me. Does anyone else disapprove?"

Hands slowly went up.

Nadir nodded. "I see," he said. "This is quite a shock, I have to admit. I mean, I guess I always knew that what I was doing was wrong, but it has taken until now, until this moment, with you fine people, to make me realise just how wayward my life has become. I want to thank you, each of you, for shining a light on my darkness. I think... I think I'm cured. Glory be to God, I think I am cured!"

"You're being sarcastic," said Bennet.

"*Duh.* Your disapproval didn't stop you from sneaking me into the city, did it? I think you've all long since fallen from your moral high ground, and you know what? You didn't have to fall very far."

"You're disgusting," said Demure.

"Yeah," Nadir responded, "I am. Big surprise there. But, even though I don't know why you want a door opened into this particular dimension, I'm going to go ahead and assume the reason you're keeping it secret is because no one else outside your little group would be in favour. Am I right? Yeah, I figured."

"That's enough," said Sebastian.

Nadir turned to him. "Says who? You? The freak in the bird mask? Who are you, freak? I can see your eyes through the glass. You're looking at me like you know me. Do you know me?"

"I know you."

Nadir stepped right up to him. The others tensed, but Sebastian didn't react.

"Who did I kill?" Nadir asked, smiling, staring right into Sebastian's eyes. "Parents? Family? Girlfriend? Boyfriend? Kids? Who? I've killed all sorts, all kinds, of all ages, and you're looking at me like I've personally hurt you. I know that look. I know it well. So who did I kill?"

Nadir peered closer. "Or was it you? Is that why you wear the outfit? Did I scar you up? Are you wearing the mask because of what I did to you?" He laughed. "If you're waiting for me to remember, I'm afraid I'm going to have to disappoint you. You all blur into one after a while."

"You won't remember me," Sebastian said. "But I remember you. And none of that means anything, because we brought you here to do a job – and you're going to do it."

"Am I?" said Nadir. "Or am I just going to walk on out of here? What are you going to do – call the City Guard? Get the Cleavers on to me? File a complaint?"

"We'll stop you," Sebastian said.

Nadir sneered. "You're too scared to stop me."

"There are seven of us and only one of you," said Lily.

"And would you be willing to kill me?" Nadir asked. "Would any of you have the guts to end my life? Because I'll tell you – I reckon I'd kill three of you before anyone laid a hand on me."

"This is getting ridiculous," said Ulysses. "Mr Nadir, we upheld our end of the deal. We got you in here. Now please do as you promised, and open the portal."

Nadir considered it, then smirked. "Sure," he said. "There's not one of you who looks even remotely competent, so I'm sure this is going to backfire on you all. It'd be a hell of a kick to contribute to that." He rolled his shoulders, and held out his hands. "Get ready, kids. This is going to be awesome."

50

It was almost two in the afternoon, and it was raining, and it was freezing, and Valkyrie's feet were so numb that when they landed in the garden behind her parents' house her ankles almost gave out. She stomped around to get the feeling back, gave the Soul Catcher to Skulduggery, and blew into her cupped hands.

"If you need some time to rest," Skulduggery said, but she cut him off.

"We're not resting. We're getting the fragments today. We've let too much time go by as it is. Come on."

She led the way inside. Her mum was out and her dad was asleep in his armchair. They found Alice upstairs.

"Stephanie!" Alice squealed, running to her. "Skulduggery!"

"Hello, little one," Skulduggery said, patting her head as she hugged him.

"Why are you here? What are you holding?"

"I'll show you," Valkyrie said, taking the globe from Skulduggery and setting it down on Alice's desk. "See this? This is a magic globe."

Alice's eyes widened as she came forward. "What does it *do?*"

"I don't know yet. Want to find out?"

"Yes!"

"Put your hand on it," Skulduggery said. "What's it like?"

"Cold," said Alice.

"Tell me when it's warm."

"OK." She frowned in concentration, then smiled brightly. "It's getting warm now!"

"Good girl. Give it a big spin, OK?"

The tip of her tongue sticking out between her teeth, Alice spun the globe as hard as she could. It rattled in its stand as it blurred – and then suddenly locked itself in place. The surface rippled. It re-formed itself, zooming in on two points of light in Ireland, and one in Scotland.

"The soul has been split in three," Skulduggery said, tapping one of the lights. The globe rippled again and changed as it zoomed in once more, and Valkyrie recognised Haggard. The light emanated from a familiar structure.

"That's our house!" Alice exclaimed. "Look, Stephanie!"

"So it is," Valkyrie said. She'd seen something like this before, but even so it was, all things considered, pretty cool. "See that light, coming from inside? That's you."

"Is it?"

"Part of you, anyway."

Alice peered closer. "Wowww..."

Skulduggery tapped the globe again and it zoomed out, then rippled and focused on a small town that became a street that became another house with a light shining within. The first lost fragment of Alice's soul.

"This is about half an hour from Roarhaven," Skulduggery said. "It didn't travel too far."

Valkyrie frowned. "It's moving. It is, isn't it? Look."

"It would appear so."

Her heart became heavy. The fragment had found a host.

"What's this one do?" Alice asked, tapping the third light. The surface rippled, focusing on Scotland, showing a city that seemed strangely familiar to Valkyrie.

"Where is that?" she asked.

"Right where I thought it might be," Skulduggery said. He

didn't sound pleased. "I imagine this is where traumatised souls tend to flee to."

"Where?"

"Meryyn ta Uul. The City Below."

"Oh," said Valkyrie, sagging. "The Necropolis."

51

They touched down on the roof of a car park. Carrying a bag containing the Soul Catcher, Skulduggery activated his façade and they took the elevator to the ground level. Valkyrie's thoughts were on fire again. She tried to remember the tune from the music box, but it remained just out of reach. She needed something to focus on. She needed words.

"How are we going to find the fragment in the Necropolis?" she asked.

"We're not," Skulduggery said. "I am."

She was aware of how fast she was speaking but she couldn't actually stop. "Then how are you going to find it? How are you going to find a part of a soul in a city *filled* with souls? It's impossible. It sounds impossible."

"Not according to Doctor Nye," Skulduggery said. "Once we've captured the first fragment, the Soul Catcher will act as a metal detector of sorts. All I'll have to do is walk the streets of the Necropolis until I find what we're looking for."

"We have to get to it fast, though. We have to. I mean, if the first fragment can merge with some random soul it bumps into, then won't the second one be at a higher risk? In the Necropolis, there are souls everywhere you turn. We should have gone there first."

"It's been six years, Valkyrie. A few more hours aren't going to make a difference."

Valkyrie nodded. Nodded again. That was true. She knew that. It made sense. Made a lot of sense.

"Are you feeling OK?" Skulduggery asked.

"I'm grand," she said.

The elevator doors opened and they emerged on to a pavement and she just followed Skulduggery. The town was small. She didn't even know its name. It didn't matter. The only thing that mattered was retrieving that fragment of her sister's soul.

They got to the house, a quiet house on a quiet street. Valkyrie went to slam her fist against the door, but Skulduggery caught her wrist. With his other hand, he gently, politely knocked.

Valkyrie nodded. She had to calm down. Had to. She was going to hurt someone if she didn't.

She took a deep breath, and smiled as she exhaled.

The door opened. A woman in a flowing dress nodded sombrely at them. She was calm, but her aura was in chaos. It writhed and twisted like a yellow snake chasing its own tail. There was a smaller aura, an orange aura, in there with it. They hadn't merged. Not yet.

"Hi," Valkyrie said. "We're here—"

The woman held up a hand. "I know why you're here."

"You do?"

"Of course." She stepped to one side and held the door open. "You're here for a reading."

Valkyrie hesitated, but Skulduggery nudged her forward, and then they were both inside a living room strewn with bowls of cheap crystals. This was the living room of a fortune-teller, and not one of the good ones, either.

"My name is Margaret," said the woman. "I'll be your guide today."

"Our guide where?" Skulduggery asked.

Margaret smiled softly. "Into the realms of the unknown."

"Oh, good," said Skulduggery.

"Actually," Valkyrie said, "we just had a few questions for you."

Margaret guided them to two chairs at a small table. "I don't like questions," she said, sitting opposite. "Questions get in the way. They lodge themselves in the spiritual pathways we'll need to traverse. Banish all questions from your mind. Happiness is acceptance."

"That's what I'm always telling her," Skulduggery said. "But will she listen?"

"That's a question," Valkyrie pointed out. "Not allowed to ask questions."

"It was rhetorical," he responded. "There was supposed to be a percontation point after it."

"Well now, I think we're both fully aware that you just made up that word," Valkyrie said, "so I'm not going to argue with you. Margaret, we're not here for a reading or to get our palms read or anything remotely spiritual like that."

"You came here looking for answers," Margaret said.

"We came here looking for you."

"Because I have the answers you seek."

"How can we have answers, though, if we're not allowed to ask questions?"

"That's a question," Skulduggery said.

Margaret smiled again. "You're sceptical. I understand. I don't even blame you. You're young, with your whole life stretching out ahead of you. You don't yet know just how fragile we are, as humans. You think you're immortal. You think spirituality is nonsense. You don't believe in psychics."

Valkyrie smiled back. "Got me there." She watched Margaret's aura as they spoke.

"I was like you when I was your age," said Margaret, "but as I got older I accepted the fact that there will always be facets of this life we will never be able to even glimpse. Six years ago, I was visited by a spirit, and it joined my own."

"What's that like?"

"Oh, it's wonderful," Margaret said. "It's not without its

282

drawbacks, of course. The spirit that attached to mine is broken, I think. I can't hear its thoughts – I don't think it has any – but I can feel its sadness. I do what I can to soothe it, and in return it grants me a certain sight. Give me your hand, and I'll show you."

Margaret held her own hands out, waiting, but Valkyrie didn't move.

"We're not here for a reading," she said. "We're here for the spirit."

"I'm sorry?"

"The spirit that bonded with you. We're here to take it back."

Margaret smiled again. "I'm not sure I understand."

"It isn't yours," Skulduggery said. "You were right when you said it was broken. It is broken, but we can fix it. We can put it back where it belongs."

"You can't just take a spirit."

"Actually," Valkyrie said, "we can."

Skulduggery put the Soul Catcher on the table.

Margaret frowned. "Who are you?"

"That doesn't matter," he said. "We didn't come here to cause you any distress, but we are going to take the spirit with us when we leave."

"Is that a crystal ball?" Margaret laughed. "No one uses a crystal ball any more."

"What's your second name, Margaret?" Skulduggery asked.

"Kennelly."

"Margaret Kennelly, don't panic."

Margaret nodded, and smiled.

"Margaret Kennelly, lie down on your couch."

"Why do you want me to do that?" Margaret asked as she got up and led the way into the living room. "Wait. What am I doing? How are you making me do this?"

"Margaret Kennelly, don't worry about it," Valkyrie told her.

Margaret lay on the couch, head on the cushions, hands by her side.

Valkyrie switched on her aura-vision again. The two souls writhed as she held both hands over Margaret's belly.

"What do I do now?" she whispered.

Skulduggery stood beside her. "You can see the souls, can't you? Can you feel them?"

Valkyrie frowned, concentrating on the tingling of her palms. "Yes," she said. "Yes, there."

"Can you draw them to you?"

"I don't want to damage them. I don't want to... disperse them."

"You're not going to," he said. "What happened to the ghost pirate was unfortunate, but it only happened because he wasn't protected by a physical shell. Besides, you're not using your lightning. You're not scared. You're calm. Feel the souls. Can you tell which one is Alice's?"

"Yes."

"Then draw it out to you."

"I don't know how."

He put a hand on her shoulder. "That's just because you haven't done it before. Magic is all about doing the same things with different intent. Magic obeys. That's why things go wrong when we panic, because we're too confused to tell it what we need it to do. Your magic wants to help you, Valkyrie. Guide it."

The auras buzzed beneath her hands. Something connected them to her skin, like static electricity. Like magnetism. A finger twitched and the smaller aura twitched with it.

Valkyrie breathed out so very slowly.

This was going to take a while.

52

It was another hour before she could create a gap between the souls. The smaller one responded easiest. That's the one she wanted. That was the fragment.

She raised her right hand – aching now – and brought the aura slowly with it. The first part of it passed through Margaret's body, like a child's drawing where they'd coloured outside the line. Margaret whimpered.

"Margaret Kennelly, remain calm and feel no discomfort," said Skulduggery.

Valkyrie used her other hand now, to coax out more of the fragment. She turned both hands, curling her fingers ever so slightly, trapping the churning soul in the space between them.

Higher, she went. Higher.

The soul fragment broke free of Margaret's physical shell and thrashed out of Valkyrie's grip, spun in the air and then darted into the Soul Catcher that Skulduggery held out. It churned with a bright orange.

Valkyrie slumped on to her back and blinked wearily at the ceiling.

"Is it over?" Margaret asked. "Did you do it?"

"She did," Skulduggery said. "How are you feeling, Margaret?"

"I... I think my connection to the spirit world is gone. I feel empty."

"The feeling will pass. You're back to your old self."

"I'm very tired."

"Margaret Kennelly, go to sleep."

Margaret closed her eyes.

Skulduggery helped Valkyrie up. She gazed into the Soul Catcher.

"Hey, little sister," she murmured.

"I think you need a break," Skulduggery said.

"No. We have to go after the next one. Then it'll all be over."

"Valkyrie, you need rest. You're about to collapse. I'll take you to Militsa's, OK? Temper needs my help with something, so I'll go off, help him and I'll be back to pick you up in the morning and we'll go straight to the Necropolis."

"Maybe a little sleep…"

He took the Soul Catcher from her and scooped her up and she put her head against him and closed her eyes. She was aware of them leaving the house by the back door and rising into the air, and that was it.

53

Temper found him on a bench beside Black Lake, throwing chunks of bread to the gathered ducks. "Hello, Adam," Temper said, sitting beside him.

"Pretend like you don't know me," Brate whispered. He still had his sunglasses on.

Temper pulled his collar up. "Can we just get to it? It's February, man. It's cold."

A guy passed them, walking his dog, and Brate waited until both were out of earshot before talking again. "Where are Skulduggery and Valkyrie?"

"On their way, but we don't need to wait. You tell me, I can tell them."

"Naw, dude," Brate said, shaking his head. "Like the song says, we're all in this together. The Three Musketeers, right?"

Temper sighed. "I guess."

A few minutes passed. Brate kept feeding the ducks and Temper kept shivering. Finally, Skulduggery appeared. Temper shuffled over to make room on the bench.

Typically, Skulduggery stayed standing. "Hello, ducks," he said as the ducks quacked around his feet.

Brate glanced up at him and whispered, "Valkyrie not with you?"

"Afraid not."

"She gonna join us later, or what?"

"She's busy on another case, Adam. We'll have to make do without her."

Brate nodded. "That's cool, that's cool. Although I was hoping that it'd be all three of you here. Safer, you know? I mean, it's not that I don't feel safe around you guys, but, like... she's Valkyrie Cain, you know? She's done some things."

"Well," said Skulduggery, "we've all done some things."

"Not like her, though."

"A bit like her."

"But she's been to, like, the dark side, you know?"

"Some of us are well acquainted with the dark side."

"Not really, though."

"Actually," Temper said, "I agree with Adam. Valkyrie *is* intimidating."

Skulduggery tilted his head. "*I'm* intimidating."

"Oh, yeah, you are – but not like her. One time I made her smile and I immediately shut up for the rest of the day in case I went too far and she gave me one of her looks."

"That's ridiculous," Skulduggery said. "I'm scarier than Valkyrie."

"Sorry, man, you're not."

"I'm a *living skeleton*."

"And she can be quite blunt."

"I don't believe what I'm hearing," said Skulduggery. "I came back from the *dead*."

"And so did Valkyrie, didn't she?"

Skulduggery let a moment go by. "It's not the same thing," he said, and brushed a speck of dust from his sleeve. "Can we focus on why we're here?"

"Yeah, sure, OK," said Brate. He looked around to make sure no one was listening, then covered his mouth with his hands and spoke. "So I think Creed is doing all this Activating stuff right here, in Roarhaven. Right in the Dark Cathedral, in fact."

Temper frowned at him. "What are you doing? What are you doing with your hands?"

"Satellites, man," Brate responded. "They got cameras on some satellites that can read your lips. Do what I do. See? Like this."

"I can see what you're doing, Adam. You're right beside me."

"May we remind you," said Skulduggery, "that you are not a spy."

"I know," said Brate. "I know. But... I mean... precautions, dude. Please."

"Maybe we should..." Skulduggery murmured.

Temper gave him a look. "What? Are you serious?"

"In case someone is observing us through a long lens. It's better to be safe than sorry."

"You kidding me?"

"We'll all do it," said Skulduggery.

"Please?" said Brate. "I'll feel a lot safer if we hide what we're saying."

Temper glowered, and put one hand over his mouth. "Fine," he said. "If we're all doing it, then fine. You think Creed is doing the Activations from the Dark Cathedral, do you? Why?"

Brate took another look around, then leaned closer, once again speaking through his fingers. "A friend of mine has a friend who works there. Nothing too glamorous, just cleaning up and stuff, unblocking the toilets, changing light bulbs and whatnot. This friend told my friend, and then he told me, that he's heard these weird noises from the vents, coming up from the ground, you know? Screams and crying and then... silence."

"Your friend has heard silence?"

"Yes."

"And what does silence sound like?"

Brate frowned. "I don't know. Quiet, I'd imagine."

"And you think this is Creed performing more Activations?" Skulduggery asked, his arms folded.

"Hey," said Temper, "hand over your mouth."

Skulduggery looked at him. "Why? I don't have any lips to read."

Temper glared.

"That's right," said Brate. "My friend says that his friend says that there's this weird feeling in the air, like electricity but not electricity, this invisible thing that doesn't affect anything, but it's still there... He says it's a bad feeling and, when the screaming and the crying stops, it goes away."

"I don't know," said Skulduggery. "As far as incriminating evidence goes, that isn't much."

"Also," Brate said, "he says there are people who go down into the lower levels and, like, don't come back."

"*That*," said Skulduggery, "is more interesting."

Brate nodded. "Or at least they don't come back during his shift."

Skulduggery sighed.

"Is that useful?" Brate asked.

"It's something," said Temper, and looked up at Skulduggery. "It's the only lead we have. And listen, we're here, the Dark Cathedral is just down the street – what do you say we take a look?"

"You're suggesting we break in," Skulduggery said.

"Yes."

"I know a secret way!" Brate said, forgetting for a moment to hide his mouth. He squealed and covered up.

"You know a secret way into the Dark Cathedral?" Temper asked.

Brate nodded. "A tunnel into the lower levels, yes. I can't go with you – if Arch-Canon Creed knew I was involved, he'd do awful, unspeakable things to me – but I can definitely show you where to go."

Temper raised an eyebrow at Skulduggery.

"You're an officer in the City Guard," Skulduggery said, "and I'm an Arbiter, and you're suggesting we commit a crime."

"What's wrong?" Temper asked. "You've broken the law before."

"Yes," Skulduggery said, "but it's only fun when I suggest it."

"Do you want me to pretend that it's your idea, or...?"

"Forget it," Skulduggery grumbled. "It sounds silly now. Let's just break into the place."

54

Valkyrie woke. Took her a moment to figure out that she was in Militsa's place. Took her a moment to remember why she was here.

She sat up. Her body was heavy. Her muscles were useless and her eyes stung so much they hurt to open. She untangled her leaden feet from the bedcovers, set them on the floor.

The door opened. Militsa came in, moving immediately to sit by her, arm round her shoulders.

"Hey, no, back to bed. You need your sleep."

"I've *had* my sleep."

"You've barely had an *hour* of sleep. You're exhausted, poppet. Look at you. You can barely open your eyes."

Valkyrie opened her eyes and smiled, made sure to keep any irritation out of her voice. "A good shower is what I need. I'm stinky, and my hair's a mess."

"I'm not arguing with you there, but—"

"Did Skulduggery tell you? About the soul fragment?"

"*You* told me," Militsa said. "He dropped you off and while I was putting you to bed, *an hour ago*, you told me all about the pirates and the mermaids and the soul fragments..."

"I told you about the mermaids?"

Militsa grinned. "Yes, you did. You don't remember any of that, do you?"

"Militsa, the last soul fragment – if we don't get it in time, it could fuse with one of the ghosts in the Necropolis."

"Skulduggery mentioned that before he left," Militsa replied. "He said it's been there for six years. One more night will hardly make a difference."

"But it might," said Valkyrie. "What if we get to it tomorrow, and we realise we were one day too late? That we were a few *hours* too late?"

"Sweetie, come on..."

"It's a part of my sister. I can't leave her there alone when I know where she is. I have to get her. I have to bring her back."

"I understand that," said Militsa, "I do, but Skulduggery's helping Temper with something and there isn't a whole lot you can do without him, now is there? Go back to sleep. You'll be bright and alert in the morning and you can get it then."

Valkyrie shook her head. "I don't have to wait for Skulduggery."

"Yes, you do. You can't walk into the Necropolis, Val. It's for dead people only."

Valkyrie took her hand. "I have a plan. But I'm going to need your help."

"I don't particularly like the sound of any of that."

"It's a good plan."

"What is it?"

"I can't tell you."

"If it's such a good plan, why can't you tell me?"

"Because you probably won't want to do it."

Militsa folded her arms. "That doesn't sound like a good plan."

"It's a very good plan. It's very clever and totally safe."

"How illegal is it?"

"Only mildly."

"Val, come on now, you know I don't do illegal things."

"But it's only mildly illegal," said Valkyrie, "which means it's *barely* illegal, which means it's practically legal. What time is it?"

"Just gone six."

"In the evening? That's perfect! We'll probably need Tanith's help on this." She grabbed her phone. "Are you in?"

Militsa looked uncomfortable. "You're going to do this tonight? I've got so much homework left to mark."

Valkyrie dialled Tanith's number. "Militsa, please."

A sigh. "Fine."

"Thank you. I'm going to grab a shower. Do you have anything to eat?"

"I'll make you something," Militsa said, resigned to her fate. She left the room as Tanith answered the call.

"Hey," she said.

"I need your help," said Valkyrie. "Can you get to Roarhaven in the next hour?"

"Shouldn't be a problem. Want me to bring my sword?"

"No," said Valkyrie. "I reckon this part should be pretty non-violent."

"Ah," said Tanith, "I'll bring it anyway."

Valkyrie gave her the details and tapped the call off. She stood, took a step towards the bathroom and the world tilted and her legs gave out and she fell.

"Val?" Militsa called from downstairs. "Was that you? Are you OK?"

"I'm fine," Valkyrie called back. "Dropped my phone."

It wasn't the best lie, but it didn't provoke a further response from Militsa so it obviously did the job.

Valkyrie lay on the bedroom floor, taking a moment to just give in to the exhaustion. She could have fallen asleep right there and then. It would be so easy.

She counted to twenty.

At twenty, she rolled sideways. Kept rolling, until she came to the dresser. She opened her drawer – the one at the bottom that Militsa had designated for Valkyrie's stuff. It had been a big deal. Beneath the fresh set of clothes, a packet of dried leaves that dulled pain. Hidden between the leaves, a little square of paper with a sigil painted on it. A little Splash of magic.

She wished she had the music box with her. It had been too long since she'd listened to that wonderful, wonderful tune, and her thoughts were growing edges.

She shook her head. She didn't have the music box. She had the Splash, and that would have to do.

Valkyrie put it on her tongue. Felt it dissolve.

Strength flooded her body. Her eyes widened, the light in the room flaring as she sat up with a gasp, every muscle knotted, her bones cracking. She sat like that until she regained control of herself, until she sank back, giggling.

She sprang up. She felt good. Strong. Capable. Her magic jumped between her fingertips.

She took a shower and washed her hair, then dressed and went downstairs to the kitchen. A cup of tea was waiting for her beside a plate on which lay a massive sandwich. Her stomach rumbled.

"Thank you," she said, sitting at the table.

"You're looking brighter," Militsa said.

Valkyrie grinned. "I told you all I needed was a shower."

55

Tanith's bike was parked outside the Museum of Magical History, and Valkyrie and Militsa met her inside, by the reception desk. The guy at the desk frowned at them.

"This nice gentleman has been telling me that they're about to close," Tanith informed them with a strained smile.

"We won't be long," Valkyrie promised, and walked quickly to the East Wing. "Tanith Low, this is Militsa Gnosis. She and I are a thing."

"Hello," Militsa said, shaking Tanith's hand. "It's very nice to meet you."

"Likewise," said Tanith. "Do you know why we're here?"

"Not a clue. She's being all mysterious."

"I've seen that happen," Tanith said, nodding. "She gets it from Skulduggery."

"Really?" Valkyrie said without turning. "I always thought he got it from me."

They arrived in the East Wing. This part of the museum was a lot less spacious than Valkyrie remembered, and now resembled a cosy old antiques shop, every surface packed with curious oddities.

"They're refitting one of the other wings," Militsa explained as they squeezed between exhibits. "Everything in there is now in here. It's a bit of a mess, to be honest. What are we looking for?"

Valkyrie stopped before the glass case in which stood a manne-quin wearing the necronaut suit.

There were two layers to it. The outer layer was a frayed, burnt, torn fabric – but it was covering something else. Something black. It had a hood, and a mask – a white skull, stylised, angular, with glass-covered eye sockets.

"This is what I need," Valkyrie said.

Militsa nodded, and looked around. "What is?"

"This."

"The mannequin?"

"The mannequin? Why would I need the mannequin? No. The suit."

"What's so special about it?" Tanith asked.

"It's designed for Deep Venturing," Valkyrie told her. "Necromancers would go exploring the realms of death and they'd wear a necronaut suit like this to protect themselves. They wouldn't need food, wouldn't need water, wouldn't need air..."

"So you put this on and you can just walk into the Necropolis?"

"Yep."

"OK. That's pretty cool."

None of this was computing for Militsa. "But it's... I mean, it's part of the museum. They're not going to just give it to you."

"I think Valkyrie means to steal it," Tanith whispered.

"Oh," Militsa responded, her eyes widening. "Oh. Right. Wow."

A lady walked by. "The museum is closing now," she said with a smile.

They smiled back. When she was gone, Valkyrie turned to Militsa. "How do you feel about that?"

"I'm not sure," Militsa said. "On the one hand, it goes against absolutely everything inside me. All my little nerve endings are screaming, *No, no, don't steal from a museum!*" Militsa laughed uneasily. "But on the other hand..."

"On the other hand," Valkyrie prompted, "you'd do anything to make me happy...?"

"I would," Militsa said. "I totally would. Well, almost. It's just, the two of you, you're used to this sort of thing. You break the rules, you break the law, you go rogue and do cool stuff... but that's not me. I'm the one who thinks that rules are actually a pretty good idea, and the world would be better off if more of us respected them and, you know, just did what they told us."

"But the rules won't let me use the suit," Valkyrie pointed out. "So the rules aren't perfect, are they?"

"I never said they were," Militsa countered. "They're just better than the alternative."

"Look at it this way," said Tanith. "The rules hold most people in check. Those that the rules *don't* hold in check, Valkyrie goes after. She finds them, beats them up, and throws them in a cell."

"Bit simplistic," Valkyrie murmured.

"But there will always be those people who are too far gone and, when they appear, the good guys like Valkyrie need to be able to transcend the rules in order to go after them. And sometimes it's not even a person. Sometimes it's a circumstance. Sometimes it's a weird suit behind a glass case in a museum that smells of dead things and disinfectant."

"I need your help with this," Valkyrie said. "And I know I'm asking a lot. I know how much you hate this kind of thing. But... please?"

"Even the thought of breaking the rules makes me feel sick," Militsa said. "And, since I feel like I'm about to throw up, I suppose that means I'm in."

Valkyrie squeezed her hand. "You're the best."

"We should probably continue this discussion away from here," Tanith said, eyeing the museum lady, who was on her way back.

They went to the restaurant across the street, sat at the window and huddled close.

"The security system is pretty standard for sorcery museums," Militsa told them. "The doors and windows are alarmed, each individual exhibit is alarmed, the floor is electrified and the air is mined."

Valkyrie tapped her finger against her chin. "Repeat that last part for me?"

"The floor is electrified and the air is mined," said Militsa. "Once the building is locked up, if any movement is detected, these tiny, microscopic mines are released and they, basically, float through the air. If you hit one and it goes off, you'd barely notice more than a spark and a slight sting. But the mines work by setting off the other mines around them, so instead of one mine and a slight sting, you get a thousand mines and your head explodes."

"That seems elaborate," said Tanith. "What if there are mice? What if mice set them off?"

"There are no mice," said Militsa, and looked sad. "Any more."

Tanith made a face. "Harsh."

"I don't suppose bringing an Elemental with us would help?" Valkyrie asked.

"The mines were introduced to *stop* Elementals," said Militsa. "Any manipulation of the air currents results in detonation."

"Could we prevent the mines from being released in the first place?" Tanith asked.

"Probably," said Militsa. "If we had the time and the resources, not to mention the know-how."

Tanith looked at Valkyrie. "Do we have any of those things?"

"Not that I'm aware of," Valkyrie said.

"Damn."

"Although..." Militsa said.

Valkyrie leaned forward. "Yes?"

"The security system is controlled by a series of sigils," Militsa said. "I saw one carved on the wall in the East Wing, just before the entrance to the Haitian exhibits. These sigils will be linked to a larger master sigil, in a secure location. If we set one of these off, the master sigil will instigate the security countermeasures."

"You're dumbing this down for me, aren't you?"

"Do you mind?"

"Not at all."

Militsa continued. "But, if I can get to the sigil in the East Wing before it goes off, I can possibly delay the signal."

"And stop the mines from being released," Tanith said triumphantly. "Which was my plan."

Valkyrie ignored her. "What about the electrified floor?"

"When it detects us, we'll have about two seconds before we're fried to three very cute crisps. But that's electronic, I'm afraid – I haven't a clue how to deactivate that."

"Then we'll stay off the floor," Valkyrie said. "OK then. I think we have the makings of a plan."

Militsa paled. "We're doing this tonight? But... I can't! I need time to prepare. I need a high-quality heat pen to do the carving, and I need to practise, and – and..."

Valkyrie gripped her hand. "A wise man once said to me, *Doers do. Triers try. Those who can't don't bother, and those who don't bother never will.*"

They both frowned at her.

"Forget it," Valkyrie said, sitting back. "I just made that up. I thought it would sound deep, but I should have thought it through a little more, and maybe made it rhyme. It's stupid. But the central point remains."

"What central point would that be?" Militsa asked.

Valkyrie pressed her hands together. "Please," she said. "Please, please, please."

Militsa sighed. "Maybe I could manage it..."

"Yes! I knew it! I knew you could!"

"Don't get too excited, OK? If I can get a heat pen, then I might know a way to possibly delay the release of the mines, if we're lucky."

Valkyrie grinned. "If, might, possibly, and another if. I don't know about you girls, but I'm feeling confident."

"I'm not," said Militsa. "At all."

"Me neither," said Tanith.

"We should form a squad," Valkyrie said. "Just the three of us. It'd be so cool, wouldn't it?" She nodded. "This is going to work."

"No, it's not," Militsa said. "We're all going to die."

Valkyrie pointed at her. "And now we have our battle cry."

56

The darkness swirled around them, and when it whipped back to Militsa they were standing in the East Wing of the museum.

Tanith sprang for the ceiling, flipping as she did so to land on her feet. Militsa scrambled on to the nearest table and Valkyrie jumped on to a cabinet. A moment later, the floor started to crackle with blue-white electricity. It was actually quite pretty.

Militsa stepped to the edge of the table and leaned against the wall dangerously.

"Careful," Valkyrie warned.

"I'm fine," Militsa said, heat pen in hand, already working on the sigil.

"How will we know when it's working?" Tanith asked.

"Not sure," Militsa answered. "We won't die, I guess. You guys should probably do your bit."

Still walking upside down on the ceiling, Tanith hurried over to Valkyrie and Valkyrie jumped and grabbed her hands. They took a moment to make sure the grip was secure.

"Ready," Valkyrie said.

Tanith took a step along the ceiling, and Valkyrie left the cabinet behind her. She hung, swaying, over the crackling floor. It was an unsettling sensation.

Slowly, Tanith carried her down the row of exhibits, her muscles straining. They got to the glass case.

"Here comes the tricky part," Tanith muttered.

Valkyrie took a deep breath, and as she let it out she raised her legs. Her foot tapped against Tanith's wrist. Once. Twice. On the third tap, Tanith released Valkyrie's left hand and grabbed her left ankle instead. Valkyrie hung there.

"I'm good," said Tanith.

Valkyrie crunched her abdomen as her right foot tapped Tanith's other wrist, so that when Tanith let go of her hand to grab her other ankle, Valkyrie stayed curled, stayed in control.

Slowly, she straightened her body.

"How's it going?" Militsa called.

"I'm hanging upside down," Valkyrie called back, feeling her face darken as the blood rushed to her head. "How are those silly little mines?"

"Staying put for the moment."

Valkyrie slid her lock pick from her pocket, and went to work on the case. It was tricky, doing this upside down, but the last tumbler fell into place and the glass door opened with a light click.

Tanith moved her closer and Valkyrie reached for the mannequin.

"Uh," said Militsa.

Valkyrie frowned. "Everything OK?"

"Um."

"Militsa," Tanith said, the strain evident in her voice. "What seems to be the problem?"

"It's not working as well as I'd hoped," Militsa said. "I think we have... We don't have long. Get back here now."

"I almost have it," said Valkyrie.

"Get back here!" Militsa commanded – and then they heard it, like the whir of an air conditioner: the mines were being released.

Valkyrie looked up, straight into Tanith's eyes. They weren't going to make it.

Valkyrie gripped the top of the case. "Go," she said, and

yanked her ankles out of Tanith's hands. Her knees hit the top of the case, almost cracking the glass. Tanith was still looking down at her. "Run!" Valkyrie shouted.

Tanith bolted along the ceiling and Valkyrie swung her legs down and dropped into the glass case, jostling for space with the mannequin. She grabbed the door, swung it shut, pulling her fingers in right before it clicked. She steeled herself for an explosion –

– that didn't come.

Valkyrie stood there, waiting. Nothing happened, and that meant they'd made it. Tanith and Militsa had shadow-walked out of there. She wished she had enough room to take out her phone and check. She breathed out, and gave a little laugh. Now all she had to worry about was herself.

There wasn't enough space in here to do much, but Valkyrie managed to turn enough so that she could start to take the suit off the mannequin. Her fingers searched beneath the torn fabric, to the black material beneath. It felt a lot like the armoured clothes Ghastly had made for her. Slightly rougher, maybe.

She tore the fabric away – it ripped easily, like tissue paper – but she couldn't find a zip or buttons anywhere. Slowly, she moved her hands up, careful not to let her elbows nudge open the glass door.

The hood seemed to be attached to the skull mask, which was smooth and hard. She *tinked* her fingernail on the glass over the eyes. Her fingers curled under the chin and found a seam, and she pulled the mask up and immediately it crumpled like cloth. The rigidity, the smoothness, was suddenly gone. She pulled the mask up further, and it disappeared into the hood, which she could now pull down off the mannequin's head.

Still no zip, though. Still no buttons.

But she could feel something on the mannequin's chest. She pulled away the grey fabric. Attached to the suit beneath was a brooch of dark metal, about the size of her palm, engraved with the same stylised skull as the mask. Valkyrie was almost sure it hadn't been there when the hood was up.

She tried to prise it off. It was cool to the touch, but wouldn't budge. She pressed her thumb against it, hard, then tried turning it. She gazed at it for a few seconds, then a thought occurred to her and she tapped it, and the suit instantly withdrew into the brooch and the brooch fell off the mannequin – and Valkyrie snatched it.

"Huh," she said.

The mannequin was now wearing the torn grey fabric and nothing beneath. Valkyrie turned the brooch over, examining its smooth underside. Not a brooch, she saw now.

She slipped the amulet into her pocket. She could figure it out later. Right now, she had to get out of this case, and out of this museum, without being killed.

First thing to overcome was the electrified floor. If Skulduggery was here, he'd just float across it like a well-dressed balloon – but Valkyrie's flying style had more in common with a barely controlled missile than a balloon. But in theory – in theory – she could do it.

In theory.

Then there was the issue of the mines. That force-field thing she did, that would probably keep them at bay. But she'd have to maintain the force field while she flew, which is something she hadn't had to do before.

But again this was something that, theoretically, she was entirely capable of doing.

At least until she lost her concentration. Once that happened, she'd drop to the floor and lose the force field at the same time, and then it'd be a race to see which security measure killed her first.

But if she could keep her focus then a few seconds would be all that she'd need to get to the door. From there, maybe she could blast her way out. Maybe.

Valkyrie nodded. So that was the plan. It wasn't a very good one, but that's pretty much how she lived her life. She'd give it a try, and improvise when it didn't work out. She was OK with that.

Placing her hand on the door, Valkyrie focused on the magic inside her. She felt it churning, and she brought it out. It expanded from her chest, passed through her skin until it was crackling all around her.

Then she pushed open the glass door and jumped out and her magic expanded even further, enclosing her in a bubble of energy even as she felt the propulsion potential at her feet, that desperate need to burst upwards, to hurtle, and her fists clenched and her eyes squeezed shut as she fought that urge and just hovered there, unsteadily.

Her breathing was shallow. Her insides were knotted. She was suddenly sweating and she needed to pee so, so badly. But she stayed where she was, hanging in mid-air, until she could open her eyes.

She could feel the mines all around her, pressing in against the force field, itching to find something physical within it that would set them off.

Turning her body to the right, Valkyrie locked her eyes on the end of the aisle and, with a series of jerky starts, moved slowly towards the wall.

Halfway there she crashed into a display stand, breaking the glass, sending the exhibits tumbling. She watched as the floor sizzled them down to charred embers. She muttered a "Sorry" and rebounded off and kept going.

When she got to the wall, she again turned her body and again followed the next aisle. She got too close to a stack of undoubtedly valuable books and scorched the lot of them. When reaching out to steady herself, she knocked over an entire stand of presumably priceless artefacts. She misjudged a burst of speed and flew way too fast and had to rise up and flip over a display cabinet.

She came down on the other side and put all her focus into staying still. Her eyes closed, her hands out for balance, her feet unsteady, Valkyrie reminded herself of someone trying to surf for the first time.

When she felt that she was in control again, she propelled herself to the doorway, got there without wrecking anything else. The corridor beyond was long and straight.

She set off. For a while, she did well, but by the time she reached the end she was ricocheting around like a pinball. She emerged, spinning slowly but uncontrollably over the reception desk. It was making her dizzy.

There was a knocking. Someone was knocking on glass.

Bit by bit, she turned round. Tanith and Militsa stared at her from the street on the other side of the window. Valkyrie waved, then wobbled, and decided not to wave again.

Militsa indicated the force field, then mimed expanding it. It took Valkyrie a moment to figure out what she was proposing, and then she nodded quickly.

Taking a deep breath, Valkyrie pushed herself up towards the ceiling, and let the force field grow. When there was enough room, she nodded again at the window, and the darkness wrapped itself around Militsa at the same time as a swirl of shadows appeared within the bubble, right beside Valkyrie.

Militsa vanished from the window and lunged out of the swirl and wrapped her arms round Valkyrie and then they were falling and the darkness was everywhere.

They fell from the darkness on to the street outside. When they hit the ground there was no life-ending jolt of electricity – there was just a thump and a groan and a little bit of pain.

Valkyrie pulled her magic in and cut off the force field. Tanith stepped into view, looking down at her.

"At least you're not dead," she said, then took their hands and pulled them both up. They were, thankfully, alone on the street. "So what do we do now?"

"First, I thank this one for saving me," Valkyrie said, grabbing Militsa and giving her a huge kiss, "and then I proudly announce that I have the necronaut suit."

Militsa staggered a little after the kiss. "Ooh, light-headed," she said, blushing, and then looked down at Valkyrie's empty hands. "But I think you might have left the suit behind, baby."

Valkyrie smiled, and took out the amulet.

"Great," said Tanith. "You nicked a badge from the gift shop."

"Not a badge," said Valkyrie. "An amulet. And I'm pretty sure what I'm going to do next will definitely probably work..."

She pressed the amulet to her chest and tapped it, and the necronaut suit flowed outwards, covering her own clothes in an instant.

Militsa's eyes widened. "Oh, wow."

Valkyrie turned to the museum window, examining her reflection in the glass. The suit was black, and tight, and it fitted her perfectly, as if it had been designed for her.

"Should have known a Necromancer suit would have a few tricks built into its sleeves," Militsa said. "It must redesign itself according to its wearer. That is *brilliant*."

"How does this feel?" Tanith asked, and punched Valkyrie in the shoulder.

"Ow!"

"Did that hurt?"

Valkyrie frowned. "Actually... not really. I mean, it's not as good as Ghastly's clothes, but... but it's pretty good, all the same. Still – don't punch me. It's rude."

"Sorry. Where's the mask?"

"In the hood."

"Let's see."

"OK, but you can't punch me any more."

"Let's see, you wuss."

Valkyrie tucked back her hair and pulled up the hood. It looked pretty cool. She searched the lining on the top, found the crumpled material and pulled it down. The moment the mask covered her face it became rigid and the entire suit sealed and Valkyrie gasped.

She felt every beat of her heart. More than that, she felt the blood in her veins. She felt her lungs and how they filled and expanded, and she felt the air as it left those lungs. She felt her skin, every bit of it, nestling against her clothes. She felt alive in a way she had never felt before.

Every inch of her was now covered. The mask was solid. The glass at the eyes was so clear it was like there was nothing there. The mask, the hood, none of it muffled the sounds around her. If anything, she could hear better now.

"This is amazing," she said. The mask didn't muffle her voice, either.

"You look awesome," said Tanith, then took her sword from her bike and stabbed Valkyrie's leg.

"Tanith!" Militsa cried.

"No cut, no blood," Tanith said, returning the sword to its scabbard. "The suit's armoured. Sweet."

Militsa glared. "You didn't know that when you stabbed her."

Tanith shrugged.

Valkyrie spent another few seconds like this, just listening to and experiencing her own body, the feel of her own *life*, before she made herself lift the mask. It immediately crumpled, and she pulled the hood down.

"That felt amazing," she said. "That felt..." She shook her head. Back to business. "All right, OK. Now I get the soul fragment back."

Militsa put her hand on Valkyrie's arm. "Are you sure about this?"

"Don't I seem sure?"

"You do, but..."

"Look at me," said Valkyrie. "I'm ready. I'm feeling strong and confident. I don't need to wait for Skulduggery. I can do it myself. You believe in me, right?"

"Always."

Valkyrie smiled. "Good. Get back home." She took out her phone and tapped out a message. "I'm just asking Fletcher to teleport me to the Necropolis. I'll call you when I'm done, OK?"

"The *moment* you're done."

Valkyrie put her phone away. "I promise."

"What about me?" Tanith asked. "You said I could help with this Abyssinia thing, but I've been sitting alone in a rented room for the last week. I'm bored, Val. Give me something fun to do."

"I have the perfect thing," Valkyrie said. "Abyssinia had a spy working as an aide for President Flanery. I know, I know, we don't usually get involved in mortal stuff, but, in this case, mortal stuff seems to have got involved with *us*. Anyway, this spy, Wilkes, has gone missing. Which might mean that Flanery knows about sorcerers.

"We've been working with a man named Oberon Guile to track down someone called Crepuscular Vies, who seems to be behind at least some of this, but we've been busy with a load of other stuff, so right now Oberon is having to do most of this on his own. Also, he's pretty hot, for an older guy."

"I volunteer," said Tanith.

"Thought you might. I'll get Fletcher to drop you off in the States when he's done with me."

"Oh, joy," said Tanith.

Militsa's eyebrows went up. "You don't like Fletcher?"

Valkyrie laughed. "Fletcher has had a tendency to drool over Tanith in the past – but a lot of time has passed since then. Fletcher's grown up."

"Yeah, right," Tanith said.

"No, he has," Militsa tried. "He's a very good teacher, and he's really responsible and mature now."

Valkyrie nodded. "Very mature."

Fletcher appeared on the other side of the street. He saw Tanith and he froze for a moment, before walking over with a seductive smile sliding on to his face.

"Hey there," he said.

Tanith sighed.

57

They appeared in the Scottish Highlands, at a doorway cut into a rock wall.

"You're sure this will work?" Fletcher asked.

"It's what this suit was designed for," Valkyrie answered.

"Yeah," Fletcher responded, "but a lot of things fail to do what they're designed for. Planes crash. Boats sink." He paused. "I can't think of a third example, but you get my point."

"I do," she said, "but I'll be fine. If I need a lift home, I'll give you a call."

"You sure you don't want me to wait out here?"

Valkyrie smiled. "Honestly? I don't know how long this'll take. Go home, Fletch. Thanks."

He gave her a hug. "Good luck," he said, and vanished.

With the Soul Catcher containing the fragment of her sister's soul in one hand, Valkyrie walked through the doorway. Down black marble steps she went, her way lit by the weak torches on the walls. It got colder. A lot colder.

She got to the bottom. The Necropolis lay before her, a vast city with a sky of rock.

She took a deep, deep breath, pulled up the hood, and pulled down the mask. The suit sealed itself. Her life, her vibrancy, shuddered through her – and she stepped over the threshold, into the City of the Dead.

58

After fifteen minutes of walking through this secret underground tunnel, Temper and Skulduggery arrived at a wall. They found a lever and pulled it, and the wall parted. They stepped out into the Dark Cathedral and the wall sealed behind them.

They watched two Cathedral Guards in black armour walking away from them, and headed in the opposite direction.

"So how are we going to play this?" Temper asked quietly. "Are we going to sneak? Are we going to—"

"We're going to walk," Skulduggery said. "No sneaking."

"But everyone knows who we are. They'll know we're not supposed to be here."

"Which means they'd expect us to be sneaking. Because we're so obviously not supposed to be here, they'll assume we *are* supposed to be here, and they'll let us pass without interference."

"Are you sure?"

"I've studied human behaviour for the last four hundred years, Temper. I know how people react."

"You two," said a Cathedral Guard from up ahead. "Stop. You're not supposed to be here."

Temper looked at Skulduggery. Skulduggery didn't say anything.

Temper smiled at the guard. "Actually, we've been invited. It's all on the down-low, so keep it to yourself, you get me? Good man. Carry on."

He went to walk by, but the guard stepped into his path. "You're a traitor. He's the enemy. We have orders to detain both of you on sight, and kill you if you resist."

"Seriously? Kill us?"

"At the slightest sign of resistance."

Temper exhaled loudly. "This is awkward. I mean, we definitely have an invitation. This is one of those embarrassing mix-ups you hear about. You know those? Ever get those? That must happen all the time."

"That has never happened."

"That strikes me as unlikely."

"We are very particular about who we let down here," said the guard. "There are many levels of security you have to pass through. How did you get this far?"

"I told you, man. We were invited. We were taken through all those levels of security you were talking about. Every single one of them. You know what I think? Personally? I think you got way too many levels. I do. I think you don't need them all. Maybe take one away. Maybe the last one – you don't need it."

"Who escorted you?"

"Tall guy. Stern. Dressed a lot like you."

"What was his name?"

"Kevin, I think."

"There are no Kevins working here."

"It was something *like* Kevin. It wasn't *exactly* Kevin. It *sounded* like – you know what? You can ask him yourself when he gets back. He's just gone to the restroom. We told him we'd meet him at the place where you're keeping all those Kith fellas. Where is that? That's a few floors down, right? Or up?"

"You're not going anywhere."

"Kevin's probably going to wait for us there, though."

"There is no Kevin."

"Well, I don't know what to tell you, OK? It was Kevin or

something that sounded a lot like Kevin. Maybe I should speak to your superior. Is he around?"

"She."

"Is she around?"

"She's upstairs."

"Can you run and get her? Then we can sort out this whole Kevin thing, once and for all. Get to the bottom of this mystery. The more I think about it, the more I'm remembering some pretty suspicious behaviour that Kevin was demonstrating. Now you got *me* wondering, you know – was he meant to be here? Have you got an intruder on the premises?"

"The sparrow flies south for winter," Skulduggery said.

Temper frowned at him. "What?"

Skulduggery caught the guard completely unawares, connecting with a right cross that spun him and sent him to the ground.

Temper stared. "Can you warn me the next time you're gonna do something like that?"

"I did warn you," Skulduggery said, dragging the guard into the shadows.

"You said something about birds and then you sucker-punched the guy."

"Now you know the phrase," Skulduggery said, coming back. "When you hear that, violence is imminent."

"We didn't need violence," said Temper. "I was talking our way out of that situation just fine."

"You were dreadful," Skulduggery said as they started walking again.

"I was in the process of convincing him. Besides, who was it who assured me no one would stop us because we were so obviously not supposed to be here? Who was it that said that?"

"I think you know who it was," Skulduggery said.

"Yeah, I think I do, too. So much for your four hundred years of studying human behaviour."

"Do you know what I've learned in all my years of studying people?"

"Is it to admit when you're wrong?"

"It's that people can always surprise you."

"So it's not admitting when you're wrong, then?"

They continued on, sticking to the shadows a lot closer than they had been.

Down they went, level after level.

It got darker. And colder. And quieter.

And finally they came to a cavern filled with thousands of smooth-headed people, all standing in perfect rows in the dark. None of them moving. None of them reacting. Just standing there.

"Well," Temper said, "you wanted evidence..."

Great lights flickered on above them, banishing the darkness and giving Temper a good look at just how many Kith were stored down here. It was a lot more than he'd thought.

Skulduggery nudged him, and they both turned.

For a man whose big secret had just been uncovered, Damocles Creed seemed remarkably chilled as he came down the stone steps into the cavern. He was carrying a towel and wearing sweatpants. Perspiration glistened off his bald head and broad chest. They'd obviously interrupted a workout. Such a shame.

"Detective Pleasant," said Creed as he neared them. "Officer Fray. I didn't hear you come in. How *did* you get in, just out of curiosity?"

"Through one of the secret entrances that are all over this place," Temper said, "and that you know nothing about. That must be so annoying for you..."

"Arch-Canon," Skulduggery said. "Apologies for the surprise visit, but sometimes that's the only way to catch evil people doing evil things."

Creed used the towel to wipe the sweat off his face. "I'm not going to debate good and evil with you, Detective. You have your priorities and I have mine."

"Mine include not lobotomising tens of thousands of innocent victims."

"You say victims, I say volunteers."

"Well," Temper cut in, "I don't think it matters much what any of us say, does it? What matters is what the Supreme Mage says when she finds out what you've been up to."

Creed flicked the towel over his shoulder, and clasped his hands before him. "The Supreme Mage has enough troubling her without being called on to decide matters of religious freedom."

"If that's how you're going to frame your argument," Skulduggery said, "it will be a very short conversation."

Creed laughed. "I'm sorry, but what exactly do you expect to happen? Do you expect the High Sanctuary to shut down the Church of the Faceless? Do you expect them to oust me from my position? Roarhaven's success depends on its bank — and its bank depends on *me*. As fearsome as China Sorrows is, do you really think she'll do something that will invariably lead to the downfall of her own seat of power? Detective Pleasant — you know her better than anyone. Is that what you expect of her?"

Skulduggery observed Creed a moment before answering. "I learned a long time ago that China tends to be two steps ahead of whoever's trying to outmanoeuvre her. Be careful, Damocles. This isn't going to go the way you think."

Creed smiled. "You should leave. Maybe try the main door this time."

"We're going to go," said Skulduggery. "But because we want to, not because you told us to."

"Yeah," said Temper.

They walked by him, to the stairs.

"Nice one," Temper whispered.

"I know," Skulduggery whispered back.

59

Never limped into study hall, her face hidden by her hair. Omen waved and Never came over, squeezing between the desks to sit beside him. The teacher on duty never even looked up from her newspaper.

"What happened to you?" Omen asked softly.

Never settled, put her bag down and with a flick of her hair she showed him the gigantic bruise on the left side of her face, a bruise that ran from her bloodshot eye down to her cut lip. Despite the injuries, she was grinning.

"Pretty nasty, huh?" she whispered. "My ribs are bruised as well. And my leg. My bum, too, but I'm not really sure how that happened, and no, you can't see it. You don't get to view the goods."

Omen leaned closer. "What. Happened?"

"Fight," she responded so only he could hear. "Huge one. Auger was brilliant, as usual, as were Kase and Mahala. But you know what, Omen? Do you know what?"

"What?"

"I didn't embarrass myself," Never said, and was suddenly bubbling with excitement. "I helped. I actually helped out. I wasn't just standing there, or teleporting uselessly around. They were in trouble and I jumped in and... and I wasn't useless."

"I doubt you're ever useless," Omen said.

Never flicked her hair back again. "You're sweet, but no, in life-or-death battles, I'm beyond rubbish. At least I have been."

"Well done," Omen said, smiling at her obvious delight.

"Thank you. Auger said I could've died."

"Seriously?"

She nodded quickly. "He said, *Don't do that again – you could've got yourself killed.* I really feel like I'm one of the team now, you know?"

"And *did* you almost get yourself killed?"

"Oh, yeah. God, yeah. Hilariously so."

"And when was this?"

"Like... three hours ago."

"And you're all right?"

"I'm right as rain, Omen, my dear."

"You're not, like, in shock or anything, are you?"

"I don't think so," Never whispered. "I mean... how would I know? If I'm in shock?"

"Are your hands shaking?"

"Everything's shaking."

"Maybe you should go to the nurse's office. Just in case."

"But I have homework to do. So much of it. I mean... I could copy someone's work, I suppose. Someone smart. Someone good. Not you, basically. But someone else. Anyone else. Literally anyone."

"Are you insulting me on purpose, or just out of habit?"

"Little bit of both," Never said. "OK, I'll go see the nurse. Toodle-pip, monkey." She sat there, and started frowning. "Why can't I teleport?"

"Can't use magic in study hall," Omen reminded her.

Never made a face. "Yikes. I *must* be in shock. OK, distract the teacher for me."

Omen looked up, but the teacher was still reading her paper.

When he looked back, Never was on her hands and knees, and was scuttling between the desks towards the door. She'd have been faster walking, Omen reckoned. And would have drawn less attention.

60

The portal shimmered in the middle of Lily's living room. It was quite beautiful in an eerie, heart-stoppingly scary kind of way. The members of the Darquesse Society stared at it, fully aware that on the other side there could very well be an entire race of Faceless Ones ready to reach through and grab them.

Sebastian nodded. "I'm ready," he said. "Let's do this."

Demure hugged him. "I just want you to know that we all think you're incredibly, incredibly brave."

"Uh... thank you."

"Anything might happen to you over there."

"I suppose."

"You might be eaten by something."

"Wow."

"Can you swim?"

"Yes."

"If you go into the water, watch out for sharks."

"I will."

"And cannibals."

"In the water?"

"In general."

"Good advice."

She released him and stepped back, wiping tears from her eyes.

"I'm not dead yet," Sebastian pointed out with a chuckle.

Demure smiled sadly. "That's the spirit," she said.

Lily stepped up. "We're counting on you. I know that's a lot of pressure, but it's all up to you now. Don't let us down."

"I'll try not to."

She tapped the beak of his mask. "For good luck," she said.

He nodded and turned, and Ulysses filled his eyeholes.

"I've never had a brother," he said. "I was the only boy out of a family of eighteen, and every time my mother got pregnant I'd pray for a boy. It never happened. But now, with you... I like to think that I finally have the brother I've waited my whole life for."

"Oh," said Sebastian. "Wow. That's... that's really nice of you."

"Did I make it weird between us? I feel like I made it weird. Maybe not a brother. Maybe a cousin?"

"Cousin's cool."

"Yeah? Then you're like a cousin to me," Ulysses said, then rapped a knuckle against Sebastian's beak. "Or a neighbour."

Sebastian turned to Forby and Tarry.

Forby nodded, and handed him the scanner, a small box with a series of tiny bulbs built into it. Sebastian nodded back. Tarry started to say something, but his phone rang and he mouthed a silent "Sorry", then answered it and left the room to talk.

Now there was an arm round his shoulder, and Bennet was leading him to the portal.

"If it gets too dangerous," he said, "come back. We'll figure something else out. We'll load up with supplies and make a proper expedition out of it."

"I'll be fine," said Sebastian. "It's going to be fine."

"Demure was right, you know. This is one of the bravest things I've ever actually witnessed."

"Yeah," said Sebastian. "Me too."

Bennet hesitated, then tapped Sebastian's beak, and allowed Sebastian to take the last few steps alone.

Sebastian stared into the swirling vortex of the portal. For all he knew, the moment he walked through, his body would be torn inside out. For all he knew, he'd disintegrate. For all he knew, there was a Faceless One waiting on the other side and the instant he saw it his mind would snap.

He took a deep, deep breath, and let it out as he stepped through the portal.

The ground on the other side was hard. Cracked. The sky was red. Dark clouds rolled.

There were no trees, no grass, no plant life at all. No animals or birds that he could see. In the distance, there were mountains. The scanner clicked and one of the lights lit up, pointing to those mountains – across all that flat, hard ground.

Sebastian stuck his head back through the portal.

"Everything OK?" Bennet asked.

"All good," Sebastian answered, then looked at Lily. "Could I borrow your scooter?"

And that was how Sebastian travelled across this alien landscape, trundling along on Lily's yellow scooter, his black coat flapping behind him, like some weird, majestic bird.

On a scooter.

61

The dead watched her.

They filled the streets Valkyrie walked upon and she moved between them, slowly. Some of them were so faint they were barely there. Others so distinct they looked almost solid. They all turned their heads to follow her with sunken eyes. The only sound in Necropolis came from Valkyrie's footsteps and the occasional whistle of the wind that found its way down here, through all that rock.

When she passed, their gazes fell on the Soul Catcher in her hands. The soul fragment inside turned in on itself endlessly. It didn't point the way like she'd hoped, and so this was taking a lot longer than she'd expected.

All night, Valkyrie had been walking these streets. She was exhausted. She could feel her hunger, feel her thirst, but the suit stopped it from becoming a problem. Her eyes were heavy and her feet were concrete blocks she had to drag along the ground. That dose of Splash had long since worn off. Coming here, as weak as she was, had been a mistake. She knew that now.

The suit was working well. It contained her life like a glove contained the hand that filled it. It kept death at bay.

But her head...

Her head was filling with voices. All her own. Shouting at her, calling to her, telling her to stop, to lie down, to give up, to take off the mask, take off the suit, let death in, let it seep in and swamp her. It's what she wanted, the voices said. It's what she thought about.

"It's what you dream about," said Ghastly.

She froze.

He stood there, solid among all those ghosts. "Take off the suit, Valkyrie. End your pain."

"You're not here," she said.

"You weren't designed to suffer this much," he said. "No one was. Your mind has broken. You're never going to get back to the person you were. She's gone."

"Shut up."

"She's dead," Ghastly said, walking with her as she moved. "It's time for you to join her, Valkyrie. Join these people. Look at them. Ghosts. They don't care. They're not tortured. You can be like them. Don't you want to be like them?"

Valkyrie stopped.

The Nemesis of Greymire was ahead of her. Standing there with that sledgehammer.

Valkyrie's breathing quickened. She was panicking. Suddenly the suit felt too tight. It was too tight and too close and the mask, oh, God, the mask, it was itching. It was itching and she was sweating and she needed to take it off, to rip it off, and her hand, her free hand, went to the mask, fingers digging at the seam, trying to pull it off, and then she'd be able to breathe again, to gasp, to—

"What are you doing?"

Valkyrie blinked.

Her fingers stopped digging.

She lowered her hand. Kes stood there, frowning at her.

"I was itchy," Valkyrie said.

"I can guess what kind of suit that is," Kes replied. "And I can guess what it does. You do know that if you took the mask off, you'd die, right?"

"I wasn't going to take it off. I just got claustrophobic. It's passed now."

Ghastly was gone. And the Nemesis. Valkyrie started walking again, Kes beside her.

"How did you know this place wouldn't kill you?" Valkyrie asked.

Kes shrugged. "I didn't. I was bored, so I thought I'd see. I do love the suit, by the way. Skulduggery seen it yet?"

Valkyrie shook her head.

"He'll probably think you're wearing it to honour him."

"He doesn't know I'm here."

"This place is so creepy... I'm assuming this has something to do with little sis?"

"Her soul has been split," Valkyrie said. "I've got one fragment with me. The second one is here somewhere. I can fix her, Kes. She's going to be OK."

"That's great," Kes said, a huge smile on her face. "That's brilliant! Can I help you look for her?"

"She won't go to you. Or... it won't. The fragment. That's why I have the Soul Catcher. Like a, a metal detector. Or a beacon. Or both."

"Cool," said Kes, looking at her weirdly. "How're you doing anyway? You OK?"

"Yes."

"You sure?"

"Yes. No. It doesn't matter."

"Valkyrie, come on. If you can't talk to the sliver of the god you were once upon a time, then who can you talk to?"

Valkyrie bit her lip beneath the mask. "I think I've gone nuts."

Kes shrugged. "No argument from me."

"Something happened. I was gassed and... and buried. I think something... broke. In my mind."

Kes frowned at her. "Seriously?"

Valkyrie stopped again and turned to her. "I'm seeing things," she whispered. "Things that aren't really there."

"Like me?"

"No. No, you're real. I know you're real. But other things. People. Ghastly. I see Ghastly. And this thing, this woman, called the Nemesis of Greymire. They're not really there, but I see them. They talk to me."

"But they're not real?"

"No."

"Then why are you whispering?"

Valkyrie leaned closer. "Because they might hear me."

Kes looked at her. "When was the last time you slept? Properly slept?"

Walking again.

"I'll sleep when I'm done here."

"Hey, hold on."

"No," said Valkyrie. "I have to keep going."

"Hold on, I said. Is it supposed to be doing that?"

Valkyrie looked down, and a sudden shot of adrenaline buzzed through her body, almost making her drop the Soul Catcher. The fragment was twisting and writhing and throwing itself against one side of the sphere. She turned slowly. The fragment kept pointing in the same direction.

"Let's go," said Kes. "Valkyrie, come on!"

Bleary-eyed, Valkyrie nodded, stumbled, then led the way, holding the Soul Catcher out in front. They hurried through the streets. The dead watched them go.

"There!" Kes cried. "Look!"

Something moved towards them. A shape, almost translucent, that distorted the air as it moved. Valkyrie wouldn't have seen it if Kes hadn't pointed it out.

Her head pounding, Valkyrie managed to switch on her aura-vision and instantly recoiled. The ghosts were so bright they hurt her eyes behind the skull mask. The city glowed, a dizzying array of colours. She forced herself to look up, and saw the piece of the soul that was flitting towards them.

Crying, Valkyrie held up the Soul Catcher and the fragment passed into it, and both fragments swirled and whirled like excited puppies and then they melted together.

Valkyrie fell to her knees. She shut off the aura-vision. The world darkened, went back to normal.

"I have to go," said Kes.

Valkyrie sniffed, and raised her head. "Already?"

"I don't have the strength to stay visible for very long."

Kes's face was suddenly pale and lined.

"Are you OK?" Valkyrie asked.

"Don't worry about me," Kes replied, smiling. "You're about to fix our little sister's soul, so you get home and you do that. I'll drop in on you when I'm strong enough, OK? Hug her for me."

Kes faded, and vanished.

Valkyrie didn't have the strength to stand, but somehow she managed it. The Soul Catcher was so heavy in her hands. She brought it up, pressed it against her mask.

"I'm going to take you home," she said softly. "Won't be long now. Won't be long."

She turned.

A woman stood there in a black robe with a porcelain face. "Who goes there?" she asked.

"My name is Valkyrie Cain."

"Why are you here?"

"My sister's soul was damaged," Valkyrie said. "It was split, and a part of it came here. I'm just getting it back."

"To do what with it?"

"Return it to my sister."

"I'm afraid I cannot allow that," said the woman. "I am called the Sentinel, and the Necropolis is a place of safety. Of peace. Once a soul seeks us out, it has found its home."

"But her soul was split. It needs to be put back together."

The Sentinel was silent for a moment. "We have considered your proposal," she said. "We agree that the pieces should be reunited, so we are willing to accept the fragments you have found." She held out her hands.

"Excuse me?" said Valkyrie.

"The Soul Catcher, please."

Valkyrie put the Catcher behind her back. "No. That's not how this works."

"I am afraid it is."

"Listen to me – even if I left this here, it still wouldn't fix the problem. Her soul was split into three. I have two pieces, and the third is still with my sister. You understand? The only way the soul is repaired is if I take these two pieces with me when I leave."

The Sentinel shook her head. "There is another option."

"No, there really isn't."

"You bring your sister here," the Sentinel said. "Her physical form will die, but her soul will be reunited."

"You're... asking me to kill her."

The Sentinel paused. "Yes."

Valkyrie surprised herself by laughing. God, she sounded insane. She looked away, chewing her lip while her mind struggled to sort itself out.

"I killed her once before," she said at last. "That's how her soul was damaged in the first place. I'm not going to do it again."

"Why not?" the Sentinel asked.

"Because she's my sister. She deserves to live."

"Life is but the first step on the journey we all must take," the Sentinel responded. "It is nothing to be especially cherished. Death is where we break free from the physical universe."

Valkyrie indicated their surroundings. "Excuse me for saying so, but you don't exactly look free to me. You spend your days haunting a place you can't leave. How is that better than living?"

"This is only a fraction of our existence."

"My sister should have a chance to grow up in the world. She should be able to feel the sun on her face. She should be able to travel, and meet people, and fall in love, and experience life before she gets to a place like this. Please, let me help her."

"Even if I wished to, I could not," said the Sentinel. "It goes against our most ancient laws."

"People break laws all the time."

"People do," said the Sentinel, "but we do not."

"I'm not leaving here without it."

"You have trapped one of us in your little cage," the Sentinel said. "Do you think we could ignore this?"

Valkyrie stared at her. She softened her tone. "It doesn't have to be like this," she said. "I came here to heal a soul. That's what we both want, isn't it?"

"It is."

"Your way, listen to me, your way can't be done. I can't bring my sister here. I can't kill her. I just can't. Do you understand me? I am unable to. This is my law. This is my unbreakable law. But my way, where I leave with the pieces I have, that can be done. It's achievable. It's simple. You just have to let me—"

"It is far from simple."

"No, no, you listen. You just have to let me walk out of here. It's easy."

"It is impossible."

"No, it isn't."

"Please," said the Sentinel, "hand over the Soul Catcher."

"No," Valkyrie said. Tears were in her eyes. "Don't do this. Please. I want my sister back. I want to help her."

"Your sister is not a thing of flesh and bone and blood," the Sentinel said. "Your sister is more than this, as are you. As is every living thing. Your view is limited because your experience is limited."

"I'll fight you."

"Why?"

"I won't give it to you."

The Sentinel reached for the Soul Catcher and Valkyrie went

to shove her, but her magic crackled round her hand and, when she touched her, the Sentinel staggered.

Valkyrie froze, and there was a moment, a moment of shock, and then the ghosts changed and became angry and they crowded her and Valkyrie couldn't help it, the energy built up inside her, churned and burned, and they reached for her and reached for the Soul Catcher and her power exploded and there were a thousand flashes of crackling light and her scream was the only thing in the world and then

62

she was flying.

The surprise broke her focus and she wasn't flying any more. She was falling, falling towards the fields and the trees and the roads beneath her.

The Soul Catcher slipped from her hands.

Energy crackled and she righted herself, swooped low and snatched up the Soul Catcher, then ascended again, passing through the low-hanging clouds. The suit kept the cold at bay. The crackling energy didn't make it smoulder or burn. She still had the hood up, still wore the mask. She could feel her heartbeat.

She'd been... where had she been? The Necropolis. Yes. She'd found the soul fragment and the Sentinel... the Sentinel...

Valkyrie piled on the speed. Her face, beneath the mask, was wet with tears, so she went faster. Faster still.

She glimpsed Grimwood House through a gap in the clouds and flew down, wincing as the thoughts in her head grew louder. She tried to stop the images from forming, but they slipped round her defences.

The Sentinel. The spirits. The city.

She landed, heavily, and stumbled to the front step. She patted her suit, searching for the door key. Cursing, she slapped the amulet on her chest. The suit retracted and the amulet fell. She ignored it, pulled the key from her jeans and turned it in the lock and the door opened and the Nemesis was there.

Valkyrie ducked the sledgehammer, threw herself back, scrambling away as the Nemesis stepped out of the house and swung again.

Valkyrie rolled, kicked at the Nemesis of Greymire's leg and the Nemesis didn't notice.

She got up, fell, got up again, the Soul Catcher in her hands. Ran into the house. Up the stairs. Got to the top.

But now the Nemesis was coming out of her bedroom and Valkyrie dived under the swing of the hammer, the Soul Catcher rolling across the floor, and Valkyrie lunged for the bedside table, managed to grab the music box as she fell. She hit the floor and opened the lid –

– and the music flowed.

She breathed out.

Her body relaxed.

The noise in her head went away.

There was nobody in the doorway. No Nemesis in the house.

Valkyrie reached across, scooped up the Soul Catcher and held it to her chest. Xena poked her head in and Valkyrie held out her hand, and the dog came over, wagging her tail happily.

63

Love, Razzia often thought, was the stupidest of all emotions.

It got in the way of just about everything there was to get in the way of. It ruined friendships and disrupted families and left a trail of trauma in its wake. Love made people do the dumbest of things for the dumbest of reasons – just because one synapse said to another synapse, *Hey, let's spark up and see what happens.*

Stupid. Just stupid.

That didn't mean that Razzia herself wasn't prone to feeling this particular emotion. She wasn't a robot, or a Hollow Man, or some kind of plant. She had feelings. Proper ones. She'd even fallen in love with a mortal, once upon a time. And what a mortal he had been. Big smile, flashy suits, total lunatic. It had got weird and she'd had to end it, but not before falling deeply, madly in love.

So she understood why Caisson had asked for help to break Solace out of Greymire Asylum. He'd been married to her, after all, before being captured by Serafina. And she understood why Abyssinia had said yes to helping him. It was love, that pesky little creature, chucking a stick in the bicycle spokes of harmony. It was love, that look on Caisson's face when they'd taken Solace from the tower. The pure kind of love, the kind that doesn't fade.

Solace herself was not what Razzia had been expecting. She'd imagined someone young and pretty and strong. She had not been expecting a frail old lady who looked like a stiff breeze could blow her off course.

But such was love. There was no accounting for it.

Razzia was in her quarters, feeding her pets, when Abyssinia turned up at the open door. She stayed there for a while, watching as the parasites snapped hungrily at the diced-up chicken. Then she came in, sat on the bed, smiling at Gretel, who by now was stealing some of Hansel's dinner.

When the plates were clean, the parasites retracted into Razzia's hands and her palms closed up, and she felt them settle inside her forearms.

"Caisson seems happy," Abyssinia said.

Razzia nodded.

"I'm glad he has someone," Abyssinia continued. "It's important to have someone in your life. It gives you meaning. It gives you purpose."

Razzia nodded again. She knew exactly what Abyssinia was talking about.

"For me, that person was Caisson," Abyssinia said. "When I was in that box, just a heart, reaching out to you all, I tried reaching out to him as well, but... but he was always too far away. That was Serafina's doing, of course. Blocking him from me. But I never stopped trying. When I finally saw my boy again after all these centuries... it was the happiest day of my life."

Abyssinia fell silent. Razzia waited.

"Solace seems nice," Abyssinia said.

Razzia nodded. "For an old chick."

"Watch it, you. I'm a lot older."

"Naw," said Razzia. "Age doesn't work like that. Young bodies tend to have young minds. It's all in the brain chemistry. Once those chemicals dry up, however, and you're faced with the irreversible onslaught of years upon your physical form, you tend to surrender to the ravages of time. So, old bodies, old minds."

Abyssinia studied her for a bit. "You surprise me sometimes. I've looked inside your mind and I know you better than anyone... yet you still surprise me."

Razzia shrugged. "What can I say? I'm a surprising person."

64

Tanith met the tall streak of goodness in a bar on Charlotte Street, the kind of place where mortals got hammered and listened to good music through bad speakers. He walked in, scratching his stubble, looked around and saw her, sitting all the way at the back. He had a nice walk. His hair was dark, going grey, but lustrous. He had eyes that crinkled when he smiled. He smiled now as he shook her hand.

"Oberon Guile," he said.

"Tanith Low."

"Pleased to meet you. Buy you a drink?"

"Already have one," Tanith said. "I'll buy you one, though." She waved over a barman, and Oberon ordered a Scotch, because of course he did.

"How much do you know?" Oberon asked after he'd taken his first sip.

"Everything up until right now," Tanith said. "Last I heard, you were about to interrogate a mercenary. Bolton. How did that go for you?"

"Wasn't easy," said Oberon. "A Sensitive would've made short work of it, but I had to resort to old-fashioned methods. Even so, I got him to talk eventually. Little while after that, I got him to actually tell me the truth. The group Bolton works for, they're called Blackbrook Services, a private military company."

"You mean a private army."

"That I do. They've been fighting wars that governments don't want to be seen to be fighting."

"How does Bolton know about sorcerers?"

"They all do. Blackbrook is the same as any army – it's got its regular grunts, and then it has its elite squad. Bolton's one of the elite, and he says everyone in his squad is well aware that sorcerers exist."

Tanith sat back. "Whenever groups of well-armed mortals find out about magic, it never ends well."

"That's what I was thinking."

"Did he say what Blackbrook has to do with this Crepuscular Vies guy?"

"Far as I can tell, he's their boss. Been secretly bankrolling the whole thing since it was set up back in the 1980s, but it's only in the last few years that he's stepped out of the shadows."

"What's he after?"

Oberon took another sip. "I do not know. But whatever it is, he's got a squad of black ops killers at his beck and call, and a whole army behind *that*, should he need it." Oberon paused, sloshing the drink around in its glass. His eyes were green. "Tanith, I have to be honest with you. I have no idea what I'm doing. I don't know where to go from here."

"That's why Valkyrie sent me," she said. "I've been through stuff like this before. You've done well, with the questioning and the interrogating and the finding stuff out. That's all good. It's all helpful. But now's the part that I'm good at."

"Which is?"

"Kicking down doors, and beating people up."

Oberon gave her another one of those smiles. Valkyrie was right. He was pretty hot. "Lead," he said, "and I'll follow."

65

Omen had pulled a sickie.

It was his first one. He thought it would have been a bigger deal, like he'd have to prove that he was genuinely feeling ill and couldn't possibly go to class.

But the nurse believed him, and told him that maybe he'd feel better by tonight, and that he should go back to his dorm room and sleep it off.

But Omen wasn't in his dorm room. Omen was in Dublin. Omen was skipping school.

Auger skipped school all the time and, now that she was a part of the team, so did Never. They were all off somewhere today and nobody knew where, and the teachers just sighed and shrugged and carried on. It was Chosen One business, they reckoned. Auger never got in trouble for it.

Omen wondered if he would.

He made it to the Spire on O'Connell Street and waited. Three o'clock came and went and there was no sign of Colleen. He started to worry. If Abyssinia had found out that they were planning on leaving, he didn't want to think what she'd do to them. The last time someone tried to leave, Jenan had pushed her to her death. He probably wouldn't hesitate to kill the others, too.

And then he saw Colleen on the other side of the road. She stared at him as he crossed over. Kept staring as he neared.

"You came," she said, when he was standing in front of her.

"Of course," Omen said. "I told you I would."

"I just... oh, I don't know. I'm not used to anyone coming through for me, I suppose. Do you have the papers?"

"Yep," Omen said, reaching for his bag.

"Not here!" Colleen said, eyes widening in alarm. "This way. Come on."

She started walking. Omen shrugged, and followed.

They didn't talk as they walked. Colleen made sure to stay ahead of him, probably so that no one would think they were together. Omen didn't know a whole lot about this sort of stuff, but he reckoned that was probably smart.

They turned on to a smaller street. There was a door open ahead of them and in they went, into the back of some restaurant. There was nobody else around.

"We should be safe here," Colleen said, turning to him. She gave a little laugh. "Oh, God, you probably thought I was leading you into a trap, didn't you? *Here, come, follow me away from everyone else where you'd be safe and step into an empty kitchen where we'll spring our ambush!*"

He laughed along with her, slightly annoyed that this had never crossed his mind.

"So," Colleen said, "the papers?"

He handed over the bag. "They're not too bad, actually. I think if I had this kind of pressure with all my classes, I wouldn't have to cheat so much. So what now? Are you all going to sneak away at the same time, or leave one by one?"

"Ah, we haven't really decided."

"Do you think you'll get away without anyone noticing?"

Colleen shrugged.

"Aren't you going to check the papers?" Omen asked. "I mean, I appreciate the faith you seem to have in me, but my forgeries have not been the best in the past."

"I'm sure they're fine," said Colleen.

They stood there, and Omen began to feel uneasy.

"Well," he said, "you'd probably better get going before anyone becomes suspicious. If you need anything else, just let me know, OK?"

"There is one more thing," Colleen said. "It's... it's kind of embarrassing, but this might be the last time I ever see you, so if I can't say this now then when can I? I... love you, Omen. I'm in love with you."

"What?"

"I've loved you for years."

"Sorry?"

"You're all I've ever wanted."

"Who is?"

"And I know I was horrible to you, and I said horrible things, but that's just because I was afraid of my feelings for you."

"Pardon?"

"I don't expect you to love me back."

"Huh?"

"But I need you to know this."

"Me?"

"I love you."

He blinked at her. "Really?"

She nodded, then stopped nodding and laughed. "No, not really. Damn, I couldn't keep that going. Wouldn't it have been, like, a twist? If I did actually love you?"

He laughed along with her, although he wasn't exactly sure why. "I suppose," he said.

Colleen put a hand on his arm, as if to steady him. "I don't love you, though."

"Yeah, I understood that."

"I could never love you."

"Well, OK."

"I hate you."

"Um."

"You're a waste of space. I have literally never seen the point of you. Your brother, absolutely. But you? Why do you even exist? You just bumble around in the background, and you're barely noticeable until you *are* noticed, and then you're just, like, everywhere, like a bad extra in a movie who you can't take your eyes off because they're literally so annoying."

"Right," Omen said quietly.

Colleen burst out laughing again. "I'm joking! Oh my God, the look on your face! I'm only joking, Omen!"

"Ha," he responded, managing a weak smile.

"I'm sorry, that was mean. That was very, very mean. But I was kidding. I don't think any of those things. No one else would have done what you've done for us. No one else would have risked it. Sincerely and genuinely, thank you."

"Well, you know, no problem."

"I bet no one else would have even believed me," she continued. "Especially after I insisted that you'd have to forge the papers without telling your friends or the people you trust. Anyone else but you, Omen, would have suspected that something was up, right then and there. They'd have thought, *Oh, hold on, Colleen's asking me to do this stuff just so I'd agree to meet her outside Roarhaven. Where I'm alone. And vulnerable. I'd better not do it because, like, I'm not stupid.* That's what anyone else but you would think, Omen."

She wasn't smiling any more. Neither was Omen.

"I should go," he said.

"Could I have a goodbye hug?"

She opened her arms, and waited.

He didn't step towards her. "I should probably just head back."

"Just one little hug?"

"I'm not much of a hugger."

"Please?"

He looked around. They were still alone.

"I wasn't being serious," she said.

"I know."

342

"Ah-ah," she said, grinning. "I didn't say which part I wasn't being serious about. Which do you think it was? Do you think I wasn't being serious about the leading you into a trap part, or the other part?"

"I'm, uh, I'm not sure. I'm getting kind of confused."

Colleen nodded. "You are quite dim. Will I tell you?"

Omen stepped back. "You know what? I'm just going to leave. Good luck with everything, and say hi to the others for me."

She dropped her arms, and looked hurt. "Dude, I'm only messing with you. I didn't mean to, like, make you uneasy or whatever."

"No," Omen said, smiling again. "You didn't make me uneasy."

"I'm such an idiot. You do all this to help us and what do I do in return? I mess with your head. I'm sorry, Omen. I hope I do see you again, but, if I don't, thank you so much for this. You are, literally, saving our lives." She took out her phone, checked the time, and put it away again. "I have to go. When all this is over, will you tell our friends that we had nothing to do with the bad stuff that's going to happen?"

"What bad stuff?"

"I... I can't tell you. The more you know, the more dangerous it'd be for you."

"Colleen, please. If people are going to get hurt, I need to know."

Tears glistened in her eyes. "So many people are going to get hurt."

"Then tell me. Right now, before you go. Tell me, and I can tell Skulduggery and Valkyrie and they can go and stop it. You'll be saving lives, Colleen."

Colleen chewed her lip.

"You chose to go with Abyssinia," Omen said. "You chose to be on the wrong side, but you changed your mind. You saw where all this was headed and you realised you wanted nothing to do with it. But this? This is your chance to be on the right side. This is your chance to do something to help people."

Colleen sniffed, and wiped her eyes. "Help people," she echoed. "That's kind of a new one for me. You probably hadn't noticed this, but usually I'm actually pretty selfish. Help people, eh? That does sound... nice. Is that the word? *Nice?* Wait a minute... I'm feeling something, something inside. Something warm. Is this..." She looked up. "Is this what it feels like to be good?"

Oh, crap. This was a trap.

He spun for the door just as Jenan Ispolin stepped through. "Hello, moron," he said.

66

Omen got out.

He didn't know how, but he got out of the restaurant, and Jenan was bleeding from his nose and shouting and running after him and this narrow little street suddenly seemed very, very long.

Lapse burst out of a doorway ahead, laughing like they were in the middle of the best prank ever. His hands were glowing. A burst of energy shot out, hit Omen in the shoulder. The impact spun him, nearly made him fall, but Lapse had never been a particularly good Energy Thrower. He'd never been able to focus enough to give his blasts much power. Two more bursts followed, each weaker than the last. Omen didn't even bother trying to dodge them as he ran. They exploded against his back with all the force of a half-hearted slap.

A year ago, Omen wouldn't have had a chance of outrunning Jenan, but he wasn't the short little ball of podge that he'd once been. All those aches, all those growing pains, had brought with them longer limbs, and the longer limbs helped even out his weight. He wasn't particularly fast, but he wasn't especially slow, either.

And then Gall came from nowhere and barged into him, slamming him against the brick wall. Omen dodged a ridiculous spinning back fist and grabbed him, twisting and throwing him into Jenan's path. They fell over each other, cursing, and Omen went to run on, but the air smacked into him, threw him sideways. He rolled through filth and broken crates.

Colleen strode up, fire in both hands and a smile on her face. The others were coming from the other direction, blocking his escape route. Omen snatched up a heavy piece of wood and hurled it. It spun as it went. He didn't expect it to actually hit Colleen but it actually did, smacking her diagonally across the face. She went down, howling, and Omen leaped over her and ran back the way he'd come. There were shouts from behind. Panic. He was going to escape.

And then Mr Lilt stepped out, waving his hand, and Omen flew backwards. He hit the ground and rolled, tried to get up, but the air was pressing down on him, impossibly heavy. Omen stopped fighting and lay there, struggling to breathe.

First Wave crowded round him.

"There are seven of you," Lilt said, his voice quiet. "Seven of the most ruthless students I could find in Corrival Academy. Seven. And you couldn't stop one measly, insignificant little nobody. You couldn't stop Omen Darkly."

No one in First Wave responded.

"I thought I'd recruited the best and the brightest," Lilt continued. "I assured Lethe, I assured Abyssinia, that the students I had picked were destined for greatness. They were worthy to stand by our side in the war to come. But to look at you now, as you scramble and flail and panic in your attempts to apprehend quite possibly the worst student I have ever had the misfortune to teach... I am disappointed. I am dismayed. He has made a fool of you, and I am ashamed to be your teacher."

The pressure keeping Omen down vanished, and he gasped in relief.

"Pick him up," Lilt said. "Try at least to do *that* right."

67

Valkyrie was feeling good.

She'd slept like the dead for close to twenty hours, and woken to a dozen missed calls and Militsa banging on her front door. She couldn't answer half of the questions that she'd been bombarded with – she only had a vague memory of finding the soul fragment, and couldn't remember at all how she'd left the Necropolis. All she knew was that when she got home she must have fed the dog and opened the music box, because it was still playing when Militsa arrived.

And now she was driving into Roarhaven, singing along to the radio and waving at Cleavers as she passed.

She'd done it. She had everything she needed to fix her sister. The Soul Catcher was safely tucked away in the secret room, back in Grimwood House. According to Doctor Nye, all she had to do was break it near to where Alice lay and the fragments would find her and sort themselves out.

And then Valkyrie was going to take some time off.

Nobody knew how Alice was going to react to having a fully functioning soul again, so Valkyrie needed to be there for her, for whatever she needed. Skulduggery would understand. He'd partner up with Temper again, and they'd handle this Crepuscular Vies thing and this Abyssinia thing and, by the time Valkyrie was ready to come back, everything would be cool.

She parked underneath the High Sanctuary. She had intended to head straight up, but instead went to the back of the car. The boot sprang open. The music box sat there, nestled in her gym bag. She opened the lid.

That tune, smoothing out her thoughts, hushing all her anxieties... She didn't know what she'd ever done without it, she really didn't.

Valkyrie shook her head, and laughed to herself. She couldn't just stand here all day. She had people to talk to. She closed the lid, then took off her jacket and draped it over the box. It was always the perfect temperature in the High Sanctuary.

She took the whirling, twirling tiles up to the foyer. Skulduggery wasn't there and she couldn't see Cerise so she told the guy at the huge marble desk that the Supreme Mage was expecting her, and off she went, wandering towards the elevators.

China and Skulduggery were supposed to be in the Room of Prisms, with all those wonderfully shiny slivers of glass that hung from the ceiling. And the throne, of course. But they weren't.

"Hello?" Valkyrie called out. Nope. No one.

She grinned.

Quickly, she climbed the steps and sat on the throne. Nice view from up here. All those slivers of glass made it impossible for anyone to sneak up. Kind of a paranoid feature, but China didn't get where she was today by embracing a casual lifestyle.

Valkyrie dug into her pocket for her phone to send a selfie to Militsa – then remembered that her phone, and her wallet and her amulet, were in her jacket, back in the car. She shrugged, got up and left the room, nodding to the Cleavers standing guard on the other side.

She finally found someone who would answer a simple question, and was told that Skulduggery and China had been last seen strolling along one of the corridors.

She found them, deep in conversation, and ran up.

"Sorry I'm late," she said, smiling.

China raised an eyebrow. "Tardiness is not like you – but Skulduggery tells me you've been quite busy lately on a personal project."

"I have," Valkyrie said. "But it's just about finished now."

"That is good news," said China, "because I'm going to need all your focus, I'm afraid. Both of you."

"You have *another* case for us to work on?" Skulduggery asked. "We're not even finished with the one we have now."

"I'm sure you can handle one more," China said. "I need you to find a traitor in our ranks."

Valkyrie made a face. "We have a new traitor? After Tipstaff? This is getting silly. If you can't trust a sprawling organisation full of centuries-old killers, then who *can* you trust, I ask you?"

China didn't react – not even an unamused twitch of one of her perfect eyebrows. She was angry. She was, in fact, furious. It was a cold fury, and it radiated outwards. Valkyrie could feel it from where she stood. Not even Skulduggery seemed to appreciate the joke. He hadn't even reacted.

"What did this traitor do?" Valkyrie asked, trying to be more serious.

"They passed top-secret information to the enemy," China replied. "Beyond top secret. The good news is that the suspect list will be short. There is a very limited number of people who even know Greymire Asylum *exists*, never mind where it is."

Valkyrie's good mood vanished.

"What happened?" Skulduggery asked quietly.

"Caisson and Abyssinia broke into the place," said China, "and left with one of the patients."

"Who?"

"You don't need to know that."

"If we don't have all the facts—"

"Just find the traitor!" China snapped, then immediately calmed herself. "That's all you need to do. Who they set free is not relevant. I'll give you whatever resources you need, but you have to—"

"It was me," Valkyrie said.

China turned to her slowly. "What?"

"They took the old woman in the tower, didn't they? In K-49."

China's blue eyes travelled from Valkyrie to Skulduggery and back again.

Valkyrie stood up straighter. "I'm sorry."

"You're sorry," China said softly.

"Skulduggery had nothing to do with it," Valkyrie said. He started to protest, but she cut him off. "Skulduggery, no. It was my decision."

A strand of China's hair fell out of place and brushed lightly across her forehead. "You're sorry," she repeated.

"Caisson had information I needed," Valkyrie said. "He promised me he would free one patient and only one, and that no one would be hurt. Was anyone hurt?"

China shook her head.

"Good," said Valkyrie. "I'm sorry, China. I am. I knew the location was supposed to be kept a secret, but I didn't have any other choice. I'm prepared to accept whatever punishment you hand out."

China nodded, pressed a point on the back of her hand. A sigil glowed briefly on her skin, then faded, and two Cleavers appeared.

China looked at them, then at Valkyrie. "Arrest her."

They came forward and took hold of Valkyrie's arms. Skulduggery stepped in to push them away.

"Don't," Valkyrie said. "Skulduggery, please."

He hesitated, then backed off as the shackles locked round her wrists. Her magic dulled. The world got smaller.

"China," he said, "you can't do this. You've fought beside her. You know she'd never do anything like this unless she absolutely had to."

China ignored him. "Get her out of my sight," she said, and they hauled Valkyrie away.

68

Mr Lilt didn't say anything as he brought Omen before Abyssinia. Omen was glad about that. It went against his nature to curse at a teacher, but with Lilt he reckoned he would have made an exception.

Abyssinia stood in the control room, looking out on to Coldheart Prison with her back to them.

"I have him," Lilt announced. "First Wave were underwhelming in their—"

Lilt suddenly groaned, his hands going to his head. Omen watched as he paled, as his legs buckled, as he fell to his knees.

"I am vexed," Abyssinia said without turning. "I am... irked. One might even go so far as to say I am irate."

Lilt curled up into a moaning, groaning ball. Omen would have run off if there was anywhere to run off to.

Abyssinia turned. "You. Boy. Do you know the American president?"

Omen wasn't trying to be cheeky, but even so he found himself saying, "Personally?"

Abyssinia didn't explode his brain. She just looked at him without really looking at him. "Do you know *of* him?"

"Yes."

"Thoughts?"

"He... doesn't come across as a very nice man."

"He's not," Abyssinia said. "He's not a very nice man at all. I want to kill him. Usually, when I want to kill someone, I kill them and immediately feel better. But he needs to stay alive in order to do what I tell him. That annoys me."

Right then, that precise moment, was not the time to be an amateur detective. Asking clumsy questions would only get him killed. And yet, Omen knew, if Skulduggery or Valkyrie or Auger were in his position, they'd find some clever way of interrogating Abyssinia without her even realising it.

"What did you tell him to do?" Omen asked.

That was a mistake. He knew that immediately. Abyssinia's gaze flickered and she noticed him now.

"You were there," she said, "in Cadaverous Gant's house, when I found my son."

"I was," said Omen, giving a nervous smile. "How is he? Is he feeling better?"

She ignored him, and Lilt got up slowly.

"Apologies, Abyssinia," he said. "I should not have walked in unannounced. I merely wished to bring the boy. I shall now take him to his cell."

Abyssinia didn't respond, and Lilt grabbed Omen and dragged him out. It gave Omen a little burning nugget of satisfaction, deep in his soul, to have seen his self-important teacher being dismissed so casually.

They went down some steps and across one of the tiers. Omen peeked over the edge. It was a long way down.

Lilt threw him into a cell and closed the door and walked away without speaking.

Omen took out his phone.

"You really think it'd be that easy?" Jenan said, appearing on the other side of the bars. He was wearing a black uniform and polished black boots. "Hand it over, fatso."

"I'm not fat."

"Hand it over, or I'll call you worse names than that."

Omen hesitated, but he finally gave his phone to Jenan.

"Oh, this is a nice one," Jenan said. "This is a really good one," and then he tossed it over his shoulder and it dropped behind the barrier and fell all the way down.

Omen sagged. All his contacts were in that phone.

"How scared are you feeling right now?" Jenan asked. "You must be terrified. Petrified. Your little mind must be racing with all the terrible things we're probably going to do to you." He leaned his head against the bars. "See, I did want to kill you. I mean, that's all I wanted. But then I realised there are way worse things to do to you than just, like, ending your suffering."

Omen shook his head. "Why me, man?"

"You interfered," said Jenan. "You spied on us."

"No," Omen said, "I mean before that. Before all this. What did I ever do to you that made you hate me so much?"

"You existed."

"That's it? That's your sole motivation? You were a bully and I was your victim?"

"You're everyone's victim, Darkly. You're weak and pathetic and pointless. You're a pointless person."

"And there's nothing more to it than that?"

Jenan sneered. "There doesn't have to be."

"I suppose not. Though it is kind of disappointing."

"I wouldn't worry about it, if I were you. You've got other things to think about. You like movies, don't you?"

"Uh... sure."

"You know in movies, when there's a twist at the end that you don't see coming? Like, *Oh my God, I can't believe he was the bad guy all along!*, that kind of thing? Well, there's a twist coming for you, too. Want to know what it is?"

"Wouldn't that spoil the twist?"

Jenan laughed. "The twist's not for you, you idiot. It's for everyone else. But it's funnier if *you* know it ahead of time, because then you get to think about it, and fully absorb what it means before it actually happens. So do you want to know Abyssinia's big plan?"

"Sure."

Jenan's grin got wider. "OK, cool. So, this whole thing, right, is about a war. Abyssinia wants to start a war between sorcerers and mortals and then, basically, rule the world. With me so far, Darkly?"

"I'm just about managing to keep up, yes."

"Good boy. She's got Martin Flanery involved in this, too. Or he thinks he's involved. From what I've heard, he's got no idea what's in store for him, but I don't really care about any of that. I care about how this all starts. Tell me, Darkly, do you want to know how the war is going to start?"

"Sure."

"It starts with us," said Jenan, tapping his chest. "First Wave. We're going to do a whole new Pearl Harbour."

"What?"

"Pearl Harbour," said Jenan. "You remember Pearl Harbour, right? It was one of Mr Lilt's favourite topics to teach. Good God, Darkly, were you not paying attention to *anything* in school?"

Omen shrugged. "It just didn't seem relevant."

"Well," said Jenan, "it's relevant now. Do you know what World War Two was? You remember being told about that? See, the war was going on, but America was staying out of it. The American people just weren't motivated enough to get involved, you know? Then the Japanese targeted an American naval base in Pearl Harbour. Surprise attack. Sank ships, killed loads... They even made a movie about it. It's great. Anyway, this riled up the American people so much that the USA finally joined the war effort. And that's what we're going to do."

Omen stared. "Abyssinia is going to attack Pearl Harbour?"

"Not Pearl Harbour, you moron. It doesn't have to actually *be* Pearl Harbour to be *another* Pearl Harbour."

"I don't... I don't understand."

Jenan sighed. "You're so incredibly dumb. You make me dumber just by talking to you. Nero's going to teleport us to another American naval base, OK? Naval Magazine Whitley is a small base in Oregon, with only two dozen mortals stationed there – and we're going to kill them all. Isn't that cool? It's going to be... I mean, I don't know how to describe it. It's going to be amazing. It's going to be the best night of my life. Can you imagine it?"

Jenan's eyes were alive with the thought. They gleamed.

"This'll be... this will change the world. The mortals are going to have camera footage of evil young people with horrifying powers killing their proud soldiers and sailors like they were nothing... And, you know, they'll have *you*."

Jenan leered. "They'll have *you*, Omen. You'll be wearing our uniform, but you'll have been injured by one of their soldiers so, unfortunately, we'll have to leave you behind. Maybe I'll be the one who gets to shoot you. I hope it's me. I've asked, and Mr Lilt said yes, but you know how things go. Anyway – that's the twist. We frame you.

"Isn't that cool? You get hauled away by the mortals and for a few days they have a real-life sorcerer to photograph, and maybe do some really painful tests on – and then we'll teleport in and kill you when you're alone in your jail cell. Providing the mortals haven't beaten you to death by then, which is a real possibility.

"So then America will, like, go nuts. And the rest of the world will go nuts. And, when the panic rises to the perfect level, President Flanery will discover where the American Sanctuaries are – and he'll bomb the crap out of them." Jenan's voice quivered with excitement. "He's going to bomb his own country. He's, like, already agreed to it. Can you believe it? It's going to be *insane*."

"And that's the big plan," Omen said quietly.

"That's it. And you play such a big part in it. Until the war kicks off, you will be the most famous person in the world. The most hated person in the world."

69

Valkyrie sat and waited. The shackles were on too tight. They chafed her wrists and bit into her ankles. She'd only been a criminal for a few hours and already she was hating it.

A door beeped. She watched Skulduggery come in. He sat on the other side of the glass. This was just like in the movies, except they didn't need phones to talk.

"I need to get out of here," she said.

His head tilted. "You're the one who confessed."

"Yeah, because my whole life people have been telling me that honesty is the best policy, but guess what?"

"People lied to you."

"People lied to me. If I'd known she'd throw me in a jail cell, I wouldn't have said anything. Why didn't you stop me?"

"This is my fault?"

"You should have interrupted me or distracted me or kicked my shin or something. I didn't know how mad she'd be. I've never seen her that angry. Well, I've never seen her that angry at *me*. Can you talk to her? I need to get out of here. I'm *this* close to fixing Alice."

"China isn't really speaking to me at the moment. I'll talk to her tomorrow. Can you spend a night here?"

"Skulduggery—"

"Just one night. I'll talk to her when she's calmed down, and

I'll convince her. You have my word. Then you can fix Alice. OK? I promise."

"You're certain you can convince her?"

"Fletcher's going to teleport me to America first thing in the morning. Tanith and Oberon have found where Blackbrook operate from. I'm going to join them and we're going to get some answers, so I'll be able to approach China with real, concrete results. I'll tell her I need you by my side. She's angry, yes, but she's not going to keep you locked up out of spite."

"OK," Valkyrie said. "That sounds like it might work."

"Just one night," Skulduggery said. "That's all."

Her cell wasn't that bad, all things considered.

It was clean. It had a desk, screwed to the wall. The mattress was thin but fine. The pillow was new. The toilet was uncomfortable, but she could handle that.

Valkyrie lay there, in the dark. She wasn't wearing the shackles that bound her magic any more, but they'd put a metal bracelet around her wrist that did the same job.

She was getting worried. She hadn't been able to listen to the music box since she'd parked. Right now, she was fine. No voices, no panicking. No Ghastly. No Nemesis of Greymire.

She just needed to stay like this. To stay calm. To fall asleep. That wasn't too much to ask. She'd been falling asleep all her life, for God's sake. She was good at it. And tomorrow Skulduggery would convince China to let her out and she could go straight to her car and open that music box. And then she could heal her sister.

The problem was she'd been lying here for hours. She didn't know how long exactly, but she guessed that it must have been around two in the morning. And the more she stayed awake, the more her mind churned. And a churning mind was not a calm mind. If she didn't fall asleep soon, she was going to start to panic, and, if she started to panic, Ghastly would appear, and if Ghastly appeared—

She took a deep breath. *No. Calm down. Calm down.*

She heard footsteps and she felt her face go cold and she sat up.

She listened as they got closer, and she relaxed. Too many footsteps. She laughed to herself. Unless Ghastly had brought along a bunch of imaginary friends, that wasn't him.

The footsteps stopped outside her door. A key rattled in the lock.

He'd done it. Skulduggery had done it. She was getting out already.

The door opened and Sergeant Yonder stepped in.

Valkyrie didn't get it. She didn't get how he could be standing there with his hands on his hips, wearing his City Guard uniform and a smile.

"They reinstated me," he said. "Commander Hoc called me himself, said the City Guard was understaffed, and needed good people like me. The Supreme Mage was forced to take me back." He laughed. "That's your friend, isn't it? The Supreme Mage? Or she *was* your friend. But she's thrown you away, hasn't she? You're a traitor now. An enemy of Roarhaven."

Valkyrie realised what was about to happen. It made her mouth dry. Her heart beat so hard she could feel it in her wrists.

"You're not so chatty now," Yonder continued. "When you were arresting me, you were all chat. You wouldn't shut up, would you, you and the skeleton? You had your witty banter thing going on. Has anyone ever told you how annoying it is to listen to that? It's like you think you're the king and queen of your own little world, and the rest of us are just here to stand around and listen to how smug you both are. Where are your jokes, Cain? Huh? Where are they? Where's the arrogance now that you're in a cell without your magic or your horror-show partner to back you up?"

He perched on the edge of the desk. "Nothing to say? That's disappointing. I told all my friends how chatty you were. You're going to make me look bad."

More City Guards came in. Valkyrie recognised two of them

from the arrest at the mortal shop – Lush and Rattan. The other man she didn't know. They all held shock sticks – like the ones Valkyrie used but bigger. Heavier. Lush handed Yonder a stick of his very own.

Valkyrie stood up slowly. It was coming. It was inevitable. There was nothing she could do to stop it from happening, and nothing she could do to defend herself. They were going to beat her. They weren't going to kill her – that would be going too far, even for them. But beating her... that was just far enough.

There was no chance she could talk her way out of it, and no chance they'd have mercy. In a way, it had already happened. That made her feel better, knowing it had already happened. It allowed her to detach.

"Careful," Yonder warned with a smile. "Any move we deem potentially aggressive shall be met with reasonable force."

His friends laughed at the *reasonable* part.

"If you're going to do it," Valkyrie said, "do it."

Yonder lost his smile. "What'd you say? What was that, Prisoner Cain?"

She wanted to repeat it, but her mouth was too dry.

He came closer. "Are you challenging my authority, Prisoner Cain?"

He jabbed his stick into her belly. It hurt, made her step back. He hadn't shocked her, though. That was coming.

"You'd better watch yourself," he continued. "Down here, we are the only law that means anything. If you upset us, we upset you. You don't want to upset us, do you?"

Maybe she deserved what was about to happen. She'd been given a choice, after all, and she'd chosen to betray the High Sanctuary. She thought maybe she'd be given a slap on the wrist. She hadn't thought she'd be shackled. Maybe she should have.

What had she learned in the last few years if not that her actions had consequences? What had she learned if not that she possibly deserved those consequences?

Valkyrie looked at them, Yonder and his little gang of eager thugs, as they lit up their shock sticks. She watched them shift their weight, narrow their eyes, and grip the weapons tighter. Their adrenaline was coursing. Their hearts were beating faster. Violence was but a moment away. They were athletes at the starting blocks, their bodies ready to spring forward. All they needed was the starting pistol.

Valkyrie licked her lips, got some moisture back into her mouth, and then she said, "Let's be having you."

Yonder swung first. The stick connected with her skull and the world flashed white and the only reason she didn't fall was because her legs were too stupid to get the message. The others crowded round as she stumbled back against the wall. Their sticks left crackling blurs in the air as they swung. She felt ribs break. Every touch jolted her into a new position that she was immediately punished for. Someone, she thought it might have been Lush, broke her jaw. She swallowed blood. She swallowed teeth. Her knee buckled – broken? – and she fell. Their boots came for her, then. She curled. More ribs broke. Her cheekbone shattered. Shock sticks rammed into her side and she screamed, arching her back, giving them more targets. They beat her until they couldn't touch her any more, until she fell into endless night. She didn't know what happened after that.

70

Omen sat and worried.

The prison buzzed outside his cell. Convicts looked in as they passed, cracked jokes, made threats, laughed about it and clapped each other on the back as they moved on.

Omen didn't answer any of them. He just sat on the bed, knees drawn in, and did his very, very best not to cry.

A big man came up to the bars and looked in.

"Oh, God," said Omen.

The big man sniffed. "Remember me, do you?" he asked. He had a cold.

Omen stood up. "You're Immolation Joe."

"Last time I saw you," said Immolation Joe, "I asked you to let me out of my cell. You were worried that I might kill you. Because of my name. And the fact that I kill people. I asked you to let me out, but you kept saying no." He paused to blow his nose. "The thing is," he said, "you were right not to. I wasn't ready to be released. Abyssinia, she released all of us a little bit later, and since then I've killed seven people."

"Please don't kill me."

Immolation Joe frowned. "Why would you think I'd kill you? Why would you automatically assume that I'd do that? There's more to me than killing. There's more to all of us than the things we like to do. I have facets, kid. *Facets*."

"I'm... I'm sorry."

"I mean, I *could* do it. There's a part of me that wants to." He clicked his fingers and stared into the flames that danced in his palm. "I'd love to just... set you on fire. I love setting things on fire." He quashed the flame. "But they've got plans for you, haven't they? Abyssinia and whoever?"

"I... I think so."

The big man grunted. "So I really shouldn't kill you. I know I shouldn't. They'd kill *me* if I did, you know? What'd that be? Would that be ironic?"

"Maybe," said Omen, though he seriously doubted it.

Immolation Joe looked away for a few seconds, and sniffed again. "I'm considering leaving," he said.

"You are?"

He nodded. "This isn't for me. Being part of an army and all? I wasn't born to take orders or to carry out... *plans*. I'm just a guy who likes to burn people. Abyssinia and that lot, they want to rule the world – but where do I fit in? If we do end up ruling the world, where am I going to be in the hierarchy? Am I going to be at the top, sitting on a throne being fed grapes, or am I going to be scurrying around with a whip somewhere, scaring the mortals and making sure they carry rocks or build pyramids?"

"Probably the pyramid thing," said Omen.

"Yeah," said Immolation Joe, "that's what I think, too." Another sniff. "I like the world the way it is. I don't hate mortals – not any more than I hate most sorcerers anyway. I eat the food they make, I watch their movies, I drive their cars. Why would I want to do anything that'd mess that up?"

"Do you think there are others like you?"

"Who are considering leaving? Yeah, probably. No one talks about it, though. Most of them, they try not to even *think* about it, what with Abyssinia being able to read their minds."

"Maybe you could, um, form a club or something."

Immolation Joe frowned at him. "Why?"

"So you could talk about it. And, if there were enough of you, maybe you could approach Abyssinia with your concerns. Like a trade union."

"Huh."

"We kind of had a trade union in school," Omen said. "Well, I wasn't involved, but some others formed a student council, and went to Principal Rubic with a list of things they'd like changed."

"How'd that go?"

"Some things were changed, I think. A little."

Immolation Joe blew his nose again, and examined the contents of his handkerchief before putting it away. "Ah, I don't know, kid," he said. "Something like that'd only draw attention to me and make it harder to leave. Besides, everyone's buzzing about the Sanctuary thing right now. There's no talking to them."

"What Sanctuary thing?"

"Just a thing," said Immolation Joe, and Omen didn't press it. "So, yeah, I reckon I'll just split. But, before I do, I owe you something."

Omen's stomach went cold. "You do?"

Immolation Joe nodded. "I asked you to let me out, and, even though I wasn't ready, you still opened my cell door."

Omen blinked. "That's right," he said. "I did."

"And I appreciated that," Immolation Joe said. "Even though it was by accident, and even though Temper Fray kicked me back in, you did let me out. So, I guess, thank you."

"Uh, you're welcome. Are you going to let me out now?"

"Yep."

"Are you going to help me get off the island?"

"Nope. I'm already doing enough for you by letting you out and not burning you alive. I'm not a charity, kid." He nodded to Omen. "Good luck." He walked away, and a moment later the cell door clunked slightly as the lock retracted.

The binding seal broke instantly, and Omen felt his magic

363

return. His first instinct was to throw open the door and run, but he had nowhere to run to. He stood there, beside the bunk, trying to imagine what Auger would do in this situation. It was obvious, really. Auger would find a way to turn the tables on the bad guys and either call for help or just take them all down single-handedly. The second option was out of the question for Omen, so that left him with the first. Call for help. Unfortunately, he didn't have his phone, and there was no other way to...

His eyes widened.

He sat on the edge of the bunk, startled by the very fact that something he'd learned in school might actually come in useful, and he did his best to empty his mind. It wasn't easy in a prison, and each time he'd get close a random thought would blurt its way across his consciousness.

He did what Miss Wicked had taught them, though, and focused on his brother's name and repeated it in his head, over and over again. He pictured Auger's face. His breathing deepened. His brow furrowed.

After ten minutes, he stopped, his head aching and his ears ringing. He waited until the pain receded a little, then closed his eyes and tried again.

Immediately there was a rush of thoughts inside his head and he latched on to something, someone, far away in the darkness.

"Auger?" he whispered. "Auger, can you hear me?"

For a moment there was nothing – and then a voice screamed in his head –

OMENWHATISTHISYOUOMEN?

– and Omen hissed in pain, the words vibrating off his very skull as he fell sideways off the bunk and he lost it, he lost the connection.

Then he heard footsteps. Slow footsteps, and a tune being whistled. 'Flowers in Your Hair'. He stood quickly.

A man with long grey hair came into view, dressed in jeans and a ripped T-shirt, with tattoos all over his arms. He had another tattoo over the lower half of his face – a grotesquely grinning mouth. His real mouth, his *actual* mouth, was also grinning.

"I know you," he said.

Omen knew him, too, from Never's description. Mr Glee, the serial killer from San Francisco. Omen was suddenly all too aware that the door between them was unlocked.

"How is she?" Mr Glee asked. "The girl I had a tussle with?"

Omen tried to answer but couldn't.

"I think about her, you know. I think about her a lot. The one that got away." He shrugged. "I'm sure we'll meet again, though. Life moves in circles, does it not?"

Mr Glee shrugged, went to move away – then turned, reached over and shut the door. It clicked and Omen's magic left him.

Whistling, Mr Glee moved on.

71

Valkyrie woke without opening her eyes.

Her body ached. Her face felt swollen. She breathed tiny daggers into shallow lungs. She was badly damaged and lying on a thin mattress, and she was cold.

Beyond the darkness were the sounds of the uninjured world. Voices and machines and phones ringing.

She opened her right eye. Her left wouldn't open.

The ceiling was cracked. The light was a boulder that rolled into her head and crashed around her skull. She closed her eye, waited for the boulder to settle before opening it again.

She saw wires and tubes. A curtain.

Her tongue was thick and heavy. She probed the inside of her mouth, felt the broken teeth. She remembered losing a tooth years ago, having it knocked out. She remembered she'd cried about it.

Her jaw was wired shut.

Valkyrie lay there, not moving, trying not to panic, trying not to feel like she was trapped in a broken body. She closed her eyes and pictured the farm back in Colorado. She pictured the mountains. The sky. She calmed herself, using all the tricks Coda had taught her.

Minutes passed and kept passing. Perhaps they became an hour.

The curtain was pulled back. A doctor loomed over her, tapping the machines that beeped, ignoring her in favour of the screens. He was thin. He looked hassled and unhappy. He'd missed a spot shaving, right at the hinge of his jaw.

He noticed her looking at him, and took a moment, like he was deciding whether or not he should speak.

"My name is Doctor Whorl," he said at last. "You arrived here early this morning. Apparently, you'd fallen down in your cell. This fall resulted in four broken ribs, one fractured zygomatic bone, a fractured patella, a fractured eye socket, a punctured lung, breaks in your jaw, your tibia, your..." He sighed. "You have sixteen broken or fractured bones. You have internal injuries. You've lost teeth. You have first-degree burns on your back, chest, sides and legs. You are being treated for all of this, and, thanks to the wonders of modern technology and ancient magic, you'll be able to return to your cell late this afternoon."

Someone called him, someone Valkyrie couldn't see, and he nodded, but before he left he looked down at Valkyrie again.

"I know you're not Darquesse," he said, his voice quiet. "I know you didn't kill all those people. I know it wasn't you who destroyed half the city." He leaned down. "But she was a part of you. So a part of you killed all those people six years ago, and a part of you destroyed half the city, and a part of you killed my friends. So I will do my job, Prisoner Cain, but I will do it slowly. I will mend your broken bones one at a time, and you will have nothing to dull the pain. I want you to suffer, you see. And I happen to know that you will. I happen to know that you're going to be falling down in your cell again tonight. So I'll see you back here tomorrow."

Then he straightened up, and walked away.

72

On the top of a hill on this alien planet, by a jagged outcrop of rock, Sebastian Tao found Darquesse.

She lay on the ground, her arms spread wide, one leg bent back at a distinctly unnatural angle. Her clothes were filthy and torn and stretched between protruding bones. Her jaw, clearly broken, hung at an angle, kept in place only by her dried and lined skin. There was so much dust in her hair that it appeared grey.

Sebastian couldn't tell how long she'd been dead. Years, maybe. He couldn't tell how she'd died, either. Her body was ravaged, obviously, but everyone knew that Darquesse had been through injuries more horrific than these. Maybe some magical disease had caused her to waste away, or some injury that not even she could heal. Or maybe she had just been beaten to death.

He lowered himself down until he was sitting beside her remains. He'd failed. He'd been sent on this mission with no way of succeeding, yet he'd failed nonetheless. Of course he had. He always failed. That was who he was. They'd placed their faith in the wrong person.

He took off his hat, lowered his head and cried.

The world was doomed. Everyone he'd ever known was doomed. The people he loved. The people he didn't. The people he'd never met and never would.

Darquesse had been the answer. The only answer. His only purpose. The only reason he'd put on this suit of loneliness, of isolation – the only reason he'd come here. It was all a waste. It was all a joke.

It was a joke, but all he could do was cry.

Sniffling, sobbing, he pushed himself up on to his knees, and pressed his hands together.

"Darquesse," he said, his voice loud in his mask, "we need you. The world needs you. We need your strength. Your power. I came here to bring you back. I don't know what to do now. I've come all this way and I don't know what to do. I... I didn't want to think about what would happen if I couldn't find you, but I never thought I'd find you and you'd be..."

Bile rose in his throat and he put out a hand to steady himself while his stomach heaved and he clamped his mouth shut. He wanted to rip the mask off. He wanted nothing more than to rip the mask off.

He could do it. He didn't know what would happen, but he could do it. What did it matter any more? He'd failed. No one would mourn him. No one would notice. Bennet, or one of the others, would maybe come looking for him eventually, but he'd be long gone by then and they could go back to their lives. Their sad little lives.

But what could he do? What could Sebastian Tao do? Where could he go? Where was there to go?

He swallowed, tasting acid, and straightened his spine. The least he could do, after all, was straighten his spine. His gloved hands rose, his gloved fingers crawling along the back of his neck, searching for the clasp.

He felt a smile, and found he was looking forward to feeling fresh air on his face. Or would he feel anything at all? There was always the possibility that the moment he undid the mask he would blink out of existence.

His fingers stopped crawling. They wouldn't move when he

commanded them. They were failing him, just as he was failing everybody else.

A shadow fell across him, and he looked up and saw a god.

It was big. The kind of big measured in skyscrapers, in mountainous peaks. It stood on two legs, its sagging grey skin mottled pink and blue. Its arms were long and triple-jointed. Its hands had three fingers and a thumb. All clawed.

From its back there sprouted the sharp, twisted bones of what may once have been wings. Spiders as big as cars scuttled on its shoulders. Its head twitched on a thick neck. The head had no eyes, no ears, no face. It just had a mouth, a dark circle rimmed with teeth.

Behind it was another one just like it. In the distance, three more.

Faceless Ones.

Not the kind Sebastian had read about. Not the kind whose appearance alone would be enough to snap his sanity. These were Faceless Ones that had taken physical form, that had channelled their power into a shell of meat and teeth. He knew this instinctively. This was a cosmic truth that some part of his mind recognised without question.

He tried to stand, but his body had grown numb. He tried to hide behind the outcrop of rock, but he couldn't even crawl. He just looked up and waited for them to notice him.

The hill shook. The very ground shook.

A woman emerged from behind a mountain, running, her footsteps like earthquakes. She was as big as the Faceless Ones, a fierce light shining through her translucent skin, through her long hair, and she crashed into the Faceless One beside the hill and gripped its wing bones, yanking it round. The spiders flew off, and the Faceless One let out a scream so loud and so sharp it threw Sebastian on to his back, his hands clutching at his ears.

The Faceless One ripped its claws through the woman's midsection and light spilled out. She ignored the wound and bit down on its neck. Its scream turned to a squeal. They staggered backwards together, locked in their embrace.

The other Faceless Ones just watched as the shining woman broke off a wing bone and used the sharp end as a dagger, stabbing and stabbing until purple blood leaked from half a dozen stomach wounds. She released the Faceless One and it stumbled and she shoved her hand into the bite on its neck. The Faceless One struggled, panicking, but all the shining woman did was plunge her hand deeper.

Then she ripped her hand back, and tore the head off the thing.

The other Faceless Ones turned, and walked away. The shining woman watched them go.

Sebastian managed to stand. He watched the light that was spilling from the woman's midsection start to fade as she healed herself.

At the same time, the Faceless One's body twitched on the ground behind her. Its neck sealed, and lengthened, and it grew a new head while the old head, the one in the woman's hand, started to grow the beginnings of what looked like a new body.

She hurled the head away from her, and the horizon swallowed it.

The rest of the Faceless One clambered to its feet. Its wounds were closed now. Its wing bone was whole again. It shuffled away and she let it go.

She couldn't be killed. Neither could they. Yet they were locked in battle.

"Darquesse!" Sebastian shouted from the hilltop.

The shining woman turned.

His heart thudding in his chest, Sebastian wished he'd thought about what to say.

"Hello," he called. "I'm from earth. The other earth, the one you're from. We need your help."

She bent over, peering at him.

"We're still alive," he said. "You didn't kill us. We made you think you did, but you didn't. We, the whole world, I mean, we need you to come back now."

The shining woman turned as she straightened, and started to walk away.

"No!" Sebastian shouted. "Please! We need you to come back! We need you!"

But one single stride had taken her far out of range of his weak, human voice, and all he could do was stare as she disappeared behind the mountain range.

The hope that had flared inside him died in an instant. Earlier, falling to his knees beside her old physical form, he had thought he could never feel worse than he did then. But to fail at a mission for which there could be no success was infinitely preferable to failing at a mission for which success was possible.

He'd failed. He'd properly failed. He'd been given the briefest of chances, but it was a chance nonetheless – and he'd squandered it. It was all his fault now. Whatever happened in the world, to the world, it was all because he'd messed up.

Yes. This was so much worse.

73

Morning time, and Tanith woke to find Skulduggery Pleasant standing over her bed.

She yelled, thrashed around and eventually settled back on her pillow.

"What the hell are you doing here?" she asked, glaring.

"I'm here to help," he told her. "While unconventional, this is still technically an Arbiter investigation."

"I mean," she said, "what are you doing in my motel room?"

"Oh. Well, I arrived and... and you weren't awake yet, so..."

"So you broke into my room?"

"I merely opened the door."

"You picked the lock."

"In order to open the door. I must admit, I was surprised I was able to. Why didn't you seal it? You can seal a door with one touch."

"Never mind why I didn't seal it. You shouldn't have picked the lock. How long have you been standing there?"

"Not long," he said. "I was sitting over there for an hour, and then I got bored so I decided to stand here until you woke."

Tanith sat up. "Skulduggery, man... you can't do that."

"Why not?"

"Because it's weird. It's frightening to wake up and see someone standing over you. How would you like it?"

"I don't sleep."

"You kind of sleep."

"I meditate."

"And how would you like it if you were meditating and then I suddenly appeared beside you?"

His head tilted. "I would be delighted to see you."

"Oh, shut up," she said. "You would not. Where's Val?"

"In jail."

"Seriously?"

"I'm feeling very positive that I'll be able to get her out later today. In the meantime, we have a job to do, yes?"

"Sure," she said. "Now get out. I'm going to take a shower."

He left the room and Tanith showered and dressed, and when she was ready to leave she grabbed her bag and opened the door and yelped in shock.

Skulduggery, standing right there, did that head tilt of his again. "Are you all right?"

"I'm peachy," she said, moving past him.

He followed. "Where are you going?"

"I'm hungry," she said. "I need breakfast."

"I'll come with you."

She turned. "No. I need food and coffee. I do not need conversation. No offence."

"Why would I be offended?"

She sighed. "I don't really know."

"You seem grumpy."

"Well, I'm not, so I don't know what to tell you."

"Were you expecting someone last night?"

"I wasn't expecting anyone," she growled. "Where's Oberon?"

"Having breakfast," Skulduggery said.

"Did you wake him up like you woke me?"

"Yes," Skulduggery said. "He was grumpy, too."

"That surprises me so much. Hold on to this, would you? I'll be out when I've eaten."

She passed him her bag, and carried on to the diner. Oberon had finished, and was paying as she walked in. He still hadn't shaved. He looked even better than he had the night before.

He gave her a smile and left, and she watched him go, then sat at a table and the waitress came over.

"Now that," the waitress said admiringly, "is a tall drink of water, you know what I mean? What can I get you, hon?"

Tanith sighed. "Coffee," she said.

They got in Oberon's car and arrived at Blackbrook base two hours later. A military compound of watchtowers and squat, functional buildings, it was cut into dense woodland, but didn't seem to have much in the way of actual people.

Skulduggery took to the air, did a quick scout around. He landed back beside them. "It appears to be deserted," he said, "apart from one building near the entrance. The security systems are inoperative. There are a few jeeps, a few transports, but everything else seems to have already been moved out – personnel included."

"So we're too late," said Oberon. "Whatever mission they're on is already underway."

"If there's someone still here," Tanith said, "we can ask them about it. We don't even have to sneak in."

So they walked right into the building near the entrance. To their right there was a desk behind bullet-resistant glass with a clerk sitting at it. In front of them were two doors – both made of reinforced steel.

The clerk frowned as they approached.

"Hello," Skulduggery said. The façade he wore had blond hair and a strange, drooping moustache.

"Who are you?" asked the clerk.

Skulduggery gave him a huge smile. "We're supposed to be here."

"What?"

"In case you were wondering if we're supposed to be here – we are. We have clearance. Proper, official clearance. What clearance level are you?"

The clerk hesitated. "I... I'm Green Level."

"Well," said Skulduggery, "we're four levels above that."

"I'm sorry, who are you?"

"Figures of authority."

The clerk reached slowly for the phone.

"Stop that right now," said Skulduggery. "I just explained to you who we are and I think I've been quite clear about the facts pertaining to our clearance levels."

"You're going to need to show me some identification," the clerk said, his hand hovering over the phone.

"Are you trying to give me an order, Corporal?"

"I'm a sergeant."

"Not for long if you keep this up."

"This is all very unusual," said the clerk. "I should check with my supervisor."

Skulduggery nodded. "I demand to see him."

"Sorry?"

"Your supervisor," Skulduggery said. "Get him down here immediately. When I walk into one of my facilities, I expect people to at least know who I am. This is ridiculous. I've never been so insulted in all my life, and neither have my friends. Have you?"

"Uh," said Tanith, "no."

"Not really," Oberon said.

"There," said Skulduggery. "So go ahead, call your supervisor. I shall be having a word. A stern word."

"OK," said the clerk, and picked up the phone.

"Wait," said Skulduggery.

"Yes?"

"Maybe I was too harsh. I do that sometimes. I overreact. I blame my upbringing. My parents didn't react very much to things

376

when I was a child, so I overcompensated. I'm still doing it to this day. What's your name, Lieutenant?"

"I'm just a sergeant, sir."

"Not for long with your attention to detail."

"My, uh, my name is Perkins, sir."

"Perkins. Like the car."

"Sir?"

"The car," said Skulduggery. "They made a car called the Perkins, didn't they? The one with all the wheels?"

"I don't think so, sir."

"Then what one am I thinking about?"

"Maybe the Ford?" Tanith suggested.

"That's not it," said Skulduggery. "It definitely sounds like Perkins. Perkins, Shmerkins, Flerkins... Hyundai! That's it! Sorry for the mix-up, Private."

"I'm a sergeant, sir."

"That's the spirit."

The clerk started dialling. "I'm calling my supervisor."

Skulduggery folded his arms and leaned his shoulder against the glass. "Good idea. Can't trust anyone these days. To be honest, I don't even know the people who came in with me. They could be anyone. Spies. Enemy agents. Assassins. Best you and me stick together, what do you say? Maybe open this door here so I can join you in there."

The clerk straightened slightly as the call was answered. "General," he said, "this is Perkins, over at the Idaho site. I have three individuals who just walked in – pretty sure they're sorcerers."

"Dammit," muttered Tanith.

"That's just rude," said Skulduggery.

"That's right, sir," said Perkins. "I'm looking at them now."

Skulduggery rapped on the glass. "You knew I was a sorcerer all along and you just let me talk. I expected more from you, Perkins, I really did."

"At once, sir," Perkins said, and hung up the phone.

"Well?" Tanith asked. "What did he say?"

"I've been ordered to leave the base," Perkins said, flicking switches, "and lock you in here."

Skulduggery shrugged. "That suits us fine. We'll be able to hunt for clues in peace."

Perkins's fingers danced over his keyboard. "I've also been authorised to release the test subjects so that they can kill you."

Skulduggery's head tilted. "I feel like this has got personal between us, Perkins."

"You're sorcerers," Perkins said, still typing. "You must be stopped by any means necessary in order to preserve our way of life."

"We don't want to interfere with your way of life," Tanith said. "We're the good guys."

"The only good sorcerer," said Perkins, "is a dead sorcerer."

The heavy doors ahead of them clicked and slid open, and soldiers came through, blinking like animals set free from a cage. They were barefoot, wore fatigues and olive-green T-shirts, and they had metal collars around their necks and sigils carved into their arms.

They saw Tanith and the others and hope flashed in their eyes. They hurried closer. Two of them had to help another who could barely stand.

"Can you help us?" the closest soldier asked. "They've been experimenting on us. Torturing us. Please, if you can just—"

The soldier caught sight of Perkins and he shrank back slightly, like he was expecting to be hurt.

"This is where I leave," Perkins said. He took out his phone and tapped on the screen as he walked for the door.

"Don't let him do that," the soldier whispered. "Please don't let him do that."

Skulduggery snapped his hand against the air and the re-inforced glass cracked into a million spiderwebs. As Perkins left through the door, he tapped the screen again, and the metal collars beeped before falling from the soldiers' necks.

Pain crossed their faces. Two of the soldiers crumpled to the floor. The soldier in front, the one who'd asked for their help, clenched his hands into fists and held them to his chest while he moaned and shook his head.

"What's happening?" Tanith asked gently, moving towards him.

He raised his head and raised his hands and she glimpsed the fresh scars that curved across his palms, palms that were now glowing from the inside. She barely had time to duck before streams of white-hot energy burst out, shredding his skin and spraying the wall with his blood. His scream was pain and rage and utter insanity.

Tanith scrambled, evading the sweep of the energy streams. The other soldiers were howling as they unleashed their magic. Tanith flipped, ran across the ceiling, following Skulduggery and Oberon over the desk and through the gap in the reinforced glass, then out the door.

"What do we do?" Tanith asked. "We can't fight them. If we fight them, we kill them, and they're not in control of themselves."

Oberon peeked back in, then jerked away to avoid an energy stream. "Who are they? They *are* sorcerers, right?"

Skulduggery shook his head. "I don't think so."

Tanith narrowed her eyes. "What do you know?"

"There's a new drug going around," he said, "called Splash. I thought it was recreational, designed to give sorcerers a hit of someone else's magic, something to make them feel good for a short while. But the Splash sigil is the same one carved into the soldiers' skin."

Tanith frowned. "So these guys are mortals? And this drug makes them into mages?"

"From the looks of things, very *unstable* mages," Skulduggery said.

They heard a car, and turned to watch Perkins speed out through the gates.

"Follow him," Skulduggery said. "The two of you. He's our only lead, and we need to know where he's going."

Tanith frowned. "What are you going to do?"

Skulduggery nodded back towards the screaming soldiers. "I'll take care of them, and contact you later."

"Come on," Tanith said to Oberon, and they ran.

74

Private Hank Mayer wasn't human any more. None of them were. Not Ramirez, not Foster, not Cruz nor Dixon.

They were pain. They were agony. Their lives burned through their hands, scorching the walls.

The people ran. The woman and the two men. Ran away from the monsters. He didn't want them to go. He wanted them to stay. He wanted them to kill him.

He'd suffered enough. They all had. He wanted someone to take the suffering away.

He was dying. The heat that was rushing out of him, it was burning up his insides. He could feel them as he staggered. His organs were liquefying. His brain was liquefying.

And yet he couldn't stop moving, couldn't stop screaming, couldn't stop hurting.

Then one of them came back. A man in a suit. He had something wrong with his face. He had a skull for a head.

Private Hank Mayer didn't care. He just wanted it to be over.

The man, the man with the skull, he understood. Private Hank Mayer knew he did. The man with the skull walked between them like he was studying them. Examining them.

When he saw that they were dying, when he saw that they were in agony, he took out his gun.

Blam, and Foster went down, and Private Hank Mayer tried waving, tried begging to be next. But *blam*, Dixon went next.

It was getting hard to see now. Private Hank Mayer's eyes were failing him.

The man with the skull aimed his gun at Cruz, who had fallen to his knees, but before he could pull the trigger Cruz screeched and all that light and all that heat burst out of his chest and out of his head and his body crumpled, silent at last.

Blam. The man with the skull put Ramirez out of his misery. Now it was Private Hank Mayer's turn. Finally.

Sobbing, Private Hank Mayer dropped to his knees and waited.

But then another man appeared, right behind the man with the skull, and then they both vanished.

Private Hank Mayer called out, begged for help, begged for mercy, and then the heat grew in his chest and his head and he screamed and he screamed and then there was nothing but sweet, blissful light.

75

Nero teleported Skulduggery right into the middle of this little cave. The moment Razzia saw the gun in his hand, she sent out one of her pets to snatch it from his grip.

Hansel retracted into her palm, dropping the gun by her feet before he did so. What a good little boy.

Skulduggery didn't move to retrieve it. He was looking around, assessing his situation, looking at the cave, looking at the weird machine in the corner. Always assessing, that Skulduggery. Smart guy.

Nero stood nearby, smiling. He was just happy he hadn't messed up. His powers had been on the fritz lately and he'd begun to doubt himself. Today was a win for him, and no mistake.

Destrier stood beside his machine, fiddling with it, making last-minute adjustments. But that was him all over. Always fiddling, that Destrier.

Abyssinia stood quietly. Razzia didn't like it when Abyssinia was quiet. It made her sad. Abyssinia had worked so hard to get Caisson back, and she'd been so delighted when it had actually happened. But now...

None of them had anticipated Caisson making plans with that old woman from the loony bin. It was all going wrong. They were supposed to be one great big family by this stage, but the lovebirds were off by themselves all the time and Abyssinia just... moped.

The only thing that looked like it might snap her out of this funk she was in was this part of the plan. Abyssinia had been looking forward to it. So had Razzia, for that matter. She quite liked Skulduggery Pleasant. He was a laugh.

Skulduggery, meanwhile, had finished his assessment, and was now making his move.

From where she was standing, Razzia had an unobstructed view of him clicking his fingers. Nero didn't, though. He didn't see the spark, or the flame, or the ball of fire, so when Skulduggery flicked his wrist and that ball of fire hit Nero's arm, all Nero could think to do was panic and howl and slap at himself. That was funny. Razzia had to suppress a giggle. In the meantime, of course, Skulduggery had crossed the distance between them and was about to grab Nero when Abyssinia held out her hand and Skulduggery arched his back, his fingers curling as she started to drain his life force.

The flames were battered into submission and, his jacket now ruined, Nero backed off, glaring.

"Please don't do that again," Abyssinia said, approaching slowly. "Nero is part of my family. I don't appreciate it when people hurt my family. You should know that by now."

She stopped what she was doing and Skulduggery gasped, and fell to his knees.

"It's good to see you," Abyssinia said. "But then you already know that." She leaned down, raised his chin with her finger. "I never could stay mad at you. Not even after you killed me."

"So all is forgiven?" he asked. To Razzia's ears, his voice sounded a little weaker.

"Not in the slightest," Abyssinia responded, walking away from him. "You cut out my heart, imprisoned me in a box, and took me away from my son. Do you really expect me to forgive you for any of that?"

Skulduggery stood. Slowly. Abyssinia watched him. Razzia watched them both.

"Maybe not," Skulduggery said, "but there were extenuating circumstances. You were a threat that had to be eliminated."

"I wasn't a threat to *you*. I may have been to everyone else, but not to *you*. When I heard that you'd returned, when I heard that Skulduggery Pleasant had come back after five years away, I was happy for you. I could admit, even back then, that I'd been a bad influence. That I'd led you astray."

"You led me nowhere I didn't want to go," Skulduggery said. "I take full responsibility for my actions."

Abyssinia smiled. "I didn't help, though, did I?"

"You did not," Skulduggery said. He was sounding stronger. Back to his old self. "But I've never blamed you."

"That... actually means a lot to me. Likewise, I didn't take it personally, what happened between us. None of it."

"You are far more gracious than people give you credit for."

"I think they're thrown by all the murdering."

"That might be it, yes. Thank you for bringing me here, by the way. Valkyrie has been trying to convince me that talking our way out of problems is the way to go. I'm not too sure about that – I'm quite old-fashioned in that regard – but I do like to keep an open mind."

"Ah," said Abyssinia. "I'm afraid you've misunderstood my intentions. I didn't bring you to this cave to talk this through and find a solution. I already have a solution: everything goes according to my plan, and I win, and everyone else loses."

Skulduggery took off his hat, brushed dust from the brim, and put it back on. "I see," he said. "That's unfortunate. Entirely understandable, of course, but unfortunate. So why am I here?"

"In this cave, you mean? This cave is important to me. I was nursed back to health in this cave. It holds a special place in my... in my history, I suppose."

"And are you going to try to kill me?"

Abyssinia laughed. "If that were my intention, there would be no *trying*, my sweet Skulduggery. There would only be a pile of bones in a nice suit. But no, this world is far more interesting with you in it. You remember Destrier, of course?"

"Of course," Skulduggery said, as Destrier waved. "A man who holds time itself in the palm of his hands."

"Well," Destrier said, blushing, "not quite. No, not quite at all. But it is my, ah, vocation, if you will? My... hobby."

"Obsession," Nero muttered.

"Tell Skulduggery what's in store," said Abyssinia.

Destrier nodded quickly, and motioned to the machine, which appeared to Razzia to be little more than a square platform with metal columns at each corner. "It's a prison," he said. "Or, actually, no. A prison *cell*. Singular. It's a..." He cleared his throat. "I have been working, with time, to isolate a moment within a given space, to, uh, to focus it, to concentrate it on what you might call a... a..."

"He's going to freeze you in time," Nero said.

Abyssinia's hands went to her hips. "Nero!"

"Sorry."

"This was Destrier's moment!"

"He was taking too long!"

"Everyone takes too long for you," Abyssinia said. "You're a Teleporter. The moment you leave, you arrive. The rest of us don't work that way. You need patience. We've talked about this."

Nero looked down. "Sorry, Abyssinia. Sorry, Destrier."

"Oh," said Destrier, "that's OK. I can be... annoying. I'm, I'm... My thoughts can get jumbled." He looked back at Skulduggery. "What Nero said was correct, though. Or correct to a degree. I can't literally freeze you in time, but I am going to slow down time so much that it doesn't make a great deal of difference."

"I see," Skulduggery said.

"We're calling it the Eternity Gate," Destrier said. "As a name, it's a bit dramatic for me, and somewhat misleading, but I've been told it sticks in the mind, and it's memorable, and... and apparently

386

being memorable is better than being, um, accurate. Anyway, I've set it to hold you for seven days. I hope you don't mind."

"Just long enough to keep me out of the action, I presume," Skulduggery said.

Abyssinia smiled. "I don't want to have to hurt you, my love. I think it's safer for everyone if you miss what's coming. Now, I would ask you to step up voluntarily, but we both know you'd try a last-minute manoeuvre, so I'm afraid I'll have to drain the fight out of you."

She held out her hand and Skulduggery seized up again. That was Razzia's cue to grab him and move him on to the platform.

"For you," Abyssinia said, "only an instant will pass, and, when I see you again, all the dominoes will have fallen. The mortal soldiers will be dead, First Wave will be on every news channel on the planet, the White House will have launched their little missiles wherever I tell them to... and I'll be here to welcome you into the new world."

"Don't do this," Skulduggery said, straightening up. "Don't—"

Destrier flipped the switch.

An energy field rose between the four columns on the platform, trapping Skulduggery inside like a mosquito caught in amber.

Destrier did a quick check. "It's working," he said. "All systems are, um, good."

Razzia peered up at Skulduggery. He appeared completely frozen.

"That is so cool," she said. "When this is over, can I have a go next?"

Destrier frowned at her. "Yes...?"

She grinned. "Bonzer."

76

Flanery needed some peace and quiet, so he left his briefing documents on the table and moved into his private cabin, shutting the door on the rest of Air Force One, with their ringing phones and constant chatter. He didn't have time for briefing documents. He didn't have time for phone calls. He didn't have time for chatter. It was Friday night. This was the world's last night before magic was revealed and everything went crazy He needed to be alone.

"Nervous?" Crepuscular Vies asked from Flanery's favourite chair.

Flanery jumped back, his heart hammering dangerously in his chest. He was seriously starting to hate how magic people kept scaring him. "What the *hell* are you doing here?"

"I'm everywhere, Martin," Crepuscular said. "Haven't you figured that out yet? So, good news. The team's in place. We're good to go for tomorrow night so long as Abyssinia fulfils her end."

"What if someone comes in?"

Crepuscular shrugged. "So what if they do? In a few days, what will it matter? When Naval Magazine Whitley goes down, you'll order the footage to be broadcast and sorcerers will be revealed to the world. Then the war starts. You'll need your own sorcerer bodyguards, of course, so I'll be by your side from that point on. We'll be inseparable."

Flanery dropped into the other chair. "When did we decide this?"

Crepuscular always looked like he was smiling, but Flanery got the feeling that he was genuinely smiling now. "This has always been part of the plan, Martin."

"Abyssinia's plan?"

"My plan."

Flanery didn't like this. Everyone seemed to have a plan except him. He chose his next words carefully. "Are you sure that's a good idea? How can we tell the American people that all the sorcerers hate us and want to kill us if I have one protecting me?"

"There'll be a few sorcerers, like me, who will bravely put our humanity before our heritage, and fight for the mortals. It'll be inspiring, trust me. The American people eat that stuff up. What's the matter? You look worried."

"I'm just... This is all happening very fast."

"No, it isn't."

"It is. It's happening very, very quickly."

"Everything in the last few years has been leading up to this, Martin. This is why you were elected president."

"I was elected president because the people were tired of the same old politicians playing politics instead of—"

Crepuscular held up a hand. "Please don't chant your campaign slogans at me. I don't think I'd be able to handle it." He observed him for a moment. Flanery didn't like being observed. "You're a funny little man, Martin. You have an enormous capacity for self-deceit. I am entirely convinced that you believe everything you say, simply because you've said it enough times. But let me remind you: Abyssinia sought you out. When she was a heart in a box, when all she could do was communicate telepathically, she looked around for someone who could do what she needed them to do. That's why you were nominated, Martin."

This was starting to anger Flanery. "I was nominated because

389

I was the best. I was the smartest and the strongest candidate the Republican Party had."

Crepuscular laughed. "She chose you because you were the weakest. You were the easiest to manipulate. You had the most secrets, and the most money, and so you had the most to lose."

"That's a lie."

"Wilkes did it all for you."

"Wilkes was a traitor and a spy!"

"Yes, Martin," Crepuscular said, sighing. "We know that. Abyssinia sent him in to guide you, and to keep an eye on you, but he still came up with the strategies, didn't he? He arranged for Magenta's son to be kidnapped so that she'd read the minds of your opponents and push your agenda through."

Flanery shook his head. "That was my idea."

"He told you about her, and he waited until you took the hint. That's not the same thing as coming up with it yourself."

Flanery didn't respond. He could feel his face burning.

"You entered into this well aware of what was coming," Crepuscular continued. "This isn't happening fast. This has been happening for the last four years. You're just nervous because now you have to actually do something."

"I'm not nervous."

"No? You should be. Abyssinia is going to double-cross you."

Flanery stared. "What?"

"You're really not very bright, are you? That's OK, that's why you have me. She's going to double-cross you, Martin. The first part of the plan will go smoothly. First Wave will attack the Naval base on the Whitley peninsula, and they'll kill everyone they find, providing you with your very own Pearl Harbour. There'll be a twist, a little more bloodshed... and, when it's all done, you'll receive the footage. Evidence, beyond the shadow of a doubt, of the existence of sorcerers. You'll broadcast this footage and you'll address the nation. You'll address the world. That's your moment. That's what you'll be remembered for. Standing at that podium, the entire world listening to every word you say, thanking the Lord that at least they have a leader as strong and as smart as you. You like that idea, don't you?"

"Yes," said Flanery.

"Well, that's not going to happen," said Crepuscular. "You'll broadcast the footage and stand at that podium – and then Abyssinia's bomb will go off."

Flanery felt the blood drain from his face. "No."

"Abyssinia is going to kill you on live television. That's how you'll be remembered."

"She wouldn't," said Flanery. "She needs me. We have it all worked out."

"What did she tell you, Martin? Can you even remember? Were you even paying attention? What did she say? War will break out, right? And she'll co-ordinate with you in secret in order to attack the Sanctuaries and take out the troublesome sorcerers, and then what?"

"She'll... she'll become leader of the sorcerers, and we'll declare a truce, and—"

"And she'll run the magical societies of the world and you'll stay in power for the rest of your life," said Crepuscular. "And, when you die, your children will take over. You'll leave behind a family dynasty that your father could only dream of."

"That's the deal."

"Abyssinia isn't any better at keeping deals than you are, I'm afraid. She doesn't want a truce. She wants to win. That's where your vice-president comes into it."

Flanery frowned. "Dan?"

"He's working with her, Martin."

"No."

"Yes."

"Dan Tucker is loyal to me."

"Not really."

"How do you... how do you know?"

391

"He told me," Crepuscular said. "He told me everything. Before I killed him."

"You killed him?"

"Yep."

"You can't just... you can't just kill the vice-president!"

"Sure I can. Just as easily as I'd kill the president. You're going to hear that he's missing in the next hour or so. Try to act surprised. Don't worry, they'll never find his body. Not unless I want them to."

"What are we going to do?" Flanery asked, the panic rising. "What are we going to do?"

"We're going to calm down, is what we're going to do. Abyssinia wants to double-cross you so you'll double-cross her first. Easy."

"Can I... can I do that?"

"So long as you have me, you can do anything."

Flanery's head dropped into his hands. It was all too much. It was suddenly all too much. "Who... who are you? Please, you've never given me a straight answer. Just tell me, once and for all, who are you and why are you helping me?"

"Who am I?" Crepuscular said, his voice surprisingly soft. "I'm you, Martin. Haven't you figured that out yet? I'm a part of you."

Flanery looked up. "What?"

"Haven't you wondered why no one else can see me or hear me? I'm not really here. This is all in your head. *You* killed Wilkes. *You* killed Dan Tucker. Why doesn't Abyssinia ever sense the truth when she reads your mind? Because you're stopping her. There's a part of you that's brimming with magic, Martin – and it is *amazing*."

Flanery gasped.

And then Crepuscular laughed. "No, only joking. I am really here. And other people have seen me. Wilkes saw me, remember?"

"Oh... yeah."

"When I killed him? Yeah, he saw me then. And I'm the one protecting your thoughts when Abyssinia goes sneaking. What, you thought you had a split personality? That's funny. That's hilarious. You crack me up, Martin, you really do." He leaned forward. "Don't you worry. Things are going to get crazy in the next days and weeks and months and, let's be honest, years, but I'm not going to let anything happen to you. You and me, we're buds. We're *besties*. You are, by far, my favourite mortal. I could... I could hug you. I could just reach over there and... and hug you. Can I? Can I do that?"

"Um," said Flanery.

"No," Crepuscular said. "You're right. It's silly. We're two grown men. We can't just hug. It's not as if we're people, with feelings."

Flanery didn't know what the hell was going on.

Crepuscular looked around. He nodded to a door behind him. "What's through there? Is that the toilet?"

"It's my bedroom."

"That'll do," said Crepuscular, and got up.

77

Another motel room. Another motel shower.

Tanith and Oberon had followed Perkins for hours until he'd finally pulled in here. They'd rented a room two doors down from him and took turns sleeping.

While Oberon went to get breakfast, Tanith sat by the window. From here, she could see into the diner as Oberon waited for their food, standing with his elbows on the diner counter. He had nice arms.

Perkins stepped out of his room.

Tanith grabbed her phone, dialled, and watched Oberon take out his phone and put it to his ear.

"Perkins is coming in," she said, and Oberon moved casually away from the counter, keeping his back to the door as Perkins entered.

"Does it look like he's seen me?" Oberon asked, his voice soft. She could hear low chatter in the background, and music playing. Country and western.

"No," she said, as Perkins spoke a few words to the waitress on his way to settling into a booth by the window. "Although I'm not entirely sure how you're going to get out of there without passing right in front of him."

"Dammit," said Oberon. She couldn't see him any more. "Our breakfast is almost ready."

She sighed. "You may as well grab a table and start eating."

"I've ordered two breakfasts."

"Better eat them both," she told him. "You don't want to raise any suspicions."

The waitress crossed the length of the window, carrying two plates, before disappearing from sight.

"Thank you," Oberon said, a little faintly. There was a pause, and then he laughed and spoke again. "No, no, both for me. Yeah. Well, you know, growing boy and all that." There was another pause, and another laugh, and when he spoke again his voice was clearer. "Our food has arrived."

"Was that you flirting?" Tanith asked, a grin on her face.

He sounded amused. "You'd know if I were flirting, because I'd be doing it really, really badly."

Tanith watched the waitress deliver a coffee to Perkins, and a car pulled up. A neatly dressed man with a tight haircut got out – a military man, by the way he moved. "Perkins might have a friend joining him," she said.

The military man went in and sat opposite Perkins.

"Can you hear what they're saying?" Tanith asked.

"Bits and pieces," said Oberon.

The new guy put something on the table, and Perkins scooped it up and slid it into his shirt pocket.

"New guy just gave Perkins a key card," Oberon whispered.

Both men got up. Perkins paid, and they nodded to each other and walked to their cars.

Tanith grabbed her bag and left the room as the cars moved to the road, waiting for a gap in the traffic. Perkins's car was indicating right. The new guy was going left.

Oberon ran to his car and jumped in.

Tanith hurried over. "What are you doing?" she asked.

"Perkins is going to meet up with Blackbrook's black ops unit," Oberon said, starting the engine. "The new guy is going to relieve one of the men watching my son. I'm sorry, Tanith – that's where I'm going."

"Absolutely," Tanith said. "I have to stick with Perkins, but you have to get your son back."

He was about to drive off. "You should call for back-up," he said. "Getting anywhere close to Blackbrook is gonna be too dangerous for one person."

"I have friends," Tanith said. "Don't worry about me. Focus on your son."

"It was very nice meeting you," he said. "I really hope I get to see you again."

She smiled back. "Likewise."

Five seconds later, he was on the road and Tanith was running towards the nearest parked car. She dialled a number before she reached it.

"Tanith," said the voice on the other end.

"Hey," she said. "Been a while. You about? I might be in need of some help."

"Where are you?"

"Outskirts of Oregon right now, heading west."

There was a pause. "I can get there by tonight."

"Thank you. I'll let you know where I end up."

She put the phone away, pressed her hand to the car door, and a moment later the lock sprang open.

78

There was no mirror in her cell, so Valkyrie didn't know how she looked. Her face was swollen, as was her knee, as was her left hand and most of her torso. Every movement brought new levels of pain.

The City Guard who'd escorted her back here hadn't said anything the entire way. He'd barely looked at her as she'd shuffled in. Valkyrie recognised shame when she saw it, which meant there were still some cops in Roarhaven with a conscience – even if that conscience didn't quite stretch so far as to compel them to do something.

She lay on the uncomfortable bed, unable to take in a full breath, and waited for the footsteps, for the key rattling in the lock, for the door squealing slightly on its heavy hinges as it opened.

She had just started to wonder if maybe they'd skip tonight's beating, maybe give her a chance to heal more, when the footsteps came.

Moaning, Valkyrie forced herself to stand. She was able to open her left eye now. Her ribs screamed at her but at least she was able to stand without support. The doctor, Whorl, had graciously begun the procedure to fix her broken jaw. It was halfway healed, and she gritted her broken teeth.

The door was heavy and solid and closed. She wanted it to

stay that way. Stay closed. Stay shut. Keep her in here. Keep them out there.

The door opened and Temper Fray came in.

"Jesus," he said when he saw her, and Valkyrie burst out crying and sagged back against the wall, and he came forward and hugged her and she gripped him and hugged him as tightly as she was able. She cried into his shoulder and he held her up, taking her weight.

When the sobs that racked her body, that sent fresh pain streaking through her spine and her ribcage, when that all subsided, he sat her down on the bed and knelt before her, his large hands holding hers.

"Who?" he asked softly. "Yonder? I heard he'd been reinstated. Him and his buddies."

She nodded. He nodded, too.

"I can't get you outta here," he said. "I want to but I can't. I don't have the authority. We'd never get past the inner gates."

Valkyrie took a deep, shuddering breath. "You can't tell Skulduggery about this," she muttered, barely able to open her mouth.

He frowned. "He needs to know."

She shook her head.

"Valkyrie—"

"If he knew, he'd break me out. China would send everyone after us both."

"Then I'll go to Commander Hoc," Temper said. "He's no friend of mine, and he's certainly no friend of yours, but from what I've seen he's a by-the-book kinda guy. What's happening to you, I doubt he'd approve."

Valkyrie nodded.

"You expecting another visit tonight?"

She nodded again.

"I'll be quick. I'll go see Hoc, then get back here. We'll barricade that door if we have to."

She went to give him a thumbs up, but her hand was broken.

He straightened. "Hang in there," he said, and hurried out of the cell. The door closed behind him.

79

Temper got as far as the stairs before Lush stepped into his path.

"You're in a hurry," she said. She was smiling. "Never seen you in a hurry before. You're always so laid-back."

He watched her, aware of footsteps coming up behind him. "You're part of it?" he asked.

Her smile broadened. "Part of what?"

Temper moved slightly so he could keep an eye on Rattan and Ferule as they approached. "What's this, then? You're here to stop me going to Hoc?"

"Why're you going to see the Commander, Corporal Fray?" Rattan asked. "There's a chain of command here in the City Guard. Any grievance you got, you take it up with your immediate superior. Who is that, in this case?"

"That would be me," said Yonder, appearing behind Lush. "You have a report to make to me, Corporal?"

Temper smiled at him. "What is it you're trying to do here? You trying to intimidate me?"

"Intimidate you?" Yonder echoed, horrified at the very thought. "Dear Lord, no. I mean, I wouldn't even know where to begin! You're Temper Fray – you're the guy who went undercover for years. You palled around with the bad guys, walking the razor's edge. At any moment, they could have figured out who you were really working for. I'm not going to be able to intimidate someone like you, Corporal."

"We could bribe you," Lush said. "Is there anything you want? Money? Maybe a promotion? We have friends, higher up. And I mean... higher up."

"We can't bribe Temper," said Yonder. "He's friends with the skeleton. He'll do the right thing, no matter the cost. Isn't that right, Temper?"

"You mind stepping aside?" Temper asked. "I have to get through."

Yonder sighed heavily. "Temper, I wish things could be different. I really do. But we're not here to persuade you not to report us. We're not going to bribe you or threaten you or intimidate you. We're going to kill you."

Temper's first instinct was to laugh, but he'd seen that look on so many faces before – faces of people who meant to do him the worst kind of harm.

"I'm one of you," he said.

"You wear the uniform, but you're not one of us," said Yonder as the others closed in. "You never were."

Temper fought the urge to lash out. "You're not thinking this through. Valkyrie's gonna talk to someone eventually. She'll tell them you were the ones who beat her."

"We're going to kill her, too," said Lush. "As soon as we get the go-ahead."

"Maybe it's tonight," Yonder said, smiling. "Maybe tomorrow. There are forces at work here, Corporal Fray, that you know nothing about."

They grabbed him and he struggled and then they put a bag over his head.

80

They drove him somewhere, loosened him up with a few shots from a shock stick, then dragged him out of the car and into a house. They pulled the bag off his head and dumped him on the ground. He blinked quickly, eyes adjusting to the light.

They were still in Roarhaven, but this was a style of house he wasn't familiar with. It was small. Furnished but empty. There were sheets covering the windows.

"Don't bother getting up," said Lush, training her gun on him. "Rattan, uncuff him."

"Why bother?" Rattan asked, frowning. "Just shoot him, for God's sake."

Lush glared. "You're a cop, aren't you? You're supposed to know this stuff. If he dies with handcuffs on, the blood is in danger of pooling at his wrists, isn't it? That'd lead someone like Skulduggery Pleasant to conclude that he could have been killed by people who use handcuffs – like us. You don't want Skulduggery Pleasant kicking down your door, do you, Rattan?"

Rattan scowled, then took the cuffs off Temper and returned them to his belt. "I could handle the skeleton," he said.

Ferule and Lush laughed, and Rattan's face went bright red. He glared down at Temper. "What's your discipline anyway?"

"That's a good question," said Lush, still smiling broadly. "I've never actually seen you use magic. Why is that?"

"I've never needed to," said Temper.

"Maybe he's not even a mage," said Ferule. "Wouldn't that be something, if he was just a little mortal man, scurrying around, pretending to be a sorcerer?"

Rattan slapped Temper behind the ear. "Tell us what you are before you die," he said, obviously relieved that they were no longer laughing at him. "Is it something embarrassing? Can you talk to plants or something? Or maybe animals. Did you devote your life to talking to animals only to discover that they don't talk back?"

Rattan laughed. The other two laughed as well. Lush's gun wavered, and for a moment it wasn't pointed directly at Temper.

He released.

The gist burst from his chest and flew, shrieking, straight for Lush, where it separated her arm from her shoulder with its first swipe and then took her face away with its second.

It twisted in mid-air, flowing back under the stream of light and darkness that connected it to Temper's chest, went for Ferule as he stumbled backwards. It grabbed him, its claws sinking into either side of his chest, and lifted him off the ground, slammed him against the wall and held him there while it tore out his throat with its teeth.

It locked its black eyes on Rattan. It screeched again.

Rattan went for his sword. The gist went for Rattan.

The gist won.

What remained of Rattan crumpled and fell, and the gist darted to the corners of the room, looking for more enemies to destroy.

When it realised there were no more, it looked, finally, at Temper.

Then it drifted downwards. Legs formed and it stood there. That had never happened before.

Despite the exhaustion, despite the rolling sweat and the trembling muscles, Temper forced himself to his feet. The gist was as tall as him now, as broad as him. It smiled with his face. But those teeth. Those claws. Those eyes.

As he examined the gist, the gist examined him. He could feel it probing his weaknesses. It was patient. It had waited this long. It could wait some more.

It smiled again, and allowed itself to be pulled back inside.

Temper's legs gave out and he collapsed. He lay on his back, breathing hard.

One more time should do it. He just had to release the gist one more time, and it would take over, and Temper would be gone forever, trapped inside his own dark side.

81

China shut the doors to keep out the rest of the world, pressed her back against them, and her apartment drank her in.

She stayed where she was for a moment, her eyes closed, her head down. She breathed in the subtle aromas that the apartment sent her way, aromas that brought to mind the days of her youth and the adventures that marked them, of mountains and rivers and romance and danger.

And of him, of course.

She straightened, squaring her shoulders, and entered the large walk-in wardrobe. She had intended to wear a dress made especially for her by Modiste Fair, that most delicate of designers for the magical and wealthy and magically wealthy, but now she thought better of it. Serafina would be coming to dinner in an extravagant gown of her own, and if China dressed to match her she would either succeed, and sour the evening from the very start, or fail, and immediately give Serafina the upper hand. This second possibility was, of course, highly unlikely, but China knew never to underestimate the inestimable Ms Dey.

She chose a single-strap Givenchy, brought it into her bedroom and placed it on the bed. She showered and her man came by to do her make-up and then her woman came to do her hair. Nothing fussy. China didn't have time for fuss.

When she was done, she dismissed them both and went to

stand on the balcony. The sun was going down and Roarhaven was turning on its lights. She liked the city at this time of day. During the sunlit hours, it was imposing. By moonlight, mysterious. But at this precise moment, when it was changing its masks, if she looked at it just right, she could glimpse its true face.

Her city. Her Roarhaven.

The force field, mere centimetres from the balcony, shimmered slightly, sending a wave of purple hue running down the length of the High Sanctuary, and China went back inside. She put on her shoes and took the elevator down to the dining room.

Serafina was, of course, early.

"My darling," she said, gliding across the floor to kiss China's cheeks. "You look ravishing."

"And you are, as ever, quite breathtaking," China responded. Serafina's dress was another marvel of human bones and couture, but less showy than the dress she had worn upon arrival. She had, in her own way, also decided to dress down this evening.

They were seated at the table and made polite small talk as their entrées were served. They advanced to reminiscing while they waited for the main course. Serafina was as skilled at deflecting certain topics of conversation as China remembered, and offered up no new insights into past events.

"And Corrival Academy," Serafina said, changing the subject yet again, "what a wonderful institution. For centuries, sorcerers have only dreamed of a school like this – and now it stands proudly in the First City of Magic. That's what they're calling Roarhaven, you know."

China arched an eyebrow. "I'm sure the Mystical Cities would have something to say about *that* title."

Serafina waved her hand. "Mystical Cities don't count, you know that. What's the use of a city of sorcerers if it only appears every forty years? No, Roarhaven deserves every accolade it receives. Credit is due to you." She raised her glass of wine in a salute.

"Thank you," said China, raising her own.

"And to Erskine Ravel, of course."

China took a sip. "Of course."

"It was his foresight, his vision that led to all this," said Serafina. "For a member of a group I used to despise and regularly try to have killed, he turned out to be quite all right in the end, didn't he?"

"His friends would disagree."

"His friends were self-righteous heathens, China. What do I care for their opinions?"

"I would imagine nothing at all. Speaking as a heathen, however, I can only say that, while I appreciate the obvious work he put into this city, I do not and cannot approve of his methods – nor his ultimate objective."

"To rule over the mortals?" Serafina asked. "But what would be so wrong with that?"

They smiled at each other, and Serafina appeared to soften.

"I do not envy you, China. Dedicating so much of your time to the tedium of bureaucracies is something I would simply not be able to countenance. You are a more selfless woman than I." She took a moment, examining China anew, and then, with her most concerned tone, said, "You look tired, my dear."

China kept her smile, and was about to answer when the doors opened and Cerise hurried in.

"Deepest apologies, Supreme Mage, High Superior," she said, bowing. "But there's a visitor who requests an audience most urgently."

"Of course," China said, frowning, and rose from her chair as Temper Fray entered the room.

China strode to the lower levels. The door opened before her and the City Guard officer straightened up when he saw who it was.

"Valkyrie Cain," China demanded.

The officer blinked rapidly. "I'm sorry, Supreme Mage?"

China stared at him. He swallowed.

"Through... through there," said the officer, pointing. "The cell at the end."

China left him where he stood and walked quickly to the last cell. She waved her hand over the lock and the door opened and she stepped in.

Valkyrie lay on the bunk. Her hair was matted, her face swollen and puckered, scraped and bloodied. Her neck was scratched. Deep bruising discoloured her arms. Her clothes were dirty and stained with dried blood.

China watched her as her eyes fluttered open. She saw China and tried sitting up, but hissed and lay back down.

"Don't move," China said, quickly crossing to her. "What did they do to you? What did they..." Anger choked off her words, and she took a moment to regain control.

"Officer!" she called. She heard running footsteps, and the nervous man appeared at the door.

"Yes, Supreme Mage?"

China spun to him. "Who did this? Did you do this?"

"Do... do what, Supreme Mage?"

"Look at her," China said, pointing. "Did you do this?"

"No!" the officer said. "I swear!"

"Who did?"

"I don't know, Supreme Mage. I've only just started my shift."

China glared. "Get a doctor down here immediately."

"Of course," the officer said, bowed quickly and deeply, and sprinted away.

China turned back. Valkyrie's eyes were on her.

"I'm sorry," China said. "I didn't know this was happening. Who did this to you?"

Valkyrie started to move. China helped her into a seated position, her back against the cold wall, and sat on the edge of the bunk beside her.

"I thought you'd sent them," Valkyrie said. Her lips were cracked. Her voice was a whisper.

"I would never hurt you," China responded. "I would never allow anyone else to hurt you. I gave orders that you were to be given proper chambers and placed under house arrest. I never meant for you to suffer, Valkyrie."

"I betrayed you."

"And you were arrested for it. You had to be punished. I hope you see that. But I didn't want this. I just didn't have any other option. Greymire... Greymire is a secret never to be told. What you did was an unbelievable breach of trust."

"I know."

"You could have come to me, you know. About your sister. I would have helped you."

A slight smile, that revealed broken and missing teeth, "You're always so busy."

"I suppose I am," China said, looking away. "You don't get an awful lot of free time when you're running the world."

"Must be lonely."

China paused. "It is," she said. "But I brought it on myself. You can't take the power without taking the responsibility." Ever so gently, she patted Valkyrie's hand. "How's your sister?"

"Haven't fixed her yet," Valkyrie said, speaking slowly. China had never seen her so drained. "Trying to decide if I even should."

"Some decisions are too big for people to make," China responded. "It's the only reason I envy the religious. They can hand over their troubles to an omniscient deity, or – in the case of the Faceless Ones – uncaring, insane deities, and absolve themselves of the burden of morality. Why struggle with the right decision when you can pick the easy one and say your gods told you to do it?"

Valkyrie winced as she shifted her weight slightly. "Sounds like you know the struggle well."

"Sometimes it threatens to become too much," China said.

"Sometimes I feel that my humanity means I'm too limited to make the kinds of decision that need to be made. What I wouldn't give for some guidance."

A tiny raise of an eyebrow. "Could use some of that myself."

China smiled. "I think we're arguing for the need for a god," she said.

"Wouldn't that be nice?"

82

"Bejant," said Temper.

"Hey, man," Bejant responded, his usual smile in place when he turned. The smile faded. "What the hell happened to you?"

"It's definitely a story," Temper said. "You on duty?"

"About to come off."

"Do me a favour? Stay on for a bit. I've got a crime scene to show you."

"What's the crime?"

"Kidnapping. Assault on an officer. Attempted murder."

"Is the officer you?"

"He happens to be, yes."

"And who are the perpetrators?"

Temper hesitated before answering. "Lush, Rattan and Ferule."

"Seriously?"

"They're all dead, by the way."

"You kill them?"

"It was them or me. Yonder gave the orders, but I get the feeling this goes a lot higher."

Bejant pulled him to one side. "Just to be clear on this one – officers of the City Guard, our *fellow* officers, tried to kill you?"

"Maybe half an hour ago, yeah."

"Why?"

"Valkyrie Cain is in custody. They were beating her. I was on

411

my way to tell Hoc and they grabbed me. They intended to kill me, and they were waiting on orders to kill Valkyrie."

"Whose orders?"

"I don't know. Yet."

"Temper, this is... this is crazy. You're saying everyone in uniform is in on this?"

"Not everyone," said Temper. "Skulduggery set up the City Guard – I'd be willing to trust anyone who came in when he was in charge. Anyone who came in when Hoc was in charge... I'm not so sure about."

"Do you have any idea what'll happen when this gets out?"

"None at all," said Temper. "Do you?"

"No," Bejant said. "But I can't imagine it'll be pretty. If you're right, if this involves more than Yonder and his little crew, you're going to have to watch your back."

"I'm used to it."

"Yeah," Bejant said, "but I'm not." He sighed. "Right, fine. Take me to the crime scene and let's shoot our careers in the face, what do you say? Take my car? It's over there."

Temper nodded and led the way. They were halfway to it when there was a noise and Temper glanced back, saw the figure who had grabbed Bejant, saw the look on his friend's face that told him there was a blade in his back, and then someone grabbed Temper around the throat and there wasn't a whole lot he could do to stop the darkness from closing in.

83

The City Guard officer ushered Doctor Whorl into the cell.

"Doctor," Valkyrie said in greeting.

China stood. "Is this the one?"

Valkyrie nodded. The doctor was taller, but even so China seemed to loom over him. "You didn't report her condition?"

Whorl was already sweating. "I tend to injured prisoners all the time. If I made a report on every single one of them—"

"Then you would be doing your job," China finished. She glared at the officer. "Remove her restraints."

He came forward, keys rattling. He took the metal band from Valkyrie's wrist and she felt her magic flood her system.

"Away," said China, and the officer scuttled out. She turned to Whorl. "Heal her."

"I, um, I can have her taken down to the Infirmary and schedule an immediate—"

"You'll be doing all that," said China, "but it seems apparent that you can start the healing immediately. Would I be correct in this assumption, Doctor Whorl?"

"I... I suppose."

"Then heal her. Now."

Whorl hesitated, then turned to Valkyrie. "Lie back, please."

"She's in pain," China said. "You'll have to assist her."

Whorl assisted. He laid Valkyrie on her back very, very gently, and then he knelt by her. His hands started to glow, and he placed them on her belly.

She closed her eyes, focusing on the warmth as it permeated her skin. She felt the damage fade. She felt the torn muscles and the burnt skin and the fractured bones start to knit together. She felt the swelling begin to go down. It was a nice feeling.

She felt Whorl's power, and she pulled it in closer to examine. For a moment, she skirted along its surface, unable to delve any deeper –

– and then a door sprang open in her mind to reveal a room she'd never known existed, and in that room the workings of his magic were written on the walls. She sensed him approaching the limits of what he could do. But she liked the feeling too much to allow it to stop.

She reached out with her own magic and latched on to his. She heard him gasp in some distant part of the world. The warmth spread through every part of her. It was almost painful. It *was* painful. But pain didn't mean the same thing any more.

Whorl took his hands away. She felt him fall back. She didn't care. She remembered how his magic worked and she kept it going. Strength flowed through her blood. Chemicals flooded her brain. She heard herself laugh.

And then the door in her mind... it started to close. It was getting difficult to remember his power. Bit by bit, inch by inch, the door closed, and the light from the room dimmed, until with a click it was over.

Valkyrie opened her eyes. China and Whorl were staring at her.

She felt better. She felt great. She sat up, swung her legs off the bunk. Stood.

Dizziness washed over her and she swayed, almost fell, but laughed again as she steadied herself.

There was no longer any pain. The stiffness had vanished from her knee, from her ankle and her shoulder. She flexed her hands.

They were no longer swollen. No longer broken. Her arms were no longer bruised. She felt her face. Her eyes. Her nose. She ran her tongue over her teeth.

She frowned, opened her mouth and did it again.

"Did you just regrow your teeth?" China asked.

"I don't know," said Valkyrie. "Did I?"

"That's not possible," Whorl said, coming closer. "The human body can't just..." He stepped away again, suddenly wary. "What did you do to me? You took control of my magic. How did you do that? How did you—"

"Doctor Whorl," said China, "you may return to the Infirmary now."

"But we have to—"

"Do you remember the contract you signed, Doctor?" China asked. "Do you remember the section forbidding you to talk about anything classed as a Red Case?"

Whorl quietened. "Yes," he said.

"I am classing this as a Red Case," China said. "Return to your ward. Do not discuss this with anyone. We will be speaking, however, about your failure to report Detective Cain's injuries. Have a good evening."

Whorl hesitated, then left without saying another word.

"Well now," said Valkyrie.

"Has this ever happened before?" China asked.

"Have I healed myself? No."

"What about commandeering another mage's power?"

"That's a first for me, too. It was weird. I understood how his power worked and I was able to, I don't know... replicate it."

China observed her a moment before speaking again. "We'll need to run tests."

"No," said Valkyrie.

"We have to understand this," China said. "A few days with my best people, that's all I'm asking."

"I'm not a lab rat, China."

China sighed. "Fine. But at the very least you need another doctor to check you over. Is that acceptable?"

"I don't know," Valkyrie said. "Do I get to go free afterwards?"

China narrowed her eyes. "You betrayed me."

"And I was nearly killed in your jail cells. Doesn't that make us even?"

"Not even close."

"China, I'm sorry. I didn't have a choice. This is my sister we're talking about. I have to do whatever it takes to help her. You *have* to understand that."

For a few seconds, China's face was unreadable. Then, "You owe me," she said.

Valkyrie nodded. "I do."

"A favour," she said.

"Agreed."

China motioned to the door. "OK then, let's go get you checked out."

"Thank you," Valkyrie said, leading the way out of the door. "But the favour cannot be anything to do with getting poked and prodded."

"You are obstinate," said China. "Don't you want to know how your powers even *work*? We still don't know, because you haven't let anyone run the tests they need to run. You don't know the limits to what you can do. What is this energy you produce? How can you fly? How can you do the other things you do? Think what this could mean. If we can learn how you did this, maybe it's something that could be taught to others. This could be the start of a whole new breed of sorcerer."

Valkyrie frowned. "Do we *need* a new breed of sorcerer? Aren't there enough already? When I started, there were Elementals and Adepts. That's all. Then I learned about monsters, and creatures, and Warlocks, and witches, and now we have Neoterics. We don't need more, and we certainly don't need to make the ones we already have even stronger than they are right now, do we?"

"Not all of them, no, but—"

"China – not everything has to be a tactical advantage."

"I never said otherwise."

"You're thinking it. You're wondering how to weaponise what I just did, aren't you?"

"Not weaponise," said China. "Utilise."

They got to the door. China waved at the officer to open up.

"I don't trust *me* to wield this power," Valkyrie told her. "I'm sure as hell not going to trust anyone else to do it."

The door opened, and Sergeant Yonder's eyes widened when he saw Valkyrie. Suddenly his pistol was in his hand and he was pointing it straight at her face. She instinctively raised her hands to chest height, palms out in surrender.

China started to speak at the same time as something flashed across Yonder's eyes. He was going to fire.

Valkyrie moved forward a half-step, both hands rising, grabbing Yonder's wrist with one hand, the barrel of the gun with the other. The gun went off and the bullet hit the ceiling, and Valkyrie wrenched downwards, snapping his trigger finger as she ripped the pistol from his grip. He didn't even have time to scream before she slammed the gun into his face three times, and then she flipped it and stepped back, aiming his own gun squarely at his chest.

He froze. She froze. Gradually, the world came back online.

"Sergeant Yonder," China said. "Well, that makes sense. Who else would be stupid enough to assault a personal friend of mine while she's in custody?"

The City Guard officer leaped out of his booth.

"Well done, officer," China said to him. "Great reflexes."

Cradling his bloody nose with his left hand, Yonder jabbed one of his unbroken fingers at Valkyrie. "Escaped prisoner!" he said, his words garbled. "Apprehend her!"

"So you weren't going to shoot her on the spot, then?" China asked. "You weren't going to murder her where she stood?"

Yonder shook his head. "Just going to take her back to her cell." He spat blood and mucus on to his shirt.

"It didn't look like you were going to *just* do anything." China nodded to the officer. "Take Sergeant Yonder here to the Infirmary. Don't let him out of your sight. When his nose is mended, put him in a cell. Valkyrie's cell, in fact. I'll deal with him later."

"Yes, Supreme Mage," said the officer, and took Yonder's arm.

Yonder shook him off, glared at China, and then at Valkyrie. "You..." he said.

"Please," Valkyrie responded. "Make things even worse for yourself. Please."

A reasonable thought must have found its way into his head, because he swallowed what he was about to say, along with a good deal more blood and mucus, and allowed the officer to take him to the elevator.

China looked at Valkyrie. "You can't help but make friends, can you?"

"People love me."

The elevator door opened and a man in a yellow jumpsuit shot the City Guard officer dead.

84

Yonder cried out, scrambled back, as Valkyrie and China both stepped into different doorways.

A voice. "Go after him."

Valkyrie peeked across at China, who held up three fingers. Valkyrie nodded. She'd counted three, as well. Three people in yellow – two men, one woman. All holding assault rifles, but not a type Valkyrie was familiar with. There had been no gunshot, either – just a snap of a hum and a flash of red and the officer had fallen.

The jumpsuits were prison-issue. Coldheart.

Soft footsteps, coming closer. China pressed the sigils on her palms and they glowed red before she moved deeper into the other room. Valkyrie stepped away from the door.

She watched the lead shooter's weak shadow move across the floor, and waited for the barrel of the assault rifle to come into view.

She breathed out. Slowly.

The barrel came round the door and she grabbed it, raised it as she stepped to meet him, blasting white lightning straight into his chest. The shooter hit the wall before crumpling.

At the same time, China stepped out beside the second shooter and put her hand to the woman's head, and a beam of red energy seared through the woman's skull. She collapsed.

Valkyrie stared. "Did you have to kill her?"

"Yes," China said, picking up the woman's gun and examining it.

"You could have subdued her."

China glanced up for a moment. "Someone wants to kill me. I kill them first."

There was a grunt, and a cry of pain, and Yonder and the third shooter came tumbling into view. They struggled for the rifle. It skittered away from them. Yonder dived for it while the shooter tried pulling a pistol of similar design from his jumpsuit pocket. It snagged, and Yonder shot him.

Yonder lay back, blood still running from his nose, his injured hand held close to his chest.

An alarm blasted for all of two seconds before it was shut off.

Valkyrie frowned. "What the hell's going on?"

China closed her eyes, accessing the Whispering. "They're... everywhere," she said. "Hundreds of them. All armed. Camera footage has them on all floors."

"What are they doing?" Valkyrie asked.

"Attacking my people, mostly." Her expression hardened. "Abyssinia. She's here with the Teleporter, in my apartment with... Caisson."

"They've come for you," said Valkyrie.

"They've got the exits sealed, and most of our operatives and Cleavers are pinned down. The Cleavers' uniforms don't seem to be adequate protection against those guns they're using." China snapped out of it, her eyes open and focusing on the rifle in her hands. "We can't let these get out. A weapon that can take down Cleavers with one shot could mean the end of the Sanctuary system around the world."

Valkyrie examined the rifle she held. Lightweight, with a scope and collapsible stock. A foregrip but no magazine. There were two small sigils etched just above the trigger guard.

"No bullets," China said. "Powered by magic. How did they do it? We've been trying something similar for years. We've

420

managed it with some of the doors and elevators and various bits and pieces in the building, but to actually power *weapons* this way..."

"Can you stop admiring it, and tell me what the sigils mean?"

"Of course," China answered, pressing the first one. "They're settings for variations of density."

The convict Valkyrie had blasted moaned and stirred. They watched him get to his hands and knees. Slowly, he stood, his back to them. He took out a pistol. It dangled by his side.

He turned, blinking stupidly, as if he was trying to remember where he was. Valkyrie held up her hand to blast him again, but China shot him with the rifle, a bolt of blue energy hitting him in the chest, and he wheeled round and collapsed.

Valkyrie snatched the rifle out of her hands. "Will you *stop* killing people?"

"I doubt he's dead," said China.

Valkyrie hesitated, then hurried over, checking for a pulse. When she found it, she stood, and glared again. "You didn't know that for sure."

"So blue is stun," said China. "Red is kill. Good to know."

"We have to get out of here," Yonder said, picking himself up.

"You don't get a vote," China told him. She turned to Valkyrie. "We have to get out of here. Once they realise I'm not in the building, maybe they'll teleport away and stop killing my employees."

Valkyrie handed her back the rifle. "Any idea how to get out without being seen? Or killed?"

"The Detention Wing has a secret entrance for the transport of especially high-profile or dangerous prisoners. It's a pod, big enough for eight people, that goes from the floor above us to just beyond Shudder's Gate."

"That's our way out," said Valkyrie. She picked up the convict's pistol. "If we're going to be using these guns, set them to stun."

China frowned. "Our enemies will not afford us the same courtesy."

"I don't care how rude *they* are," Valkyrie answered. "I care how rude *we* are."

China sighed. "Very well."

Valkyrie stuffed the pistol into her waistband and hefted the rifle. "Yonder, you hear me?"

"Yeah, yeah," he muttered, making a show of pressing the sigil. "There. Happy?"

"Ecstatic." She walked up to him. "And if I think for a moment that you're about to shoot either of us—"

"I won't."

"You didn't let me finish."

"I won't, though."

"Let me finish," she snarled, and Yonder fell silent. "Thank you. If I think for a moment that you're about to shoot either of us, I'm going to break all of your *other* fingers, do you understand me? Every single one of them."

"OK," he mumbled. "I got it."

"Good. How's the nose, by the way?"

"It's really sore."

"It does look painful," she said, and slapped it. Yonder howled, and Valkyrie left him to his howling and walked to the staircase door.

Once Yonder had quietened down again, Valkyrie opened it a crack. No bad guys. No sound. She stepped through, the stock of the rifle firm against her shoulder. She swept the staircase overhead, finger against the trigger guard. When she was sure there were no shooters lying in wait, she gave China the nod.

"Where did you learn all this?" China asked, joining her, her own rifle dangling.

"Skulduggery, mostly," said Valkyrie. "Tanith, some."

China shook her head. "They didn't teach you this stuff. You're moving like you're military."

"Just some things I picked up."

"During your time in America?"

Valkyrie looked at her. "Were you spying on me, China?"

"Not at all," China answered. "I was keeping an eye on you – as much as I could."

"I really don't appreciate that."

"It was only for the first few years," China assured her. "Just until I knew you weren't going to be too lonely up on that mountain."

The door opened again and Valkyrie turned to Yonder. "You're on point," she said.

He paled. "You want me to go first? What if there are bad guys up there?"

Valkyrie frowned at the question. "Then they'll shoot you," she said. "Obviously. But it's better that you get shot instead of me or China."

"It's very much preferable," China agreed. "Now hurry up, Sergeant. There are people being killed as we speak."

85

Yonder led the way up the stairs a lot slower than Valkyrie would have liked.

She overtook him as he reached the landing, and crept over to open the door. She could hear shouting and gunshots – the Sanctuary agents returning fire, presumably.

"Are the cameras picking up anything nearby?" she whispered to China.

China closed her eyes, and a look of intense annoyance crossed her face. "They're taking out the cameras," she said. "They must have a tech mage with them. There are only a few left, and..." She opened her eyes. "All the cameras are offline."

"Wonderful," said Valkyrie. "Where's the escape pod?"

"Turn left out of the door, through the next door, keep the wall on your right until you come to the statue of the Cleavers. On the heel of one of these Cleavers is a switch that opens the door behind you. The pod is right there. It'll seal once we're in, and we'll be at Shudder's Gate in seconds."

"OK, then," Valkyrie said. "Let's go."

She crept out, keeping to the wall, moving low. They got to the doorway. The sounds of fighting were louder here. She peeked round. All seemed fine.

Holding the rifle to her shoulder, she moved on until she

reached the next corner. There, across a wide-open space, was the Cleaver statue.

She motioned to China to stay put, and peeked again. No bad guys, but this was such an obvious ambush point that Valkyrie found herself hesitating. Then she thought of the tune from the music box and it relaxed her – and she broke into a run.

Red bolts sizzled by her and she swerved away from the statue and slid behind the opposite corner. Three shooters, maybe more, and they all had a clear shot of anyone trying to get to the statue.

Unless something took their minds off it.

Valkyrie got to one knee, peeked, ducked again as they sent another barrage of bolts her way. She looked over at Yonder, and nodded back towards the statue.

Yonder understood, and shook his head violently.

She nodded. Once. Insistently. He glared – finally nodded his agreement.

Valkyrie popped up, firing, and Yonder broke into a sprint. He lost his rifle somewhere along the way, nearly tripped over it, but managed to keep going. He dived behind the statue and Valkyrie ducked back again.

She watched him feel around for the switch. The secret door opened behind him.

Valkyrie slid her assault rifle across the floor and he scooped it up, rejoining the gunfight. She took the pistol from her waist-band, fired at the convicts as China ran across the open space. Valkyrie leaped up, still firing, and together they ran for the pod as Yonder jumped in ahead of them.

He turned, smiling.

Valkyrie screamed his name, but the doors slid shut a heartbeat before she collided with them.

China grabbed her, pulled her down behind the statue. She thumped her hand against the switch, but nothing happened. They looked at each other.

"Really should have seen that coming," said China.

"What do you suppose the chances are of him sending the pod back to us when he gets out?" Valkyrie asked.

China arched an eyebrow. "Slimmer than me, darling."

A bolt from one of those fancy rifles sizzled past them. The shooters were closing in, guns raised.

China clasped her hands, twisted them and pulled them apart, stretching a thin wall of sparkling energy between them. "This is usually enough to stop a bullet," she said, and started to rise. A bolt of red went straight through the shield and she dropped down again, the wall of energy sputtering out. "Dammit," she said.

"My turn," Valkyrie muttered. She stuffed the pistol back in her waistband and pulled her magic into her hands, her fingertips tingling. The tingling turned to a steady itch and she straightened, holding a wall of crackling white energy before her.

She felt each one of the red bolts hit the shield – each impact was like an extra heartbeat deep within her chest – but the shield held and the bolts didn't pass through.

China got behind her, and they started walking. China began slapping her back. "Your clothes are starting to smoulder," she said.

"Yeah," Valkyrie responded. "That happens."

One of the shooters tried to outflank them, but he ran right into China's line of fire. He dropped, unconscious, and the other two stopped shooting. They stepped out from behind cover, rifles still up, and followed Valkyrie and China as they backed into the corridor. The big one had a machete in his belt.

"Do either of you idiots know the trouble you're in?" China asked. "Do you have any idea who you're dealing with?"

"Sure we do," said the bigger one. "You're China Sorrows and she's Valkyrie Cain."

"No," said China. "I am the *notorious* China Sorrows and she is the *infamous* Valkyrie Cain. We're more than you boys can handle, so do yourselves a favour: put down your weapons and walk away."

The smaller convict grinned. "Naw, don't think so. Killing her and capturing you will *make* us. After this, we'll be up there in Abyssinia's inner circle – making the decisions and reaping the rewards." He nodded to his friend. "This is where we hit the big time."

They threw down their rifles. The smaller one took a pair of brass knuckles from his jumpsuit – the bigger one took out the machete. Shadows swirled, and swallowed them.

Necromancers.

Valkyrie dropped the shield and spun, but they had already shadow-walked behind her, and the smaller convict gathered a fistful of darkness and flung it at China. It scooped her off her feet, slamming her to the wall.

The bigger convict wrapped his shadows around Valkyrie, pinning her arms to her sides and squeezing her legs together. The shadows constricted, and she almost toppled as the breath was forced from her lungs.

China got an arm free, managed to flick a dagger of red light into the bigger convict's shoulder and he grunted, stepped back, the shadows that held Valkyrie dissipating. Valkyrie sucked in air and returned the favour, sending a bolt of white lightning into the smaller convict's chest. He went flying, and China dropped to the ground.

The machete came for Valkyrie's head and she lunged to meet the arm that swung it, the edges of her hands striking the big convict's forearm and biceps. The machete clattered to the ground and he tried to pull away, but she had him now, and her arm was wrapped round his and she was firing elbows into his face. She turned his nose to mush and took him to the floor and continued striking him until he went limp.

She straightened. China was already walking away, machete in one hand, rifle in the other, and Valkyrie had to jog to catch up.

"Our next way out?" she asked.

"The main elevator or the service elevator," China said. "Both of which will probably be heavily guarded. Which leaves us with the stairwell."

"So up we go."

"I know Abyssinia. She'll have a little squad of her best shooters on the top landing. Keep in mind that this section was designed to prevent a prisoner breakout. If they even hear a *footstep*, they'll destroy us and there'll be nothing we can do about it."

"Is there a fourth option?"

"Not for me."

"What does that mean?"

They arrived at a small hatch. China passed the rifle to Valkyrie before sliding the tip of the machete behind the hatch door. She started to pull the machete slowly back. "This shaft leads to an air vent," she said.

Valkyrie frowned. "How big is the air vent?"

"You'll fit."

"I'm kind of claustrophobic."

"You'll be fine." China glanced at Valkyrie's shoulders. "Although it might be a tight squeeze."

"I'm really not good with small spaces."

"Well, I didn't ask you to put on all that muscle," China said, giving the machete a final tug. The hatch door sprang open. China dropped the machete and took her rifle back. "You'll crawl through."

"I don't like crawling."

"I have an aversion to it also. But you'll crawl through the shaft, until you reach the vent. Then you'll fly."

"I'm not very good at the flying thing yet."

"Luckily for you, the vent goes straight up, so I doubt you'll veer too far off course. You'll need to stop at the third opening, then crawl along that shaft until you come to a section you can drop through. You'll be in the car park."

"And how are you going to get out?"

"Oh, that's easy," said China. "I'm going to walk up the stairs after you've disposed of the squad of gunmen."

"Assuming they don't kill me."

China smiled at her. "They won't kill you. You're Valkyrie Cain. You'll outlive us all. After that, we'll get in a car and we'll drive right out of here."

Valkyrie hesitated, then hunkered down and peered into the shaft. It was dark, and looked small.

"Oh, God," she said, and started crawling.

The vent was just up ahead, so the first part wasn't so bad. She just focused on the fact that in a few seconds she'd be able to stand. Her breathing was calm. Her heart wasn't hammering at her chest. She was doing good.

She got to the vent. It was narrow – scarily so – but it did, as China had said, go straight up. Unfortunately, it also went straight *down*, too, servicing the floors below. Something China had neglected to mention.

Grumbling to herself, Valkyrie inched forward, reaching out to lay her hands flat against the far wall of the vent. Her head and shoulders emerged next, and cold air hit the perspiration on her brow. She leaned out further, bringing her knee out from under her, bracing the sole of her boot against the outer edge of the shaft.

She shifted her body forwards and upwards, straightening her leg, bracing the other foot now, too, until she was standing at an angle. She looked up, saw the opening of the next shaft.

She bent her knees, was about to take off, but chickened out at the last moment. She'd never done it like this before. If she did something wrong and ended up falling, it was going to hurt like hell.

She took a breath, raised her head, charged up her magic – and jumped.

Her magic kicked in immediately, white energy bouncing off the four walls of the vent like she was in a microwave about to explode, and she shot upwards, ricocheting all the way, speeding past the first opening and the second opening and then reaching madly for the third while she cut the jets. She managed to get both arms into the shaft and she hung there for a moment, legs dangling, before she pulled herself in. Her clothes were smouldering again.

Valkyrie crawled on. Her shoulders brushed the sides of the shaft. That was getting to her. Her hair was in her eyes. That was getting to her, too. She stopped. This *was* the third opening, wasn't it? She'd been going so fast, she could easily have missed one. If she was in the wrong shaft, then maybe there was no way out. Her hands curled into fists. She might crawl and crawl and it'd get hotter and hotter and her panic would rise and keep rising and there'd be no way out.

Her skin sparked.

"No," she whispered. "No, no."

Energy crackled along her arm.

She bit her lip. Bit it hard and focused on the pain. She needed to calm down, to reduce her panic, to understand that she was going to be fine and she was going to find the way out and she'd be standing up and free to move and everything would be—

Her anxiety spiked again and lightning crackled up and down her body.

She lay down flat, resting her forehead on the backs of her hands. She closed her eyes. She forced herself to breathe slowly, and reached out with her mind.

She found Abyssinia.

86

Valkyrie slipped into Abyssinia's mind, just like she'd done before – quietly and without fuss.

Like a thief in a museum, she trod carefully, avoiding the thoughts that roared like thunder all around her.

A section of Abyssinia's memories lay open, brought to the surface by the return of Caisson. Valkyrie sneaked in and let herself go, let herself fall between moments. She saw the moment Abyssinia found him, experienced the joy, the sheer happiness that came with it. Then there was nothing – no sight, no sound – and she knew these were the years Abyssinia spent in that box, deep in the bowels of Coldheart Prison.

She fell beyond them, out of the darkness and back into the warmth of the light, of Caisson as a young boy, laughing, and Abyssinia caring for him, loving him, raising him. And Caisson was a baby now, bundled in animal hide, and Valkyrie fell further, and further...

And she saw Caisson's father.

87

Valkyrie opened her eyes. She was back in the ventilation shaft. For almost a full minute, she didn't move, didn't make a sound.

Then she said, "Oh, wow."

Slowly, she got to her hands and knees and started crawling again, following the shaft round a corner. She heard voices and slowed down, making sure she was as quiet as she could be.

Light spilled from a grate ahead of her. She reached it, looked down, saw nothing but a concrete floor below her. No voices nearby.

She tried lifting the grate, but had to drop her elbow on to it – heavily – to get it to swing open.

She dropped into the car park, immediately ducked behind a car and took a deep, shuddering breath. This was better, out in the open like this. This was much better.

There was a sign for the stairwell, pointing to her left. Keeping low and scuttling from car to car, she followed it. She stopped moving when two convicts strolled by. When they were gone, she moved again.

Valkyrie was almost to the stairwell when she realised her car was parked nearby. She took a detour, found her car and opened the boot. She grabbed her phone to call Skulduggery, but the signal was being blocked. Right then. She pressed the amulet to her chest and the necronaut suit flowed over her own bloodstained clothes. She fixed her shock sticks in place, and then she opened the music box.

She closed her eyes, let the delicate tune wash over her.

Ohh, this was better. This was what she needed. Just a little bit of calm. Just a little bit of confidence.

Not too long, though. She couldn't afford to lose much time here. This was an urgent situation and it required her to be at her sharpest. Just five more seconds. Five more.

That's all.

She opened her eyes and flicked the lid down. That was dangerous. Valkyrie laughed. She'd have to be careful of that in the future.

She hurried off. The gunmen. Yes, she had to take out the squad of shooters on the stairs.

She found the door to the stairwell, opened it quietly. She heard whispers, and took a peek. They were a little below her, peering down. She grinned, and readied her pistol.

She burst in, leaping over the stairs as she fired downwards. She got most of them before she even hit the wall, then fell on to the two shooters left conscious. There was a lot of cursing and yelling and a scramble, but their rifles were too big to manoeuvre and Valkyrie shot them point-blank.

She lay there for a moment, a grin on her face.

"Valkyrie?" China called up.

Valkyrie poked her head over the edge, and waved, and China hurried up to her.

"I've changed my mind," China said.

"About what?"

"We can't leave. *I* can't leave. You go if you want."

"I'm not going anywhere."

China nodded. "This is my home. I can't run from my home just because I have uninvited guests. What do you do when you have uninvited guests in *your* house, Valkyrie?"

"Oh, I never have any guests," Valkyrie answered. "I have very few friends."

China sighed. "You kick them out," she said. "The answer is, you kick them out."

They kept going up. They got to ground level and found Fletcher slamming a golf club into a convict's shin. The convict went down, screaming, and Fletcher sent him to sleep with another swing.

"You should yell *fore* when you do that," Valkyrie said, walking over. "Makes for a cool story you can tell at parties."

"Oh, I'm glad to see you two," Fletcher responded. "What's the plan? Do we have a plan? I need a plan."

"Take us to my quarters," China said.

Fletcher looked apologetic. "Ah – I can only teleport to places I've been before. The highest I've ever been in this place is the twenty-seventh floor."

"That will have to do," said China.

Fletcher nodded, and vanished for a moment. When he re-appeared, he was shrugging. "OK, looks clear from what I can see." He held out his hands. Valkyrie and China both took one, and an eyeblink later they were on the twenty-seventh floor, at the elevators. There were voices – shouts, in fact – coming from some-where, but they were too far away to make out what was being said.

"This way," China said, walking quickly. "There's an elevator that they might not know about."

"What's it like on other floors?" Valkyrie asked Fletcher as they followed.

"Pretty scary," he replied, "but it could be worse. Our side is putting up a fight, as you'd imagine."

They got to a corner and Valkyrie peered round, then motioned for them to keep following.

"Nero's working overtime," Fletcher continued. "I can feel it in the air whenever he teleports. He's moving the – well, the *troops*, I suppose, wherever they're needed before our guys can react."

"Can you take him?" China asked.

"I'm sorry?"

"Can you find Nero and can you kill him?"

Fletcher hesitated. "Supreme Mage, I'm a teacher. I'm not a killer."

China turned suddenly and Fletcher almost walked into her. "We can't let him continue," she said. "They're here because Nero teleported them here. They're winning because of him. Teleporters are the most valuable sorcerers in any battle. They have Nero. We have you."

"Nero's a Neoteric," said Fletcher. "He can do things I can't."

China turned on her heel and they resumed walking. "Because he cheats," she said. "Because he doesn't have the training you do. He doesn't have the discipline. He has *tricks* that you don't, this is true – but his power is unstable. You just need to push him."

"I really don't think I'm the guy for this," said Fletcher.

"You're telling me," someone said from behind them. Valkyrie and China whirled, firing, but Nero, wearing a black trench coat, simply teleported to their right, and grinned.

"I thought I sensed you nearby," he said to Fletcher. "Old man Renn, come to spoil the fun."

"Old?" Fletcher said, appalled. "I'm twenty-seven." He disappeared, and reappeared a moment later, carrying a baseball bat.

Nero laughed, teleported away, and returned with an axe.

They walked towards each other.

"I owe you one," Fletcher said.

"You mean that time I stuck that knife in your back?" Nero asked. "You didn't find that funny? I know I did."

"Your coat is ridiculous."

Nero laughed again. "No, it isn't."

"You look like you read *Catcher in the Rye* and then raided your parents' wardrobe. Yeah," Fletcher said, hefting the bat, "I read books now."

He swung the bat and Nero blocked and teleported behind him and Fletcher whirled, teleporting to his right as he did so, the bat crunching into Nero's leg.

Nero roared in anger and was suddenly dropping down from above, but Fletcher vanished, the axe barely missing him, and charged into Nero as he landed. The bat skittered away and they tumbled to the floor, wrestling for the axe, appearing and disappearing faster than Valkyrie could process.

"Let's go," said China.

Valkyrie grabbed her arm. "We can't just leave him here."

"Do you want to get involved in *that*? Do you have any idea where they're teleporting *to*? They could drop us into a volcano and they wouldn't even notice. Come on, Valkyrie. This is Fletcher's fight. Not ours."

China continued on.

After a moment, Valkyrie followed.

88

Up they went.

They reached the thirty-third floor and stepped into a corridor littered with dead convicts, with Serafina Dey standing there in another weirdly awesome dress.

"Finally," Serafina said, "some decent conversation. These people have not been helpful in the slightest. They kept trying to kill me, and then had the gall to protest when I started killing them. These are Abyssinia's people, aren't they? Is she here? With the boy?"

"Yes," said China.

"They've come to kill you, haven't they?"

"I would expect so."

"And to think," Serafina said, "I was going to waste my time hunting for him when all I needed to do was wait for him to come here to murder you."

"I'm glad my predicament has been of benefit to you," China said. "It means this day is not a total waste."

"I know you're being sarcastic," Serafina responded, "but I can't help but agree. So, you're going to confront them, are you?"

"If you want to accompany us—"

"Oh, I do."

Doors opened behind them and shooters came through, filling the air with those lethal red bolts. China dropped her rifle and tapped her shoulders, then flung her arms wide and a blue wave took the closest convicts off their feet. Valkyrie threw lightning at the others. When they were down, she realised Serafina was appraising her.

"You have power," she said. "Excellent."

Valkyrie didn't like the way she was looking at her. She preferred it when she was being ignored.

Two more shooters stormed in. Valkyrie raised a shield and China crouched behind her, but Serafina was exposed. It didn't seem to worry her all that much.

With bolts of red sizzling all around her, Serafina held her hands up like she was praying, then flicked them apart. The shooters slammed into the walls on either side of the corridor.

The first to recover grabbed his rifle. Serafina pinched her thumb and forefinger together and raised her hand, and the shooter was picked up off his feet. He struggled, eyes wide, grasping at whatever was holding him, but Serafina flicked her hand again and he hit the ground with enough force to break every bone in his body.

The second shooter tried to run. Serafina closed her hand and he jerked to a stop, his arms and legs pressing into each other, his body twisting. He screamed as Serafina squeezed, and then the scream was cut off and he dropped like a sack of broken twigs.

China brushed at something on her dress. "We're trying not to kill them," she said.

"Are we?" Serafina asked. "Whyever are we doing that? Is that your idea, girl?"

"The name's Valkyrie."

"Is it your idea, I asked?"

"Yes."

"It's a silly one," Serafina said, walking onwards. "I shan't be doing it."

"And you thought I was bad," China muttered, and followed.

They continued like this, floor after floor, getting shot at, shooting back, Serafina making arch comments. Valkyrie lost her pistol somewhere along the way and just started hurling lightning at people. It was more satisfying anyway.

On the forty-sixth floor there was the crash of a door opening, some startled cries, and then the unmistakable sounds of people getting punched. Valkyrie hurried to the corner, looked round, watched Skulduggery beat the hell out of four shooters who were panicking too much to offer any kind of challenge.

When he'd stomped the last one's head into the floor, Valkyrie made herself known. "Where have you been?"

"Trapped," he responded, adjusting his hat slightly as he came over, "in an ingenious device that slows time. A truly remarkable feat of engineering, if I'm being honest. I don't think I've ever been in a more impressive trap in all my years of being trapped in things. It really was quite something. I would have been held there for a full week if I hadn't managed to escape."

"And how *did* you escape?"

"I'm not sure. I think it broke down, actually."

"Hmm," said Valkyrie. "So not all that impressive, then."

"It was very impressive at the time," Skulduggery countered. "You know, before it stopped working. I came straight here to convince China to release you, and found the whole place overrun with killers. But you managed to get out of your cell, which is a nice surprise. How did you manage that?"

"We'll have time for explanations later," said China, as she and Serafina came round the corner. "We've been caught off guard, but I believe we have retaken the initiative. By now, Nero has hopefully been neutralised, which means Abyssinia's army has lost its manoeuvring capability. It also means that Abyssinia is stuck here."

Skulduggery tilted his head. "And do we know where she is?"

"We do," said China. "Would you like to come with us?"

"By all means, lead on."

89

Valkyrie was expecting an ambush.

The doors to China's apartment were wide open. Two Cleavers lay dead outside. China discarded the rifle like it was a toy she'd grown bored of, and led the way in. Serafina was to her left, Valkyrie and Skulduggery to her right.

But there was no ambush. Instead, Razzia and Caisson were standing there, waiting for them.

China froze when she saw them. Caisson stared at her.

"My boy," China said softly.

Caisson said, "No. You don't get to call me that." He was different to when Valkyrie had last seen him. Calmer. A lot calmer.

"You don't have to be a part of this," China said. "You can walk away. I'll see to it that nothing bad happens to you ever again."

Caisson's eyes flickered to Serafina. "You'll protect me from her, will you?"

"I'll protect you from everyone," said China.

"And who, I wonder, will protect me from you?"

Before China could answer, Abyssinia walked in from another room, examining the ceilings and the walls as she did so. She had a smile on her face until she saw Skulduggery. "You're not supposed to be here," she said, dismayed. "How did you free yourself?"

Skulduggery shrugged. "I think the Eternity Gate needs a little fine-tuning before it's ready for the mass market. It still has a few bugs in its system."

"This is... unfortunate," Abyssinia said. "I didn't want to have to kill you. That's why I trapped you there. To save you."

"Thank you, Abyssinia," Skulduggery said, "but I'm long past saving."

Abyssinia shook her head, like she was ridding herself of sad thoughts. A smile reappeared as her eyes settled on China. "You have a lovely home," she said. "It's not necessarily to my taste, but lovely, even so. Naturally, I'd have to change the colour scheme, replace the furniture, generally make it fit for royalty before I move in."

"You're going to take over, are you?" China asked. "That's your big plan?"

Abyssinia smiled. "That's part of it. But I'm not actually here for me. I'm here because my son needed to come. For closure, as they say these days. Caisson, my dear, how are you feeling?"

"As usual," he muttered, "I'm conflicted. And a little overwhelmed. But, before we go on, hello, Valkyrie."

"Hi," Valkyrie said back.

"I don't want to kill you," he said. "I just want to be clear on that."

"I appreciate it."

"But you other three," Caisson said, "you're the three people I hate most in this world. I want to kill *you*. I want to kill you so incredibly violently." His hands clenched into fists, then sprang open. "Skulduggery Pleasant: you murdered my mother. Serafina: *you* had me tortured for decades. You ensured that each moment was pure agony. And China. Oh, China. You'd protect me, would you? But you betrayed me. I really don't know which one of you I want to kill more."

"Serafina," Skulduggery and China said at the same time.

"In fact," Skulduggery continued, "I don't think I should be on that list at all. Yes, I killed Abyssinia, but look. She got better."

"After a few hundred years of being a heart in a box," Abyssinia said.

"You're standing here with us now, aren't you?" Skulduggery said. "*That's* the important thing."

"It's all connected," Caisson said to Skulduggery. "You made sure I grew up without a mother. You made sure that *she* raised me instead." His eyes locked on to China. "*You* told me I was like a son to you. We pretended that I *was* your son. And then you handed me over to *her*."

"Finally," said Serafina, "we get to me. I'm not going to deny what you're saying, Caisson. I'm not going to make excuses. I had you tortured. The broken person you are today – you owe it all to me. And now I'm here to take you back."

"Oh," Caisson said, "you are, are you?"

"You killed Mevolent, you filthy little murderer. You killed my *husband*. I'm not done with you yet."

Caisson snarled and raised his hands, and Valkyrie stepped between them.

"Don't," she said. "Don't do this."

"Move out of the way, Valkyrie," Caisson said. "I don't want to hurt you, but I will if I have to."

"Abyssinia lied to you."

"Excuse me?" Abyssinia said.

Valkyrie ignored her, and focused on Caisson. "Everyone's lied to you. Everyone has treated you terribly. I can't imagine what it must have been like to lose your mother. I can't imagine having to pretend that you were someone else, that your mother was someone else. I've been told how you fell in love with Solace, and about how Serafina snatched her away. They told me how you sneaked back into Mevolent's castle to rescue her. About how you were the one who killed Mevolent." Valkyrie glanced at Abyssinia, and Abyssinia frowned. She looked back at Skulduggery, hesitated, then continued. "Abyssinia lied to you, Caisson. You were raised believing that Lord Vile was your father."

Caisson's eyes narrowed. "Because he was. My mother and Lord Vile joined Mevolent's army together. They *were* together. There was no one else." He looked at Abyssinia. "Tell them."

Abyssinia didn't appear to have heard him. Her eyes were on Valkyrie. "How did you know?"

"How did she know what?" Caisson said. "Mother. How did she know what?"

"You looked inside my mind," Abyssinia said softly.

Valkyrie blushed, like she'd been caught eavesdropping.

Finally, Abyssinia looked at her son. "I did it to protect you."

Caisson took a step back. "What? What did you do?"

"If the truth got out," Abyssinia said, "you would have been hunted down. They wouldn't have stopped until you were dead."

"Lord Vile is my father."

"No, Caisson. He isn't."

Skulduggery tilted his head.

"This is highly entertaining," Serafina said, clearly loving every bit of it. "So who *is* the father?"

"Caisson—"

"Answer the question!" Caisson snarled. "If it isn't Lord Vile, then who is it?"

Abyssinia looked him dead in the eye, and gave a slow, wistful smile. "Joining Mevolent's army was everything I had worked for my entire life. My father, the King of the Darklands, had practically raised him, had taught him everything he knew, and, as a reward, Mevolent killed him, and had my mother and my siblings killed also. He would have killed me, too, only I escaped. I was but a child. My heritage had been ripped from me. My destiny lay in tatters. I didn't know what revenge was, but I knew I wanted it. It drove me. It consumed me.

"When I encountered Lord Vile, I saw in him a weapon I could wield, and we happily joined the army of the man who had butchered my family, so that I could get close to him and, eventually, kill him, as he had killed my father and my entire family. In my naivety, I thought I could control Vile, have him pick off my enemies, my rivals in the Diablerie while I rose to the top. But Lord Vile could never be controlled. Not really. When I realised that, I knew I had to make other arrangements. I had to form new alliances. My friendship with China was one such alliance, but I had others. I had plenty of others.

"The night of the feast, the night Lord Vile and I planned to kill Mevolent, was the culmination of all my scheming. I had finally, I thought, manoeuvred myself into a position where the others would accept me as their new leader. We would kill Mevolent, we would kill Serafina – and then I would take over. I would no longer be the Princess of the Darklands. Finally, I would be the Queen, and my family would be avenged."

Abyssinia's smile grew shaky.

"Mere hours before I was due to give Lord Vile the signal to attack, I discovered I was pregnant. This changed... everything. My destiny opened up before me. Instead of avenging my fallen family, I could start a new one. I could walk away, leave the hatred and the ambition and the anger behind me. I didn't have time to tell Lord Vile about any of this, of course, and we all know what happened then."

"Far be it from me to point this out," Serafina said, "but you still haven't told us who the unfortunate father is."

"Have I not?" Abyssinia asked, frowning. "Oh. Forgive me. It was your husband, Serafina. It was Mevolent. In all my manoeuvring, it seems I manoeuvred a little *too* close to the man I hated beyond all others."

Serafina paled, and Caisson's legs gave out. He fell to his knees and Abyssinia reached for him, but he slapped her hand away.

"I'm sorry," she responded. "If Mevolent had found out that he had a child, he would have had you slaughtered."

"But I killed him," said Caisson. "*I killed my own father.*"

Abyssinia didn't have anything to say to that.

"You're lying," Serafina whispered.

"I do not lie," said Abyssinia. There were tears in her eyes, but her tone was defiant.

Serafina stormed across the room and Abyssinia went to meet her, and Nero appeared, sweating, stumbling to the floor.

Razzia grabbed him, hauled him up. "Get us out of here," she said. "Now."

Just before Serafina and Abyssinia collided, Abyssinia disappeared, along with Caisson and her little gang of followers.

Serafina screamed in rage.

90

Serafina swept from the room and Valkyrie watched her go.

"The cameras are coming back online," China said, staring into the middle distance. "The Coldheart convicts are... They seem to be surrendering."

"They don't have Abyssinia in their minds any more, telling them what to do," Valkyrie said, and looked at Skulduggery. He was unusually quiet. "Everything all right?"

He didn't answer immediately. "Abyssinia has sacrificed most of her followers. She attacked us and lost."

"So?"

"So that's risky," Skulduggery said. "That was a risky move. Abyssinia wouldn't risk sacrificing that amount of people if victory wasn't assured in some form or..." He straightened. "There's a bomb."

"I'm sorry?"

"What did you say?" China asked, looking round.

"On any ordinary day," said Skulduggery, "what would be the chances of sneaking a bomb into this building?"

"Virtually non-existent," China answered. "Apart from all our regular security measures, the Whispering has been modified to detect explosives."

Skulduggery nodded. "So Abyssinia would have to distract us with something huge, something crazy – like a full-scale attack that would set off every alarm you had. Are the shields still up?"

"Yes."

"That could interfere with a signal, so an attempt to detonate the bomb remotely might not be successful. It must be on a timer."

"Skulduggery," said China, "I'm telling you. If there were any explosives in the High Sanctuary, I would already know."

"Besides," said Valkyrie, "wouldn't a bomb kill Abyssinia's own people, too?"

"She's already written them off," Skulduggery replied. "She came in here personally because of Caisson, because he wanted the opportunity to watch China die – but that wasn't the primary intent. When she spoke to me yesterday, she said the Sanctuaries will collapse into chaos. The only way that would happen is if the High Sanctuary is destroyed."

"But Abyssinia was practically appraising the place," Valkyrie said. "Planning to redecorate. Why would she be even joking about moving in if she's going to blow up the building?"

Skulduggery tilted his head. "Because not all bombs are explosive." He turned to China. "Scan for a device in the middle levels. Somewhere central. It might have an energy signature you don't recognise."

"Give me a moment," China said. Her eyelids began to flutter.

Valkyrie turned to the sound of running footsteps. Cleavers. And Fletcher, out of breath and bringing up the rear.

"Stairs," he gasped. "They're awful."

"What happened with Nero?" Valkyrie asked. "He looked exhausted."

"I think I may have... short-circuited him. He started to... lose control." Fletcher sucked in a deep breath, and exhaled. "Basically, I beat him, and I'm pretty sure I broke him."

China opened her eyes. "Found it," she said. "Fletcher, twenty-fifth floor. Now."

All of them, Cleavers included, laid a hand on Fletcher's back and the next instant they were in a corridor junction. China took a moment to orientate herself, then led the way to a windowless room with a black box, about the size of a car battery, sitting on a table.

"What are we looking at?" Fletcher asked.

"It's a bomb that targets organic life," Skulduggery said, walking round the table slowly. "A long time ago, Abyssinia came up with the idea for this, based on her own ability to drain the life force from living things. If this goes off, it could kill everyone in the building and not disturb a single chair."

"That's OK," said Fletcher, "I'll just teleport it somewhere it can't hurt anyone."

Skulduggery held up a hand. "We don't know how sensitive it is. Teleporting it could set it off."

"Everybody out," China said. "I can contain it." She started carving a sigil into the wall with her fingernail.

"Are you sure?" Valkyrie asked, stepping out into the corridor with Skulduggery and Fletcher.

"Perfectly," China responded. "Talk among yourselves while I work. Or run away. Either is acceptable."

Fletcher waited a moment. "So we're staying, are we?"

"Yes, we are," said Valkyrie, keeping her voice low.

"Skulduggery," China said as she worked, "Abyssinia presumably came here to kill us all because she's about to launch her grand offensive and she requires the Sanctuaries to be destabilised just when they'll be needed the most. Do we know yet what this grand offensive is?"

"From what I can gather," Skulduggery said, "she's going to send First Wave to attack an American military post. This will reveal magic to the world, which will then push the American people towards war with sorcerers – which is where President Flanery comes in, I would imagine."

China didn't stop carving sigils. "How wonderfully diabolical of her. Do we know which military post?"

"We do not."

"Cleaver, bring one of the convicts in here."

The Cleaver nodded, and left.

"Caisson's life is in danger," China continued, her voice a little softer.

"Yes, it is," said Skulduggery. "Who do you think she'll send after him?"

"She'll want it to be done right. She'll send her sister."

"Wait," Valkyrie said, "I'm missing something."

"Oh, good," said Fletcher, "I thought it was just me."

"Once word gets out that Caisson is Mevolent's son," Skulduggery said, "Serafina's followers will flock to him. She may have been the wife of their messiah, but Mevolent's own flesh and blood would inspire a deeper sort of loyalty. The Legion of Judgement could very well be hollowed out and all her power and influence would desert her."

"So Caisson has to die," Valkyrie said, "and Serafina's sister is going to kill him? The same one we met on the steps?"

"That's Rune," said China, "and if she wanted to kill someone, she'd kill them face to face. But Serafina has another sister, one who worked as an assassin during the war. I expect she's setting out to track Caisson down even as we speak."

"But Caisson will be OK, won't he?" Valkyrie asked. "He's got Abyssinia watching over him. I don't care how good this assassin is, she won't be able to get past Abyssinia. Right?"

"Right," said Skulduggery. "Caisson is perfectly safe."

"So long as he stays with Abyssinia," said China.

Valkyrie hesitated. "He... he didn't look too pleased with her."

"No, he didn't."

The Cleaver returned, pushing a shackled convict before him. A mage came with them.

"Excuse me," the mage said, "could we borrow Mr Renn for a while? We've got enemies that need transporting straight to the cells."

"Absolutely," China said, finishing up the final sigil.

Fletcher hesitated. "Are you sure? Maybe I should stick around in case you need a quick evacuation."

"Nonsense," China said, stepping out of the room. "You see? I'm all done. Go and help with the clean-up."

Fletcher followed the mage out, and China looked at the convict.

"And what is your name?"

The convict glared at them all. "I'm not telling you nothing. You can—"

"Clerihew Montgomery," Skulduggery said. "Imprisoned for two counts of murder."

Clerihew snarled. "They had it coming. You all have it coming."

"That's nice, dear," China said. "Put him in this room, please, Cleaver."

The Cleaver shoved him in and China tapped her arm. The sigils on the walls lit up, activating the force field. His eyes widened when he realised he was trapped.

"As you probably already know," China said, "that is Abyssinia's life-force bomb. When it goes off, this force field should contain it and ensure that we, out here, are perfectly safe."

Valkyrie didn't like this *should* business.

China continued. "You, however, will die instantly. Your life will be drained from your body, and you will be reduced to nothing more than a dry and empty husk."

"You... you can't do that," said Clerihew. "That's not allowed."

"I'm the Supreme Mage," China replied. "I can do whatever I want. The thing is, though, the bomb's on a timer, and we have no way of knowing when it will detonate. Any moment now, I should imagine."

"That's murder. You'd be murdering me!"

"Technically, Abyssinia would be murdering you. I just wouldn't let you out. But here's the good news. You don't have to be murdered at all. It's true. I will drop the force field and you can walk out right now – and all you have to do is tell me which military post Abyssinia is planning to attack."

Clerihew shook his head. "But I don't know."

"I'm afraid you'll have to be a bit more forthcoming in order to escape."

"No, really, I don't know," Clerihew said. "She never bothered to tell us. Why would she? We're not involved in that stuff, the planning stuff. She points and we go, that's the drill. I don't know, OK? I don't. You got to let me out."

"I believe I was quite clear on the rules, Mr Montgomery."

"Oh, God, please."

"China," Valkyrie said, "we don't know when it's going to go off, so maybe you should let him out."

"Yes!" Clerihew said. "Yes, let me out!"

"Not until you tell me the name of the military post," China said calmly.

"I don't know it! I swear to you! Please! All I know is it's a base and it's got sailors on it! Get a Sensitive down here to read my mind – they'll know I'm not lying! Please, let me out!"

Valkyrie looked to Skulduggery for help.

"If Clerihew tells us where we can find Coldheart Prison," he said, "we might be able to locate this naval base ourselves."

China pondered the proposal, and nodded. "Yes," she said. "That is acceptable. Mr Montgomery?"

"It's nearby!" Clerihew said. "Just off the coast of Dublin, over a little island, called, um... Aw, jeez, I can't remember! It's a small island!"

"Dalkey Island," Skulduggery said, "Bull Island, Colt Island..."

Clerihew shook his head. "No, no. It has these weird little things on it! Not kangaroos, not koalas—"

"Wallabies," said Valkyrie. "Lambay Island."

"That's it, yes!" Clerihew said, pointing at Valkyrie. "Abyssinia wanted it close in case anything went wrong! She's going to leave it there while everyone goes and does this American thing! Please, for the love of God, will you let me out now?"

"Of course," China said. "I am nothing if not a woman of my—"

She stopped talking. The bomb had started to hum.

Clerihew stared at it, pressing his back against the force field. "Let me out, please," he said quietly.

"China," Valkyrie said, tugging at her arm, "let him out."

"I'm afraid I can't," China said.

Clerihew spun. "You said. You said you'd let me out if I told you and I told you so please let me out!"

"The bomb is armed," said China. "It could go off at any moment."

"Drop the force field," Valkyrie said. "It'll just take a second."

"And, in that second, the bomb could go off. Mr Montgomery, I'm dreadfully sorry, but it appears I won't be releasing you today."

Clerihew stared. "You said. You said!"

"Dreadfully sorry."

The bomb went off.

There was no sound. There was just a flash that made the force field turn a bright blue, and Clerihew stopped panicking. He just stood there, mouth open, eyes open, and then he crumpled, like he was a collection of scaffolding that was falling in on itself. The force field burned like that for another moment, struggling to contain the forces that had been unleashed, before it returned to normal.

Valkyrie stared.

Skulduggery stepped forward, examining the force field. "It held," he said.

"You doubted me?" China asked.

"I doubt everyone. We're lucky it held."

"I knew it would."

"You hoped it would."

"He died," Valkyrie said quietly.

They looked round at her.

China hesitated. "I did intend to let him out," she said at last.

Valkyrie nodded. "I know."

"It was just unfortunate timing."

"OK."

"We'll talk about this later. Right now, we've got to find out which naval base Abyssinia is going to attack. I can send a team of mages and a Cleaver squad to Coldheart—"

"We can get there quicker," Skulduggery said. "Valkyrie, are you with me?"

Valkyrie pulled her eyes away from Clerihew's lifeless body. "Always," she said.

91

Coldheart was almost empty.

There were maybe thirty convicts remaining. The others had been left behind somewhere. Omen didn't know where, but from the snippets of conversation he'd been able to piece together, their plans had not been working out and some of the convicts were worrying.

Also, the "weirdo with the scars", who Omen assumed to be Caisson, had walked out. Abyssinia, apparently, was not happy about any of it.

First Wave were still here, unfortunately. Jenan came up with Lapse and Gall to shackle Omen's hands and take him down to where everyone had congregated. Mr Lilt was here, and so was Razzia. She gave Omen a smile and waved to him. He didn't know what to make of that.

Jenan shoved Omen ahead of him and Gall stuck his foot out. Omen tripped. Gall laughed. Omen got to his knees and Jenan cuffed the back of his head.

"Stay," Jenan said.

Omen stayed.

Abyssinia and Nero walked in. First Wave, and the remaining convicts, went quiet.

"My children," Abyssinia said, then paused, her eyes downcast. When she continued, her voice was softer. "And you *are* my children. Each and every one of you makes me proud. We have been through so much in our short time together that you are now family to me – and you know the lengths I will go to for family."

There were smiles and nods all round.

"We have suffered losses," Abyssinia said. "As you know, the raid earlier did not go as planned and the bomb... they must have found the bomb. The Supreme Mage still lives and the High Sanctuary still functions. Many of our friends have been captured. For this, I blame myself. I beg your forgiveness."

Omen watched Nero. He was sweating. He looked sick. More than that, he looked like he was in pain.

"But we will see them again," Abyssinia said. "We will free them from their shackles, and they will take their place by our side in the sun. It is time, my children. The night is finally upon us."

There were cheers.

When they'd died down, she continued. "You know that we shall be targeting an American naval base. Whitley is a quiet little peninsula in Oregon, and what they do at the Naval Magazine there is they stock battleships and submarines with food and fuel and munitions, and they send them off. There are twenty-seven active duty personnel stationed there this very night – and the brave members of First Wave are going to kill every last one of them.

"The watchtowers, sentries, and the boat patrols have already been eliminated, and communications and alarms have been cut. Most of the sailors are already asleep in the barracks. You will go in. You will kill whoever you find there. You will let the security cameras see you. This is important. I want your powers on full display. When this gets broadcast around the world, I want the mortals to quake in fear at what a few teenagers can do. *If the children can do this*, I want them to say, *what can the adults do?*"

Everyone Omen looked at was beaming at the thought. It was insane.

"Mr Lilt," Abyssinia said, "do you have any words of encouragement for your students?"

Lilt stepped forward. "Tonight is a special, special night," he said. "It is the night you've been waiting for. It is what you've been building up to. It is the first step towards war, and the first step towards our great victory. And it all starts with you. I'm so proud of each and every one of you."

The members of First Wave were hugging and holding hands. Their chests were swelling.

"The Dead Men, the Diablerie – history will forget them all," Abyssinia said. "History will never forget First Wave. You will be the heroes of the new world. You will be legends." Her eyes found Omen. "And you, little boy, you will have your role to play also. Your name might not be remembered in years to come, but your face will strike fear into the hearts of mortals everywhere. You will be the one they interrogate. The one they dissect. You are, in your own way, vital to our cause. My throne will be built on the bones of my enemies, but it will be built from the sacrifices that will be made at Naval Magazine Whitley. So thank you, Omen Darkly. And thank you all. Now go, and know that my love goes with you."

Nero and Lilt came forward, and they all waited to teleport.

But something was wrong with Nero. He vanished without them, then came back, frustrated. It was clear that he hadn't meant to do that, but no one said anything.

"Link hands," he snapped. First Wave did so, and Jenan grabbed a handful of Omen's hair. Omen scowled in pain, and, after a few more seconds of trying, they finally teleported.

92

They flew through the cloaking field, and Coldheart Prison appeared before them.

Valkyrie landed, ready for gunfire, for alarms, for *shouting*, at least. But there was only the sound of the wind and the sea beneath them.

Skulduggery led the way to the Beast, the biggest and ugliest of the buildings on the hovering island. The door was open. Once inside, Skulduggery raised his hand to the air.

"It's impossible to say for sure," he murmured, "but it would appear the prison has been evacuated."

"We'd better search quickly, then," Valkyrie said, moving past him. "Once the Cleavers get here they're likely to stamp anything resembling a clue to dust."

They started with the control room.

"You're quiet," Skulduggery said as he skimmed through computer logs.

Valkyrie went through a handful of files left out on one of the desks, looking for anything related to a military base. "Am I?"

"Is everything all right?"

She glanced up. "Can't this wait until after we've saved the world?"

"Of course," he said. "Of course."

He went back to searching. She frowned at him. "How are *you* doing?"

"Me?" he said. "Fine. Why?"

"You sound angry."

He looked up. "You answer me, I'll answer you."

She sighed. "I'm still kind of reeling over that guy China killed."

"In her defence, it was an accident."

"Yeah," said Valkyrie. "Maybe. OK, now you. Why are you angry?"

"Why wouldn't I be angry? You were almost beaten to death in that cell and I was nowhere around."

"You were trapped in a time-slowing thing."

"I should never have let them arrest you."

"You didn't really have a choice. We may be super-cool Arbiters, but we're not above the law. China had every right to arrest me, and there's no one to blame for what happened in that cell except for Yonder and his friends. I'm quite looking forward to seeing him again, actually."

Skulduggery stood. "We're not going to find anything here and we're wasting time." He went to a diagram on the wall beside the door. Valkyrie joined him.

"What are we looking for?"

"Somewhere comfy," he said.

"In a prison?"

"The most comfortable area in a prison will be the guards' quarters. Abyssinia will have commandeered them for herself and her lot, so they'd all be in the same area... here." His gloved finger jabbed the diagram, and Valkyrie didn't even have time to figure out where that was before he was stalking away and she was following along behind.

"That wasn't what I meant, by the way," she said as they walked. "When I asked how you were doing? I wasn't talking about how you felt about what happened to me. I was talking about Caisson and the whole... Mevolent being his father thing."

Skulduggery didn't look back. "I told you he wasn't my son."

"But there had been a possibility."

"You're wondering if I'm upset about it. I'm not."

"That's cool," she said. "It's just... it was a chance at having family again."

"I already have family. I didn't need the possibility of a son I never knew about."

Valkyrie frowned. "What family do you have?"

"I've got over four hundred and fifty years of family," he answered as they went up metal stairs, "provided to me by siblings, cousins, aunts and uncles. For all I know, I'm surrounded by family at all times."

"But do you have any, like *close* family members?"

"Yes," he said.

"Who?"

"An older brother."

Valkyrie came up alongside him as he walked. "You have an older brother? Who's still alive? And you haven't mentioned him before *now*?"

"You've never asked. I ask you questions about *your* life all the time, but, once I'd answered what it was like to be a skeleton, you seemed to lose interest."

"Oh, God. Oh, God, you're right. I'm a terrible friend."

He patted her shoulder. "You're just a little narcissistic, that's all."

She gaped. "Coming from you, that's horrible."

"I know," he said happily. "But of course you're narcissistic. Why wouldn't you be? You're as unique as I am. I've never heard of anyone doing what you did when you healed yourself."

"And now China wants to do experiments on me. She's not going to, is she? I mean, she wouldn't. I know she's, like, one hundred per cent China Sorrows at all times, but she's my friend, too. She does actually care about me – ignoring the time she had me arrested."

"She does seem to care," Skulduggery admitted. "But you can expect her to try to persuade you to do a few blood tests, a couple of scans, some chopping off of body parts..."

Valkyrie waved her hand. "I'm fine with all *that*, it's the written work I'd have objections to."

"That's just what I told her."

They got to the guards' quarters. The rooms were pretty bare, but they started to search them, one at a time.

"It must have been weird for her to see Caisson again after all this time," Valkyrie said loudly as she searched. "Do you think it registered on whatever emotional scale she uses?"

"I'd say so," came Skulduggery's reply from another room.

"I know we joke about it a lot, how we can never trust her, but I think she's proven herself. I mean, hasn't she? She tends to do right by us."

"Are you sure about that?"

Valkyrie checked under a bed, then straightened up. "Oh, come on. You can't doubt that the three of us are on the same side."

"I've thought China was on my side so many times over the years," Skulduggery said, "only to be corrected by China herself. I should have learned it by the time I was thirty. I should definitely have learned it by the time I was a hundred and ninety. By the time I was three hundred—"

"OK, I get your point."

"I could go on."

Valkyrie went to the next room. "You knew her when you were a young man, then?"

"Her and her brother," Skulduggery responded.

"Mr Bliss scared the hell out of me."

"Really? I always thought he was funny."

She raised an eyebrow at the wall. "Somehow that doesn't surprise me. What age were you when China joined up with Mevolent?"

"Thirty," he said. "Her family were prominent worshippers of the Faceless Ones, so she had always flirted with joining Mevolent's cause – but I was thirty years and five months old when she made it official."

"Your memory is that precise?"

"I had just met my future wife a few months earlier. That year sticks out."

Valkyrie smiled. "Fair enough."

"Five years later, we were at war, and China and I were suddenly enemies."

"But then flash forward four hundred and something years, and look at you now! Trust has finally been established!"

They both emerged from doorways. There was only one room left to search.

"China still has secrets," Skulduggery said.

Valkyrie shrugged. "Don't we all?"

Skulduggery folded his arms. "What do we know about Solace?"

"Well, from what China told us, she was one of Serafina's handmaidens. She fell in love with Caisson and ran off with him. Serafina found her again, dragged her back, and Caisson went to rescue her. In doing so, he – unknowingly – killed his own dad."

"After which, Serafina went straight to China," Skulduggery said, "and China surrendered Caisson, a boy she had raised as her own son, without a fight."

"Which is weird."

"And, once Serafina grabbed Caisson, China had Solace committed."

Valkyrie frowned. "She what?"

"China's the one who put Solace in Greymire Asylum," Skulduggery said.

"Why?"

"I haven't been able to find that out yet."

"Well... Solace must have had a breakdown or something,

461

right? Her boyfriend has just been taken away from her, so I suppose it's understandable that she'd be upset."

"I imagine Caisson was more than a boyfriend," Skulduggery said. "As near as I can work it out, they got together in 1770, when Caisson was twenty-five."

"But... but he didn't kill Mevolent until, like..."

"1929."

"So you're saying Caisson and Solace were together for, uh, wait, let me—"

"A hundred and fifty-nine years."

Valkyrie slapped Skulduggery's shoulder in annoyance. "I would have got it."

"Of course you would."

"Caisson and Solace were together for a hundred and fifty-nine years. Well then, *no wonder* Solace went crazy. *Anyone* would have. She found someone she could love for a hundred and fifty-nine years and then this arrogant cow who wears a human skull as a headdress swoops in and takes him away to be tortured."

"There's more to it," Skulduggery said. "I don't know what it is yet, but there is something more."

"With China, there always is."

Skulduggery moved to the last room, and froze. Valkyrie frowned, and joined him.

A small table was filled with machine parts. There were shoes under the bed. A toothbrush in a glass.

"These are Destrier's quarters," Skulduggery said. "Every other cell has been cleared out because they were evacuating. But not this one. Why is that?"

Valkyrie looked round. "Because he's still here."

93

Omen wasn't very impressed with Naval Magazine Whitley so far but, considering the fact that the only thing he'd been able to see had been a map on the wall of this little office, that was hardly surprising.

According to the map, Naval Magazine Whitley consisted of a 1,750-foot pier, a load of warehouses, a bunch of military and administrative buildings – one of which he was currently in – and a hundred or so dome-like structures dotted across the peninsula. Also, a lot of trees and hiking trails.

Omen had expected gun emplacements on the outer edges of the base. What he was seeing instead was a visitor's centre and a souvenir shop.

Lapse let the blinds fall back against the window, and turned to Omen. "Won't be long now," he said.

Omen didn't respond, and Lapse's face soured.

"Fine," he said, "don't say anything. Sit there and sulk."

"What would you like me to say, Lapse?" Omen asked.

"I dunno," Lapse said. "Something. Anything. That's the first thing you've said since we got here."

Omen shrugged. "I'm just not used to talking to you. We never really chatted much in school."

"Well, this is different, isn't it? We're about to attack a frickin' *naval base*."

"If you can call it that."

Lapse frowned. "What's that supposed to mean?"

"This is supposed to be a new Pearl Harbour, right? Wasn't Pearl Harbour full of ships and soldiers? This place is... it's a loading dock."

"So?"

"When Jenan was telling me about it he made it sound like it was gonna be epic. How many soldiers are here?"

Lapse snorted. "You don't get soldiers in a naval base, idiot."

"Soldiers, sailors, whatever. How many?"

Lapse shrugged. "Twenty-seven."

"That's all?"

"Twenty-seven is enough, Abyssinia says. She says anything more and it'd be hard to contain it. Man... the moment that signal comes, I'm outta here, and I'm gonna get some blood on my hands."

"And how do you feel about that?"

Lapse grinned. "Excited. I mean... I mean, I am *buzzing.*"

"You seem nervous."

"What? I'm not."

"But you seem like you are. A lot of nervous energy."

"That's excitement."

"If you say so."

"*If you say so,*" Lapse echoed. "Do you think I'm stupid, is that it? You think you can convince me I'm nervous even though I know I'm just excited? You're not that clever, Darkly. Fact is, you're not clever at all."

"Yeah, you're probably right. Auger's the clever one."

"Big shock there."

"If Auger were here instead of me, you'd be unconscious by now," Omen said. "He would have found a way out of these shackles and you'd be, like, in a heap in the corner of the room with a broken jaw or something."

"He'd never get out of the shackles."

"He's the Chosen One, dude."

"I don't care, *dude*. People think way too highly of your brother. They think he can do anything, that nothing can beat him."

"Nothing *can* beat him."

"I'd beat him," said Lapse, jabbing his thumb into his chest. "I would."

Omen laughed. "You'd barely beat me."

"What are you even *on*? I'd smack the hell outta you."

"Oh, really?" said Omen. "Like you did when you all turned up to catch me, and had to wait until Mr Lilt arrived and did it himself?"

Lapse strode over. "I'll beat the hell out of you now, if you like."

"Oh, sure," Omen said, grinning. "Fight me when my hands are shackled. That'll prove it."

Lapse grabbed Omen's shirt, hauled him to his feet and pinned him against the wall. "You're gonna want to be shutting up now."

"I thought you wanted me to talk."

"I've changed my mind."

"Yeah, thought you might."

Lapse leaned in. "And what's *that* supposed to mean?"

"Nothing."

"Go on, tell me."

"You talk tough, Lapse, but we both know—"

Lapse punched him really hard in the shoulder. Omen twisted his body and couldn't stop the groan, but he followed it with a laugh.

"You think you're being clever again," said Lapse. "You think you can tease me into taking off your shackles."

"The word is goad."

"The word is shut the hell up," Lapse said, and punched his other shoulder.

"You think you can manipulate me?" Lapse asked. "You honestly think anyone would fall for this little game you're trying to play?"

"*You're* falling for it."

"You just admitted it!" Lapse exclaimed. "You just told me that's exactly what you're trying to do!"

"So?" Omen asked, straightening up again. His shoulders throbbed.

"Here's the really funny thing," said Lapse, leaning in again. "Even if I did take off those shackles, which I'm not gonna do, you'd still have to fight me in order to leave. And you really think you'd stand a chance of winning?"

"*You* obviously do, or else my shackles would be off by now."

Lapse prodded him in the chest. "I'm not taking off the shackles, all right?"

"Because you're scared."

"No," said Lapse, his face growing redder and redder, "because you don't take shackles off prisoners just to prove a stupid point." He walked back to the window.

Omen stayed where he was, and kept smiling.

Lapse looked outside, then glanced back and narrowed his eyes. "Stop looking at me."

"Sorry."

"And stop grinning."

Omen made a show of trying to stop his smile.

Lapse stormed over, turned Omen round and slammed his face against the wall. "Fine," he said, the key sliding into the shackles. "You want me to beat you up? You want it so much, great. Then the shackles go back on and nothing will have changed except now you've got a broken jaw and a busted nose."

The shackles dropped and Omen turned. Lapse raised his fists.

"Just step back there," said Omen. "Let's have some room to do this."

Lapse retreated to the middle of the office.

Omen followed, bouncing lightly on the balls of his feet. "Right then, should we set some ground rules?"

"No ground rules," Lapse said. "This isn't training, this isn't

Combat Arts class. This is real life. There are no ground rules in real life."

"Good point. OK, sorry, let's get this started."

Lapse grinned. "This is gonna hurt."

Omen held up a hand. "Hold on, wait, sorry. What if I hurt *you?*"

"Not gonna happen."

"Yeah, but what if I do? I mean, I get it, you hate me, you want to hurt me, but I don't really want to hurt *you*, so maybe we should come up with a signal if you want to give up."

"I'm not gonna be the one giving up."

"Well, you don't know that, now do you? Yeah, you're bigger and stronger and you'll probably win – but what if I get in a lucky shot? What if I, like, knee you in the groin? That'd put you down, wouldn't it?"

"Not necessarily."

"But it would hurt, right? And now I'm realising that the only way to probably beat you, probably, is to knee you in the groin repeatedly. Like, over and over again. Until there's nothing left."

Lapse looked appalled. "You'd do that?"

"I'd have to," said Omen. "I mean, there are lives on the line, right? I can't let your groin stand between me and saving lives."

"I suppose."

"Do you really want that to happen?"

"No."

"Me neither, man. So what are we going to do?"

"You could... you could put the shackles back on."

Omen winced. "Ah, well, see, now that I'm *out* of them, I don't want to go back *into* them. So again, there'll be a fight and, well... your groin."

"Christ."

"Whichever way this goes, it looks like your groin is in for a nasty time."

"But that's only if you get me," said Lapse, "and you won't

have the chance because I'm gonna knock your head off before you even get close."

"Ah, now, that doesn't help," Omen replied. "Now that I know what you're going for, I'll just cover my head with my arms, and *then* knee you in the groin."

"Then I won't go for your head. Maybe I'll knee *you* in the groin."

"So, we'll just be two guys with their arms over their heads, trying to knee each other in the groin?"

Lapse dropped his hands. "Then what do you suggest?"

"I don't know," Omen said. "It started out as a good idea, but now I'm not so sure." He looked at the door. "I mean... I could leave."

"What do you mean?"

"You could let me walk out."

"Without a fight?"

"The fight complicates things," Omen said.

"But I can't just let you leave. I'm meant to be keeping an eye on you."

Omen frowned. "Or..."

"Or what?"

"I'm not sure if this makes sense, but I think it might," Omen said, speaking slowly. His words started to speed up. "OK, so, in order to leave, we have to fight, yes?"

"Yes."

"But fighting would be painful, and would probably result in your groin being destroyed."

"Not forever."

"Oh, God, no, not forever. I wouldn't do that to you. It'd get better eventually. Here, I'll rephrase. Fighting would result in your groin being temporarily destroyed – which, to me, still sounds like a bad deal."

"Me too."

"But we're the only ones here – so we don't actually have to fight, do we?"

"What?"

"Why don't we just skip that part, and move on to me leaving? Then you wait for a few minutes for the pain to die down, wink wink, and then come after me."

"You don't have to say *wink wink* if you're actually winking."

"Yeah, sorry. So what do you reckon?"

"I dunno."

"Listen, is it a perfect solution? Probably not. But I think it solves most of our problems."

Lapse sighed. "Yeah. OK." He went over to the door, opened it, and stood aside to let Omen out.

Expecting Lapse to grab him or punch him at the last minute, Omen walked up... and stepped outside.

It had worked. It had actually worked.

Part one of his amazing escape was a roaring success. Now for part two. The tricky part. The part where he saved the day and managed to not get killed while doing so.

94

The main strip of the naval base was well lit but here, between all these administrative buildings, it was dark, and full of shadows.

From where he huddled, Omen could see right across to where the Pacific Ocean sploshed against the ridiculously long pier, with its four enormous mobile cranes. He could see the warehouses, which were a lot bigger than they'd appeared on the map, and, set well back from them, the military buildings, which included the barracks, where all those sailors lay sleeping.

Omen started sneaking forward.

He needed to raise the alarm before First Wave launched their attack. Get all those sailors to grab their guns and come outside. He was pretty sure First Wave would collapse in a whimpering heap if that happened. Admittedly, that would risk exposing magic to the world, but it was probably the best way to save lives.

Saving lives had to come first, Omen reckoned. Saving lives had to always come first.

He whirled when he heard running footsteps. Lapse sprinted straight for him.

Omen held his hands out, and Lapse lost the violence in his eyes and stopped just short of a collision.

"I got you," Lapse said.

"Well, yes," Omen replied, his voice less shaky than he expected.

"But that really doesn't do us much good, does it? We'll just go right back to where we were."

"Oh, yeah."

"You've got to give me a good head start, you know? How about this? I go this way, and you go that way. When you meet Mr Lilt or the others, tell them I escaped and you're hunting for me."

"What if I catch you again?"

"Unless you've got someone else with you, let's just pretend we don't see each other."

Lapse sighed. "Yeah, OK. Which way are you going?"

Omen pointed.

"Fair enough," said Lapse, and ran in the opposite direction.

Omen carried on, moving quickly but quietly and sticking to the darkness. The closer he got to the barracks the better he felt. It was OK. It was going to be OK. It was all going to be ohhh crap.

He ducked back as Jenan and Gall walked into view. It was a miracle they hadn't seen him. He took a peek. They were strutting around, throwing fireballs. He didn't know what they thought they were doing until he saw the security camera and realised they were performing. They carried on until they were out of sight.

Omen stayed where he was. The attack hadn't started yet. First Wave probably needed to work themselves up to the slaughter. That was good. That bought him some time.

He closed his eyes, pictured Auger's face and repeated his name in his mind. He'd managed to form a connection back in Coldheart, if only for a moment. He could do it again. He had to. Lives were depending on him.

He controlled his breathing and tried to build a tunnel with his thoughts.

It wasn't working. He furrowed his brow against the doubt that came creeping. It'd take over if he let it, that doubt. It'd overwhelm it like it always did and he'd have to give up. Like he always did.

But not this time. This time it was too important. He needed to believe that he could do this. He *could* do this. He didn't even have to do much because his brother was the Chosen One, for God's sake. Omen just had to do the bare minimum and then trust that Auger had been trying to communicate with him since that attempt in the cell. His brother would have known he was in trouble. He'd be ready. Omen may have had precious little faith in himself, but he had all the faith in the world in his brother.

DUDE.

Omen hissed, hands clutching his head.

DUDEWHEREAREYOU?

His foot slipped and he fell backwards.

DUDEWHEREAREYOUAREYOUOK?

"Stop shouting," Omen muttered, his eyes squeezed shut against the pain.

SORRYSORRYAREYOUOK?

"Talk slower."

NOTTALKINGTHINKING.

"Then think slower."

There was a blessed moment of peace before Auger replied.

IS THIS BETTER?

"Barely."

DUDE WHERE ARE YOU? NO ONE AT SCHOOL'S SEEN YOU.

Omen swayed on his feet. "I'm with First Wave."

YOU JOINED THEM?

"What? No. They kidnapped me. I was in Coldheart. Now I'm in America."

WHAT'S GOING ON?

"You need to get Skulduggery and Valkyrie and, like, the High Sanctuary. Jenan and the others... they're going to kill everyone on this base."

WHATBASEWHERE?

"You're speeding up again. It's called Naval Magazine Whitley. It's a small base for restocking ships and stuff. Abyssinia wants them to kill everyone."

OMEN?

"What?"

OMEN, I CAN'T HEAR YOU.

Omen narrowed his eyes and focused on the tunnel between them. "Can you hear me now?"

YES.

"I don't know what to do. Do I raise the alarm?"

IF YOU DO, THE SOLDIERS ARE GOING TO KILL EVERYONE IN FIRST WAVE.

"I don't think they're soldiers, I think they're sailors."

DUDE, DOESN'T MATTER.

"Sorry."

WE CAN SAVE EVERYONE. NO ONE HAS TO DIE. I'M COMING, OK? I HAVE NEVER WITH ME. HOLD ON A SECOND.

Omen waited.

NAVAL MAGAZINE WHITLEY. WE HAVE IT ON MY PHONE. YOU'RE CLOSE TO SEATTLE.

"OK, cool. Now what happens?"

NEVER SAYS SHE'S VISITED A PARTICULAR BRIDGE IN SEATTLE. SHE'S... SHE'S STILL TALKING ABOUT THE BRIDGE.

"Yeah."

DID YOU KNOW SHE WAS SO INTO BRIDGES?

"Never does love bridges."

LISTEN, WE'RE GOING TO START TELEPORTING TOWARDS YOU. IF IT'S A CLEAR NIGHT, WE WON'T BE LONG.

"It's clear."

THEN WE'LL BE TEN MINUTES OR SO. FIND SOMEWHERE TO WAIT.

"I can't just *hide*, Auger. I have to stop the others before they hurt anyone."

THEY'LL KILL YOU.

"I have to try."

STAY WHERE YOU—

"Auger, listen to me. Start teleporting. In the meantime, I'm going to do what I can."

DUDE, I KNOW HOW SCARED YOU ARE. I CAN FEEL IT.

"I can't just sit by and do nothing while people get hurt."

A pause.

WE'LL GET THERE AS FAST AS WE CAN.

"Thank you."

PLEASE BE CAREFUL.

"I will."

AND PLEASE, said the voice from the other side of the world, *DO NOT TRY TO BE THE HERO.*

95

Temper woke.

He was outside, and he was cold, and it was raining, and he was wet. His magic was bound, as were his arms and legs, and his mouth was gagged. The wind was strong. He opened his eyes.

Yep. He'd pretty much known it. He was strapped to a table on a platform that jutted out from the side of the Dark Cathedral. Roarhaven sprawled out far below him.

He'd seen this table, or ones like it, a thousand times. It was oak, and carved into every centimetre of it were ancient prayers in ancient languages. It was an Activation table. It was where the Kith got lobotomised.

Two Dark Priests from the Church of the Faceless helped Damocles Creed into his vestments. They were all drenched from the rain.

The door to the platform opened and two people came forward. Temper couldn't see their faces at first, but finally they stepped into the light and he recognised Abyssinia's son, Caisson. He was with a stooped, elderly woman.

"Caisson," Creed said, his giant hand landing heavily on Caisson's shoulder, "it is good to see you out in the world. You look well. You look healthy. It's heartening to see that my sister failed in her mission to break you down."

"Your sister?" Caisson said, eyeing that hand distrustfully.

"My apologies," said Creed, stepping back and bowing slightly. "My name is Damocles Creed. I am the Arch-Canon of the Church of the Faceless. I have friends everywhere, and they talk to me, and I have heard so much about you that I feel we are already friends."

"You mentioned a sister," Caisson said.

"Of my many siblings in this world, the one you surely know of is Serafina Dey."

Caisson's eyes narrowed, and the elderly woman clutched his arm.

"This is no trap," Creed continued quickly. "My goals and my sister's goals are not compatible, I assure you."

None of them had even looked over at Temper this entire time. He started making noises. They ignored him.

"What do you want, Mr Creed?" the elderly woman asked.

"Merely to talk. Perhaps to seek an alignment."

"What kind of alignment?"

Creed smiled down at them both. "My sister's presence in Roarhaven is as unexpected as it is unwelcome. As Mevolent's wife, she inspires a certain *following*, shall we say. This following draws numbers from my own congregation."

"We just want to be left alone," said Caisson.

"Of course," Creed responded. "That's the most any of us can wish for, isn't it? A quiet life? As I said, people talk to me, so please don't be alarmed by the things I know. But if I may offer some unsolicited advice? Caisson, you're never going to be left alone. Not only are you the *son* of the mighty Mevolent, you are also the *killer* of the mighty Mevolent."

Caisson tensed. "How do you know these things?"

"I told you, people talk to me. Information like that, it travels faster than you'd think possible. It's only a matter of time before it gets out, and once it does you will have as many people wanting you dead as worshipping you."

The elderly woman stood in front of Caisson. "What do you

476

want, Mr Creed? My husband has just had a lifetime of lies torn open in front of him. I have just escaped from ninety years of confinement. We are both tired, sir, and impatient, and we do not appreciate your riddles."

"No more riddles, then," said Creed. "Your lives are in danger. If you proclaim your allegiance to the Church of the Faceless, you will have our full protection, and we will ask nothing else of you."

"You think we need your help?" Caisson asked softly.

"I do."

"Mr Creed, we don't care about the Faceless Ones."

"But they care about you. They care about all of us."

Caisson's lip curled. "That's not what Mevolent taught."

"That is true," said Creed, "which is why I opposed him from the very beginning. Mevolent's interpretation of the message, his reading of the Book of Tears, is so far from the truth as to be downright lies. The Faceless Ones are not cruel, uncaring gods whose very appearance would turn you insane. They merely have a power we don't fully understand yet. There are deeper complexities at work here – deeper beauties. All I ask is that you allow me to demonstrate what I mean. Afterwards, you make up your minds. If you can't see what I'm talking about, you walk away. But if you do... then join me."

"The son of Mevolent joining your church would steal followers from Serafina," the elderly woman said.

Creed nodded. "I suppose it would, but I promise that is not my primary motivation."

"This demonstration," said Caisson, "what is it? What do you plan to do?"

Creed indicated Temper. "Our guest here has a very particular strand of DNA. One in seven people share this strand, or at least a variation of it. I'm going to Activate that strand here, tonight, and, if it's strong enough, it will unlock the Faceless One that is lurking within."

Temper made more noise, and shook his head, and Caisson frowned at him. "He's going to turn into a Faceless One?"

"A hybrid, of Faceless One and human," said Creed. "If it works."

The old lady peered closely. Temper tried to catch her eye. "And if it doesn't work?" she asked.

"Then his face will melt off and his brain will be wiped clean."

The old woman finally caught Temper's eye, and shrugged. "OK," she said. "Let's see what happens."

96

Omen crept through the shadows next to the storage sheds. In the clearing ahead, First Wave stood. They didn't much look like the instigators of a war.

Colleen and Perpetua huddled together while the others stood apart. Sabre was puking into a barrel, and everyone looked pale, nervous. Terrified, even.

Everyone but Jenan. From his vantage point, Omen could see the look of anxious determination on Jenan's face. He was looking straight ahead, but at nothing. His lips were moving, ever so slightly, and Omen was seized by the absolute certainty that Jenan was envisioning all the ways he was going to kill people.

But the others... the others weren't killers. They had maybe deluded themselves into thinking they were, convinced themselves that they were capable of murdering some sailors in their sleep, but the sharp angles of reality were now pushing against these little bubbles. All that was needed, for those bubbles to start bursting, was one final push.

Omen straightened. If he could take out Jenan, fast and without fuss, the others would snap out of it. He knew they would. He'd tell them that it wasn't too late, that they had committed no crimes, not yet. They could go home. Back to their families, back to Corrival Academy, back to normal life.

All he needed to do was knock Jenan Ispolin the hell out.

He took the first step of a sprint and then sank back into the shadows.

"What are you doing here?" Jenan asked as the remaining Coldheart convicts walked from between the buildings.

Omen shrank even further back.

"Abyssinia sent us," said one of them, a particularly mean-spirited convict from Birmingham. Omen had seen him pass his cell. Slyboots, he thought his name was. "We're just back-up, in case you need us."

"We're not going to need back-up," Jenan replied, a little angrily. He was watching his moment of glory begin to fade even before it had started. "They're a bunch of mortals. They don't pose a threat."

Slyboots grinned. "I don't think Abyssinia is worried about the sailors. I think she's worried about you lot. Seems to me you don't much look like a pack of merciless killers."

There were a few laughs from the ever-growing throng, and Jenan's face burned.

"Abyssinia has been training us for this," he said. "She knows what we're capable of."

"That one," Slyboots said, pointing at Sabre, "is pukin' in a barrel. That doesn't instil in me an overwhelmin' sense of confidence."

"It's just jitters."

"Looks a lot like fear."

Jenan spotted Mr Lilt in the crowd. "Sir," he said. "Tell him. Tell him this is *our* mission."

The convicts all turned to Lilt, who seemed to shrink under their gaze, and didn't say anything.

"We *know* this is your mission," Slyboots said, smiling easily. "We're merely here as well-wishers, to give you a little encouragement should you need it. Now, with that bein' said, if you start to screw this up we will immediately and without ceremony take over and butcher this base ourselves."

Jenan stepped up to him. He was taller, but the convict was sturdier, and he wasn't quaking with rage.

"This is a First Wave mission," Jenan said, his voice strangled. "We are the ones who are going to strike a blow for sorcerers everywhere. We are the ones who are going to go down in history as the people who kicked off the war that will change the world. Not you. Not a gang of criminals, who are so inept, so useless, that they were set to spend the rest of their sad, pathetic lives in prison before Abyssinia took pity on them and let them play outside. We are the future. We are *your* future. Pretty soon, you're going to be taking orders from us – so I'd advise you to get used to the idea, and back the hell off."

"Of course," said Slyboots. "You're the boss, Mr Ispolin. In fact, we believe in you so much that we wanted to help. Bring out the mortal."

A sailor, in blue and grey fatigues, came stumbling from the shadows. Two convicts followed, grinning.

"We got you a present," Slyboots said. "Your first victim. All yours to murder."

Omen watched as the members of First Wave paled.

"Go on," Slyboots continued, sneering. "I thought this is what you were trainin' for."

"Maybe you should start 'em off," the other convict said, chuckling.

"No," Slyboots answered firmly. "This is an honour for the children. For the First Wave. The best and the brightest. Come on, kiddies. Zap him. Set him on fire. Do *somethin'*. If you can't kill this one, what chance do you have of killin' the twenty-six others, lyin' in their beds?" He walked up to Gall, put a hand on his shoulder. "Go on, my little friend. This is your chance. Start off the slaughter with a bang. No?"

He moved over to Perpetua. "What about you, darlin'? You gonna do it? You gonna smash this pathetic mortal's face in? Want me to get you a rock, or do you fancy doin' it with your bare hands?"

Perpetua bit her lip, trying not to cry. Slyboots grinned again, and moved over to stand between Sabre and Disdain.

"We don't hear much from you two," he said. "This is your chance, I reckon. Start us off, get your names out there, build a bit of a reputation. What do you say? No? Too much for you? Ah, don't worry about it."

Slyboots took hold of Colleen's hand, and raised it to point at the sailor. "Here. I'll help you. How are you at Energy Throwin', eh? Go on. Give it a go. Aim straight for his head, or straight for his heart. Or, if you wanna be really cruel, you can start with his limbs and work your way in."

He took his hand away. Colleen's whole arm was shaking.

She lowered it.

Slyboots shook his head. "I'm disappointed in you, sweetheart. I really am. So that leaves us with Mr Ispolin." He turned to Jenan. "Now, we all know you can do it, you murderous little psychopath. Lord knows, it's all you've been talkin' about for the last few months. So here it is. The moment that you've been waitin' for. Your classmates seem to have bottled it. The reality of killin' is a lot different to the fantasy, isn't it, my little cherubs? But Jenan here, he knows what's what. You won't get a little thing like morality stoppin' Jenan Ispolin! You know who his father is, right? He's a big muckity-muck in some Sanctuary or other. But he is *nothin'* compared to junior here. Jenan Ispolin is gonna remake the world – and it all starts when he kills this little sailor-boy."

Jenan had his eyes on the sailor the entire time. Omen watched him step forward, his right hand glowing with energy.

The sailor stared at that hand in horrified amazement. When Jenan raised it, the sailor took a step backwards.

"Do it," Slyboots said. "Do it, or we'll have to. You understand? If you little kids can't handle the awesome responsibility that has been bestowed upon you, then we shall be forced to step in. Either you start the killin' – or we do. Make up your mind, Jenan."

The sailor took another step back.

A stream of energy erupted from Jenan's hand and hit the sailor in the arm, spinning him round, and suddenly the sailor was bolting.

"He's messed it up," Slyboots said loudly. "All right, lads and ladies, it's up to us! Kill 'em all!"

The convicts cheered and started running, and Omen ducked back, barely scrambling behind cover as a few ran by.

He stayed where he was, in the darkness.

Hiding.

"Ah, damn," he whispered as he got up.

A convict passed and he followed along behind, sneaking between buildings. He didn't know what he was doing. This was a convicted criminal he was following. Probably a killer. What could he do against a killer?

Omen had to turn back. He had to. So why were his feet moving forward? Stupid feet didn't know what the hell they were doing, going this way and that, even though his legs were shaking and his heart was hammering and his bladder was full and his skin was way too sensitive. His shirt was scratchy. His left sock had lost most of its elasticity. Everything was horrible and he was going to die.

A figure disengaged itself from the shadows as the convict passed, and hauled him out of sight.

Omen froze.

He waited a moment, wondering what he was supposed to do, then he started forward slowly.

The convict lay in the shadows. Unconscious or dead, Omen didn't know. Another convict passed ahead of him.

The figure dropped from the roof and the convict crunched underneath him and lay still. Omen ducked down, waited a moment, then peeked out.

It was a man in his thirties, with a beard, wearing black. A shadow fell across him and two convicts ran into Omen's line of sight. The bearded man met them, grabbed them, spun them and broke them, and when he was done he moved on in a crouch, and Omen lost him.

Omen turned round, went the other way. He wasn't needed. There was someone else on the scene and they were handling things a lot better than he ever could, so it was time to sit down and hide and wait for back-up.

Footsteps. Movement. A convict in front of him, sneaking into one of the buildings. It was Slyboots. Oh, great. Oh, wonderful.

97

Slyboots slipped in through a doorway, and there was a cry and a crash from inside. Omen got to the door, took a breath, took another one and ran in.

An office. Filing cabinets and phones. A man in uniform, an officer, on the floor, bleeding from the head. Slyboots standing over him, fire in his hands, ready to kill.

"Stop," said Omen. He shouldn't have said anything. He should have just run at him. Now Slyboots was looking round. Now he was grinning.

"You're supposed to be locked up."

Omen squared his shoulders. "I escaped."

"I can see that. So what are you doin'?"

"I'm going to stop you."

"From doin' what?" Slyboots asked. "From killin' this sailor? Afraid not. I'm gonna kill him, take you back to wherever you're supposed to be, and then carry on killin'."

"Get help," said the officer from the floor.

"Shut it," said Slyboots, and gave him a kick that knocked him into unconsciousness.

Omen rushed him. Slyboots actually seemed surprised when they collided, but, as Omen struggled against him, he started to laugh. That was infuriating.

Slyboots threw him off and Omen came right back. His fist

looped in and caught the convict on the cheek, made him bellow as he backed off. Fury washed across Slyboots's face and he lunged, and Omen dodged, caught him with a left hook to the ribs and a graceless punch to the back of the head that nearly broke his hand. Slyboots turned and Omen tried to give himself space, but his hip hit the edge of the table and he couldn't go any further. The punches came then, and Omen ducked what he could and soaked up the rest, and then the air whooshed and Omen flew backwards over the table, hitting the wall and dislodging framed certificates as he fell.

Slyboots grabbed him by the shirt and the hair and hauled him up, then sent a knee crashing into his side.

Omen dropped, gasping for a breath, his muscles in spasm, contracting around his lungs.

Now, a voice in the back of his mind said, *would be a perfect time for Auger to arrive.*

And that's when Auger arrived.

He ran in and leaped, and he sailed clear over the table and his knee hit Slyboots in the chest and Slyboots smashed into a filing cabinet. Omen's brother kicked at Slyboots's knee and hammered at his neck and, when Slyboots tried to grab him, Auger broke his arm and rammed an elbow into his chin, and Slyboots crumpled.

Auger pulled Omen to his feet. "What did I say about being the hero? Pretty sure I said don't do it."

Omen wheezed. "Did you not see me losing that fight?"

"You don't have to win to be the hero."

Never came staggering in, her tired eyes widening when she saw Omen. "You're alive," she said.

Omen frowned. "I'm fine. Are you OK?"

She looked dreadful as she came over, pale and perspiring. She hugged him.

"She's had to do a lot of teleporting," Auger said. "She's pretty much wiped."

She broke off the hug, and thumped Omen, then hugged him again.

"Ow," Omen said, confused.

"She's angry with you," Auger explained. "We were off, y'know, stopping some bad guy from doing some bad things, and suddenly I hear you in my head, and then nothing. So we get back to school and no one knows where you are, but no one's worried because it's you and they all think you're just wandering around."

"Like a ridiculous puppy," Never mumbled, collapsing into a chair.

"Exactly. I try to get in touch with you but I can't make contact and... well, here we are now. What's the situation?"

"There are thirty or so Coldheart prisoners here to kill everyone," Omen said.

Auger waited for more. When there was none, he said, "That it?"

"Yeah, basically. Who did you bring?"

"Just us."

Omen frowned. "Not even Kase or Mahala?"

"We didn't have time to find them."

"Did you try Skulduggery and Valkyrie?"

"They're not answering their phones."

"But have you alerted China, at least?"

"These are good plans," said Auger. "You stay here with Never and decide who to call. I'm going to try to stop Jenan and his little band of morons, OK?"

Omen frowned. "Is Never asleep?"

Auger checked. "Yep," he said, and scooped her into his arms. "This has happened before. She'll be out for a few hours and then wake up starving." He carried her behind the desk and laid her gently on the floor. "Stay with her, OK?"

"I'm coming with you," said Omen.

"Dude, it's not safe."

"There are too many of them. I'm coming and I'm not arguing about it."

Auger took a moment. "Fine," he said. "But stay behind me at all times."

"I'll be so far behind you you'll be wondering why I'm even there, OK? Now let's go."

98

Destrier's workshop was small and dark and untidy and he was at the centre of it, sitting at a desk, poking at a piece of machinery with a screwdriver.

Skulduggery and Valkyrie walked slowly in.

"Hello," Skulduggery said.

Destrier looked up, bit his lip, then went back to work.

"You don't seem too surprised to see me," Skulduggery said, "even though I was supposed to be in that Eternity Gate for another six days. Was it shoddy workmanship that released me early, or was it something else?"

Destrier shrugged, released his lip and bit it again.

"Do you want to know what I think?" Skulduggery said. "I think you sabotaged your own machine, Destrier. I think you wanted me to get out, because you want me to stop Abyssinia. Am I right?"

Destrier looked away.

"It's OK if that's what happened," said Valkyrie. "We understand. We do. Abyssinia's plan is going to hurt so many people."

"Too many," Destrier mumbled.

"Yes," Skulduggery said. "Too many. You sabotaged the Eternity Gate so that I could stop her. Thank you, sincerely. But I'm going to need you to tell me which naval base she's planning on attacking. Do you know the name of it? Can you tell us?"

Destrier looked up, but didn't say anything.

"You're one of us," Skulduggery continued. "You don't want innocent people hurt. The High Sanctuary would love to work with someone like you, someone with your vision. Would you like that, Destrier? The best equipment. The best workshops. The best everything."

Destrier smiled. "I could... I could continue with my work? My projects? I could do my projects?"

"Absolutely. Would you like that?"

"Yes, indeed," said Destrier. "Yes, indeed, I would."

"The naval base," Valkyrie pressed. "Do you know what it's called?"

Destrier nodded. "Naval Magazine Whitley," he said. "In Oregon."

"Thank you, Destrier," said Skulduggery. "We have to go now, but there'll be Cleavers coming and they'll take you—"

"There's a bomb," Destrier interrupted. "In the tunnels beneath the White House. I... I helped Abyssinia make it."

"Can it be disarmed?"

Destrier went to another table full of junk, started searching through it. He picked up a TV remote control and held it out to Skulduggery. "Point and press the off button," he said. Skulduggery reached for it, but Destrier took it back. "Wait," he said, frowning. "No. This is for the television."

He rummaged again until he'd found a second remote, identical to the first. "This one," he said, nodding. "This one definitely."

"You're... sure?"

"Yes."

"Maybe we should take both," Valkyrie said. "Just in case."

Destrier frowned again. "Then how will I change the channel?"

"Oh, Destrier," Abyssinia said from behind them.

They turned, Skulduggery pocketing the remote as he did so. Abyssinia, Nero and Razzia stood there. Abyssinia looked upset. Nero looked sick. Razzia looked crazy. None of them attacked.

"Is this what always happens?" Abyssinia asked. "Do all children betray their mothers?"

Destrier looked crestfallen.

"Has Caisson betrayed you?" Skulduggery asked.

"Caisson has been led astray," Abyssinia said. "Solace is the problem. She convinced him to go. I know she did. He wouldn't have left if she hadn't talked him into it. He said..." She laughed. "He said he couldn't trust me any more. He said that I'm the one who betrayed *him*. He said I was just like everyone else, that I had let him down. Everyone apart from Solace, of course. Solace had never let him down. Solace is suddenly the only one he can trust. What has she done for him? She was locked away in Greymire Asylum while he was being tortured. I'm the one who got him away from Serafina. I'm the one who ensured his safety when he was a boy, who sacrificed my life to save his, who then rescued him all over again. I'm his mother!" she roared suddenly. "I would *never* betray him!"

"Children can be ungrateful," Skulduggery said.

"How can he not understand?" Abyssinia asked, starting to pace. "How can he not see that if Mevolent suspected for one moment that Caisson was his son, he'd never have stopped hunting him? I didn't *want* Mevolent to be the father. I got close to him to learn his secrets, not to start a family."

She hurried over to Skulduggery, her hands grasping the lapels of his jacket. "I wanted you, Skulduggery. I wanted you to be his father – in whatever form you took. You would have been a good father to him. He would have looked up to you."

Slowly, gently, Skulduggery prised her fingers loose, and she nodded, and stepped away.

"Solace has convinced him that all this changes things," she said, quieter now. "But it changes nothing. It doesn't alter who he is."

Valkyrie hesitated. "He's just found out that he killed his father. He's going to need some time to adjust."

"Is your father still alive, Valkyrie?"

"Yes."

"Do you like him?"

"Yes. I love him. He's my dad."

"I don't know if I loved my father," Abyssinia said. "I admired him. I know that. And I definitely respected him. He made sure that everyone respected him. He was a beacon of love for everyone, I think, but... But maybe I was too young to feel anything but scared." She looked over at Skulduggery. "Did you love your father?"

He didn't answer immediately. "No," he said.

"I bet you learned from him, though. I bet you learned how to be a better father to your child than he was to you. My father..." She laughed again. "He cared about our heritage. That's what he prized above all else. We were the Kings and Queens of the Darklands. We had the blood of the Faceless Ones in our veins, and our destiny lay before us. We would be worshipped as gods."

Abyssinia cleared her throat and turned away from them. When she turned back, she was calmer. "Before I was born, there was a prophecy about how the King of the Darklands would face the Chosen One in a battle that would decide the fate of the world. The prophecy didn't specify who would win – but my father knew that he could only be killed with the Obsidian Blade."

"And what's that?" Valkyrie asked.

Abyssinia smiled. "It's a dagger. A thing of legend. It began with the Big Bang, they say. Isn't that right, Skulduggery? You know the story, don't you?"

"The universe came into existence," he said slowly, "but, upon expanding, a part of it snagged. Reality continued to grow, but there was a small gap. Tiny."

"Isn't that wonderful?" Abyssinia asked, reaching out to touch Valkyrie's arm. "Can't you just picture it? Now imagine eons passing, and this gap drawing particles of matter and sprinklings of dust until it attains a weight of its own. This speck of nothingness, entombed in rock, drifts through the cosmos until it falls to earth as a meteorite."

"Where it's subsequently found by the Faceless Ones," Skulduggery said, "and forged into a weapon as they fight among themselves, long before the first Ancients appear on the scene. When the infighting stops, and the Faceless Ones are united, they hide the Obsidian Blade on an alternate earth in another dimension."

Abyssinia took over. "But the blade infects that earth, and the planet becomes something known as the Void World. Because the Obsidian Blade destroys everything it touches so *completely* that it wipes it from existence."

"Oooh," said Razzia.

"So the Obsidian Blade is a God-Killer," Valkyrie said.

"It's the *first* God-Killer," Abyssinia responded. "The only one worth anything. And my father knew that it was the only thing capable of killing him. According to the Darkly Prophecy, it would be a thousand years before he faced the Chosen One, so he took this as a guarantee that, for a millennium, he'd be indestructible. He killed two of my brothers just after they were born because he couldn't allow a male heir to live. He couldn't permit the possibility of a son usurping him. Providing he found and destroyed the blade or, alternatively, killed the Chosen One once he'd been identified, my father fully expected to live forever."

"But his protégé had other ideas," Skulduggery said.

"Indeed," said Abyssinia. "Indeed he had. Mevolent had no intention of helping my family become gods. Unlike, my father, he wanted to bring the Faceless Ones back. He was entrusted to lead a team of Shunters in the search for the blade. When the Void World was finally discovered, my father was overjoyed. His immortality was within reach. All he had to do now was find out how to destroy the weapon."

"Let me guess," Skulduggery said. "Mevolent used the Obsidian Blade to kill him."

"He used it," Abyssinia said. "Of course he did. I was watching from the shadows, and I will never forget the look of surprise on my father's face when Mevolent plunged that dagger into his side. And, as he struck, his people killed my mother, my sisters... They came after me, but loyal servants bundled me out of the castle and substituted a body for my own, and I watched Mevolent take what was rightfully mine."

She fell silent. Seconds passed.

"Family can be tricky," said Razzia.

Abyssinia's face crumpled. "I didn't want any of this for Caisson. I wanted him to be free. To be happy."

Skulduggery hesitated. "Maybe he has a chance of that now," he said. "He's with someone he loves, someone who loves him back. Maybe this is the freedom you've always wanted for him."

"Maybe," Abyssinia said softly. "And maybe getting as far away from me as possible is the best thing he could have done. He has no interest in our heritage. He doesn't want to be King. He just wants to have a family." She wiped tears from her eyes. "He's better off without me."

"Aw," said Valkyrie awkwardly, patting her on the shoulder, "don't say that."

"It's true," Abyssinia replied. "I... I failed him, even before he was born." She took Valkyrie's hand, and pressed it to her face.

99

Valkyrie swam in an ocean of memories that were not her own.

She'd done this before, with Cadaverous Gant and with Abyssinia herself – but this was different. Abyssinia had invited her in, and now she was directing her, and Valkyrie plunged beneath the surface and kicked for the light.

She was in the hall, in the great hall in Mevolent's castle, and she was making a speech while they all looked on.

Serpine was there, and Vengeous, and China. Others, too. She knew them all. Serafina sat at Mevolent's right, and Valkyrie stood at Mevolent's left.

No. She was Abyssinia. She was...

Lord Vile waited for her signal. At Valkyrie's command, he would drive his sword through Mevolent's back and she would take control of his army. She was the only one who could. The only one who dared.

But... things were different now. Her plans had changed. Hours earlier, she had discovered that she was pregnant. Oh joy of joys! Her life opened up before her.

Mevolent had robbed her of her family. He had murdered her father with the Obsidian Blade, the first of the God-Killers, a weapon that wiped whatever it cut from existence itself. But he had also given her the chance to have a new family of her very own.

The universe, it seemed, was not without a sense of humour.

And then, of course, it had all gone wrong, and Valkyrie discovered that Vile had betrayed her when his sword was driven through her back instead of Mevolent's. While everyone watched silently, Vile lifted her off her feet and took her to the window, and he flung her through.

She fell, twisting, her screams snatched away by the wind. She was strong, she was powerful, but the rocks broke her. She looked up at the stars, unable to move, unable to even touch her belly, and she wept for her child and waited for death to claim her.

But it was not death who claimed her that night.

An old man with a cart came upon her. He picked her up, carefully, and he took her to a cave, far away from the war. He used medicines and herbs and a knowledge of the old ways, the old magics, and he brought her back from death's door.

When she was able to speak, Valkyrie asked about her unborn child, and the old man smiled, and told her that the child still lived within her, and that child was a boy.

But the herbs and the old ways were not able to repair the damage the sword and the fall and the rocks had done, and Valkyrie began to slip back towards the doorway that stands between this world and the next.

Before she died, she said, she needed to know the old man's name.

The old man said he had no name, and Valkyrie looked upon the face of her father.

The Obsidian Blade had sunk deep into his side the night Mevolent betrayed him, he said. He had staggered away and Mevolent had let him go, confident that the weapon would do its work.

But Valkyrie's father, the Unnamed, the King of the Darklands, had knowledge of powers that Mevolent could scarcely dream of, and he used these powers to slow the blade's effects, and in doing so he sank into a deep, deep sleep.

He told Valkyrie that when she became pregnant he awoke from his slumber. An old man now, weak and dying, he travelled until he found her. He could not use his magnificent powers, he said, without hastening his own end – and so he was here to pass those powers on to his only surviving daughter, to allow her to live, and, in doing so, he could finally die.

Valkyrie wept, and thanked him, and told him she loved him.

And her father told her to trap his soul in this Soul Catcher, and, when her son was of age, to end the boy's life, and allow her father to live again in the boy's body as the King of the Darklands reborn.

And Valkyrie, mere moments away from death herself, agreed to his terms.

Her father gave her his power. It filled her completely and her body was mended and she tasted immortality.

Her father died and, true to her word, she caught his soul in the Soul Catcher. The wound he had received centuries ago from the Obsidian Blade was finally able to continue its work, and it spread across the old man's body and the body went from existence and became nothing.

Abyssinia left the cave. She was as strong and as powerful as her father had once been, and her family had a path to greatness once again.

100

"Do you understand?" Abyssinia asked, eyes searching Valkyrie's. "I need to know that someone understands. Do you understand?"

"I do," Valkyrie gasped. "I understand."

"Good," Abyssinia said. "I wish things had been different. I wish we could have been on the same side."

"So why don't you join us?" Skulduggery asked. "You've got what you wanted. You came back, you rescued Caisson – you can stop now. You can help us. Call off the attack."

"No, no," said Abyssinia. "I don't have what I want at all. I want them to worship me, Skulduggery. I want the world to bow down. I am the Princess of the Darklands."

"But, if you continue down this path, we'll have to stop you."

"You won't be able to."

"Caisson—"

"You're right," she said. "Caisson is gone. He has his own path to take now – which is how it should be. Now I've got to focus on my plans. On *the* plan." She looked at Destrier. "Are you coming with me, my child? Or staying with them?"

Destrier didn't answer, and Abyssinia saddened further.

"Of course," she said. "You must do what you feel is right. I bear you no ill will."

"Wait," Razzia said, "you can't be serious. Mate, come on."

"No, Razzia," Abyssinia said, "Destrier will be staying behind. It's his choice, and we have to respect it."

Razzia didn't respond to that, but her lower lip wobbled.

"Nero," Abyssinia said, "please take us away."

"Nero can barely stand," said Skulduggery. "Look at him. He's losing control of his power, Abyssinia."

"He's fine."

"He's broken. He doesn't know what he's doing any more."

"Shut up," Nero murmured. He teleported away, then came back in a slightly different place. He sagged and Razzia caught him before he fell.

Skulduggery started forward and Abyssinia raised a hand. "Don't," she said. "I can drain your life, Skulduggery – you know I can – before you can take your next step."

"I might be faster than you think," Skulduggery said.

"You might be. But is Valkyrie? You don't want to see her body crumple, Skulduggery. I know you don't. Let us go. Let this happen. Nero, can you teleport us?"

Nero managed to stand on his own. "Hell, yes," he said.

Abyssinia smiled sadly at Skulduggery. "I'm sure I'll see you in the battles to come," she said.

Nero flickered. The flickering spread to Abyssinia and Razzia.

Then to Skulduggery.

And then to Valkyrie.

And in an eyeblink then they were outside somewhere, at night, only Valkyrie and Skulduggery were on one side of a stack of boxes and Abyssinia was on the other with Nero and Razzia.

Skulduggery grabbed Valkyrie's arm and pulled her down.

"Are you OK?" she heard Abyssinia ask.

"No," came Nero's voice. "I'm... I'm sorry. I can't focus..."

"You need rest. Find somewhere to lie down – somewhere secure. Razzia, you and I have business to attend to."

"You got it, boss."

Footsteps moved away. Valkyrie looked around. They were

on the military base. Well, holy hell. What were the odds of that?

"I planned all of this," Skulduggery whispered.

"Oh, shut up."

101

So far, Auger had taken down three convicts – all silently. Omen had taken down no convicts – and still he made more noise than his brother. The universe, he reckoned, just hated him. It just did. When he was born, it couldn't even see its way clear to give him quiet feet.

Auger held up a closed fist. Omen had played enough video games to know that meant stop moving, so he did. And he listened to the unmistakable sound of people getting hurt.

They crept forward, took a peek around the corner.

A woman whirled between four convicts. With every movement, there was a fresh cry of pain, and they jerked and staggered and fell, until only the woman remained standing.

The blonde hair. The brown leather. The sword. She could be only one person.

"Tanith Low?" Omen said, hurrying forward.

She spun, sword up, and he stopped moving immediately. "I'm Omen Darkly. This is Auger. We know Skulduggery and Valkyrie?"

She lowered the sword. "Are they here?"

"Well, uh, no," said Omen. "We don't know where they are."

"Damn," Tanith said. "These charming guys at my feet – they're Coldheart inmates, aren't they?"

"Yes, they are. There's about thirty of them here. They want to slaughter all the sailors and start a war. We're here to stop them."

"You two?"

"Um, yes."

Tanith shrugged. "Fair enough. Four is better than two."

Auger frowned. "There are two of you?"

There was a sudden squawk, and a convict came tumbling from the shadows. He hit the ground and stayed there – dead or unconscious, Omen couldn't tell. The bearded man walked out after him.

"Boys," said Tanith, "this is Dexter Vex. Dexter Vex, these are the Darkly boys."

Dexter Vex, one of the Dead Men, big and strong and unsmiling, dressed in jeans and a T-shirt despite the cold.

"The inmates aren't our only problem," Tanith said. "There's a private army called Blackbrook. They're heavily armed mortals, trained for dealing with sorcerers and I haven't a clue how they fit into all this. But they're not the good guys."

"We need a plan," said Dexter. His voice was hoarse, like it hurt to talk.

Tanith nodded. "We identify the convicts' leaders, and take them down. Maybe that'll discourage some of the others." She looked at Auger. "Who's the leader?"

Auger looked at Omen.

"Um," said Omen, "Abyssinia is the overall leader, obviously, but she's not here, I don't think. Parthenios Lilt is overseeing First Wave, so I suppose maybe he'd be in charge. Maybe?"

Tanith nodded. "Dexter, you and Auger do what you can. Auger's a Chosen One, so he can handle himself. Omen, I'm going to need you to point out this Lilt guy, so you're coming with me. That cool?"

"That's cool."

"Then let's get going."

102

Valkyrie pulled the mask down over her face. It sharpened the night as she moved through it, and caught sounds she might have missed. Footsteps ahead, coming up on the other side of this wall.

She pulled a shock stick from its mooring on her back and swung it into the head of the convict who appeared at the corner. The stick sparked and the convict went down and she returned the weapon to its place before its electric-blue glow gave away her position.

More sounds up ahead. A scuffle. She hurried towards it, arriving just as Skulduggery smashed his elbow into some guy's face. She joined him.

"How many?" she whispered.

"Six," he replied softly.

"I got four."

"I'm sure you're trying your best." He was looking at her oddly.

"What?" she asked.

"It's a little unsettling, that's all. Talking to you while you're wearing a skull mask."

She moved on. "Now you know how I feel, every single day."

He followed after her. "Honoured? Privileged? Blessed?"

An energy stream cut through the air between them and swept sideways, into her arm. Valkyrie hissed, spinning away as

Skulduggery collided with the Energy Thrower and the stream was cut off.

Valkyrie checked the suit. Her arm was sore, but on the suit there wasn't even a mark.

"You'll do," she murmured.

103

Omen felt better scurrying about in the dark with Tanith Low.

Tanith wasn't doing much scurrying, if he was being honest. She crept and sneaked and stole through the shadows, as silent as a ghost, as agile as a cat, and as deadly as a cat ghost. She dispatched convicts quickly and quietly. It was, quite simply, amazing to watch.

Whereas Omen scurried. His little feet took little steps. He didn't dispatch any bad guys. None of it was even a little bit impressive.

But, of course, she had the advantage that she could run up the sides of buildings and across rooftops while Omen had to stay at ground level. And he had to clamber over obstacles while Tanith just... flipped. It was unnerving, watching her move. It was also awesome, and Omen felt himself falling a little bit in love.

While she was moving across one of the rooftops, she turned and looked down, giving him the order to stay put. He nodded and she went on to deal with whatever lay before her. Omen looked around, making sure no one was about to jump out at him. And Mr Lilt jumped out at him.

Omen fell back, tried to shout for help, but Lilt was on him in an instant.

"Not a sound," he said.

Omen nodded.

"Mr Darkly," Lilt said, "you surprise me. I didn't think you had it in you to escape. Of course, that idiot Lapse was guarding you, wasn't he? He couldn't have been that difficult to outsmart." He raised his hand to Omen's face, and flicked his nose. "You're annoying," he said. "Telling one's students they are disliked is generally frowned upon in teaching circles, but I feel I am allowed, just this once. I don't like you, Omen. I never have. You would have grown up to be such an unexceptional sorcerer. In that respect, it's a good thing that you won't live to see next week. It just means there'll be one less mediocre mage in the world."

"Can... can I say something?"

"If you promise not to scream."

"I promise."

"Then go ahead."

"You're a terrible teacher."

Lilt chuckled. "Is that right?"

Omen tried to glare defiantly, but he couldn't keep it up. "No," he said glumly, "you were actually a very good teacher."

"I know," said Lilt. "But it's nice to be told, just the same. I'm going to stand you up now, and shackle you somewhere so that you can be dissected by mortals in a few days. OK?"

"Yes, sir."

Lilt stood, took hold of Omen's jacket and pulled him to his feet. Immediately, Omen punched him in the groin.

Lilt groaned, doubled over, and Omen whacked him in the jaw. That spun him, and Omen kicked the back of his leg and Lilt dropped to one knee, still groaning. Omen ran round, tried to kick him in the stomach, but Lilt grabbed his foot, held on to it as Omen struggled to tug it back.

His eyes watering, his face pale, an impossibly long groan still in the process of dragging itself out between his lips, Lilt managed to topple Omen. Omen lashed out frantically, but Lilt just held him down and crawled up, placing one knee over Omen's midsection, using one hand to pin Omen's right arm, and raised the other one, clenched into a fist, ready to bring it down.

Omen snapped his free hand against the space between them and the air rippled and Lilt flew backwards. He tumbled, head over heels, came to a stop and cursed, and was just lurching to his feet when Tanith walked by him.

She did something, jumping into the air and spinning crazily upside down, and somehow her foot zeroed in on his chin and Lilt went down in a twisted heap and Tanith landed and kept walking.

"You OK?" she asked Omen.

He pointed. "That's Lilt."

She looked back, and nodded. "Nicely done, but I no longer think taking out their leader is going to stop them. Looks like we might have to take them all down, one at a time. You up for that?"

"Yes," he said.

"Then why are you shaking your head?"

"Am I?"

Tanith's gaze shifted and Omen turned and jumped back as two skeletons emerged from the darkness.

He put his hand over his thumping heart. Skulduggery. Of course it was Skulduggery. Skulduggery and a lady skeleton in a hood.

The lady skeleton stared at him. "What the hell are you doing here?"

Omen frowned. "Valkyrie?"

Valkyrie pulled the mask and the hood away and glared at him. "I told you to stay out of America."

"This... this isn't my fault," Omen said. "I was kidnapped."

Valkyrie loomed over him. "I don't care. When I tell you to do something, I expect you to do it, even *if* you've been kidnapped. Do you understand me?"

"Yes," he said meekly.

She looked at Skulduggery. "We have to get him out of here."

"We don't really have time," Tanith said, "and we need all hands, Val. We have Dexter and Auger and that's it."

Valkyrie's glare turned heat-seeking. "Auger is here *too*?"

"Omen," Skulduggery said, "you stay with one of us at all times, do you understand?"

"Yes, sir," Omen said, avoiding Valkyrie's eyes.

"Tanith," said Skulduggery, "what's the situation?"

"The convicts are here to kill all mortals," Tanith said. "There are a few who look like they didn't sign up for wholesale slaughter, but most of them seem to be enjoying themselves."

"What about First Wave?"

Omen spoke up. "Apart from Jenan, they're not hurting anyone."

Skulduggery looked back to Tanith. "And Blackbrook?"

"Dexter and I followed Perkins to a staging area nearby. Three Blackbrook trucks are waiting there – don't know what for. They had eyes on this place so we thought we'd come take a look."

They looked round as Auger and Dexter Vex jogged up to join them. Dexter nodded to Skulduggery, who nodded back, and nodded to Valkyrie, who hugged him. "Good to see you," she said.

"They're gathering outside the barracks," Dexter told them, indicating ahead. "There's a vantage point on the roof of the mess hall, if we can get up there."

"I'm sure I can manage that," Skulduggery said, and they all started moving.

Omen kept up. He was sure Auger felt right at home, but he felt like a stupid kid hanging around with a bunch of adults – yet at the same time it was kind of thrilling. Now that he had seasoned warriors all around him, he could actually relax a little and start to appreciate how cool this all was.

Skulduggery swung his arms and the air took them all upwards to the mess-hall roof, and Omen had to stifle a giggle.

104

Razzia quite liked Naval Magazine Whitley. She liked the buildings, because the buildings had names. They were called barracks, and armouries, and latrines, and things like that. And she liked the pier. That was huge. And all the cranes. And all those little domes dotted around the peninsula, the concrete domes that held all the bullets and the bombs. They were supposed to be called magazines, but everyone called them igloos. Which was fun.

She followed behind Abyssinia, straightening her bow tie as she went. She'd worn her best tuxedo tonight. Her hair was perfect and her make-up was to die for. It was worth all the effort, of course. Tonight was special.

The Coldheart army – for that was how Abyssinia referred to the ragtag bunch of criminals – had brought the First Wave kiddies to the square with the flagpole, the one right in front of the barracks. Only Jenan had actually hurt someone. Razzia had expected that. The others were too soft, too undamaged. They had their prejudices and their snobberies, but, deep down, they were just normal kids, as plain and nasty as any others.

But Jenan... Jenan had the eyes of a killer, and a life of bitterness and entitlement to propel him towards bloodshed. Razzia had seen his type before.

He was too tightly coiled to really wonder, at first, why he and his little friends were suddenly surrounded, but a look of confusion did break across his sweaty face when he saw Abyssinia. He didn't even glance at Razzia. She didn't mind that.

Then the First Wave kids were in the centre, and Abyssinia and Razzia and the others were standing round them, and Jenan's expression changed from confusion to anger. He jabbed his finger at the other members of First Wave. "They were never going to do it!" he screeched. "But *I* will!"

Abyssinia put her finger to her lips. "Keep your voice down, please, Jenan. You'll wake the sailors."

"Give me a chance," Jenan said, only a little bit less screechy. "I'll do it."

"I know you would," Abyssinia said, in that warm way of hers. "Your determination is impressive."

Jenan turned that accusing finger to the Coldheart army. "We don't need these criminals. Let me do it all. I'll go in there right now and kill *all of them* on my own."

"My dear, sweet Jenan," said Abyssinia, "I'm not here to blame you. I've been very impressed with you, I really have. And the rest of you, my lovely children, don't be afraid. I'm not disappointed in any of you."

"You're... you're not angry that we didn't kill anyone?" Colleen asked, her voice shaking.

"Not even in the slightest," said Abyssinia. "I've been informed that we have suffered some losses, so there are people here – probably sorcerers, probably in league with Skulduggery Pleasant and Valkyrie Cain – who are working against us. Who might even be watching us right now. And that's fine, too. This will do. This will do nicely."

"Can we go?" Colleen asked.

Abyssinia smiled. "My dear... I'm afraid there are elements to my plan to which you have not been privy."

"We're starting a war," Jenan said angrily. "We kill everyone in those barracks and we release the footage and there's a new Pearl Harbour. What other element is there?"

Abyssinia smiled sadly. "A compromise," she said. "President Flanery – a very disagreeable man – is incapable of seeing the virtues of being a victim. He has a need to project strength at all times. When I suggested that sorcerers attack a military base, he demanded instant retaliation."

Colleen's voice was trembling. "What does that mean?"

The Coldheart army parted, and six men in black body armour, with helmets hiding their faces and automatic weapons in their hands, came through.

"These gentlemen are soldiers, or *contractors*, as they prefer to be called, from a mortal army called Blackbrook," Abyssinia said. "We reached a deal, the president and I. I would send a group of headstrong young sorcerers into a military base and they would kill and maim and destroy – like villains in a storybook – and then the mortals would fight back – like the heroes – and stop them. Only we can't have sailors from the US Navy fighting back, because we need to kill them all. So we make these nice Blackbrook contractors into the heroes who, regrettably, arrive too late to save the base, but just in time to kill the villains. Is it perfect? No. But I get what I want and the president gets what he wants, which is a lot of rich mortals becoming even richer."

The contractors surrounded First Wave, guns up and ready to fire.

The kids screeched and clutched at each other. Only Jenan had no one to hold. He spun in a crazed circle, eyes flitting from muzzle to muzzle.

"What are you doing?" he roared. "What are you doing?"

Abyssinia stepped back. "Tonight will announce to the world that sorcerers exist, that they are all irredeemably evil, and only by going to war will the mortals stand any chance of survival."

"You can't do this!" Jenan screamed. "My father's a Grand Mage! You can't!"

"Thank you for everything you've done," Abyssinia said. "Your sacrifice will not be in vain, and your names will be remembered."

The contractors flicked the safeties off on their weapons. There was a moment of dreadful, wonderful silence, where nothing moved, and nothing breathed, a moment made all the more beautiful by the storm of violence that was about to be unleashed. Razzia knew that storm well. Razzia lived in that storm.

But the contractors turned as they opened fire, away from the First Wave kids, and Razzia saw bullets hit Abyssinia, saw Coldheart convicts jerk and fall and scream, and, before she could even shout, the dark muzzle of a gun was pointed at her and fire blossomed from within.

105

Valkyrie watched as the Blackbrook contractors turned their guns on the Coldheart convicts. She saw Abyssinia stagger back under gunfire, saw Razzia fall.

The doors to the barracks burst open but instead of sailors streaming out, there were more Blackbrook guys, firing into the surging, panicking crowd of mages.

Some convicts fought back. Fireballs and streams of energy hit the Blackbrook troops, but their uniforms protected them from the worst of it. Those convicts got bullets in return, hundreds of them, angry little bees that weren't going to be stopped by paltry human flesh.

Jenan ducked and ran, but the rest of First Wave huddled together and cried – right in the middle of a goddamn firefight.

Skulduggery stood up. "Omen, stay here. The rest of you, save those kids," and then he jumped off the roof.

Valkyrie followed him down.

She blasted a convict and charged a contractor. They struggled. The contractor thought Valkyrie was trying to take his weapon, but all she was doing was pulling up his sleeve so she could press her hand against his skin.

She let him have it, a full blast of lightning, and moved on before he'd even fallen.

Tanith and Dexter were with the First Wave kids, dragging

them off the street. Valkyrie turned and bullets peppered the back of her suit, making her gasp as they drove her forward a few steps. She turned the stagger into a run, got round the corner before she was hit with another salvo.

She risked a peek. Convicts and contractors were separating, ducking for cover. Abyssinia waded through what was left of them, hurling the Blackbrook troops through the air, demolishing them where they stood, soaking up the bullets that found her and healing instantly.

Another contractor came forward, holding a ridiculously bulky rifle. He dropped to one knee, took aim and fired. Gouts of steam erupted from the barrel on four sides and spots of black ink exploded upon Abyssinia's chest. The ink, or whatever it was, instantly spread to her sides and across her back, meeting at her spine. Binding sigils glowed from that blackness.

The contractor let the bulky rifle swing free by its strap, and whipped a pistol from his holster. Bullets tore into Abyssinia's shoulder, spun her round, a look of astonishment on her face.

Muttering to herself, Valkyrie ran forward. Her lightning hit the contractor. His uniform soaked up most of the damage, but at least he dropped the pistol.

She crashed into him, knee to his chest. He made a whooping noise as the air left his lungs. She grabbed his helmet with her left hand, yanked it to the side, and punched him in the neck. His legs gave out and he crumpled, and she pulled the helmet off and sent him to sleep with a kick to the head.

"He bound my magic," Abyssinia said, clutching her shoulder, blood running down her arm.

"Yeah, yeah," Valkyrie muttered, hauling her to her feet and dragging her on.

106

Abyssinia wouldn't stop poking at the bullet wound.

"Quit it," Valkyrie whispered, slapping her hand down.

The woodland was dense where they were, and completely silent. The only sounds were the gunshots, the screams, the shouted orders coming from the naval base. Every creature in the woodland was keeping their head down.

"How did he do that?" Abyssinia asked. "How was he able to bind my magic?"

"You've got Destrier making cool new weapons for you, right?" Valkyrie whispered. "Blackbrook obviously has someone else making cool new weapons for them, too. Now keep your voice down."

"Good advice," someone said, and Valkyrie whirled and cursed as Skulduggery emerged from the darkness.

He crossed to Abyssinia, sitting with her back against a tree, and peered at the sigils glowing from the black ink.

"Huh," he said softly. "Projectile binding sigils. That's deeply unsettling."

"Valkyrie saved me," Abyssinia told him.

"That was very nice of her," Skulduggery said. "I think, to pay her back, you should go to prison for the rest of your life."

Pale and sweating with the pain, Abyssinia managed a smile. "You wouldn't put me in prison, my love. You have too much fun with me out in the world."

"You're responsible for everything that's happened tonight," Skulduggery said. "Whatever might have been between us at some stage in the past means nothing, do you understand me? You came here to murder innocent people."

"Only mortals."

"They're still people."

"Only barely."

"You would have murdered the First Wave kids, too," Valkyrie reminded her. "But it looks like you were double-crossed. By President Flanery, of all people."

Abyssinia grunted. "And I was all set to double-cross *him*. I had everything planned out."

"Let me guess," Skulduggery said. "You kill him on live television, yes?"

That got a chuckle. "You know me so well. The plan was he would sit in the Oval Office and make his announcement to the world that evil sorcerers had attacked the brave sailors of Naval Magazine Whitley – and then I would set off the bomb beneath his feet. Every living thing within a three-kilometre radius of the White House would have had their lives drained from them in an instant. It would have been glorious."

Valkyrie stared at her. "Why? Just... why?"

"Sacrifices must be made," Skulduggery said. "Isn't that right, Abyssinia? With Flanery gone, Vice-president Tucker would take over – and I bet you've taken up residence in his mind, haven't you?"

"Am I that predictable? With Tucker in charge, I could control the mortal response. You see? I would control *both sides* of the war. I would guarantee a victory with the *minimum* loss of life."

"But Flanery got there first," Skulduggery said.

"He did. When I wasn't able to locate Tucker in the last few days, I should have suspected that something was wrong. I just didn't think Flanery to be so cunning."

"Don't feel too bad," Skulduggery said. "He's had help." He looked at Valkyrie. "We need an idea of what's going on and how many we're dealing with."

Valkyrie started walking. "I can do that."

He held up a hand. "You can do that from here."

She frowned. "You want me to do it psychically? Skulduggery, come on, I haven't the first idea how to do that."

"You didn't know how to read people's minds, either," Abyssinia said, "but you managed that, didn't you? Sit down."

Valkyrie hesitated, then did so. She closed her eyes.

"Reach out," said Abyssinia, "just like you do when you read a mind. But, instead of focusing on one person, you're allowing yourself to take more in. It's going to be scary; you're going to want to block it out. Resist that urge."

"I don't think it's working," Valkyrie murmured.

"It will," said Abyssinia. "It's like talking to someone in a crowded room. You can concentrate on that one voice, or you can sit back, and let all those other voices in, too. Can you hear them?"

"Yes," Valkyrie whispered.

"Without latching on to any of those voices, who can you hear?"

"Sorcerers," Valkyrie murmured. It was hard to maintain this link that had formed between her and her surroundings. The more she grasped at it, the further it slipped. She relaxed, and let it flow through her. "I don't know them. They're frightened. Angry. Excited. Mortals. The Blackbrook guys. Scared but... intent. Disciplined."

"Go further," Abyssinia said.

"The kids," Valkyrie said. "First Wave kids. They're terrified. Tanith and Dexter, they're with them. They're in trouble. They're fighting."

"Razzia," said Abyssinia. "Nero. Can you sense them?"

"They're alive," Valkyrie said. "Razzia's hurt. She... she knows she's dying."

Abyssinia's voice caught. "My poor girl."

Valkyrie searched for the Darkly brothers. Her head was pounding. She was about to give up when she found them.

She opened her eyes. It took a moment for her vision to clear.

"Valkyrie?" Skulduggery prompted.

She stood. "Auger's hurt. Omen's in trouble."

"I'll help them."

"You stay with Abyssinia," Valkyrie said, heading for the base. "I'll go."

107

Naval Magazine Whitley was strangely quiet for a base under attack.

The bodies of Coldheart convicts, and a few Blackbrook contractors, lay in the open like spilled rubbish. Valkyrie kept away from the brightly lit areas, stayed close to the walls of the administrative buildings and kept moving.

A piece of wall sprang at her and she ducked, darting behind a parked car. The rear windscreen exploded. She crawled towards the front, then got to her knees and risked a peek. Immediately, she ducked again, and the next bullet punched through the bonnet and thunked into the engine.

Keeping low, Valkyrie moved to the back again, settling into a sprinter's crouch. She took a few breaths to ready herself, energy crackling around her, and then pushed off.

She ran for the corner and she could feel the rifle sights tracking her, catching her, and before the finger squeezed the trigger she lifted off, diving into the air, swooping up and looping round and coming at the armoury from the opposite angle. The sniper on the roof was tracking her lightning trail. He dropped his rifle, going for his pistol instead, and she landed in front of him and rolled and came up in a charge, her shoulder slamming into his chest.

They fell back, the pistol spinning off somewhere. He shoved her off and tried to get up, but Valkyrie leaped on his back. Her arm went round his throat and her legs went round his waist and she tightened her hold. She held it. His struggles weakened.

She heard gunshots close by.

She abandoned the choke and jumped up. He gasped, turned over, and she hit him full force with a shock stick. He went to sleep and she returned the stick to her back as she ran to the edge of the roof.

Omen and Auger.

Auger was hurt. Omen was helping him run between the warehouses. Behind them, Blackbrook contractors swarmed.

It was happening. It wasn't exactly as she had seen in the vision – that had taken place in a town – but it was close enough. And she knew what would happen next, unless she stopped it.

Valkyrie sprang from the roof.

There were five contractors. She'd never stop all of them from firing. She changed direction, pulling her hood up and the mask down. It solidified round her face.

She landed beside the Darkly boys and lunged in front of them as the contractors opened fire. Bullets slammed into her. She glanced over her shoulder, saw Omen dragging Auger on. A few more steps and they'd be round the corner.

The contractors advanced. Still firing. Bullets peppered her legs, her belly, her chest. They jabbed at her shoulders and arms. They hammered at her head.

She was forced to step back under the barrage. Her knees were weakening.

Another glance, just as the brothers disappeared round the corner. Now Valkyrie could bring her arms in to protect her head as she shut her eyes and sank down, making herself as small as possible as the contractors began to surround her.

There was a slight lull. She heard magazines being ejected.

She looked up and flung out her arms and lightning danced on the tips of her splayed fingers. It reached across to the first contractor and immediately to the next and then it joined with the lightning that was reaching to the contractor on the other side, and this all happened one by one and yet all at once and suddenly all those contractors were being flung backwards off their feet. They landed and rolled.

And started to get up.

Valkyrie kicked the nearest one in the head. She did the same to the next one. She tore the gun away from the third one and swung it so hard into his helmet that he collapsed and didn't move.

She turned. The last two contractors were standing and about to open fire.

And then the Darkly boys tackled them from behind.

It was a mad scramble for Omen, but Auger spun with elbows and kicks, and in a moment both contractors were unconscious.

Omen got up. "I had him," he said.

"Course you did," said his brother.

"You're shot," Valkyrie said to Auger.

"I'm OK," he responded. "I mean, obviously, I'm not, and it hurts like hell, but I'll be OK until I get to a medic. Where should we go?"

"This way," Valkyrie said, starting to walk. "Stay close to me."

They got back to the barracks. Tanith and Dexter arrived at the same time, escorting the First Wave kids, who looked scared and stupid and ashamed. They avoided looking at Omen and Auger as they approached.

Whitley was quiet. No guns were firing. Nobody was shouting. The enemy contractors, and the convicts, appeared to be down. Razzia had manoeuvred herself into a sitting position against the flagpole.

Skulduggery emerged from the woodland. Abyssinia came with him, clutching her injured arm. The ink round her torso was starting to flake off, but the binding sigil still glowed. She ran to Razzia's side.

"My beautiful girl," she said, dropping to her knees. "What did they do to you?"

Razzia coughed up some blood. "Reckon they killed me, fair dinkum..." She laughed. "Fair dinkum," she repeated softly. "Man, I love being Australian..."

"We'll make them pay," Abyssinia said. "I'm going to rip out Martin Flanery's spine."

"That's if you can find it," Razzia replied, and laughed again.

Abyssinia brushed a strand of hair out of Razzia's face. "They're all going to die," she promised.

"It's over, Abyssinia," Skulduggery said. "All of it."

Abyssinia shook her head. "My destiny will not be denied."

"You don't have a destiny. You may have the blood of the Faceless Ones in your veins, but so do a billion other people."

Abyssinia stood. "I'm on a different level."

"No, you're not. I've been doing some digging in the last few days. Caisson and Solace... they had children."

Abyssinia blinked. "Caisson didn't tell me that."

"They were together for a hundred and fifty-nine years. As far as I can tell, they had a lot of children."

Razzia managed a smile. "Look at that. You're a grandma."

Abyssinia had a weird, faltering smile on her face that disappeared completely when Skulduggery continued.

"Damocles Creed has been searching for the Child of the Faceless Ones for centuries. You know that, right? It brings me no pleasure to tell you that he got his hands on one of your grandchildren, and he Activated her."

"No," said Abyssinia.

"She's Kith now. She's standing somewhere with all the others."

"Then I will end his life as surely as—"

"You're missing my point," Skulduggery said. "If you had any special blood in your veins, your grandchildren would have it, too. When Creed Activated her, she would have become the Child of the Faceless Ones. Instead, she became just another Kith."

"I am the Princess of the Darklands. My father—"

"Was an extremely powerful sorcerer," Skulduggery said, "far beyond the capabilities of anyone around him. Until Mevolent rose up. Your father was powerful, Abyssinia, but he wasn't a King of the Darklands. There's no such thing. Everything you've done has been based on the idea that you're special, that you're destined for greatness, destined to lead. Maybe he lied to you, or maybe his father lied to him. That's the trouble with family legends. Who knows how true they are? Who knows how warped they've become as they've travelled down through the generations?"

"My family is royalty."

"Your family is powerful. But that's not the same thing."

"No. No, you're wrong. I know who I am. I can feel it in my blood." Abyssinia took hold of the band of ink that dimmed her power. It started to tear.

"Abyssinia, stop," Skulduggery said, stepping forward. Valkyrie did, too. And Tanith. And Dexter.

"I can't let you stand in my way," Abyssinia responded. "None of you." The ink tore further. It was about to come off.

Skulduggery pulled his gun. "Don't make me do it. Don't make me kill you."

Abyssinia gripped the last threads of ink with both hands, and smiled. "You won't kill me, my love. Not again."

He thumbed back the hammer.

Abyssinia tore the ink apart and Skulduggery fired and Abyssinia's head snapped back.

And then she righted herself and healed the wound and laughed. "Told you," she said, and looked at them all. "So... who's going to throw the first punch?"

108

Valkyrie rolled to a stop.

"Huh," she said.

Skulduggery was down. Tanith was down. Dexter was down. Now it was only Valkyrie, trying her best to get up.

She stood. OK. Good start. She was on the pier. She could hear the ocean behind her.

Abyssinia walked up, unhurried. Valkyrie gathered her strength, and went to meet her.

Abyssinia hit her and it was like a mountain picked up a freight train and used it as a bat, because the world cracked and juddered and Valkyrie was moving backwards and sideways all at the same time.

She shook it off. Tried to. The grogginess lingered as she worked to convince her body that everything was OK. She didn't think it believed her.

Abyssinia was circling. Valkyrie didn't like that. She didn't like being the prey in any scenario.

She reached out with a streak of lightning that spun Abyssinia in place, but, when she charged, Abyssinia was ready. Valkyrie missed her grab entirely, and was rewarded with a wrecking ball of a punch to the ribs that not even the suit could protect against. She tried to back off, but Abyssinia wasn't finished with her. A pair of jabs rocked her brain in her skull, and a lazy kick to the chest sent her to the ground.

Abyssinia smiled down at her. "Don't feel bad. You've never faced anyone like me before."

Valkyrie believed it. Nevertheless, she got up. Because she was that stupid.

She caught Abyssinia with a sustained blast of lightning, and, before she could respond, Valkyrie went at her with the shock sticks. They beat an impossible rhythm against her head, her arms, her torso, her knees, an impossible rhythm that Valkyrie tried to sustain, but her ribs, and surely there were one or two that had been broken by that punch, were screaming at her to stop.

So she backed off, the shock sticks glowing brightly in her hands. Abyssinia licked at her lower lip. Blood glistened on her tongue.

"Ow," she said.

This wasn't going to work. If Valkyrie had any chance of beating her, she needed a running start. Or maybe a flying one.

She returned the sticks to her back and magic burst from her in crackling coils as she shot into the air. Abyssinia had hit her like a freight train and a wrecking ball. Valkyrie planned to combine the two and return the favour. She glanced down to make sure Abyssinia was still in position, standing there on the pier.

Instead, Abyssinia was flying next to her, and grinning.

Before Valkyrie could do anything more than jerk back in surprise, Abyssinia put on an extra spurt of speed and flew past her, cracking her fists into Valkyrie's chin as she went.

Valkyrie spun, fell, tumbled. The ground came for her.

Energy crackled and she pulled up, skimming the road beside the warehouses. She tried to rise above a parked jeep, but her foot caught at the edge and she cursed as she went sprawling over the roof and crunched to the pavement on the other side.

She lay there, in pain, waiting until she could breathe again. She turned on to her back. Abyssinia stood on the jeep roof.

"You can fly," Valkyrie muttered.

Abyssinia gave her another smile. "My father could fly. My father could do many things. Which means I can do many things."

"Yeah?" Valkyrie said, letting her hand flop back so that it was touching the jeep. "Can you dance?"

Her lightning passed through the metal frame and locked Abyssinia's legs straight while the rest of her seized up and trembled for several seconds, before she toppled backwards, falling to the street on the other side of the jeep.

Not even allowing herself a moment to savour that small, petty victory, Valkyrie got to her feet. Slowly.

"You're a sneaky one," said Abyssinia, smoothing down her hair. She was already standing. Of course she was.

Valkyrie walked round the jeep, in no great rush. When they were face to face, Abyssinia gave her another smile.

"Shall we continue?"

"Give me a second," Valkyrie said, probing her side and closing her eyes in pain. "You broke a couple of ribs."

"I'll wait."

"Thank you," said Valkyrie, looking up, and twin streams of energy erupted from her eyes and hit Abyssinia in the face.

Abyssinia screamed, tried to turn away, covering her head with her arms, but Valkyrie pushed further, harder, the skin round her eyes sizzling, and Abyssinia's legs buckled and she was on the ground now with Valkyrie standing over her, pouring everything she had into this final, desperate effort.

Abyssinia kept screaming.

The streams thinned, and sputtered, and Valkyrie cut them off and stumbled against the jeep. She was done. She didn't have anything more.

Abyssinia lay before her, unmoving. What few strands of silver hair there were left smouldered and smoked.

Valkyrie sank to her knees. She couldn't even keep herself upright. Her arms were too heavy to lift, her mouth was dry, her stomach was empty and rumbling, and all she wanted to do was sleep for a year. Abyssinia chose that moment to sit up.

Valkyrie didn't have anything to say. She just watched as charred skin flaked and fell away, revealing the newly regrown skin beneath. She watched as the silver hair sprouted and lengthened.

Abyssinia blinked and smiled at her. "I can see why Skulduggery likes you," she said.

"Go away," Valkyrie whispered.

Abyssinia got up. "You tried to kill me," she said. "You actually tried to kill me. I didn't think you were capable of such a thing."

Valkyrie looked up at her. "Can't let you kill Auger. Just a kid."

"I don't want to kill him, Valkyrie. I don't want to kill anyone. But I have to. For the world to be the way I want it to be, people need to die. That's not something I'm going to enjoy, but it is something I've come to terms with."

"Please," Valkyrie said, "don't make me stand up."

"You don't have to. Stay down there. You've fought enough."

Valkyrie grunted. Started to get up.

Abyssinia sighed. "If you try to stop me, I'll have to kill you."

Valkyrie didn't answer until she was standing. When she had the energy, she said, "Can't let you kill him."

"Would you prefer me to kill you and *then* kill him?"

Valkyrie raised her fists. "Let's be having you."

"You poor girl," Abyssinia said, and reached between Valkyrie's fists to grab her, then launched her through the air.

The road smacked into her and Valkyrie rolled along for a bit before coming to a gasping, painful stop. She tried to get up but couldn't.

"If I leave you here," Abyssinia said, "will you let me kill the Darkly boy in peace?"

Valkyrie put both hands flat against the ground, then blew out a deep breath and started to push herself up.

Abyssinia shook her head as she came forward. "I'll make this quick," she said. She put a foot on Valkyrie's back to push her down, then gripped her head.

Someone stepped out in front of them.

"Stop hurting her," said Auger.

"Run," Valkyrie moaned.

Abyssinia released her hold on Valkyrie and straightened.

"It's me," said Auger. "In case you were wondering. I'm the one they say is going to battle the King of the Darklands."

"I won't let you harm my son," Abyssinia said.

"I understand," said Auger. "So, if you're going to kill me, kill me. Leave Valkyrie and everyone else out of it."

Abyssinia walked up to Auger, noting the blood on his shirt. "You're injured," she said.

"I've never been shot before."

"What do you think?"

"I don't like it."

"You're a brave boy," said Abyssinia. "Coming out here; it's noble. I wish I didn't have to do this."

"I'll make it easy for you," Auger said, and threw a right cross that broke his fist when it landed. He howled, staggering back and clutching his hand.

Abyssinia smiled sadly. "I like people who go down fighting," she said.

Valkyrie didn't have the strength to throw a stone, but she could still throw her thoughts. Using the same pathways Abyssinia had invited her in through earlier, Valkyrie swooped into Abyssinia's mind and filled the space with images of Auger's neck being snapped.

The same way Cassandra and Finbar and the others had planted false memories in Darquesse's mind, so Valkyrie planted a short, unsubtle sequence in Abyssinia's.

First, she kills Auger. Then she watches his body fall. Then she walks away.

Auger, the real Auger, the one who was still nursing his broken hand, frowned at Abyssinia as she stood there, almost frozen.

But then she turned to Valkyrie, and a smile broke out. "Ohh," she said. "Ohhh, you sneaky little thing. You almost had me there. You almost did. That was a good effort. For a moment, I believed I was actually watching him die. That was good. So where'd he go? Where's he hiding?"

Valkyrie frowned. "What?"

Abyssinia walked over. "Auger," she said loudly, "what's the point in hiding if I know all I have to do is hurt Valkyrie and you'll come back out to save her?"

"I'm right here," Auger said.

Abyssinia sighed, and lobbed a light kick into Valkyrie's side that jangled her broken ribs.

"Hey!" Auger shouted.

Abyssinia turned. "Auger Darkly! I'm going to count to three and then I'll have to kill her!"

"She can't see me," said Auger. "Valkyrie, what did you do to her? You've got to let her see me again. Valkyrie!"

"One!" shouted Abyssinia.

Auger clicked his fingers and threw a fireball. It exploded across Abyssinia's back and she whirled.

"Where are you?" she said. "Why can't I... Ohhhh." She looked back at Valkyrie. "Bravo. You've hidden him from me. How on earth did you manage that? You never cease to impress me, you really don't. It shouldn't take me long to overcome your little block, but even so..."

Auger threw another fireball. "I'll lead her away," he said, backing off.

"Just go," Valkyrie told him. "Get out of here."

Auger nodded. "And I'll take her with me."

He threw two more fireballs and Abyssinia swatted them out of the air and laughed as she followed him.

Valkyrie tried to remember how she'd healed herself in the

cell, just a few hours ago. She tried to remember what she'd felt when she reached into Doctor Whorl's magic. But the memories were too slippery to hold on to, and her thoughts were too manic. They yipped and barked like a pack of small dogs.

She turned slowly on to her side, and froze. The Nemesis of Greymire was at the end of the pier, and walking this way.

"Let it happen," said Ghastly, crouching beside her.

Valkyrie ignored him. Carefully, she raised herself up on to one elbow, then brought her legs in. Got her knees under her.

"You don't have to keep fighting," Ghastly said. "Abyssinia was right. You can just stop. You know you can. You want to."

Kneeling now. Taking a breath and holding it, Valkyrie raised her right knee off the ground and planted her foot in its place. That hurt.

"How much longer do you think this can continue?" asked Ghastly. "How much more can you punish yourself? Haven't you suffered enough?"

"Go away," Valkyrie muttered.

"Stop fighting. Stop resisting. Stop running. Let the Nemesis reach you. Let her swing that hammer. Just once. Once is all it takes. And then you'll be at peace. Wouldn't that be lovely? Wouldn't you welcome that?"

Valkyrie heaved herself to standing. Tears sprang to her eyes and she grabbed her side and sobbed with the pain – but she didn't fall.

Ghastly stood in front of her. "You hate yourself," he said. "You hate yourself for what you've done. Not just to Alice, but to all of them. All the people who have died because you wanted adventure. No excuse will ever be good enough to wash away that sin."

The Nemesis was getting closer. She dragged the sledgehammer along behind her. It rumbled across the concrete.

"I don't want to die," Valkyrie said.

"Yes, you do," said Ghastly.

She fixed him. With a glare. "I'm not going to die."

"Yes, you are."

"You know what? OK then. The Nemesis there, she's my guilt, is she? Fine." Valkyrie walked towards her, doing her best to keep her back straight. The Nemesis brought the hammer up into a two-handed grip.

Valkyrie stopped right in front of her. "This is what Greymire does to people, isn't it? Gives them their own private Nemesis to run away from?"

"Yes," said Ghastly.

"Only they can never escape it, can they? Sooner or later, it catches up to them."

Ghastly nodded. "And it kills them."

"And what are you? My conscience?"

"No. I'm just your insanity."

"Yeah," Valkyrie said, "I *must* be nuts, wasting my time with this nonsense. Hey, Nemesis, if you're going to kill me, then kill me. Otherwise, I've got stuff to do."

The Nemesis raised the hammer high overhead.

"Accept it," Ghastly murmured.

"I'm standing here, aren't I?"

The Nemesis of Greymire let the hammer go back a bit further, and then swung it down, straight for the top of Valkyrie's head.

109

It was raining harder as the Dark Priests finished anointing Temper with their foul-smelling oils, and they removed the gag from his mouth and Creed came forward.

"All my hopes lie with you, my friend," Creed said, speaking loudly to be heard over that wind. "What you do here tonight... it humbles me."

"I'm not doing anything," Temper said.

"No," said Creed, resting a hand on Temper's chest, "you are doing everything."

"Yeah, that's not what I meant."

"Your sacrifice will be noted in the annals of the Church."

"Tell me something," Temper said, straining at the bonds that held him. "Just between us. Have you actually worked out what the chances are of me being the Child of the Faceless Ones? We know it's in my DNA, but it's been in *plenty* of people's DNA, and now they're all Kith. Have you worked out the odds?"

Creed's expression didn't change. "Yes," he said.

"So you know that it's pretty unlikely that, when you Activate me, I'm gonna turn into what you're looking for. What is practically a certainty, though, is that after this I'll be taken down to your basement and stuck there with all the others. Right?"

"We have to try, Temper. Sooner or later, I will find someone strong enough to withstand the process. If it's not you, then that simply means we are one step closer to finding the person we're looking for."

The bonds were too strong. Temper stopped struggling. "And what if there is no one out there with genes that are strong enough, and you're lobotomising all these people for nothing?"

Creed smiled gently. "It's not for nothing, Temper. It's never for nothing. This process... it gives people hope. You used to understand that."

"No. I used to believe you. There's a difference."

"I will lead you back into the light."

At Creed's instruction, the Dark Priests painted familiar sigils across Temper's chest. Temper knew each and every one of them, as he himself had painted them on the chest of many a willing acolyte who had then gone on to be hidden away somewhere. His past. His dreadful, shameful past that itched away beneath his skin, somewhere he could never scratch.

When it was done, the Dark Priests stepped away, and Creed looked over at Caisson and the old woman.

"The prayers have already been intoned," he said. "We are now ready to proceed. I must warn you, however – if he is not strong enough to withstand the process, the resulting physical transformation can be... distressing."

"We are prepared," the old woman said, a little too eagerly.

Creed bowed. "Then, with your permission..."

The old woman smiled, but Caisson took a sudden step forward.

"Stop," he said.

Creed paused for a moment. "Is there something wrong?"

"This... isn't right," Caisson said. "He's... You're torturing him."

"No," Creed responded. "No, that isn't what's happening."

"Yes, it is," said Temper.

The old woman put a hand on Caisson's arm. "My love," she said, "we are merely observers."

Caisson stood up straighter. "No. When I was a prisoner, it was the torturers I understood. They were hurting me because they wanted to, they liked it or they were told to. It was the others I could never understand, the people who passed, who walked by, who looked in. I could see the shock in their eyes, the horror on their faces... but they never did anything. They walked on. They never came back. I'm not... Mr Creed, I'm not walking on. You cannot hurt this man. You cannot hurt anyone. Not any more."

"My love," said the old woman. "This man is the enemy."

"He's not my enemy. He has never harmed me. He has never harmed you, either."

The old woman scowled. "They have all harmed me."

Caisson detached himself from her grip. "No," he said. "They haven't. You want that to be true because then your hatred can be everlasting. But it is not true. China Sorrows put you in that tower. It is China's sin, and hers alone."

"They allowed it to happen," the old woman said. "They allowed her to keep me there, to numb my mind with that infernal contraption."

Caisson held her face in his hands. "You say that, but nobody knew where you were. You have rage inside you, as I have. But we've got to focus that rage on the people who deserve it."

She brushed his hands away. "Do you see me? Do you see how old I am? Do you see what they have made me?"

"My love—"

"No!" she roared. "You do not love me! You cannot! I used to be beautiful! I used to be magnificent! They took that away from me! They took my youth away from me! They took you away from me!"

Temper saw it out of the corner of his eye – a figure, climbing up on to the platform. One of the Dark Priests saw it as well and the figure whirled, the tip of a spear ripping across his throat, and then the spear was darting through the rain and it passed right through Caisson's chest.

The figure leaped backwards off the platform and disappeared, and the old woman screamed as Caisson fell to his knees.

110

The Darkly kid – the tubby one, not the Chosen one – bundled up his jacket and pressed it to the gunshot wound in Razzia's belly. "You're going to be OK," he said as the blood immediately started to soak through.

Razzia looked up at him. Her position, lying on the ground like this, gave her a new perspective on things. First and foremost, all those cranes on the pier. They looked even more impressive from down here.

The second being the Darkly kid. He was doing his very best to save her life, even though they were on opposite sides, and he must have been worried sick about his brother.

"We'll get you to a doctor," he said. "You're going to be fine. Stay with me. Just stay with me."

"You're weird," Razzia said weakly. "You realise we're... enemies, right?"

He shook his head. "I don't have enemies."

"That Jenan kid hates you."

"Apart from Jenan, I don't have enemies, and you're just a person who's been hurt. Do you have any way to call Mr Nero? He could teleport you to a hospital or something."

"No hospital."

"I really think you should go to a hospital, though. I mean, I have first-aid training, but..."

She smiled. "I'm a goner. There's no coming back from this."

"Does it... does it hurt?"

"Naw," she said. "It's fine."

He nodded. "Good."

She laughed a little. "Of course it bloody hurts, you dingbat. Doesn't it look like it hurts? Look at all that blood. That amount of blood doesn't leak out of a person without there being some pain involved and a great big hole that's not supposed to be there."

"Oh," said the Darkly kid. "Sorry."

Her pets squirmed listlessly in her arms. That was the worst bit. She didn't mind the thought of dying. She'd always known it'd happen sooner or later, and she'd done way too many stupid things to ever think she'd have a quiet death. But Hansel and Gretel didn't deserve to die with her.

"You have any pets, mate?" she asked.

The Darkly kid shook his head.

"Want some?"

"We're not allowed to have pets in Corrival," he said, "and my parents aren't too keen on animals."

She coughed up some blood. He did his best to wipe it off her chin.

"Cheers," she said.

He nodded.

"But with these pets no one even has to know you have them," she said. "They're very good at hiding."

"What are they? Mice, or something?"

"Naw, not mice. Parasitic Murder Tentacles, or Murdacles, for short."

"Are they... are they the things that come out of your hands?"

"Yep."

"No, thank you."

"Aw, Murdacles make great pets, though. They each have their own little personality. And they're great for grabbing a tinnie that's on the other side of the room or, like, killing people."

"I don't drink, and I don't want to kill anyone."

"Not yet, no, but I'm pretty sure both of those things'll change the older you get."

She heard footsteps. Running footsteps. The Darkly kid looked up, but she didn't have the energy to turn her head so she just waited as they got closer.

"Are you OK?" the Darkly kid asked whoever it was.

The Chosen One came to a stop beside them. "Nero," he said. "You seen him? Do you know where he is?"

The tubby one shook his head. "Haven't a clue. What's going on?"

The Chosen One hunkered down beside them. He tore off his jacket and bundled it just like his brother had done. Then he gently lifted Razzia's head off the ground and slipped his jacket under her as a pillow.

"Abyssinia's son is hurt," he said. "Like, dying. She was chasing me, and there was a whole thing where she couldn't see me, but she got over that, and she grabbed me, and then she had this psychic flash that Caisson was hurt. She's panicking. I said I'd help her find Nero."

This didn't make sense to Razzia. She frowned. "But she... she wants to kill you."

"Yeah," said the Chosen One.

"But she wants to *kill* you."

"Well, yes," said the tubby one, "but her son is dying."

Razzia looked at them both. The Chosen One, with his great hair and square jaw, was just a kid. Just a teenage boy. And the tubby one... well, was he really that tubby? He had a few extra pounds on him, and he wasn't chiselled like his brother, but he was just a normal kid. Two normal kids helping people who'd had every intention of killing them just a short time ago.

"You're both weird," Razzia decided.

Nero appeared, turned unsteadily and saw the Darkly brothers crouching over a bleeding comrade, and he lunged. Before Razzia could speak, the Chosen One grabbed him, spun him into a chokehold.

"Abyssinia needs your help!" the Chosen One said quickly. "Please don't panic!"

"Calm down, Nero," Razzia said. She was slurring her words. That wasn't good.

Nero stopped struggling and the Chosen One released him – warily.

"Caisson is hurt," the Chosen One explained. "Abyssinia needs you to take her to him."

"Where is she?" Nero asked, eyes narrowed. His face was pale. He looked sick.

"She needed a little peace and quiet to get a fix on his position. She said she'll meet us here when she has it."

Razzia's gaze moved beyond them and above them, and she watched Skulduggery Pleasant drop from the sky.

"Where's Valkyrie?" Skulduggery asked before he'd even landed. His suit was dirty and torn at the shoulder and he didn't have his hat.

"She's OK," the Chosen One said. "I mean, she's hurt, but I led Abyssinia away before things got too serious."

"And what's happening here?"

"I, uh, I think we've called a truce," said Omen. "Caisson is hurt and Abyssinia's searching for him. You know, psychically."

Skulduggery knelt beside them, started examining Razzia.

"It's not good, is it?" she asked softly.

"It isn't."

"I'm going to die, right?"

"Yes," he said, without hesitation. That's what she liked about him. No nonsense.

"What's going to happen to my pets? This isn't fair. Not their... not their fault their mum got herself killed."

Skulduggery brushed her hair off her face. "You're in pain. I can end it for you now if you'd like."

She managed a smile. She was sure she had blood on her teeth, but she didn't mind a little blood. "No, thanks," she said. "I've survived this long without rushing towards death. Figure... why should I change the habit of a lifetime now?"

He tilted his head. "I always liked you, Razzia."

"Always liked you, too."

Everyone looked round as someone new approached. Valkyrie's voice: "Glad to see you're still alive."

"Same to you," said Auger.

Valkyrie came into view, holding her side and looking all beaten up. She stopped behind Skulduggery, put a hand on his shoulder as she leaned over to peer at Razzia.

"Hey," she said.

Razzia wriggled her eyebrows because she didn't have the strength to do anything else.

"Your tuxedo rocks."

She didn't know where the strength to give a goofy smile came from, but it came from somewhere very deep.

Valkyrie straightened and Skulduggery stood, and Razzia knew Abyssinia was approaching.

Skulduggery held up both hands. "A truce has been called," he said. "We won't stop you."

Abyssinia hurried into view. "I want you to come with me," she said. "There are people around Caisson, I don't know who they are." She saw Razzia and covered her mouth with her hand. "Oh, my child..."

"Omen and Auger," Skulduggery said, "stay here. Find Tanith and Dexter, help them round up the First Wave kids. Nero, the rest of us are ready to teleport. Abyssinia, where are we going?"

"A church," said Abyssinia, "or a temple. Made of black stone and black metal."

"The Dark Cathedral," said Valkyrie, taking Omen's place by Razzia's side. "Roarhaven."

"They're outside," Abyssinia said. "On some sort of platform."

Nero nodded, and vanished. A few seconds later, he was back. "Found them," he said, looking unsteady on his feet.

They waited. Nero's hands went to his head. Nobody said anything.

"I'm ready," Nero said, and teleported.

111

Night in Ireland was very much like night in America except the clouds were blocking out the stars and it was colder and it was raining. Still, at least Razzia now had a new surface to bleed on, so that was nice.

There were a load of people talking and arguing and making threats and a whole lot of movement. Only Razzia and Valkyrie stayed still and stayed quiet.

The hostile voices calmed. Most of them. From where she lay, Razzia couldn't see Solace, but she could hear her wails of anguish. There was a large, brutish-looking man with a shaven head standing around, and Skulduggery was freeing Temper Fray from a big wooden table. And there was Abyssinia, kneeling by Caisson, his head cradled in her arms.

"My boy," she said. "My beautiful boy."

Caisson's eyes were closed. Razzia knew a soon-to-be-corpse when she saw one. If she'd had a mirror, she'd have pointed to herself – but right now Caisson was ahead of her in the race to the finish line. The blood that spilled from the wound in his chest had slowed to a trickle. Abyssinia wrapped her arms round him and sobbed, her forehead pressed against his.

"I'm sorry," she said, as Solace's wails dipped to a strained sobbing. "I'm sorry, my beautiful boy. I'm so sorry. My beautiful little boy."

She held him so tightly that Razzia expected to hear his bones pop. She'd never been the sentimental type, or the type to really understand other people's emotions, but she wished she could have gone over there and held Abyssinia as she held her son. Instead, all she could do was lie there and watch with the others as Abyssinia's heart tore itself in two.

The last signs of strength left Caisson's body, and Razzia knew he was dead.

Abyssinia raised her head to Nero. She didn't have to say anything. He nodded and teleported away.

"Don't," said Valkyrie.

Abyssinia glared, and Valkyrie stood up slowly. Temper came over, took Valkyrie's place by Razzia's side. Razzia smiled at him, and he smiled back.

"Don't," Valkyrie repeated. "Don't do it. Let your son rest. Doesn't he deserve that? Doesn't he deserve to be allowed to rest after a lifetime of suffering?"

"He's dead," said Abyssinia, her teeth bared.

"So let him stay that way," Valkyrie replied. Her voice was gentle. "The promise you made to your father... you don't have to be bound by it. You don't have to do it. You're not alone, Abyssinia. You have grandchildren. They probably have children of their own. You could have a huge, loving family out there and they can help you heal."

"My beautiful boy didn't deserve to die like this."

"No, he didn't."

"He should be breathing. He should be walking around."

"Putting your father's soul into Caisson's body will not bring Caisson back."

"I just want to see his eyes open."

Nero appeared, holding a Soul Catcher that pulsed with a soft, swirling grey light.

"You never loved your father," Skulduggery said, stepping forward. "You told us that. You were scared of him. Everyone was scared of him. If you bring him back, you'll bring back that fear. That fear will never replace the love that you have for your child. It won't fill the emptiness, any more than anger would, or vengeance, or hatred. Abyssinia, please, let Caisson go. Hold your love for him in your heart and keep him alive in your thoughts but don't – do not – do this."

Abyssinia sniffed, and slowly let her son's body lie flat on the ground. "My father saved my life," she said. "And I made him a promise."

She snatched the Soul Catcher from Nero's grip and, before Valkyrie could unleash her lightning or Skulduggery could push at the air, she crushed it with one hand.

The grey light, suffused with swirling smoke, exploded outwards and dived straight into Caisson's chest.

112

Valkyrie watched Caisson's eyes snap open.

But of course it wasn't Caisson. It was the King of the Darklands. It was the Unnamed.

He stood up slowly, the broken shards of the Soul Catcher falling from his shirt. Abyssinia stood, too, and took a step back. Valkyrie and Skulduggery also took a step back. Everyone did.

The King held his arms away from his sides, his fingers splayed, like he didn't want his body parts to touch. But gradually the arms lowered, and the fingers relaxed, and he released the breath he'd been holding.

Valkyrie's aura-vision showed that grey light struggling to fill the King's new body. Abyssinia's aura, deep and strong and brimming with power, throbbed beside her father's weakness. She was watching him with wide eyes. There was no relief on her face at seeing her son's eyes open once again. There was only trepidation.

The King licked his lips. He blinked. His brow furrowed as he looked down at the wound in his chest. Blood was starting to spill again.

He looked up, to Abyssinia. "Daughter," he said.

"Father," Abyssinia responded, and stepped into his arms.

He breathed in, and Abyssinia gasped, and Valkyrie watched the power leave her body and flow into his.

She switched off the aura-vision in time to see Abyssinia stagger backwards, eyes glazed, while the King's new body repaired itself instantly. In that cave, hundreds of years ago, he had given his power to his daughter. Now he had taken it back.

He looked at Abyssinia as she stumbled. Nero grabbed her, kept her up. He looked at Creed, and at Skulduggery, and at Valkyrie. He narrowed his eyes at Valkyrie.

Then he rose into the sky and kept going, until he was claimed by the darkness.

Abyssinia managed to stand. "Flanery," she snarled to Nero. And they vanished.

113

Flanery flicked off the TV in the Residence for the sixth time that night. He couldn't focus on it. On any of it. The news pundits talked about policies and leaks like the American people cared about any of that stuff. They tried to turn everything he did into some sort of scandal, tried to paint him as the bad guy when really they should have been chanting his name.

They'd regret these criticisms. He'd make sure of it. Martin Flanery was a man who remembered his enemies. Even after they'd all fallen in line, as they surely would, he'd remember all the times they opposed him.

Nothing they said tonight mattered, of course. Tomorrow it would all be swept away with the news coming out of Whitley. That's what the headlines would be about. That's what the whole country – the whole world – would be talking about. And then it'd be about him. Then they'd all be looking to Martin Flanery to guide them through the terror of the wizards, the horror of the witches.

He checked his watch, a Vacheron Constantin that he'd worn for his inauguration. They cheered for him that day. They'd cheer for him again.

The operation would be well under way by now. It was a risk, having all those people killed, but you didn't get very far in life without taking risks. He'd learned that from his father.

And what a risk he was taking now. If handled incorrectly, it could be disastrous. If the war happened and people found out how he'd been involved, he could be impeached. Maybe even jailed. He was sure they'd try to find some way to pin the deaths of anyone who died on him. Of course they would. The mainstream media hated him.

But if he handled it correctly, if he did everything right, then no one could stop him. He'd win a second term and there probably wouldn't even be anyone to run against him. The country would insist that he stay on for a third term, and a fourth. He'd never have to give up this power. America wouldn't want him to.

He was hungry. He needed some chicken.

He got up and went to the phone, but Abyssinia and the man with the bleached hair were standing in his way.

Flanery froze. She was supposed to be dead.

He spun on his heel, ran for the panic button. He couldn't remember the last time he'd run. It was a long time ago.

The man with the bleached hair appeared in front of him and Flanery stumbled away. Nero, that was his name.

"I'm going to kill you," said Abyssinia, walking over. Her silver hair was plastered to her head. They were both drenched. They dripped on the carpet.

Flanery backed away. "Why? What happened? I don't know what happened."

"Did you really think it would be easy?" she asked. "Did you actually think it would work?"

"What would work? I don't know what happened."

"Were you actually sitting here, expecting those mercenaries to succeed in killing me?" Abyssinia asked.

"What mercenaries?" Flanery asked, bumping up against the wall.

"Their weapons," the crazy woman said, "and their uniforms... You've been working on this for a while. You had this planned. You. The idiot. The moron."

548

She knew he'd ordered it. She knew because obviously he'd ordered it. There was no escaping the truth. He may as well come clean.

"I don't know what you're talking about," he said.

"You can't help but lie, can you, Mr President?"

"I'm not lying. I don't know what—"

She touched him, her fingertips to his shirt, and he felt a rush of coldness, like all the warmth was draining from his body.

She took her hand away and he sagged.

"In a lot of ways," she said, "you were the perfect president for my little scheme. Narcissistic. Corrupt. Completely amoral. But in other ways you were the worst. You're too stupid to hold a thought. Too limited to be truly cunning. With Tucker, at least, I had to infiltrate his mind. But you? You were ready to betray your country, to betray your world, for the first offer that came your way."

"I'm not stupid," said Flanery, trying to straighten up. "I've got one of the great brains."

"Then you should put it back where you found it." She raised her hand to his face, like she was going to drain the warmth out of him again, but then lowered it. "Skulduggery said you had help. What did he mean by that? Who has been helping you, Martin?"

Flanery found the courage to smile. "Wouldn't you like to know?"

She slapped him. Hard. Right across the face. It snapped his head round. His legs buckled and he peed a little and he found himself on the floor, looking up at her, thoughts all jumbled.

"I helped him," Crepuscular Vies said from across the room.

Flanery was suddenly overcome with gratitude – not a sensation he was used to. He liked the way the freak drifted from the shadows. He liked his casual walk. He liked the way he oozed confidence. He especially liked the way Abyssinia and Nero regarded him warily. But alongside his gratitude, there was also a part of Flanery that hated Crepuscular for being able to be that ridiculously intimidating. Those were qualities Flanery wanted for himself.

"I don't know you," said Abyssinia.

"But I know you," said Crepuscular.

Abyssinia watched him. "You gave Blackbrook their orders."

"And you survived," Crepuscular responded. "Did *they?*"

"Your soldiers are either dead or being led away by Cleavers as we speak."

Crepuscular shrugged. "That's unfortunate. A lot of training went into that squad. But they don't know anything that would lead back to me, so I suppose I don't really care. But there is the small matter of killing you..."

"I'll take care of this guy," Nero said, and in the blink of an eye he was behind Crepuscular, but Crepuscular was already turning, and Nero made a sound and his eyes went wide. He lurched back, the knife in his hand falling. There was another knife, though, and this one was sticking out of his belly.

When Abyssinia saw this, she made a sound like a wounded animal and ran to him. Crepuscular shoved Nero into her arms and she held him, and lowered him to his knees.

"Oh, no," Nero said.

"You'll be OK," Abyssinia told him. "You'll be all right. Can you teleport? Can you focus?"

"Oh, no," was all Nero said.

Crepuscular's eyes were on Abyssinia. "You've lost your strength."

She stood, and didn't answer.

"I have one of those guns," Crepuscular continued, "the kind that binds your magic? I thought I'd need it to take you down. But look at you. You're not even a fraction of the woman you once were."

"I'm strong enough to kill you," Abyssinia said.

She lunged at him and he stomped on her knee and it cracked

loudly. Flanery burst out laughing as Abyssinia went down, screaming. Finally, Flanery got to see her scream.

"You've been strong for too long," Crepuscular said. "You've forgotten how to be vulnerable." She reached for him and he grabbed her wrist and twisted. "No, no," he said. "You're not going to steal any of my strength. I'm going to need it for what I have planned."

He rammed his knee into the back of her arm and her elbow snapped and she screamed again.

Flanery got up. Fixed his hair, then his tie and his jacket. His cheek still throbbed. He walked over, casually, oozing confidence. He stood beside Crepuscular and waited for Abyssinia to raise her head and look at him.

"You thought you were playing me," he sneered. "But I was playing you the entire time. There's still going to be a war, but it's a war that I'm going to win."

"There won't be a war," Crepuscular said.

"What?" said Flanery, frowning. "Why not?"

"Because there weren't any sailors killed."

"I don't... I don't understand."

"I had a change of heart," Crepuscular said. "Revealing magic, pitting mortal against mage... We'd be juggling too many variables – and I know how much you hate juggling variables, Martin. I couldn't do that to you. So I pulled a few strings, got some sailors sent home on leave, got a few Blackbrook contractors to patrol in their place..."

"But the camera footage..."

"I'm sure the Cleavers are already deleting it."

Panic rose in Flanery's chest. He didn't want to get flustered in front of his vanquished foe, but he couldn't help himself. "But what about my re-election? This was going to get the country on my side. You promised me! You promised!"

His voice was high. He was aware that he was whining but, again, he couldn't help it.

"Calm down, Martin," Crepuscular said.

"This was going to make them respect me!" Flanery screeched. "This was going to make them love me! You promised! You swore!"

Crepuscular twitched, like he was going to lunge, and Flanery squealed and fell back over a chair.

Crepuscular adjusted his bow tie ever so slightly. "We don't have the second Pearl Harbour that we were hoping for," he said. "So we'll hold off for a bit. It's no big deal. We can show magic to the world at any time. Yes, we were planning for a spectacle so grand it would turn every right-thinking mortal into a magic-hating warrior of virtue – but hey-ho. Them's the breaks, Martin." He held out his hand. Flanery hesitated, then allowed himself to be pulled to his feet.

Crepuscular brushed dust from Flanery's shoulder. "There," he said. "Looking mighty presidential, if you don't mind me saying so."

"At least we still have the witch," Flanery said, doing his best to assert some authority.

Crepuscular winced, and walked over to the other room. "Magenta. Her name's Magenta. And we kind of lost her."

Flanery stared. "What? But she... she read minds. She influenced senators and... She got my policies through Congress! She got me elected!"

Flanery had to wait until Crepuscular came back. He was holding a big, awkward-looking gun. "Hey, come on now, *you* did that, Mr President. You got yourself elected because the people love you. Don't start doubting yourself."

"What happened? How did we lose her?"

Crepuscular walked up to him, put his hand on Flanery's arm. "Someone broke her out of where she was being kept," he said. "I say, let her go, you know?"

"But her son," Flanery reminded him. "We have her son."

"The son's gone, too. Hey, it's unfortunate, but do we really need her any more? I say no. I say, we're fine on our own. It's not the end of the world, Martin. We're still working on that one."

"You're doomed," said Abyssinia.

Crepuscular looked back at her. "Haven't I killed you yet?"

She ignored him, looked straight to Flanery. Her face was tight with pain, but she still managed a smile. It was all teeth. Like a shark. "Skulduggery Pleasant knows about what you did," she said. "He won't forget it. He doesn't give a damn that you're president. He's coming for you, Martin."

"No," Crepuscular said, "but we're coming for him." He shot her with some kind of paintball thing. It hit her leg and the black paint wrapped itself round her thigh. Strange symbols glowed.

Crepuscular handed Flanery the gun, and picked up the knife that Nero had dropped. He knelt in front of Abyssinia, tapping the tip of the blade against her chest. She didn't even try anything. She was broken. Defeated.

"Do it," Flanery whispered. "Kill her."

Crepuscular chuckled, and pushed the knife into her chest.

Abyssinia didn't make a sound, but her eyes widened and her mouth opened as blood deepened the red of her outfit. Crepuscular whispered something in her ear, and amazingly her eyes widened even more. Then she slumped back, and Nero raised his head, looked at her.

"Oh, no," he said again, and he vanished, and took Abyssinia with him.

114

Razzia died less than a minute after Abyssinia teleported away.

Valkyrie watched from across the platform. She died clasping Temper's hands. Slowly, tenderly, Temper picked her up and carried her body out of the rain, disappearing through the doorway. It was then that Valkyrie realised that Solace was no longer on the platform with them. The only people left out here, in the rain, was Valkyrie and Skulduggery and Damocles Creed.

"You have to leave," Creed said, with the temerity to actually sound bored. "You're all trespassing on Church property."

Valkyrie didn't know what to do. Didn't know what she *could* do. It had all gone horribly wrong. She wanted to punch someone, wanted to hurt someone, wanted to find someone to blame. So she marched over.

"You," she said, snarling up at him. "You're under arrest."

"I am?" Creed said, his face impassive.

"You've been conducting illegal experiments with the Kith."

"That is a gross mischaracterisation of a deeply spiritual practice."

"You've been lobotomising innocent people."

"Your ignorance is as sad as your petulance, Detective. I believe you will find that the practice of Activation is covered in the Religious Freedom Act."

She stood within punching distance and looked up. He was smiling at her. "You find this amusing, do you?"

"I find you amusing," he said.

Skulduggery came over to pull her away and she whipped her arm out of his grip. "You're under arrest! Damocles Creed, I'm placing you under arrest!"

"I have committed no crime."

"How about kidnapping? Or what, you want to tell me that Temper volunteered for this?"

"He did," Creed answered, "many years ago. I have the papers he signed, a contract, if you will, giving the Church permission to Activate him."

"We all know he walked away from that."

Creed raised an eyebrow. "The contract is still valid. If anyone should be pressing charges, it should be me. None of you have permission to be on Church property. Believe me, the Supreme Mage will be hearing about this."

Valkyrie wanted to throw him from the damn platform and listen to him scream all the way down.

Creed sighed, and pressed his hands together. "But you're emotional. You look like you've been through quite an ordeal. So I will not call the City Guard, and I will not have you arrested. You are free to leave, at your leisure. Go in peace, and may the Faceless Ones bathe you in their love."

He bowed, and walked from the platform. The door into the Dark Cathedral closed after him.

"Skulduggery," Abyssinia said.

They both whirled.

Skulduggery ran to Abyssinia as she lay there with a knife sticking out of her chest. He dropped to his knees and cradled her in his arms, just like Abyssinia had cradled Caisson.

Nero slumped over beside them, and didn't stir.

"Flanery's still alive," Abyssinia said weakly. "I met his... his friend. He did this to me. He knows you. He said he's coming for you."

"Then I'll be waiting," Skulduggery replied, "and I'll give him your regards when I kill him."

"How... how did you do it?"

"Do what?"

"Pretend to love me."

His head tilted. "Who said I pretended?"

Abyssinia smiled. "I'm not easy to love. My son died hating me. My father... abandoned me. My devoted followers... where are they? You pretended. Of course you did."

"China is sending healers up here. Just hold on."

"I loved *you*, though," Abyssinia said. "I loved you so much. When we were together, we could do... anything. Thank you for that. Thank you for pretending." She traced her fingers along his cheekbone. "But I have to tell you, I preferred you... as a bad guy."

"I know you did."

"You were always so good at being bad."

"I changed my ways. You can, too. It's not too late."

She gave a laugh that obviously hurt. "It's far too late, my love. But... thank you for lying." She was silent for a moment. "Valkyrie?"

"I'm here." Valkyrie went over and knelt by her.

Abyssinia took her hand. "Take care of him. He's been through a lot, and he's not... nearly as clever as he thinks he is."

"I may not have ears," Skulduggery said, "but I can hear you just fine."

Valkyrie ignored him, and nodded to Abyssinia. "I will."

"Even if that's true," Skulduggery said, "even if I'm half as clever as I think I am, that's still twice as clever as either of you."

Abyssinia's voice was growing softer. "He needs someone to guide him. He gets these... ideas in his head and he thinks they're good ones... They seldom are."

"My ideas are excellent," Skulduggery said.

The fingers that gripped Valkyrie's hand tightened. "He needs a conscience. He needs to be reminded of what it is to be... alive. You've got to be that for him, Valkyrie. And he's got to be that for you."

"We will be," Valkyrie said softly.

Abyssinia released her hand, and Valkyrie slowly stood up and stepped back. The rain stopped.

"I shouldn't have... brought him back," Abyssinia said to Skulduggery. "I don't know what... what I was thinking... That was a moment of insanity."

"We're all allowed to go a little insane when the world drives us to it," Skulduggery said.

"Surely... surely I couldn't have expected him to be grateful? Surely I couldn't have expected him to show me love? He has... never shown me love. My father's obsession with his own legend... warped everything he touched. Of course Mevolent moved against him. Someone had to. Back then, my father was a monster. He... he is a monster still. But my mother. My sisters... When Mevolent killed them, he broke my heart and tore apart my soul. I never thought I'd find love again. I thought I'd never be in one piece again. But now... I'll leave this world as I came into it.

"Thank you," she said to Skulduggery. "Even if you were pretending to love me... thank you."

Valkyrie left them to their final moment together, and walked to the edge of the platform. Roarhaven twinkled beneath her.

115

Tanith met Skulduggery by the side of the road.

It had stopped raining, thank God. Three days of rain since Abyssinia had died, but now the blue was finally pushing the grey back across the horizon. A bit late for Tanith's bike, though, splattered as it was with three days of mud.

Unlike the Bentley. She wondered how long he'd been waiting for her here, wondered if maybe he'd turned up early just to give it a sneaky polish. She wouldn't put it past him.

She leaned the bike on to its kickstand, took off her helmet and hung it off the handlebar. Skulduggery was leaning against the car, wearing a façade.

"How did you do it?" she asked.

Skulduggery raised an eyebrow. Tanith could never quite tell if his facial gestures would have convinced her if she hadn't known the face wasn't real. "I'm not entirely sure," he said. "We sat down and we talked, and I told her the people she'd imprisoned weren't members of Black Sand and that she knew it. And then she agreed to release them."

"Just like that?"

"Apparently so."

"And she didn't ask for anything in return?"

"Not a thing."

"So... I don't have to turn myself in, then? China doesn't even know I'm involved in any of that?"

"I wouldn't go so far as to assume anything," said Skulduggery. "China knows an awful lot about an awful lot. But, the fact is, your friends are out of prison, and you don't have to take their place."

Tanith crossed her arms, and leaned back against the Bentley beside him. "I'll take that as a win," she said. "Thank you. A lot of good people have been reunited with their families."

"Are you sure about this?" he asked. "About what Black Sand is doing? Actively fighting against the Sanctuaries—"

"Not Sanctuaries," Tanith said. "Just the one, the High Sanctuary. Just China."

"You could work *with* her."

"She's too powerful, Skulduggery. You do see that, right? You see how far she's gone?"

He didn't say anything.

Tanith sighed. "She's dangerous. She wants to control it all. If you sided with us..."

"I have other priorities," he said. "Right now, China is a known quantity, as much as such a thing is possible."

"And if she makes a move that you don't approve of?"

He hesitated. "Then we'll see what happens."

Tanith looked out across the fields. "It's been good seeing you again," she said. "I've missed you guys."

"And we've missed you. Are you moving on? Back to Africa?"

"Eventually. I'm going to let things cool down a bit before my return."

"Have you heard from Oberon?"

She nodded. "He's doing good. His son and his ex are free and he's helping them set up their new lives under new names."

"Any idea how he got past the Seven-As-One?"

"Not a clue – but he's a man of hidden talents, that guy."

A tractor trundled by. They watched it until it was gone from sight.

"So," Skulduggery said, "seeing as how you've suddenly got some free time on your hands, would you be interested in a little side project?"

She looked at him. "Take off the face and talk to me."

He deactivated the façade. "The King of the Darklands is out there. We need a way to stop him."

"I thought Auger Darkly was going to stop him."

"Auger Darkly is going to *fight* him," Skulduggery corrected. "There's no guarantee he's going to win. So, we need to either find a way to stop the Unnamed before the prophecy comes true, or find a way to help the Chosen One emerge victorious."

"What can I do?"

"The Obsidian Blade killed the Unnamed the first time round," Skulduggery said. "I'm going to need you to find it, so it can kill him again."

116

Gripping the bar with both hands, Valkyrie planted her feet flat on the ground, took a moment to settle herself, then exhaled as she lifted. Her arms trembled and she waited for that to stop.

"Balance it," Panthea said, standing behind her. "Good. OK, go ahead."

Valkyrie brought the bar down, inhaling as she did so. It tipped off her chest and she immediately pushed it back up again. Then it came down, and then it went up. Inhaling on the drop, exhaling on the push.

The gym buzzed around her. She was used to working out alone, in silence, driven by the voices in her head. Here it was easier. Here it was Panthea's voice she was listening to, and Panthea wasn't nearly so critical.

"That's it," Panthea said. "Nice. Stay at that pace."

Valkyrie's arms were starting to shake. She enjoyed that. That was when she knew she was pushing herself, when her body was telling her, *No, that's enough now, let's just stop and go for a coffee.* She ignored the shaking and kept going.

"Three more," Panthea said. "Just three more, that's all. Come on, you have them in you. One. That's it. Push yourself. These are the important ones. Two. Nice." She moved in and her hands appeared beneath the bar, ready to catch it if it fell. "One more, Valkyrie. One more. Come on... Three! Well done!"

Panthea gripped the bar and helped Valkyrie put it back on the rack. Valkyrie's arms dropped and she laughed.

"Good girl," Panthea said. "That was impressive. Take some water."

Panthea moved away to note something down in her logbook, and Valkyrie swerved her upper body out from beneath the barbell and sat up on the bench. She wiped her brow with her towel and took a long gulp from her water bottle, noting with amusement how suddenly hard it was to lift her hand that high.

Panthea took her to the mats after that for a cooldown, and they chatted a little, while people worked out around them. Valkyrie thanked her and headed to the showers. When she was dressed, she slung her gym bag over her shoulder and headed homewards, sipping from a protein shake that had aspirations of being a milkshake, but couldn't quite make it. She slowed as she approached Haggard.

Finally, she pulled in by the side of the road and stared at the steering wheel. Her mind was clear. There was no internal debate. Not any more. Abyssinia had seen to that.

I'll leave this world as I came into it.

Alice deserved to have her soul repaired. Happiness wasn't everything. Without the dark, there was no light. She deserved to know sadness, and regret, and pain, and sorrow. She deserved to miss the people she loved when they were gone, because only then could they live in her memories. She needed to be human, as frail and as damaged as that was. It wasn't Valkyrie's place to protect her sister from every bad thing – it was only Valkyrie's place to try.

She put the car into gear, pulled back on to the road, and continued on to Haggard.

When she walked into the house, both her parents were home and Alice was waiting for her with a little purple suitcase.

Valkyrie had to laugh. "What's this?" she asked.

"My suitcase," Alice answered, frowning at her big sister's

stupidity. "It has my clothes in it for tomorrow, and my pyjamas, and my teddy bear, in case I get lonely, and it has three books in case I get bored, even though I know I won't get bored, and it has my hairbrush and my toothbrush, which is electric, and hair clips and a plastic bag in case I need to put something in a plastic bag, and an apple and a banana, in case I get hungry."

"You won't get hungry," Valkyrie said. "Tonight you get a pizza."

The smile that spread across Alice's face seemed never to stop.

"Bye, Mom," Alice said, giving Melissa a hug. She lunged at Desmond. "Bye, Dad."

"Bye, squid-face," Desmond said, kissing the top of her head. "Have a good time."

Alice bounded over to Valkyrie. "I'm ready!" she announced.

"Cool," said Valkyrie. She hesitated.

"Everything all right?" Melissa asked.

Her parents looked at her – interested. Attentive. Loving.

"Yes," Valkyrie said slowly.

Desmond laughed. "Are you sure?"

"I may have something to tell you."

Her mum glanced at her dad and raised an eyebrow. "Is it bad or good?"

"It's... it's not bad. It's not bad news. It's just, I don't know... it's just news. Something you don't know and something I think I should tell you."

Desmond frowned. "Oh, God. Does it have anything to do with..." He wiggled his fingers in the air, his incredibly subtle code for "magic".

"No," said Valkyrie.

He smiled, relieved. "So the world is safe, then?"

"Yes. Well, as safe as it ever is."

His smile vanished. "What's that supposed to mean?"

"Nothing. We're safe. We are."

"Is there an apocalypse coming?"

"Not that I'm aware of."

"What's an apocalypse?" Alice asked.

"It's a load of bad things happening," Valkyrie said. "But there isn't one, so we're fine."

Alice shrugged, satisfied with the answer.

"So what do you have to tell us?" Melissa asked.

Valkyrie's insides churned and she felt so stupid because she knew they'd be fine with the whole thing – but she also knew that when she told them they'd view her differently. Not in a bad way, never in a bad way – but from this moment on they'd have an extra bit of information that they'd have to absorb into what they already knew about her, and that would change things.

She didn't want them to think of her differently. She liked how they thought of her now. It was warm and loving and under-standing, even about the whole magic side of things.

It had been a huge adjustment, after all, when they'd found out about that. They'd had to drastically change how they thought about her, then, and, compared to that, this was nothing. This was barely worth mentioning. Even so, the words caught in her throat.

So she found new words, and blurted, "I have a girlfriend."

The kitchen went quiet.

"Oh," said Melissa.

The kitchen went quiet again.

Valkyrie watched her mother absorb the information, and watched her father butt up against it.

"But I thought you liked boys," he said, confused.

"I still do," Valkyrie responded.

"She's bisexual," Melissa told him.

"Oh!" Desmond said, nodding like he'd figured it out himself. "Best of both worlds, eh?"

Melissa came forward, hugged Valkyrie and kissed her, right above the ear. "We're proud of you, we love you and I'm sure we'll love whoever you love. Won't we, Des?"

Desmond came over, hugged them both. "I always wanted you to be a lesbian," he said. "This is the next best thing."

Valkyrie laughed, surprised at the tears in her eyes.

"I don't understand anything you're saying," Alice said.

"I'll tell you in the car," Valkyrie promised.

117

They drove to Grimwood, and sang songs the whole way. "Crazy World" by Aslan came on, though, and Valkyrie's voice cracked with emotion halfway through the second chorus, so she changed the station. After a few moments she'd got herself back under control and started singing again. Alice didn't notice.

When they entered the house, Alice hollered Xena's name and Xena came bounding into the hall and Alice dropped to her knees a moment before the dog collided with her. They went sprawling across the floor, Xena a whirling tornado of excitement and Alice the giggling focus of its energies.

Valkyrie watched and made herself laugh. She hoped they would sprawl forever.

But that's why she went for a workout that morning. That's why she pulled over to the side of the road. That's why she sat at the kitchen table for a chat. Because she was delaying it.

But she couldn't delay it any longer.

When both Xena and Alice had settled down, Valkyrie took Alice into the living room, and asked her to lie down on the couch.

"What are we doing?" Alice asked.

"We're just going to rest," Valkyrie said, kneeling beside her, "but before we do... Alice, I love you. Before you came along, I didn't know that I needed a sister. I thought my life was full. But it wasn't. I can look back now, and I can see that there was a gap that I would never have known was there if you hadn't been born."

Alice giggled. "You're being weird."

Valkyrie smiled. "Yes, I am. But sometimes you have to be weird. I love you, sweetie. I wish we could have had a normal life, and I wish I could have spent more time with you, and I'm really, desperately sorry that I went away for all that time. I missed you every single moment I wasn't here."

Alice nodded automatically. "I missed you, too," she said.

Tears in her eyes, Valkyrie leaned over, kissed her forehead. "You're such a sweetie. I'm sorry for everything that happened. I'm sorry for what I did. And I'm sorry for this. But no matter what, my darling, darling sister –" and here Valkyrie started properly crying – "please remember that I love you more than anything or anyone else in the whole entire world. Alice Edgley, fall asleep."

Alice closed her eyes and slept, and Valkyrie curled up and sobbed. Xena came in, nudged her with her snout, tried to lick her face. Valkyrie wrapped her arms round the dog and hugged her until the crying stopped, and then she kissed the top of Xena's head and gently shooed her away.

She stood, took the skull amulet from her pocket and pressed it to her hip, and the suit flowed over her. It was slightly different this time around, as if it knew what was required of it and designed itself accordingly. Valkyrie pulled up the hood, and pulled down the mask.

She picked up the Soul Catcher and turned away from Alice to shield her, and then she sent her magic crackling through her hands and the Soul Catcher exploded.

Shards of glass bounced off Valkyrie's chest and mask as the swirling orange light burst free, twisting through the air. For one terrible, horrifying moment, Valkyrie thought it was going to disappear through the ceiling, but it turned suddenly, sensing home.

She stepped back, watching as it dipped and dived straight into Alice's chest.

Valkyrie tore off her mask and activated her aura-vision.

Her sister lay there, sleeping gently, and her aura burned as brightly as any Valkyrie had ever seen.

Valkyrie sat downstairs, waiting for her sister to wake, her eyes on the music box on the coffee table. The lid was down, the music box silent.

She could have done with just a few seconds of that tune. She was nervous, sitting down here. Her anxiety was starting to bite. It wouldn't take much to calm her nerves. All she'd have to do is reach forward, flick up the lid and, after a few seconds, close it and sit back and everything would be good.

But if Alice called out during those few seconds, would Valkyrie even hear her? And of course there was no guarantee that those "few seconds" wouldn't stretch to an hour. Or more.

It had happened before. That wonderful, soft, lilting tune had a tendency to draw her in while the world rushed by around her.

Besides, when Alice woke she'd need Valkyrie to be alert and responsive, and the music box, while brilliant and amazing and so incredibly helpful, also dulled Valkyrie's emotions in ways that weren't always helpful. She'd have to be careful about using the box in the future. She wouldn't want to get overly dependent on something like that.

She blinked, realising that night had fallen and that she was sitting in darkness. She got up, leaving Xena asleep on the couch, and went through the house, turning on lights. She got to the kitchen but the kitchen wasn't a kitchen and there was a girl sitting on the edge of a bed.

Valkyrie jumped in shock and the vision wavered, started to fade.

"Hold on, hold on," she grumbled, and calmed herself, and the image grew solid again.

The girl was sitting with her head down, blonde hair falling over her face. She was wearing black – the kind of clothes Ghastly Bespoke used to make for Valkyrie.

She stood. She was tall. Strong. Maybe fifteen or sixteen years old. She tied her hair back into a ponytail. She was pretty, too. Had a look of determination. Had a look of...

Valkyrie frowned. "Alice?" she whispered.

The girl spun, eyes wide, teeth bared – but frowned.

"Who is that?" she asked.

"Can you hear me?" Valkyrie said, stepping closer.

It was Alice. Older. Bigger. But Alice.

"I can hear you," she said, eyes fixing on to Valkyrie's. "I can see you, too, but you're faded." She hesitated. "Valkyrie?"

Valkyrie sobbed, and her knees went, and she collapsed and Alice rushed to her, tried to pick her up, but her hands went right through Valkyrie's shoulders.

"Valkyrie," Alice said, crying now herself. "How is this happening?"

"You're a vision," Valkyrie said with a half-laugh. "You're in the future. Where I am, you're eight."

"That's... that's eight years ago."

"Are you OK? Tell me you're OK, please."

"I'm fine," Alice said. "I'm good. I love you so, so much. So much has happened!"

"I don't know how much we should say. Anything you tell me could mess up the way things are meant to unfold. The future isn't set."

"This science-fiction stuff can really do your head in, can't it?" Alice said, grinning.

"It really, really can." Valkyrie should have cut the vision off right then and there. She knew that. But... "So you're a sorcerer now?"

Alice laughed, and wiped her eyes. "Yes, I suppose you could say that. Magic's in our blood, isn't it? It's what we were born to do."

All the energy left Valkyrie's body, and she sat, her legs curled beneath her. "I thought I'd be doing you a favour by keeping it from you."

"Yeah, I know, but you can't cheat destiny, dear sister. I'm about to step out that door – I don't know if you can see it, but there's a door over there – and face down my arch-enemy. Can you believe it? I have an arch-enemy! Me!"

Valkyrie wanted to reach out and grab her. "Do you have help? Alice, you can't do this alone. You need to—"

"I've been doing this for years," Alice said, smiling gently. "Don't worry about it, OK? I've got our Edgley family heritage on my side. We not only have magic in our blood, we have a very specific *type* of magic. I can feel it bubbling within me." The smile faded. "But I'm... I'm about to change."

"What do you mean?"

"I have to win. I've got no choice. This is the last stand, you know? Either we win this battle, or they do – and we can't afford to let them win. The world actually hangs in the balance."

"How are you going to change, Alice?"

"I'm not... certain. I don't think I'll be me any more."

"No. No, don't do it."

"It's OK. I'm OK with it. We've all got to sacrifice something for the future we want." She turned her head, listening to something Valkyrie couldn't hear. "I have to go."

"Who is it?" Valkyrie asked, getting to her feet as Alice straightened. "Who are you fighting? Tell me and I'll stop them here, in my time, before they're even a threat."

"You can't prevent this," Alice said sadly. "This has been written in the stars. The final battle between the Child of the Ancients and the Child of the Faceless Ones."

"I can help you."

"This is my fight. I really have to go." Alice started walking away. "I love you, Valkyrie."

"I love you, too."

"I miss you every single day."

And then the vision was over, and the kitchen was the kitchen again, and Alice was calling her name from upstairs.

For a long moment, Valkyrie didn't move. She couldn't. Her feet were locked in place. She couldn't even answer. Her throat was too constricted.

And then she was moving, running for the stairs and suddenly she was across the landing and at the bedroom door, about to burst in...

But she stopped. And gently turned the handle. And stepped in.

"Hi, sweetie," she said. "Is everything OK?"

Alice was sitting up in bed. Her face was in darkness. "I don't know," she said. There was something in her voice. A hitch. A catch. "I don't feel well, I don't think."

Valkyrie pushed the door open wider, and the light from the landing swept slowly across the bed until it uncovered Alice's tear-stained face.

"I don't know what's wrong," Alice said, her mouth turning down, and Valkyrie rushed over to her.

"Oh, baby," she said, sitting on the bed and wrapping her arms round her sister. "It's OK. You're OK. I've got you, you hear me? Everything's going to be fine. I love you so, so much. I'm not going to let anything bad happen to you ever again. I promise, sweetheart. I promise."

She held her sister close, and hugged her tight, feeling every one of her sister's sobs as they echoed through her own body, and she sang to her. "Crazy World" by Aslan.

118

It was a Sunday. Omen and Auger were back at home, back in Galway, back at the big house in the country. Auger's bullet wound was healing well. He barely felt more than a twinge, he said. But he'd always been a fast healer, even without magic.

Conversation in the Darkly household was restricted, unsurprisingly, to the King of the Darklands. For all the assurance, all of the effortless confidence they'd demonstrated over the years, Omen suspected that Emmeline and Caddock Darkly had secretly believed that Auger would never have to actually embrace his destiny. Maybe they thought it would all be averted before it arrived. His parents had always loved the prestige of having a Chosen One in the family – but now Omen saw real worry in their eyes. The years were ticking down, and in the last few days the future glimpsed in the prophecy had only become more likely. More real.

They took their frustration out on Omen, of course. Nothing he did was right. Everything was commented upon. The glory he'd shared with his brother over their Naval Magazine Whitley heroism had been as short-lived as he'd expected. Their constant sniping chipped away at him. Got him down. But he was used to it. Their priority had to be Auger. Had to be.

In two years' time, once Auger had faced the King of the Darklands – as prophesised – and kicked the crap out of him – as expected – then the Darkly Prophecy would be over and Omen's parents could open their hearts to both brothers.

Omen was sure this would happen. He was looking forward to it. He actually had dreams about it.

But that day was still two years away, and right now it was Sunday, and it was half-term break, and Omen had been at home for five days and his parents were getting sick of the sight of him, so he was in his room, lying on his bed and making his way through a stack of comics that Never had dropped over a few hours earlier. He heard his mother come up the stairs. Her shoes – high heels, even at home – clicked pleasingly as they passed his door. They stopped at Auger's room, and Omen heard a delicate knock. A few moments passed, and she knocked again.

She strode back. Knocked sharply on Omen's door. "Where's your brother?"

"Um, I don't know," Omen said.

"Find him. Lunch is ready."

Omen hopped off the bed and walked quickly to the door, but, even as he opened it, his mother was already heading down-stairs. He watched the top of her head disappear. He'd been hoping for a glance from her. Not even a smile. A glance would do.

He checked the rest of the house, then went outside to the training hall. This is where they'd spent most of their time as kids – Auger learning from the best combat instructors in the world, and Omen trying to be an adequate sparring partner. He'd never succeeded, of course, but he knew Auger appreciated it, nonetheless.

This afternoon, the hall was quiet. The punchbags hung like stalactites. The weapons were racked.

There was a trail down between the trees that led to a little clearing where Auger liked to go sometimes to think. Omen didn't need places like that because Omen's thoughts were pretty simple.

He wouldn't have liked to have the kinds of thoughts that required places. Those thoughts were probably deep and scary and the sort to give you nightmares.

Omen hurried down the trail. It was bright day, and dry but cold, and Omen's thin fleece didn't do a whole lot to keep in the warmth. He passed the tree stump that usually had an axe buried in it. A moment later, he got to the clearing and Auger wasn't there, but he heard someone behind him and turned and Jenan Ispolin ran at him, the axe in his hands.

Panic exploded, and dread and terror. Jenan's face was a portrait of hatred and he kept getting closer. That axe kept swinging. Omen didn't know what to do, but he knew that if he backed off he was dead so he lunged forward, grabbing Jenan, pulled him over his hip.

It was a clumsy throw and they both went down, but the axe spun away. Omen got up and Jenan got up and Jenan reached behind him, to his waistband. Took out a knife, showed it, didn't smile, laugh, say anything, but wanted Omen to see the knife. Wanted Omen to know what was coming.

Omen didn't shout for help. To shout for help was to lose focus.

Teeth bared, Jenan stepped in. Omen shot both hands down, managed to grab the wrist before the blade reached him. Jenan's other hand seized Omen's fleece and Jenan powered forward, slamming Omen into a tree. Omen twisted to one side and pulled and the knife went into the trunk. Omen threw an elbow and then he tackled Jenan, pushing him away from the tree and away from the knife.

They turned and turned again, feet sliding in the leaves and the twigs and the dirt. Jenan snarled and snapped, straining to gain the advantage. Omen knew enough to conserve his energy.

A feint, and Jenan went low, arms encircling both of Omen's legs, and he lifted. Omen had a brief moment to shift himself higher before he was slammed to the ground. The shock ran up his spine and did its best to empty his lungs, but he'd been expecting it, and now he had the makings of a triangle choke.

Jenan recognised the move. He stalled it, pulled back, protecting himself. Omen abandoned the triangle and swivelled into an arm bar. Almost got it, too, but Jenan had always been good at the technicalities. Omen released it, kicked Jenan away. Got up.

Jenan was breathing heavily through his mouth. He lashed out, his fist crunching, Omen's head rattling. Swung again. Another strike. Swung again. Another one.

Omen retreated, covering up, wilting under the onslaught. Jenan in control now, asserting his dominance. Threw a kick. Threw another. Now he spun.

Omen stopped faking and grabbed him, picked him up mid-spin, dumped him to the ground on his left shoulder. Jenan crumpled and moaned. Started to get up. Omen threw a kick of his own – low, and to the face. Jenan tumbled back, then lurched up, and fell again under Omen's fists.

Omen stopped, crouched over him, Jenan's face a bloody mess. Enough. Look at him. He'd had enough.

He stood. Stepped away.

"Auger," he said, though he meant to shout. He turned to the trees and tried again. "Auger!"

No response. He turned and Jenan was right there and he stuck the knife in. Omen made a sound.

Omen fell, sliding off the blade on to the ground. Clutched at his belly. All that blood, staining his fleece.

Looked up. Jenan staring down at him, at the mess he'd made, at all that blood. Not in shock, though. In his eyes, something else. Triumph and... happiness.

On the far side of the clearing Omen saw a lion charging through the undergrowth except it wasn't a lion, it was his brother, and Auger leaped from that side to this, an impossible distance, and Jenan whirled and Auger's knee hit him and Jenan's knife was somewhere between them and they went down and rolled

575

and rolled and Auger rolled free and he had a knife sticking out of his chest.

"No!" Omen screamed. "Auger! No!"

Jenan moaned, turned over. Holding his shoulder. Face tight. Started to get up.

Someone, somewhere, calling out for Auger. For Omen.

Omen on his knees. Not able to straighten. Spine curved to keep the wound closed. All that blood.

Eyes on Jenan. Jenan standing. Omen standing, Omen moving, feet clumsy, crashing. Tangle. Curses. Hands in his face. Fingers in eyes. Omen biting.

Punching.

Pounding.

Jenan wasn't moving any more. Jenan barely breathing.

And then.

His name. Someone shouting his name. He tried to answer, but fell sideways instead. He looked around. Started crawling. Before he reached Auger, his strength left him and he collapsed.

His brother's eyes were open. Blinking. His arm, outstretched. Omen reached out.

Before their fingers touched, Omen fell into darkness.

119

China lay beside him. It was a cold night, the fire in the hearth having long faded to glowing embers, but the bed was warm, and the sheets were soft, and his presence was comforting. All through her childhood she'd had trouble sleeping, plagued as she was by the stories her parents would tell her of the Faceless Ones. Once, when reflecting over that day's sermon, her mother had smiled and asked her, *Doesn't that comfort you, knowing our gods are out there, watching over us, reaching out with unknowable fingers, aching to come home? Doesn't that make you feel happy?*

And China had said, *No, Mother, it gives me bad dreams,* and her mother's face had changed in an instant and China had spent the next three days on her knees, praying to the Faceless Ones, begging their forgiveness.

Since that day, she had hidden her fears from her parents and suffered those nightmares in silence – but here, in this bed, by his side, she sank into sleep gratefully, knowing she would surface in the morning, untroubled by half-remembered visions of doom and damnation.

This, she thought, was what happiness was. Love and contentment. At nineteen years old, she had found the love of her life, someone who cared not for her beauty or her status, but who loved her for the jokes she made, and the things she said, and the things she did and wanted to do. He was a kind man, fierce with others but gentle with her. Her parents, were they to learn of this, would do their best to tear them apart, but he offered her something they never did, and so, smiling, with her hand on his back, she fell, once again, asleep.

She woke while it was still dark. Her hand was still on his back, but his back, like the hearth, had lost its heat.

China lay there. Her body was heavy.

His back was cold.

Slowly, she raised her heavy head off the pillow as she moved her heavy hand up to his shoulder. She said his name and he didn't answer. But he always answered her. He always did.

She pulled him gently towards her, and turned him on to his back. His arm fell limply, as if it had no bones. His chest was still – it did not rise and it did not fall. His eyes were open, and looked to the ceiling. He did not see her. But he always saw her. He always did.

A low, guttural sound twisted up from her belly and burned through her chest and emerged from her lips, a sound of pain not yet comprehended, the beginnings of loss and despair and utter helplessness and it would not stop and she wanted to hold him and shake him, but her body moved away instead, her knees rising to her chest, her hands in her hair, her eyes on his great unmoving form, and the sound turned to a wail that turned to a scream that turned to a roar of pain and unfathomable emptiness and

China woke, her body stiff, the sheets wrapped around her, staring at the empty side of the bed.

Her bed. Her apartment. Her High Sanctuary.

She was here. Now. She wasn't nineteen any more. She wasn't in that little hut on the mountainside. It was a dream. Just a bad dream.

China sat up. Took a deep breath. She hadn't dreamed about that night in a long time. She had refused to even think about it. It was the stress of everything, piling in on top of her, that was dredging up all of these bad memories. She'd have one of her Sensitives take care of it in the morning, to scrub the nightmares from her mind. But why wait? She reached for the phone, and froze.

There was someone standing at the foot of the bed.

It was an old woman. Hunched. China couldn't see her face but she could feel her eyes on her.

China met those eyes.

"We found each other after all these years," said Solace, "and now he's been taken away from me and I'm never getting him back. All that time I was trapped in that tower, my mind numbed by that infernal music box, there was always a part of me that knew he was out there and that, given a chance, he would find me. That hope kept me alive through the loneliness. Through the madness of that place."

She wasn't really here. A sliver of moonlight came through from the window and the old woman didn't cast a shadow.

"Caisson's was the only love I have ever known," Solace continued, "and you knew that. Yet you still betrayed him, and you put me in that tower so I couldn't help him."

"I loved him, too," China said carefully. "I raised him. But I did what I did to protect you."

She could feel the old woman's sneer. "You're twisted," Solace said. "Your heart is blackened and sour. You betrayed Caisson and you put me in that tower and then you chose to forget about us both. You buried us as memories, and on our graves you built an empire."

The old woman leaned forward. "Power is the only thing you care about, the only thing you love, and I'm going to take it all away from you. Every last bit of it. Sleep well, Mother. I'll see you soon."

She stepped back and faded to moonlight, and China was alone again.

120

Lily's scooter ran out of petrol ten kilometres from the portal, so Sebastian abandoned it in the dust and started walking.

Lily wouldn't be happy. None of them would be happy, since he'd failed and everything, but Lily especially wouldn't be happy. She loved that scooter. She'd made him promise to bring it back. Just another way in which he'd screwed up. Just one more reason for people to hate him.

He was maybe four kilometres to the portal when he realised he'd forgotten his hat.

"Damn," he said. It was quiet. That word was the only thing he could hear. So he said it again. "Damn." A bit louder, that time. He opened his mouth wider. "Damn."

He raised his head to shout at the red sky and the heavens beyond.

Darquesse hovered there.

Sebastian froze.

The desiccated corpse watched him. It held his hat.

"Please help us," Sebastian said. "Please help me. We need you. We need you to come back and we need you not to kill us. You were tricked in order to make you leave. We had to do that. You understand, don't you?"

The corpse offered no reply.

"But the world faces a threat no one is ready for," Sebastian continued. "You are the most powerful being we know. You are an impossible being, in the same way the Faceless Ones are impossible. But we think – I think – that you can be on our side. I think you have a spark of humanity inside you. Even now, even after everything you did back on my world, even after you thought you'd destroyed us all... You're still one of us, Darquesse. We need you."

The corpse floated down. Its feet sank gently into the dirt before him.

Sebastian cleared his throat and puffed out his chest. "Or you can kill me," he said. "If all you're going to do is come back and finish what you started, if all you're going to do is wipe us out, then you may as well just kill me now. Just get it over with."

He took a breath and held it as he winced, waiting to be turned to dust with a click of the fingers.

But the corpse didn't click its fingers. It looked at him, with its dried-out eyes sitting in their sunken sockets, as if it was considering his proposal.

Then those eyes cleared, and colour came back to the skin as the body regrew the meat on its bones and radiance rippled through its black hair. The corpse took a breath and became a person, tall and strong, and wearing a peculiarly dispassionate version of Valkyrie Cain's face.

121

It was a sunny day.

Valkyrie took that to be a good sign. After everything that had happened, after all the hardship and pain and loss and guilt, today was the day when it could all turn around. She was going to get good news today, news that would spur her on in her adventures.

For that's what they were. Gallivanting around the world with Skulduggery, fighting bad guys, saving lives, doing magic, flying, dealing with people from alternate dimensions... if all that wasn't adventuring, she didn't know what was.

She was going to enjoy it again. From this day on, she'd meet each new challenge with a grin. If she grinned enough, she was quite sure she could keep the bad thoughts away. There was no amount of guilt, no amount of self-loathing, no amount of pain that couldn't be kept at bay with a grin and a witty line. And the music box. The music box helped. She fell asleep to the music box every night now, and woke fresh, and calm, and ready for the challenge.

Things were good. Corrival Academy was on its half-term break, so she was spending more time with Militsa. She was enjoying her new training regime with Panthea. Alice was still crying and her parents didn't know what to do, but the necronaut suit was working out well, and Valkyrie had pretty much decided to keep it. She had made a hefty – anonymous – donation to the museum, and one of these days she'd talk to the people in charge and confess her little crime, and she was confident that they'd understand – especially if she offered to make another hefty donation right then and there.

Yep, today was the day she got back control over her own life, and it started here, with this conversation.

Dusk was waiting for her, standing on the same rooftop in the Fangs where she'd met Caisson.

"Thanks for coming," she said.

He didn't react to that. He just looked at her. "Are you sure you want to know this?"

She smiled. "I'm sure. Whatever it is can't be any worse than what I've been through already. So come on – what did you see in my blood?"

He looked away, over the rooftops. "I had only been a vampire eight years when I came upon a door," he said. "It was in the middle of the countryside and I was starving for blood. When a vampire is that hungry, he can sense living creatures nearby. It's like hearing a gurgling stream."

Valkyrie liked the way he talked.

"The door was wooden, and set into the ground, secured with a metal lock. I had very little strength, but I managed to prise the door open just enough to slip through, into the darkness. Wooden steps led me to a single, vast room. Filled with people. They were naked, and staring straight ahead, and they didn't move.

"I thought, at first, that it was a mirage brought upon by my hunger, but no. These people were real, and they were here. I grabbed the closest, and sank my teeth into his neck." Dusk shivered slightly. "His blood was... different. There was a power in it. A potency. I didn't like it. It tasted... sour. So I moved on to the next, and the next, and the next, and they all had this taste. This power. It made me sick. It almost killed me."

"And what does this have to do with me?" Valkyrie asked.

He turned to look at her. "When I drank from you, I tasted that same power, but magnified. The power they held in their blood was nothing compared to yours. They were echoes. You were the song."

"I'm not sure I—"

"I learned later who they were," Dusk continued, "and I learned who put them down there. A man I believe you have had dealings with. Damocles Creed."

Valkyrie looked at him and said nothing.

"Those people were what is known as Kith," Dusk said. "When I drank from you, I knew. The legends are wrong, Valkyrie. You are not descended from the Last of the Ancients. You are descended from their enemies. You have their power and you have their blood. You are a Faceless One."

He stood up on the ledge and turned to her. "I'm sorry," he said, stepping backwards and leaving her alone.